The shining splendor of our Zebra Lov... reflects the glittering excellence of th... Lovegram whenever you buy a histori... guarantees the very best in quality a...

D0400559

"YOU'RE BEAUTIFUL, DANNY, DID YOU KNOW THAT?"

Stunned, Danny looked into Brant's eyes. She had never seen them so intensely blue and vivid, his gaze so searing. Suddenly, she found it hard to breathe, and her heart raced. He kissed her then, his mouth closing softly over hers. She leaned into him, shivers of pleasure running over her.

He raised his head and gazed down at her, his eyes smoldering with desire. "Help me, Danny," he whispered. "Stop me. Because Lord knows I can't stop myself."

But stopping Brant was the last thing Danny wanted. She dropped the towel between them and slipped her arms around his shoulders. With a groan, Brant dropped his hands to her back and molded her soft body to his long length. His hands moved back up in a lingering caress that took her breath away. He brought his mouth down on hers in hot, fierce demand, a kiss that seared through Danny and seemed to melt her very bones, sending the world reeling dizzily around her . . .

LET ARCHER AND CLEARY
AWAKEN AND CAPTURE YOUR HEART!

CAPTIVE DESIRE (2612, $3.75)
by Jane Archer

Victoria Malone fancied herself a great adventuress and student of life, but being kidnapped by handsome Cord Cordova was too much excitement for even her! Convincing her kidnapper that she had been an innocent bystander when the stagecoach was robbed was futile when he was kissing her until she was senseless!

REBEL SEDUCTION (3249, $4.25)
by Jane Archer

"Stop that train!" came Lacey Whitmore's terrified warning as she rushed toward the locomotive that carried wounded Confederates and her own beloved father. But no one paid heed, least of all the Union spy Clint McCullough, who pinned her to the ground as the train suddenly exploded into flames.

DREAM'S DESIRE (3093, $4.50)
by Gwen Cleary

Desperate to escape an arranged marriage, Antonia Winston y Ortega fled her father's hacienda to the arms of the arrogant Captain Domino. She would spend the night with him and would be free for no gentleman wants a ruined bride. And ruined she would be, for Tonia would never forget his searing kisses!

VICTORIA'S ECSTASY (2906, $4.25)
by Gwen Cleary

Proud Victoria Torrington was short of cash to run her shipping empire, so she traveled to America to meet her partner for the first time. Expecting a withered, ancient cowhand, Victoria didn't know what to do when she met virile, muscular Judge Colston and her body budded with desire.

Available wherever paperbacks are sold, or order direct from the Publisher. Send cover price plus 50¢ per copy for mailing and handling to Zebra Books, Dept. 3628, 475 Park Avenue South, New York, N.Y. 10016. Residents of New York and Tennessee must include sales tax. DO NOT SEND CASH. For a free Zebra/ Pinnacle catalog please write to the above address.

LAUREN WILDE

SWEET TEXAS WILDFIRE

ZEBRA BOOKS
KENSINGTON PUBLISHING CORP.

For Betty—
Good friend, wonderful neighbor
and loyal fan.
Thanks!

ZEBRA BOOKS

are published by

Kensington Publishing Corp.
475 Park Avenue South
New York, NY 10016

Copyright © 1992 by Joanne Redd

All rights reserved. No part of this book may be reproduced in any form or by any means without the prior written consent of the Publisher, excepting brief quotes used in reviews.

If you purchased this book without a cover you should be aware that this book is stolen property. It was reported as "unsold and destroyed" to the Publisher and neither the Author nor the Publisher has received any payment for this "stripped book."

First printing: January, 1992

Printed in the United States of America

Chapter 1

Brant Holden reined in his mount and sat in the saddle, gazing at the panoramic view before him. It was something that he did time and time again, ever since he had ridden to this high mesa east of the Pecos River. In his four years in Texas, he had seen the deep, mysterious swamps along the Sabine River, the thick pine forests of the eastern part of the state, and the rolling hills of central Texas, but this sight was something that awed him. With the land lightly sprinkled with cactus and low-growing mesquite brush, he could see clear to the horizon, seemingly to the very ends of the earth itself. With its vastness, its emptiness, its silence, there was a feeling of infinity here that both humbled him with its sheer size, and inspired him.

Brant felt alive and totally free. For his entire adult life, before he came here, he had been searching for something, something vague and ill-defined. Now he knew what it was. He had been looking for a place to put down his roots, a place to tame, to conquer, to call his own, an accomplishment that would be bought by his own sweat and toil, his own brute strength and fierce determination, not something that had been given to him on a silver platter by his affluent father. He, too, wanted to be a success in life, but in his own way and by his own choosing. No, he wouldn't be rejoining the army in the fall when his enlistment was up. His challenge in life and his future lay here in Texas.

A quiet peace fell over Brant at his decision. Then, from the corner of his eye, he spied something in the distance. He turned and looked at the line of black smoke rising ominously in the azure blue sky. Something was burning over there. Something big. Had it been to the south of him, where the Chihuahua Trail and the stage line ran, he might have thought a wagon train or stage had been attacked. Out here, in these wide open spaces, a man could see as far away as fifty miles. But the only thing that could possibly be in that direction was one of the isolated ranches. He wagered that the Indians had been up to their usual dirty work and some poor settler had been chosen as their target. The peace that he had been feeling fled, and it was replaced with dread. Grim-lipped, he turned his mount towards the line of smoke. It was his duty as a man, as well as an officer of the United States Cavalry, to offer his assistance. He could only hope that he wasn't too late.

It was almost three hours before Brant arrived on the scene. By that time, his horse was lathered and blowing hard from the steady run, and sweat was trickling down Brant's forehead and back from the hot sun. He knew he was too late before he even reached the smoldering, blackened rubble of what had once been a ranch house. The Indians didn't linger over their raids. They struck swift and once their murder and rampant destruction was done, fled like the wind.

6

Brant reined in and looked about him, seeing that the Indians had even burnt the corral, the charred mesquite logs that lay on the sandy ground clearly marking its perimeters. And that rubble that lay off to the side must have been a bunkhouse, Brant thought, while the smaller smoking ruins in the back was what was left of an outhouse. The red bastards had burned every damn thing in sight. The only thing left standing was the blackened stone fireplace of the main house.

What about the people, Brant wondered. Had they been inside the ranch house when it was set afire? There were no bodies to be seen. If that were the case, he fervently hoped they were already dead before the house was set to the torch. He couldn't think of a more horrible way to die than being consumed in a flaming inferno.

He looked at the ground around him, noting bitterly that there wasn't an arrow in sight. The Indians didn't need their primitive weapons any more, not with the filthy Comancheros providing them with repeating rifles and ammunition. For the most part, they had better guns than the army.

Spying a darkened spot on the ground a few yards from him, Brant dismounted, walked to it, and crouched. Brushing his fingers over the wet sand, he saw they were smeared with blood. Had it come from one of the Indian wounded, or had it come from one of the settlers that the Indians had carried off as a captive? If so, he pitied the poor soul. They would have been better off dead than subjected to one of the hideous tortures that the red man could devise. A shiver ran through him.

"Okay, mister, keep yer hand off yer gun, stand up, and jest turn around real slow like. Otherwise, I'll blow you to hell and back."

Brant's head shot up at the sudden sound of the voice.

7

It hadn't been the deep voice of a man. Slowly, he rose and turned, squinting against the bright light as he looked into the sun. In the shadows of the shade of a mesquite tree, about a hundred feet from him, he could barely make out the outline of a boy standing there. And the boy was holding a rifle on him, the long barrel glittering in the patches of sunlight that filtered through the lacy leaves.

"I didn't think there were any survivors," Brant said, taking a step forward.

The rifle spat fire and smoke, the sharp crack reverberating in the air as the bullet kicked up dirt less than an inch from his foot. "Goddammit!" Brant thundered angrily. "What in the hell is wrong with you? I'm not an Indian! If you hadn't missed, you would have shot me."

"I didn't miss, mister. If I had wanted to hit you, I would have. That was just a warning shot. Take one more step towards me, and the next one will be smack-dab between yer eyes."

With the gun pointed menacingly at him, Brant didn't doubt that the boy would at least try to do just that. "Why are you holding a gun on me?"

"Cause I know what you are. Some of that no-count trash come a-sneaking around to see if the Injuns left anything fer you to steal. Well, you can be on yer way, mister. There ain't nothing left."

Brant heard the catch in the boy's voice at the last words. His anger fled, to be replaced with compassion. "No, son," he said gently, "I didn't come here to rob the dead. I saw the smoke and thought maybe I could help fight off the Indians. I'm sorry I arrived too late."

"Yeah, I jest bet you did," the boy answered sarcastically. "And don't call me son!"

"I didn't mean any offense," Brant said in a soothing tone of voice. "And I can understand your fear of strangers, particularly after the terrifying experience you just went through. Now if—"

"I ain't scared of nobody! I jest want you to git outta here—and git fast!"

"I told you I didn't come here to rob the dead," Brant answered in exasperation. "I came to help. I'm a cavalry officer."

"You ain't a-wearing no uniform."

"No, I'm not," Brant admitted, "because I'm not on duty at the present time. I'm traveling from Fort Concho to Fort Davis, where I've been reassigned. I'm Captain Brant Holden, of the 4th Cavalry."

"Shore you are. And I'm Saint Peter and this here is the pearly gates."

"You still don't believe me?"

"Shore don't."

Brant was seething with frustration. It was demeaning for an officer of the United States Army to be held at bay by a mere boy. "Look at the brand on my mount. That should convince you. He's army issue."

Danny glanced at the brand on the gelding's hind-quarter that read U.S.-4C. Other than knowing it was a brand she had never seen before, it meant nothing to her. She couldn't read. "That don't mean nothing. You could have stole it from the army."

"And the saddle?" Brant countered. "Do you think that's stolen too? That's a McClennan saddle, named after one of our generals who designed it. Only the cavalry uses them. And if you'll let me go to my saddle-bags, I'll show you my uniform. Or if you need more proof, I'll even let you read my orders."

Danny was beginning to have doubts. Maybe she had misjudged the man. He certainly didn't look like low-down riffraff. To the contrary. He was the neatest attired and by far the most handsome man she had ever laid eyes on. Tall, broad-chested, taut-bellied, and lean-hipped, his face was clean shaven, and it was a face of such masculine beauty that her breath had caught in her throat when he had turned to face her. She had never seen such perfect features, or such a well-shaped mouth on a man. But there was nothing weak about it, not with that strong chin and the firm set of his lips. No, he was all man and then some. And those eyes. She had never seen such blue, blue eyes. She didn't think anything could be that blue. And his hair, where his hat was pushed back on his head, shone in the sunlight like a shiny, brand-new gold dollar. Yes, he was the best-looking male she'd ever seen. Why, he was downright pretty, and just looking at him made her belly flutter strangely.

But that didn't mean she could let her guard down, just because he was easy on the eyes and better kept than most of the men she'd seen. He could still be a low-down snake in the grass. Which was why she still had her gun peeled on him. No, it wasn't just his appearance that was giving her doubts. It was the things he'd said. First, there was his horse. Folks out here branded cattle, but not horses. And then there was that funny-looking saddle. She'd never seen such a dinky thing. Folks around here would be downright embarrassed to be caught riding on such a stingy piece of leather. Why, it wasn't hardly big enough to put your rump on. And then there was the stranger's speech. It had a peculiar clip to it, and he talked fast as a scared jack rabbit could run. Yet, with his deep voice, the sound was easy on the ears.

10

"Where're you from, mister?" Danny asked. "You talk funny."

Brant had known that the boy had been judging him and had patiently waited for his decision, but now he hesitated to tell him he was a Yankee. In the eastern part of Texas, Confederate sympathies ran high. As far as they were concerned, the war was still on and every Yankee was their enemy. But west of San Antonio, the population seemed to be divided. There were just as many who had sided with the Union as against. Since he had no idea where the boy's sympathies might lay, he braced himself for possible repercussions and said, "I'm from the East. Philadelphia, to be exact."

The stranger being a Yankee didn't bother Danny. She had never understood the war between the North and South, nor had she concerned herself with it. Oh, it had saddened her that her older brother had gone away to fight in it and never returned, but she had never understood why he had gone in the first place. Her family didn't own any slaves, and her full energies had been concentrated on surviving in this remote, dangerous frontier, and not worrying about something going on way out yonder that didn't even concern them. No, it was the way the man had looked her directly in the eye when he had answered her that impressed her. Everyone knew a thieving polecat was shifty-eyed.

"I figured you was a greenhorn, the way yer a-wearing the gun backwards in your holster," Danny commented.

Brant sensed the boy was beginning to trust him. He laughed, saying, "That's the way the cavalry carries its side arms."

"Well, if that ain't the stupidest thing I ever heard," Danny replied with obvious scorn. "How're you gonna make a quick draw like that? Lessen you're all south paws."

"We're not interested in making a quick draw. We're soldiers, not gunfighters. We're here to put down the Indians, not fight outlaws."

Yep, Danny thought, that sounded just like something a stupid greenhorn soldier would say. In Texas, a body couldn't be too fast on the draw. Just ask any Texas Ranger, and he'd done a heap more Injun fighting than any of these Yankees. Hell, those tenderfoots knew as much about fighting Injuns as a hog did Sundays. Yep, he had to be a soldier, just like he said he was.

Danny lowered her gun, saying, "Sorry I took a shot at you, mister, but there's some purty mean polecats a-running 'round these parts."

"I understand," Brant answered, breathing a sigh of relief. "But what I'm curious to know is how did you—" Brant stopped in mid-sentence as Danny walked from the concealing shadows, his mouth falling open in shocked disbelief. Recovering his senses, he blurted, "Why, you're a girl!"

"Shore am."

Again Brant's eyes quickly swept over her. No, he corrected himself, she wasn't just a girl. She was a full-grown woman, and the snug shirt and pants hugged every womanly curve and hollow like a second skin. In an age where women, even those of high quality, bared their shoulders and a good deal of their bosoms in their low-cut ball gowns, Brant had thought himself immune to the sight of blatant femininity. But strangely the male attire this girl was wearing seemed to accent her female attributes even more so than exposure, leaving almost nothing to the imagination, and despite his good breeding

12

and rigid self-control, he found himself becoming aroused. Filled with self-disgust, he tore his eyes away from the provocative sight, saying, "Excuse me for staring, but I thought you were a boy, dressed the way you are."

"I figured that. You had a mighty surprised look on yer face when I walked out, sort of like a pot licker a-sniffing a prairie dog's hole and a-getting his nose bit by a snake."

Brant frowned. "Pardon me, but just what is a pot licker?"

"Why, a hound dog," Danny answered, as if it were the most stupid question in the world.

Brant smiled, thinking he probably did look as foolish. He directed his attention to the young woman's face. To his surprise, he found she was actually pretty. Her flawless complexion was tanned a golden color from exposure to the sun, and there was a light sprinkling of faint freckles across the bridge of her pert nose, both of which would have mortified any of the well-bred ladies of his class back east, who fiercely protected their lily-white skin as if it were their most precious possession. Her jet black eyes were alert and shining with intelligence, the dark, sooty lashes incredibly long and thick. Her mouth was a little too generous for the current mode of fashion, but Brant found it as provocative as her shapely body, particularly the full lower lip that seemed to be begging to be kissed. Knowing he was once more on dangerous ground, he tore his eyes away from her mouth, to find himself gazing at her hair. He had never seen such a thick mane, or such a glorious color. It seemed to turn from burnished brown to red, then back again as the light caught it. She had pulled it back and tied it at the nape of her neck, but rebellious curls had escaped and framed her face, making it look delightfully unruly. Altogether, she had a wild beauty about her that bordered on the exotic. He was fascinated.

"You're a-gawking again, mister," Danny said bluntly.

Brant jerked his eyes away, feeling acutely embarrassed. "Forgive me. It's just that I'm still shocked to find a woman here. How did you manage to escape?"

"I didn't escape. I wasn't here. I was down at the creek over yonder," Danny explained, pointing to a line of cottonwoods about a mile away. "I heard gunshots and saw the house was surrounded by Injuns. I reckon there must have been at least thirty of them red devils. When they stopped a-shooting, I knew my brother was dead and there wasn't nothing I could do to help him. So I hid down by the creek until they rode away. I found him a-laying right here," Danny said, pointing to blood-soaked sand. "He didn't even git inside."

"What about your cowhands? I thought I saw the rubble of a bunkhouse."

"Yep, we had a little bunkhouse. Had a couple of Meskins a-working fer us 'till a month ago. As soon as the Injuns started their spring raiding, they lit out of here like a bunch of turpentined cats."

"Then there was no one on the ranch but you and your brother?"

"Yep, it's just been the two of us since Pa died ten years ago."

"Where's your brother's body?"

"I was a-burying him back there behind the mesquite when you rode up, next to my ma and pa."

"When did your mother die?"

"When I was born."

At that moment, Danny looked very small and defenseless, something that struck a strong protective cord deep within Brant. He wanted to take her in his arms and comfort her, something that, for him, was extraordinary. He was a tough, battle-seasoned soldier who had seen more than his share of death over the past ten years, a man not given to emotionalism by his very nature. He struggled to subdue the strange impulse, but it was more the knowledge that this feisty girl would probably not welcome his show of compassion, than his own natural reserve, that deterred him. Instead he said, "Show me where the graveyard is. I'll bury him for you."

"I can do it," Danny answered stubbornly.

She's just like all these frontier settlers, Brant thought, fiercely independent. "Then I'll help you. Surely, you'll allow me that much."

Danny frowned. Somehow, the golden-haired stranger had made it sound as if she would be doing him a favor, and not the other way around. "Well . . . all right, then," she agreed reluctantly.

As they walked towards the mesquite tree, Brant asked, "What's your name?"

Danny shook her head, thinking only a greenhorn would out-and-out ask someone's name. You were supposed to ask what they wanted to be called. She sure hoped he didn't make that mistake with some man running from the law. He was liable to get his fool head shot off. "Danny Morgan."

"Danny?" Brant asked in surprise. "Is that a nickname for Danielle?"

"Nope, it's a nickname for Daniel."

"Your father named you a man's name?" Brant asked in disbelief.

"He shore did. He already had the name picked out

15

'fore I was born, so he jest put that handle on me anyway."

"He wanted two sons?" Brant surmised.

"Nope, he wanted four. Can't have too many boys on a ranch, you know. But I didn't let him down. I'm jest as good a cowhand as any of my brothers were. I can rope and brand and herd cows jest as good as they could. And I'm a dad-blasted better shot than any of 'em were," Danny said, patting the six-shooter strapped to her hip. "Pa said so himself. Said I was the best waddy screw in the whole lot."

"Waddy screw?" Brant asked, his nose wrinkling in distaste. "Why did he call you that?"

"That's jest another name for cowhand that folks 'round here use."

Brant knew that Danny's father must have made her feel inferior because she was a female. Apparently, she had shown the old man her stuff and was proud of her accomplishments. While Brant found the idea of a woman cowhand appalling, he couldn't help but feel an admiration for the spunky girl walking beside him. "Then you had two other brothers. Where are they?"

"Don't rightly know where Jake went. He took off for California ten years ago. And Joe never came back from the war. I reckon he got himself killed."

"You never heard for sure?"

"Nope. All we ever heard was he was a-missing in action. Leastways, that's what Mr. Perkins at the general store said. He read the letter to us."

Which meant that his body was never found, or was so badly mutilated that it couldn't be identified, Brant thought grimly. As commanding officer of a squadron during the war, he'd had to send a few of those letters to

16

next of kin himself. He was glad Danny had accepted the worst. It was certainly better than clinging to false hopes that your loved one might show up some day. Yes, she was down to earth as well as tough.

As they walked beneath the gnarled limbs of the mesquite tree, Brant saw the roan standing in the distance. "Is that your horse?"

"Yep, that's Red. I reckon it was a good thing I was a-feeling lazy this morning and decided to ride to the creek, 'stead of a-walking. Otherwise those dad-blasted 'Paches would have run him off with the rest of our horses."

Brant stopped in mid-stride. "Apaches? You mean Comanches, don't you?"

"Nope. Those Injuns were 'Paches."

"You're sure?"

"'Course I'm shore!" Danny said hotly. "I ain't no greenhorn. Consarn it, I know the difference between a 'Pache and a Comanche! Those Injuns weren't dressed in buckskins. They was a-wearing calico shirts, breech-cloths, knee-high moccasins, and those bright colored rags they wear around their heads to keep the hair outta their eyes."

It was obvious to Brant that Danny was much more knowledgeable about Apaches than he was. He'd been fighting Comanches since his arrival in Texas, and if truth be known, he'd spent more time chasing them than fighting. "I wasn't doubting your word, Danny. It's just that I'd been led to believe that the Apaches stayed west of the Pecos River."

"They did, 'til awhile back. My brother said that this used to be 'Pache country a long time ago. Then the Comanches came and chased them across the Pecos. For

17

a long time, that's all we seen was Comanches. But here lately, the 'Paches are back.''

And Brant knew why they had come back to their old territory. Ever since President Grant had finally bowed to the pressure General Sheridan was exerting on him to let the army do their job and keep the Indian Bureau out of their business, the cavalry here in Texas was making the first headway against the Comanches since they had been sent back to Texas after the war. A great deal of the credit went to Colonel Ranald Mackenzie and the 9th Cavalry of Negro troopers that the Indians called "Buffalo Soldiers." Operating out of Fort Griffin, Fort Concho, and Fort Richardson, Mackenzie kept his men in the field, giving the Comanches no respite. The government policy of "feed 'em in the winter and fight 'em in the summer" was finally out. Now, instead of the Comanches raiding against their old enemies, the Texans, every summer, then slipping back into the Indian Territory under the protection of the Indian Bureau and fattening up on government rations, the army had the authority to seek them out in their winter lairs, and the cavalry's new tactics were beginning to pay off. For the first time, the army had the Comanches on the run. That's why they had deserted this area. But it didn't seem to help the settlers here much. As soon as they left, the dreaded Apaches came back, Indians that Brant had heard were the most savage, cunning Indians on the entire Northern Continent, and Fort Davis, his destination, lay in the heart of *Apacheria.*

When they reached the graveyard, Brant was shocked to find that Danny had already dug the grave and halfway buried her brother. It seemed impossible that such a small girl could have dragged a grown man that distance

18

and dug a hole that deep in a little over a few hours. He was amazed at her strength. Seeing her pick up the shovel, he took it from her, saying, "Let me shovel for awhile."

"I said I could do it, mister," Danny replied tightly.

"I know," Brant answered in a soothing tone of voice, "but you also promised to let me help. Let me start, and you can finish it. You must be tired."

Danny was, although she would have never admitted it. The muscles in her arms and back were aching something awful, and there were blisters on her hands. But she had been determined to get her brother buried before dark. Otherwise, she would have to contend with an ugly pack of hungry wolves.

Reluctantly, she relinquished the shovel and sank wearily to the ground beside the grave, watching as the golden-haired stranger filled the gaping hole. He had said that he was an officer, someone that she had pictured in her mind as being weak and puny, because Joe, on his one and only furlough from the Confederate Army, had said the officers sat on their rumps while the soldiers did all the work. But this man was powerful and well muscled. She could see them bunching on his back and upper arms beneath his shirt. The sight made her belly flutter strangely again. He sure did peculiar things to her.

"How come the shovel wasn't burned?" Brant asked as he tossed a shovelful of dirt into the grave.

"I took it with me to the creek this morning so I could dig fer worms. That's what I was a-doing down there, a-fishing."

Brant had tossed his hat aside to dig, and Danny sat admiring his thick, golden hair while he worked. It had a natural wave to it and curled behind his ears, ears that sat

19

flat against his well-shaped head and didn't poke out like most of the waddies that drifted through the area. And his skin wasn't pale, either, like all of the greenhorns she'd seen. One thing she purely couldn't stand was a pasty-faced man. It made them look sickly. No, the stranger's skin was just as tanned as hers. Yep, he sure was a fine-looking man.

Because Danny had been so occupied with admiring Brant, she didn't realize that he had finished covering the grave until the chore was accomplished. Seeing him tossing aside the shovel, she took notice, then glared at him and said in an accusing voice, "I was supposed to finish it."

Brant pasted an innocent look on his face and lied adroitly, "I got so carried away that I completely forgot. Forgive me."

Danny shot him a suspicious look. He had a way of getting around her that didn't set easy with her. When she said she wanted to do something, she gol-durn meant it. She'd have to keep an eagle eye on him. He was as smooth-talking as a sneaky card shark.

Brant ignored Danny's glare and asked, "Do you want to put a cross on the grave?"

Danny looked down at the mound of dirt and frowned, then answered, "Nope, I reckon that ain't necessary. The Almighty knows Pete was an honest, hard-working, God-fearing man. Reckon he'll judge him by that, and not some cross on his grave."

"Would you like to say any words over him? I have a Bible in my saddlebags. I could read the Twenty-third Psalm, if you like."

"Nope, I don't reckon that's necessary either. My folks weren't much fer a-preaching and all that. The Big Man upstairs would think it kinda strange if I started a-gushing

20

off religion now. 'Sides, he ain't got time to listen to all that. Like I said, he knows what kinda man Pete was. All them fancy words ain't gonna change his a-judging. You can't fool him."

Brant was touched by Danny's simple faith. Nor was he shocked by her apparent lack of grief, for he had seen no tears. He'd been in Texas long enough to know the settlers didn't mourn their dead like they did back east. As soon as the body was in the ground, they went back to their daily chores. It wasn't that they were callous or unfeeling. In this harsh land where survival was a moment-to-moment struggle, extended grieving was a luxury they couldn't afford. Nor did they grieve openly. To them, it was a private affair.

"Would you like to be alone with the grave for a few minutes before we leave?" Brant asked, thinking to give Danny her privacy.

Danny's head came up like a shot. "What are you a-talking about, a-leaving?"

"I'll escort you to the nearest town."

"You gotta be plumb loco if you think I'm a-leaving. This ranch is my home. I ain't a-going nowhere!"

Brant was stunned, both by her announcement and the fierce expression on her face. Finally recovering, he said, "You can't stay out here, a woman all alone."

Danny's black eyes flashed dangerously. "What's my being a girl got to do with it? I told you I can do anything my brothers can do. I'm jest as much a man as they were!"

Brant's gaze swept over Danny's obvious womanly curves. Maybe in spirit you are, he thought, but not in body. But he realized that he had made a serious mistake by throwing Danny's sex in her face. Apparently, to her, it was a stigma that she had worked hard to overcome all her life. But still, like it or not, she *was* a woman, and a damned appealing one at that, fair game for any gang of outlaws, or party of raiding Indians passing through. If he thought it would do any good, he'd tie her to her saddle and forcibly take her to the next town, but he knew as soon as he left her, she'd make a beeline back to this ranch. No, she wasn't a woman who could be forced. He'd have to reason with her.

"Danny, I can understand you not wanting to leave your home. I'd feel the same way. But you have no shelter, no where to sleep."

"I've slept in the open before."

"You have nothing to eat," Brant argued.

"I can shoot game," Danny countered.

"But what will you do when the game plays out and winter comes? You can't go on living like that indefinitely."

Danny frowned, and Brant pressed his advantage. "You strike me as an intelligent person. With all the Apaches and outlaws running around here, you'd be constantly fighting them off. What will you do when your ammunition plays out?"

Danny's face drained of all color. Without ammunition, she'd be at those varmints' mercy. And she didn't have any money to buy any more. Their stash of money had been burned in the fire. Dad-blasted, why hadn't Pete taken the sale of their last herd in coins, instead of those consarn greenbacks? Angry tears glittered in her eyes. "Dad-gum those redskins! Why'd they have to steal our herd? I could have sold it fer a fresh start. And it took us two years to round up those ornery longhorns. Two dad-blasted years of a-chasing them down! If they wanted beef to eat, there's plenty of it out here on the hoof. They didn't have to take ours!"

22

So she doesn't have any money, Brant thought. Unless her brother had some put aside at a local bank she doesn't know about. "They didn't steal your longhorns to eat. They stole them to sell to the ranchers in New Mexico and Arizona."

"Are you a-talking about white men?" Danny asked in a shocked voice.

"Yes."

"But they got our brand on 'em. Those ranchers would know they've been stolen."

"Yes, they know they're stolen, and they know where the Indians got them and how. But they turn a blind eye and buy them anyway."

"Those dad-blasted polecats!" Danny said angrily, whipping her hat off her head and throwing it violently on the ground. "They should've been hung 'fore they was born."

Brant was prone to agree. The ranchers' willingness to buy the stolen Texas cattle was making the army's job all the harder. If the Indians didn't have a market for their stolen goods, they couldn't buy guns and ammunition, which started the whole cycle all over again, and all because of the white man's greed. But just let them be the target, instead of the Texans, and those ranchers would be hollering so loud for the army to do something that you could hear them all the way to Washington.

Brant bent and picked up Danny's hat and rifle. Handing them to her, he said, "We'd better get going. Maybe we can reach town before nightfall. Then we can post a letter to your nearest of kin, so that they can send you money for passage to wherever they might be."

"Ain't got no kinfolk," Danny calmly announced.

"No one at all?" Brant asked in disbelief. "No

23

aunts, or uncles, or cousins?"

"Not that I know of."

"What about your brother in California? Do you know where he is?"

"Nope."

"He never sent a letter, saying where he had settled?"

"Couldn't send no letter, 'cause he can't write."

Things were getting much more complicated than Brant had anticipated. "What about some of the other ranchers in this area? Do you have friends among them?"

"Nearest ranch I know of is fifty miles away. Don't know those folks, but maybe they could use a good waddy."

"Danny, if you're thinking of hiring out as a cowhand, you may as well get that notion out of your head right now," Brant said in a firm voice. "You may be as good a cowhand, or better than most, but no one is going to hire a woman cowhand."

"They won't have to know I'm a woman. I could cut my hair."

Cut that beautiful mane of hair, Brant thought in horror. "Absolutely not! You'll do nothing of the sort," Brant said in his best commanding voice.

Danny's black eyes narrowed. "Now, you jest back off, mister," she said angrily. "You ain't straw boss here, and I ain't one of your troopers to be a-ordering 'round. Ain't nobody gonna tell me what I can and can't do."

Brant fought down his rising exasperation. "All right, I can't tell you what to do," he admitted grudgingly, "but I can tell you this much. Cutting your hair isn't going to fool anyone. You still have a woman's body, and there's no way you can hide that."

Danny was very aware of Brant's eyes on her breasts, making her feel peculiar again, all tingly like. "I could take to a-wearing a coat all the time."

"And don't you think they'll think that a little odd, especially in the heat of the summer?" Brant's gaze dropped to her legs. "Besides, that won't hide your legs, and whether you like it or not, no cowhand has legs shaped like yours. Why, you're not even bowlegged."

Danny's chin stubbornly rose another inch. "I could start a-walking that way."

Brant's patience was at an end. She was undoubtedly the most obstinate human he'd ever had the misfortune to run across. He threw up his hands in disgust and said, "All right! Do what you damn well want to! I guess you're not as smart as I thought you were."

Danny didn't know why, but for some strange reason, she wanted this man's approval. "Nope, I reckon you're right," she admitted reluctantly. "I couldn't fool those cowhands fer long. The first time they saw me a-sneaking into the bushes and a-squatting, 'stead of a-standing to pee, they'd know I was a girl."

Brant knew Danny didn't mean to be crude, that like all country people, she was just being blunt. They spoke of the acts of nature in a much more straightforward manner than polite society did. But none the less, his face turned red, making him feel like a naive youth.

To his relief, Danny didn't notice. She turned and walked to her horse, saying over her shoulder, "Well, I reckon you're right. I'd better be a-heading for town. But it ain't necessary for you to escort me. I can take care of myself."

Brant shook his head, thinking he was in for yet another argument. Dammit, why did she have to be so independent? He swept up his hat and quickly caught up with her, saying, "I'll ride along with you anyway. With the possibility of those Apaches still prowling around, two guns are better than one."

Danny couldn't fault his reasoning, but she hated being beholden to anyone, particularly when she didn't need protecting. "You a-going that way, anyhow?"

"Yes. I need to pick up supplies," Brant lied.

"Well, I reckon in that case, there ain't no harm in us a-traveling together. But don't be a-thinking that we'll make it 'fore nightfall. Not lessen you're a-planning on a-riding like a likkered Injun. It's thirty miles away."

"That's the nearest town?" Brant asked with a stunned expression on his face.

"Yep."

Brant shook his head, thinking that he would never adjust to the great distances between places in this vast, empty country, then, returning his attention to the problem at hand, asked, "Do you have any friends there that you can stay with?"

Danny frowned, then answered, "Well, I reckon Rose is my friend. She'll probably let me stay with her fer a spell. Leastways, 'til I can decide what I'm gonna do."

Thank God, there was someone he could leave her with, Brant thought. He was beginning to fear that he was stuck with a homeless woman on his hands, and even if she insisted she didn't need protecting, he felt responsible.

Before Brant could even offer to help Danny mount, she was in the saddle, frustrating his good manners and leaving a deep scowl of disapproval on his face.

"What's the matter?" Danny asked. "What're you a-looking so sour about?"

26

"I was going to help you mount."

"Help me git on my horse?" Danny asked in disbelief. "Why?"

"It's considered good manners for a gentleman to help a lady mount her horse."

"Well, maybe those sissy ladies need help, but I don't. Hellfire, I've been a-riding since I was knee-high to a grasshopper." Danny gazed off in the direction where Brant's horse waited. "Swing up behind me, and I'll give you a lift to yer horse."

"Thank you, but that's not necessary," Brant answered a little stiffly, thinking her offer to aid him not at all appropriate. A man might make such an offer to a woman, but not vice versa, and he was certainly capable of walking that short a distance. "I'll get my mount and be right with you."

Within a few minutes, the two were riding away, leaving a thick trail of dust in their wake. Suddenly Danny wheeled her mount and gazed back at the blackened rubble that had once been her home. Brant turned his horse and reined in beside her.

"I'm a-coming back someday. I ain't gonna let no redskins chase me off fer good. Somehow I'll git money fer a fresh start. I'll be back. I won't fergit you."

It wasn't until Danny's last words that Brant realized that she had been talking to the land, and not him. As she turned her horse and rode off, Brant gazed thoughtfully at her back. He knew she'd keep her vow. He couldn't imagine how she'd manage, but he knew she would. She was the most determined person he had ever met.

He put his spurs to his horse and galloped off after her.

Chapter 2

Danny and Brant camped that evening by a stream in a grove of scrubby oaks that Danny called a "shinnery." It soon became obvious to Brant that she was accustomed to camping out. Before he had even finished unsaddling and tending to his mount, she had finished with hers and had a fire going.

As Brant tossed his saddle, saddlebags, and bedroll down by the fire, Danny asked, "What grub are you a-hauling with you?"

"I've some bacon and cornmeal. And of course, there's coffee. But I'd better warn you. It's army issue."

"Ain't no coffee I can't drink," Danny assured him. "I'll take that cornmeal. I can make ash cakes outta it. But you can keep the bacon, 'cept for a slice or two fer the cakes. I'll shoot us a couple of jack rabbits I seen out yonder."

Brant couldn't believe his ears. He'd emptied his carbine more than once trying to shoot a jack rabbit. They had to be the swiftest animals on earth, and once more, they didn't run in a straight line. They zigzagged all over the place.

Danny picked up her rifle and walked from the grove of trees. Brant followed, curious to see if she could actually bring down a jack rabbit. The sun was just going down, casting long shadows over everything. Then, as something darted from a clump of cactus, Danny's gun flew to her shoulder, and she fired. The jack rabbit went up in the air from the impact of the bullet, did a complete somersault, and landed with a thump.

"That's yers," Danny announced. "Now I'll shoot one fer me."

A moment later, another jack rabbit went darting across the plain, bounding this way and that as it ran directly away from them. All Brant could see was its tail and huge ears sticking up. It seemed an impossible target. From this distance, it was hardly as big as a gold dollar, to say nothing of its rapid, erratic movement. Again, Danny demonstrated her remarkable marksmanship, and a second rabbit went flying through the air.

Danny turned and grinned at the dumbfounded expression on Brant's face. "I told you I was a good shot," she said in a smug voice.

"Yes, that *was* extraordinary shooting," Brant admitted, still staring in disbelief out at the prairie.

"Well, we'd better git out there and fetch 'em, 'fore it gits too dark to find 'em," Danny drawled, strolling off.

Later, back at the camp, the two skinned and gutted the rabbits. Brant was no novice at the chore. He'd skinned many a cottontail, squirrel, deer, and antelope. But Danny had hers dressed and on the spit over the fire before he was even halfway through. Compared to her, he was a greenhorn, Brant thought in self-disgust as he washed the blood from his hands in the small stream a few minutes later.

When he returned to camp, the coffee pot was on the fire, and Danny was frying a slice of bacon in his tarnished frying pan. Brant sat down and watched while she tossed out the bacon, then mixed cornmeal, salt, and water in the pan and stirred the mixture. "You got any sugar with you?" she asked.

"No, I'm afraid not. I don't use it in my coffee."

"I don't either, but just a dash keeps these ash cakes from a-tasting so plain."

Danny patted the cornmeal mixture into little cakes, wrapped them in oak leaves, and slipped them into a hole she dug with a stick beneath the ashes of the fire.

"They actually bake in there?" Brant asked in amazement.

"Yep. Ain't you ever seen no one make ash cakes?"

"No."

"Then what're you a-hauling cornmeal fer?"

"We make a mush out of it for breakfast."

Danny's small nose wrinkled. "That don't sound very tasty to me."

"It isn't," Brant admitted. "But it doesn't taste any worse than the other field rations we eat. Each man is issued a pound of hardtack, three-quarters of a pound of bacon or salt pork, an ounce of coffee, and a little salt each day. When we get cornmeal and beans, it's a luxury."

Danny had had a hard life, but she had never gone hungry. She was a little shocked at the skimpy fare the army fed its cavalry. "You could shoot game," she suggested.

30

"We do, if there's any around." But never jack rabbits, Brant added silently. "Then we make soup and pound our hardtack into crumbs and dump them into it."

"What's this hardtack you keep a-talking about?"

"The most god-awful stuff you ever tasted. It's an unleavened biscuit made from flour and water, and it's so hard that you can't chew it, not without risking knocking your teeth out. It has to be soaked first, and then it's rubbery. The troopers call it 'floortile,' and as I said, it's so hard that the only way you can crush it is by pounding it with your gun butt. So you see, this fare we're having tonight will taste like a feast to me."

When the rabbits were toasted to a golden brown, Danny took Brant's one and only tin plate, slid a rabbit on it, slipped a few ash cakes beside it, and handed it to him, saying, "Well, dig in, partner."

"No, you take the plate," Brant objected politely, shoving the plate back into her hands. "I'll eat out of the frying pan."

Brant picked up the pan and slid the second rabbit onto it, but when he tried to slip an ash cake from the hole, he burned his fingers.

"Let me fish 'em out fer you," Danny offered, putting down her plate. "There's a trick to it. You have to be as fast as a card shark a-slipping an ace up his sleeve while he's a-dealing."

Danny's slender fingers went in and out of the hole like flashes of lightning. She handed the skillet back to Brant with a big grin on her face.

"Thank you," Brant said, then sank to the ground and placed the skillet over his crossed legs. He pushed the toasted oak leaves aside, picked up the ash cake, and put it into his mouth. He couldn't believe the taste. "Why,

31

these cakes are delicious," he commented.

"They're even better with butter on 'em."

"You had a milk cow?" he asked in surprise. The few ranchers he had met around Fort Concho had sworn they would just as soon drink poison as milk. They raised cattle for their meat and hides, and nothing else. Even their children didn't drink cow's milk.

"Nope, but ever now and then, we'd milk one of the heifers during calving season, so we could have butter."

"You said you had longhorns. Wasn't that rather dangerous? Those horns are wicked, and those are wild cattle."

"Well, I ain't a-saying they exactly stood still fer it. Took one of us to milk 'em and the other to hold the bucket in place. And those consarn cows won't let you bring down the milk either. We had to let the calf bring it down fer us. Then we'd have to stake him and milk as fast as blue blazes, with him a-bawling something awful and that heifer jest a-stomping and a-kicking the whole time. We didn't do it very often. Not lessen we had a mighty hankering fer butter."

Brant imagined not. He'd go without butter for the rest of his life before he'd tangle with an irate longhorn cow. "Where did you learn to cook?"

"Pete taught me. He was twelve years older than me, so he remembered some cooking he'd learned from our ma. The rest he jest picked up on his own. He was jest about the best danged cook in these here parts. Every hand we ever had said he cooked the best vittles they'd ever eaten."

Danny turned her attention to her food, eating with a gusto that would have put Brant's troopers to shame. Then, as she licked her fingers when she had finished,

32

Brant stared in shock at her atrocious table manners. But the longer she licked, the less he thought about Danny's manners, or lack of them. The sight of her little pink tongue flicking in and out was disturbingly erotic.

"What're you a-gawking at?"

Brant startled and jerked his eyes away guiltily. He was too much of a gentleman to correct Danny's manners, and he certainly wasn't going to tell her the shocking, ungentlemanly things he had been thinking. "I was just surprised that you finished eating before me."

Danny grinned sheepishly. "Yeah, I reckon I did make a pig of myself, a-wolfing down that food like there ain't gonna be no tomorrow, but I was as hungry as a bear jest a-coming outta his lair at springtime." She glanced at the coffeepot, then asked, "You want a cup of coffee?"

"No, I'll wait until I've finished eating."

"Then I reckon I'll go ahead and have a cup," Danny said, rising and reaching for the pot. "That way, I'll be through by the time you're finished, since we only got one cup." She grinned across the fire. "Lessen you're a-planning on a-drinking from that frying pan too."

Brant chuckled, answering, "No, I don't think so."

Danny poured herself a cup of coffee and sat back down, Indian fashion, a position that Brant thought shocking for a woman, even if she was dressed in pants. She took a big sip, then spat it out on the ground, saying, "Gol-durn! That's the foulest stuff I ever tasted! What's it got in it? Sawdust?"

Brant couldn't blame Danny for spitting out the coffee. Only his good manners had kept him from doing the same the first time he had tasted army coffee. His eyes twinkled with amusement as he said, "I warned you that it was army issue. That's Santos coffee, and yes, it

33

does rather taste like burned sawdust, with a little quinine thrown in."

"Can't the army give you nothing better than that poison to drink?"

"Apparently not. Believe it or not, you get used to it after a while."

"Not me," Danny said in an empathic voice, tossing the coal-black brew in the cup on the ground. "I'd never git used to it. I'd jest as soon drink kerosene."

When Brant had finished eating, he drank a cup of coffee, while Danny watched as if she expected him to drop dead at any minute, much to his amusement. Tossing the dregs out, he picked up the frying pan and rose, saying, "Give me your plate, and I'll take these down to the stream to wash out."

Danny didn't object. She'd shot the meat and done the cooking. It was only fair that he wash the dishes. In camp, everyone should pull their weight, even a green-horn.

When Brant returned, Danny had untied her hair and was trying to comb it out with her fingers. Brant came to a dead halt at the sight of Danny sitting on the ground with her long hair hanging to her waist around her like a tumbling waterfall of riotous curls, the firelight playing over it picking up its glorious reddish highlights.

Seeing him staring, Danny said in disgust, "Ain't it jest about the most fly-away stuff you ever seen? It goes every which way but what I want it to. I'd a-cut the ornery stuff a long time ago, 'cept every durn time I even thought about it, Pete would have a regular conniption. Got some dad-blasted burrs in it while I was a-hiding down at the creek," Danny explained, viciously tearing

34

one from a long strand hanging over her shoulder. "Now I'll have a heck of a time a-trying to git 'em out."

Brant hadn't realized that he had been holding his breath until he started to speak. The words came out in a rush of air. "I've a brush you can borrow."

Danny's eyes lit up. "Shore enough?"

"Yes, but it's a man's brush. It doesn't have a handle on it."

"Shucks, I ain't never had a brush with a handle on it. Me and Pete always used the same one. If you don't mind me a-using it, I'd shore appreciate it."

Brant walked to his saddlebags, pulled out the brush, and handed it to her across the fire. Danny gaped at the gleaming metal on the top and sides in wonder, then asked, "Is this real silver?"

"Yes, it is," Brant answered tightly. "It was a gift from my father."

He couldn't have sent me a plain wooden one, Brant thought in renewed disgust. Oh, no, it had to be pure silver. That was just like the Old Man. Everything had to be ostentatious. He flaunted his wealth and used the power it gave him ruthlessly. Except Brant was one man who couldn't be bought and wouldn't be forced to bow to the Old Man's wishes. At eighteen, he'd rebelled and joined the army in a deliberate act of defiance. And the Old Man still hadn't learned that he couldn't run him like he did everyone else. His father still thought he'd bring him to heel.

Unaware of the angry expression on Brant's face, Danny ran her fingers over the engraving on the top of the brush and asked, "What's this say?"

Her question tore Brant from his dark brooding.

"Those are my initials, B.C.H."

Brantley Carelton Holden, Brant thought bitterly. Oh, yes, the Old Man had to even pick the most ostentatious name he could think of. Nothing plain and simple for *his* son.

Danny laughed, saying, "I thought they was a word." She ducked her head in the first show of embarrassment that Brant had seen. "I can't read, you know. I reckon you think I'm stupid 'cause I ain't had no book learning."

Brant had already guessed that Danny was illiterate from the other things she had told him. He hadn't been particularly surprised. It wasn't until he had joined the army and left his affluent and privileged life behind him that he had realized the shockingly high rate of illiteracy that existed in this country, not only among his troopers, but among the general population. The farther west he went, the more illiteracy he had found. Education seemed to go hand in hand with a man's economic status, a higher education such as his a decided luxury. Brant had never looked down on those who hadn't had the same opportunities as he. In his opinion, the shame was not theirs, but the state governments' that made no effort to improve the lot of the greater majority of their citizens.

"No, Danny, I don't think you're stupid just because you can't read or write. That has nothing to do with intelligence. You just never had the opportunity to learn."

Danny was immensely relieved. She wanted this man to admire and respect her, wanted it something fierce. That was why she had tried to impress him with her shooting. He was just about the most beautiful man she had ever seen, and he talked so pretty and had such pretty manners. And he was neat as a pin and his boots so shiny she could practically see her reflection in them, instead of being all muddy and scuffed-up like the cowhands she knew. Why, he even smelled good, of soap and leather and sunshine, while most of the waddies she knew smelled worse than a tomcat's spray.

She raised her head and smiled broadly, saying, "I reckon that's the gospel truth. I can't help it if I never had any book learning, any more than you can help a-being a greenhorn."

Brant's lips twitched with amusement. He wasn't quite as green as Danny thought. He'd picked up a few things since he'd come to Texas. But being with Danny was an education in itself. She had passed on information which would be useful if he planned on staying in Texas. Now he knew that cowhands in this area were called waddies; hounds, pot lickers; and everyone unsavory, a polecat. Curious about the last, he asked, "Why do you call the worst people you know polecats? Because of their foul smell?"

"No, because they're the most dangerous and meanest four-legged creatures 'round these parts. If you ever run into a polecat, mister, you'd better high tail it fast, or blast it to hell, 'fore it bites you."

Brant frowned. "I wasn't aware that skunks bit people."

"Those dad-blasted mad ones do. They'll plumb tear you apart. But all it takes is jest one bite, and you're a dead man. Might as well put yer gun to yer head and kill yerself right then and there."

"Are you saying the skunks around here are rabid?" Brant asked in a shocked voice.

"I don't know what you greenhorns call it, but we call 'em mad out here. Skunks are one critter we don't fool 'round with. And skunks aren't the only ones that can git it. So can dogs."

Brant wondered at the sad expression that crossed Danny's face at her last words. Then, as she brushed her long hair, he leaned back against his saddle and watched. He knew he was staring, but he couldn't seem to help himself. Her hair was absolutely beautiful, and there was something strangely sensuous about watching her brush it. It was all he could do to keep from walking to her and burying his hands in that glorious mass. When Danny put down the brush and tied it back in place, he felt a keen disappointment.

After carefully removing any hairs and the burrs caught in the bristles, Danny handed the brush back to Brant, saying, "Thanks, mister."

Brant accepted the brush, noting that it was still warm from the heat of her hand. "I wish you'd call me by my name, and not mister. That makes it sound like you don't like me."

Oh, she liked him all right. More and more by the minute. She blushed in embarrassment, giving her cheeks a rosy flush as she admitted, "I would, 'cept I fergot what it is. Didn't pay no never mind when you ran it past me."

"It's Brant. Brant Holden."

"Brant," Danny said softly, testing the sound of the name on her ears. "That's a mighty purty name. I ain't never heard it 'fore."

The soft sound of Danny saying his name sent a shiver through Brant. It was almost as if she had reached out and touched him intimately. "It's not a common name," he answered in a voice that was suddenly hoarse.

"What's wrong with yer voice? You sound like you got a frog in your throat."

Damn, she picked up on every little thing, Brant thought. Quickly, he cleared his throat, then said, "Nothing's wrong. Sometimes that army coffee leaves my throat feeling scratchy."

"It's a dad-blasted wonder you got any throat left," Danny commented. She rose, stretched out her arms, and yawned. Brant found himself gaping at her high, proud breasts that seemed to be all but knocking his eyes out of his head. His mouth and throat turned dry; his heart suddenly raced.

Totally misinterpreting the expression on his face, Danny said, " 'Cuse me for yawning in yer face like that, but I'm plumb tuckered out. Reckon I'll go to bed now."

"Wait a minute. I'll get my blanket for you."

"Oh, I couldn't take yer only blanket. That wouldn't be right."

"I'm carrying two with me. This early in the spring, you never know when one of those—what do you Texans call them? Northers?—might come through."

"Yep, they're about as sneaky as a cardsharp with five aces up his sleeve. It can be jest as warm as toast one minute, then cold enough to freeze the horns off a billy goat the next. Why, I even seen one come through in July. Hailstones as big as hen's eggs bouncing all over the ground like a bunch of dad-blasted balls. Had to get off my horse and sit under him to keep from a-being beaten to death. Poor old Red. He was so banged up he couldn't hardly walk for a week. Why, those consarn things even tore up my saddle. Looked like some likkered-up fool had taken a hammer to it."

While Danny was expounding on Texas weather, Brant had walked to his blankets, unrolled them, and carried one to her. As he stepped around the fire to hand it to her, Danny shrieked, "Watch out where you're a-walking, you dad-blasted fool! You almost stepped on Charlie!"

Brant glanced around at the bare ground all around him, then asked, "Charlie? What in the hell are you talking about?"

"Sorry I cussed you out, but I was scared you'd squash him. Charlie is my pet snake, and I keep him in this here bag," Danny explained, patting the canvas bag she had snatched up just in the nick of time.

Brant had seen the bag hanging at Danny's side by a shoulder strap while they were riding. He had assumed that it was a gaming bag of some sort. "You have a pet snake?" he asked in disbelief.

"Shore do," Danny answered with a big smile on her face. "I've had him since he was a baby." She reached into the bag with one hand, saying, "Come on out here, Charlie, and meet my new friend."

Brant watched with revulsion as Danny pulled the snake from the bag and proudly held the reptile up by the neck for him to see, while the rest of its two-foot-long body twisted and writhed in the air. "You don't need to be scared of him," Danny said, mistaking the look of revulsion on Brant's face for one of fear. "He's jest a harmless grass snake." She gently stroked the snake's head with one finger, making a shiver run up Brant's spine, saying, "Say howdy to my new friend, Charlie."

Charlie's forked tongue flicked in and out. Apparently Danny considered that a greeting, for she smiled and said in a pleased voice, "That's a good boy." Setting the snake on the ground, she said, "Now you go on and see if you can't rustle yerself up some vittles. But you'd better be back 'fore breakfast," she warned as the snake slithered off into the bushes, "'cause I ain't a-gonna come looking fer you."

Brant was relieved to see the snake gone. He was city-bred and hadn't even seen a snake until he joined the army and gone on his first field maneuvers. Since then, he had seen many, but he had never gotten over his revulsion of them. Nor had he learned the knack of telling a poisonous one from a nonpoisonous, except for a rattler, whose warning noise was a dead giveaway. For that reason, whenever he saw a snake, he made it a point to either give it a wide berth, or shoot the hell out of it.

"You don't like my pet, do you?"

Brant heard the hurt in Danny's voice. "It's not that I don't like him," he lied politely. "It's just that he's hardly what I would expect for a pet."

"Why not? He don't bother nobody. He don't bay at the moon all night, like hounds do, or git to fighting with the other snakes and making a awful racket, like cats do. He's real quiet and mannerly. Why, I don't even have to worry 'bout feeding him. He fetches his own grub."

Brant handed the blanket to Danny, saying, "Well, I guess it's everyone to their own tastes. Back at Fort Concho, where I was stationed before I was transferred, there were some pretty unusual pets too. Besides the scores of dogs running around, several people had wild birds they had captured, while one man had a buffalo calf and another had a pet fawn. The commanding officer's daughter even had some pet mice, until they escaped from the shoe box she kept them in and ate some of her mother's unmentionables. Then she made her give them away."

Danny wondered what unmentionables were, but it was Brant's last words that caught her attention. "There ain't nobody that could make me give Charlie away," she said with a fierce expression on her face. "He's my friend."

Brant understood. Danny had picked up Charlie for the same reason the soldiers and their families did their various pets. In this isolated, lonely country, the animals gave them companionship. And for the better part, army people were just as fiercely protective over their pets as Danny was. During his years at the various forts, he'd seen some terrible rows between neighbors over their pets.

"Will he actually come back?" Brant asked, taking more interest in Danny's unusual pet.

"Shore he will. Jest as soon as he's ate his fill, he'll crawl right back into his bag. It's his home."

"You said you had to go looking for him," Brant reminded her.

"Well, sometimes," Danny admitted. "But that's jest a game he plays with me. I can tell he's tickled to death when I find him."

"Oh? How?"

" 'Cause he smiles at me."

Brant almost burst out laughing at the idea of a snake smiling, but he knew if he did, Danny would be furious. She was deadly serious. He turned away, so she couldn't see his lips twitching, saying over his shoulder as he walked to pick up the second blanket, "How do you know it's a he?"

"I don't. I jest named him Charlie 'cause I liked the name."

Danny shook out the blanket Brant had handed her and held it up, seeing the same letters and number printed across it that had been burned into the flank of Brant's horse. "Do you army people brand everything?" she asked.

Brant laughed, answering, "Just about. Any and everything that's army issue. My horse, my blanket, my saddle, my saddlebags, my eating utensils, my canteen, my guns, everything except my personal belongings and uniforms, but only because, as an officer, I have to buy my own. Even our army wagons are labeled with the company's insignia, on both the wagons and the canvas that covers them."

"Why brand everything? Injuns don't steal all that stuff, too, do they?"

"The army does that everywhere, not just here in the west. The Indians aren't the only thieves around. If everything wasn't marked, the soldiers would just walk away with it, or for that matter, a good deal of the civilians too. They seem to think, because it belongs to the government, that it isn't stealing. As an officer, I'm accountable for everything issued to my troop, and that includes anything lost or damaged, as well as stolen. I have to be able to prove it was a justifiable loss. One time, when we were out in the field, a mule ate one of my trooper's dog tents. It took me six months and fifty pounds of paper work to prove to Washington that it was a justifiable loss. I could have killed that mule with my bare hands, except then I would have had to account for it. And mules aren't counted as government property. They're actually placed on the rolls, just like soldiers. If

43

I'd deliberately killed that mule, they would have probably court-martialed me. But there for a few weeks, I was seriously considering it, despite the consequences."

Danny burst into laughter. She didn't understand a few of Brant's longer words, but she got the jest of the story. Brant had heard her laugh before, short little laughs, but this was long, spontaneous laughter. He had never heard a woman laugh so openly, and it was a joyous sound that made his spirits soar. Suddenly he was laughing with her.

When both had regained control, Danny said, "I didn't know mules would eat tents."

Brant shook his head in disgust, saying, "Mules will eat anything. Water barrels, wagon wheels, tin cups, saddles. They're even worse than billy goats. And don't ever get too close to a mule's head. He'll take a bite out of you for pure spite. Those Missouri mules are the meanest creatures on earth."

Both occupied themselves with spreading their blankets on the ground. Brant finished first and sat back on his heels, looking across the fire that had almost burned down. What he saw was an excellent view of Danny's well-shaped buttocks in her skin-tight pants. Feeling his heat rise, he tore his eyes away and lay down, rolling with his back to her. But he couldn't resist the temptation of just one more peek.

He glanced over his shoulder to see Danny was standing with her back towards him, shimmying out of her snug pants. He sat bolt upright, asking in alarm, "What in God's name do you think you're doing?"

Danny looked over her shoulder in surprise and answered, "Why, I'm taking off my duckins. I can't sleep with those dad-blasted buttons poking me all night."

The pants fell to the ground, and Danny stepped out of them. To Brant's relief, she was wearing a pair of crude underwear that came to her knees. Then she turned, and just beneath the tail of her shirt, stenciled from one curving hip to the other, were the words, ROUGH AND READY, in bold, red letters.

Brant stared at the lettering. Considering it's location, it seemed highly suggestive, and combined with the sexual tension that Danny had already aroused in him, it was too much. "Where in the hell did you get those?" he blurted out harshly.

Danny was taken aback by Brant's sudden outburst. And he looked almost as if he was angry. Bewildered, she answered, "Why, they're my drawers. I made 'em."

Suddenly, Brant remembered where he had seen those words. They were the trade name of a brand of flour sold in every commissary, trading post store, and general store in Texas, but he had never dreamed that the settler women made drawers from the flour sacks. Nonetheless, knowing why such a seemingly blatant invitation was printed on Danny's drawers didn't detract from their provocativeness. He tore his eyes away from the sight and looked directly into Danny's face, saying, "You shouldn't be stripping down to your drawers in front of me, Danny."

"Why not?" Danny asked, still bewildered. "You can't see nothing."

"Because, where I come from, it's not considered lady-like, nor is it here in Texas. Respectable women don't go traipsing around in their underclothes, nor do they allow a man to see their lower limbs and ankles."

"Limbs? Are you a-talking about my legs?"

"Yes."

45

"What'd you call them that fer? I ain't no tree!"

"That's what polite society call them. It's considered as ill-mannered for a gentleman to call a woman's lower extremities her legs, as it is for you to prance around in your underwear."

"I wore my drawers in front of my pa and brothers all the time," Danny countered.

"Family is different. They're used to seeing you that way since you were a little girl. But other men might become . . . well, aroused by the sight."

"What's that mean? Aroused?"

A flush crept up Brant's face. He shouldn't be having this conversation with her, he thought. It was embarrassing. Christ! Hadn't anyone told her anything about men and women, about sex and passion. "That means a man might become inflamed."

Danny puzzled over the strange word. "You mean, het up?"

"Yes," Brant replied with a sigh, relieved that she had finally understood.

The puzzled expression on Danny's face deepened. "I don't know why they should get mad about it."

Brant lifted his head and rolled his eyes in a silent appeal for help from heaven, then snapped, "That's not the kind of heating up I'm talking about!"

"Well, it sure sounds to me like it is!" Danny snapped back. "'Cause that's jest what you're a-doing, a-gitting mad!"

"I'm not mad. I'm just . . ." Brant took a deep breath to calm himself, then said, "Look, let's just say that it's considered bad manners and leave it at that."

"Does that mean I have to sleep in my duckins?"

"No, it just means to keep your lower body covered

46

after you've taken off your . . . What did you call them? Duckins?"

"Yep. That's what the waddies call 'em."

That figures, Brant thought. Well, he might be able to conform to the west Texan's unique vocabulary to the extent of calling a cowhand a waddy, but he'd be damned if he'd call his trousers duckins. For Christ's sake! If his troopers heard that, they'd laugh him right out of the service.

"Is this better?" Danny asked from where she had rolled up in her blanket on the ground.

"Yes, it is."

"I didn't mean to act tacky. I reckon I jest didn't know no better."

Brant felt like a first-class heel. Danny hadn't been the one getting out of line. He had. "I know, Danny. I didn't mean I thought you were tacky. I was just trying to teach you a little lesson in manners. I hope you don't mind."

"Nope," Danny answered with a good-natured grin. "I reckon I could learn a few more manners. Like I said, I don't want nobody a-thinking I'm tacky."

Brant frowned. Danny thought tacky meant ill-mannered? He had thought she'd meant someone with low morals. Hell, he'd never figure out the west Texan's peculiar vocabulary. He lay back down and rolled up in his blanket, then glanced across the glowing coals at Danny, seeing that she was laying flat on her back with her hat over her face.

"How old are you, Danny?"

"Twenty-two," came the muffled answer.

She was a woman full-grown, both physically and chronically; yet, she seemed so childlike in so many ways, despite her self-sufficiency, Brant thought as he

47

gazed up at the stars. For all of her strengths, she had a naivete about her that made her seem very vulnerable. She had called him her friend, but the thoughts going through his head had been more passionate than friendly. The admission filled him with self-disgust. He was an officer and a gentleman, but for some strange reason, Danny seemed to bring out the worst in him. He couldn't understand how she could be so childlike and yet so damned desirable. The two should be at odds, but in Danny they combined to make her all the more irresistible. It was a good thing he'd be leaving her behind tomorrow. She was too much of a temptation for him.

Chapter 3

When Brant and Danny rode into town the next day, Brant couldn't believe his eyes. It consisted of three saloons and a run-down general store that sat perched in the middle of the prairie with one lone scraggly mesquite tree for company. There was no blacksmith's shop, no barber shop, no hotel, no post office, no stables, no jail house, and as far as Brant could tell, the only inhabitants were a pack of mangy dogs, all barking and snapping at their horses' heels.

"You call this a town?" he asked Danny in disgust.

"Yep, that's what folks 'round here call it."

"What's its name?"

"It ain't got no name," Danny answered in exasperation. "I done told you. We jest call it town."

They pulled up before a hitching rail in front of one of the saloons and dismounted, the dogs all around them still barking and snapping. Danny took off her hat and started hitting at them with it, saying, "Slap 'em in the nose with yer hat. That's the only way you're gonna git rid of the pests."

Brant did as Danny directed and found that it worked. The dogs ran away with their tails between their legs and howling as if they had been mortally wounded.

"There's Rose now," Danny said excitedly, drawing Brant's attention away from the rapidly retreating pack of dogs.

Since there was only one person visible, Brant was left to assume that the woman who had just stepped through the swinging doors of the second saloon was Rose. He was shocked. Her gaudy, low-cut, knee-length dress, heavily made-up face, and henna-dyed hair clearly marked her as a saloon girl. This was Danny's friend?

Seeing Danny walking up to her on the boardwalk, Rose smiled broadly and said, "Well, howdy, honey. How're you doing?"

Before Danny could answer, Rose looked up and saw Brant standing by the horses, then frowned and asked Danny, "Where's Pete, honey? Didn't he come with you? And who's that fella with you? A new hand?" A worried expression came over the older woman's face. She dropped her voice, asking, "Honey, you didn't go sneaking off with that young fella, did you? I know he's as handsome as Lucifer, but Pete will skin you alive if you done something like that."

"Pete's dead," Danny said in a tightly controlled voice.

"Dead?" Rose asked in a shocked voice, her face draining of all color beneath her heavy makeup and giving her complexion a horrible pasty look. Then, seeing the pain and misery written all over Danny's face, she took the girl's hands in her own and said, "Oh, honey, I'm so sorry to hear that. How'd it happen?"

Danny blinked back sudden tears. Dad-blasted, she

hoped she didn't start crying and embarrass herself. Only sissies cried. She tried to answer Rose, but found she couldn't say a word because of the lump in her throat.

Brant stepped up behind Danny, saying to Rose, "Their ranch was attacked by Apaches yesterday. They killed her brother, burned everything to the ground, and stole their herd. She only escaped being killed because she was down at the stream when it happened."

Rose pulled Danny protectively to her side and glared at Brant suspiciously, asking in a hard voice, "And who are you, mister? I ain't never seen you 'round here."

"He's my new friend, Rose," Danny said, her need to protect Brant from Rose's obvious hostility quickly overriding her grief. "He saw the smoke and came to help, only he got there too late. He helped me bury Pete. He's a calvary officer on his way to Fort Davis."

Rose glanced at Brant's oval belt buckle with U.S. stamped in the middle of it and then down at his high black boots. She knew just where to look. Soldiers might wear civilian clothing while they were on leave, but they always kept on their belts and army boots that were comfortable and well broken in. She smiled sheepishly and stepped forward, saying, "Sorry, mister, if I seemed unneighborly at first. A body can't be too careful around strangers, particularly a young girl like Danny here. I shore appreciate you helping her out."

"Captain Brant Holden, at your service ma'am," Brant answered with a slight nod of his head. "And I was more than happy to be of service to the young lady."

Yep, he was an officer all right, Rose thought, with his fancy manners and cultured speech. And no one but a gentleman would call a tomboy like Danny a lady and a disreputable person like her ma'am.

51

"Brant rode with me into town, since he was a-heading this way, anyways," Danny informed Rose. "He said it was too dangerous fer me to stay out on the ranch by myself, and I reckon he's right. All mine and Pete's money got burned up, and I ain't got any to buy more ammunition with. I ain't scared of those redskins, but I can't fight 'em off without bullets. I was a-wondering . . ." Danny hesitated. She hated asking anyone for a favor, even a friend.

"Wondering what?" Rose prompted.

The kind expression on Rose's face reassured Danny. And it wasn't like she really had a choice. She had to have someplace to stay for awhile, until she could recover from the shock of losing Pete and her home and decide what to do. "I was a-wondering if I could stay with you."

A shocked expression came over Rose's face. Seeing it, Danny quickly said, "Jest for a spell. Jest 'til I can figure out what I'm gonna do."

Rose shot Brant a desperate, "help me look," then said, "Well, now, honey, that's something I'll have to think over."

"Why do you have to think it over?" Danny asked in bewilderment, feeling a little hurt. Then as a sudden thought occurred to her, she asked, "Is it 'cause of Charlie?"

"No, honey, Charlie don't have nothing to do with it. It's jest something that needs to be thought through, and all this came kinda sudden-like. I tell you what. Why don't you go 'round back and wait in the kitchen while the Cap'n and I go inside and have a drink? After hearing about poor Pete, I shore could use one to calm my nerves. Then maybe I can think straighter."

"I'll come in with you," Danny offered.

"No, you won't either," Rose said in a firm voice. "You know Pete never allowed you to set foot in the saloon, and jest 'cause he's dead don't mean I ain't going by his rules no more. Now, you go 'round and wait in the kitchen. I'll be there shortly."

Danny shot Rose a resentful look and stomped away. Just as she was about to step off the boardwalk, Rose called, "And you tell Cook I said to give you a big piece of that gingerbread he jest took outta the oven."

Danny whirled, her black eyes sparkling with excitement. "Cook made gingerbread today?"

"He shore did. He must have known you was coming, since it's yer favorite. Now you hurry along, 'fore it gits cold."

Danny made a flying leap from the boardwalk and disappeared around the corner of the saloon. "Come on in, Cap'n," Rose said with a worried expression on her face. "You and me gotta have a long talk."

Brant followed Rose through the swinging doors, then stopped and glanced around him. The inside of the building looked like all the other saloons he'd seen in Texas. A long bar stood at one side, with a pair of mounted longhorns flanked by pictures of half-naked women hanging on the wall behind it, and the rest of the room was filled with low tables and chairs. As usual, huge brass spittoons were scattered everywhere, for a good half of the Texas male population chewed tobacco. A haze of smoke still hung in the room, made by the other half of the male population, and the saloon smelled of that, stale liquor, cheap perfume, and old sweat. Then Brant's eyes settled on a rickety staircase at the back of the room. His gaze followed the steps up to the second story at the rear of the building, then slowly swept over the closed doors that lined the landing.

"Yeah, I know what you're thinking," Rose said with a deep sigh, seeing the hard expression coming over Brant's face and knowing that he was thinking this was no place for Danny. "Now you know that this ain't jest a saloon. It's a chippie house, and I'm a chippie. You know it, I know it, but that little gal don't. Danny doesn't have no idea of what goes on here."

Rose turned and walked heavily to the bar, saying to the bartender who was occupied with drying glasses there, "Sam, hand me my special bottle and a couple of glasses."

The bartender reached under the counter and placed the whiskey bottle on the counter, then shoved two clean glasses across it, saying, "Is something wrong, Rose? I've never seen you drink this early in the day."

"Yeah, there shore is. Pete Morgan is dead. Apaches hit his ranch yesterday."

The bartender almost dropped the glass he was drying at the shocking news. Then he asked, "What about his little sister?"

"She's okay." Rose motioned to Brant, saying, "This is a cavalry officer on his way to Fort Davis. He saw the smoke, but got there too late to help old Pete. Danny was down at the creek when it happened. He brought her here. She's out back."

"Thank the Lord," the bartender muttered, then shook his graying head, saying in a sad voice, "but poor old Pete. He was such a quiet, peaceful fella. Never got rowdy, like some of these cowhands." A visible shudder ran over the man. "Apaches! Goddamned!"

"You look like you could use a drink yerself," Rose said, noting the bartender's ashen face. "Have one on the house, but don't say nothing to the girls. You know how nervous Injun talks makes 'em."

Rose turned and walked to a table, saying as she passed Brant, "Come on, Cap'n. Let's sit here in the corner by the window."

When they were seated, Rose poured whiskey into the two glasses, shoved one across the table to Brant, then lifted her glass into the air, asking, "What's that toast you cavalry officers have? Here's to the next man that dies?" Rose shook her head, saying, "Jesus, you cavalry fellas must be plumb loco, or the bravest men on earth to fight those savages."

"We're neither. We're just soldiers with a job to do."

"Yeah, and right now, believe it or not, I'd trade what I gotta do for yer job." Rose lifted her glass to her mouth and drained it with one swallow. Setting it down, she looked Brant in the eye, asking, "What am I gonna tell Danny? She can't stay here with me, and I ain't got the guts to tell her why, either. Why, she'd be shocked! I don't think she even knows about such things. Oh, I'm shore she's seen animals mating. After all, she lives on a ranch. And maybe she's figured out on her own where babies come from. But she's still jest as innocent as the day she was born. If she knew what goes on here, she'd think badly of Pete, and me too. Now, maybe I deserve it, but Pete don't. He raised her the best he could, and there wasn't nothing he wouldn't have done for her. But he was jest like all these cowhands, lonely and hungry fer a woman, but too damn shy to even talk to a decent one."

55

"How did you meet Danny?" Brant asked.

"After her pa died, Pete brought her with him. Didn't want to leave her out there on the ranch by herself. He made her sit on that bench outside the general store and wait fer him. She thought he was jest drinking and playing cards. He didn't do it very often, maybe every six months or so, and consarn it, every hard-working cowhand has the right to stay out with dry cattle every now and then."

Brant frowned, then said, "I beg your pardon?"

"Shucks, I plumb fergot you're a Yankee. That's what the cowhands call making a night of it—staying out with dry cattle. Except Pete never came at night, only in the afternoons. He always made sure he had Danny outta town before the rough crew showed up. Anyway— getting back to how I met Danny—one day I saw her sitting out there on the bench in the cold and invited her back to the kitchen, where it was warm. 'Course I didn't tell her this place was mine. I didn't want her to know I ran a saloon, much less a chippie house. So I told her I worked here serving drinks." Rose chuckled, saying, "I'm telling you, she let loose like a regular gusher. Almost talked my ear off. I figured she must have been lonely too. Anyway, I told Pete he could leave her in the kitchen from then on and he started coming more often. I got where I really looked forward to Danny's visits. You can't help but like her. Oh, I know she talks rough. That's 'cause she's never been around no one but men and me. But she's so natural and fresh, so full of enthusiasm and life. And she don't have a mean bone in her body, and is as honest as the day is long. She don't know the meaning of deceit or hypocrisy."

Rose paused and gazed off thoughtfully, then said, "She's innocent that way too. Social wise. She don't know how narrow-minded, mean-mouthed, and backstabbing some of these so-called decent folks can be. She thinks all the mean people are the outlaws and redskins. She's jest as vulnerable as a new-born lamb that way. She may be frontier wise, but she shore ain't people wise. She's jest too damned trusting when it comes to ordinary folks.

"Goddammit!" Rose swore, hitting the table with her fist and sending dust flying everywhere. "I shore wish I could keep her here with me. But even if I could fool her, I couldn't protect her. There're men coming in and out of here all the time, and even if I made it clear she was off limits, I couldn't control 'em when they got all likkered up. In case you ain't noticed, Cap'n, she's a right purty girl, and she's done a heap of filling out in the last few years. I sure can't keep her locked up in that kitchen. Besides, she needs to be 'round decent people."

Brant fervently agreed. "Don't you know anyone respectable in this area who might be able to take her in?"

"Nope. Those few ranchers around here have all they can do to feed and protect themselves and their families, particularly with those damned Injuns raiding every time you turn 'round. To tell you the truth, there was more people out here in the fifties, but the Injuns got so bad during the war, with the army gone and all the men away fighting in the war, that most of the settlers just pulled out. A few hardies have come back, but it ain't what it used to be."

Brant knew what Rose was saying was fact. During the Civil War, the Texas frontier had actually receded because of the Indian depreciations, almost as far back as San Antonio. And Brant wasn't surprised that Rose had been in this country for some time. He'd already figured out she was well into her middle years. The heavy makeup she wore couldn't hide her wrinkles, and more than a few of her gray hairs had eluded the henna dye she used. But he had come to like the prostitute because she thought so highly of Danny and had befriended her. "What about that general store across the street? Maybe that family could take her in, or if nothing else, hire her as a sales clerk with room and board?"

"My God, no! That's the last place you'd want to leave her. There ain't no family, and the owner is nothing but an old lecher."

Brant frowned. It seemed they had a bigger problem on their hands than he had anticipated. "Is there a church anywhere around? I'm sure the parson and his wife would take her in. They're committed to helping the homeless."

"Hell, there ain't no church within two hundred miles of this place. Once in a blue moon, a jockey parson comes riding through, pitches his tent down the road, preaches hell and damnation for one night, and then goes on his way. Then about every five years or so, a Padre comes from San Antone, marrying all the Meskins who'd been living together since the last time he passed through and baptizing all their kids." Rose paused, then said, "'Course, I do have a little money saved up. Enough to pay for Danny's stage fare back to San Antone and hold her for a spell until she finds a job. Don't know if she'd take it though. She's a proud little thing."

Brant leaned across the table and said in an emphatic

voice, "Whatever you do, don't offer Danny money, not even as a loan. She'd take it, buy a few provisions and some more ammunition, and head right back to that ranch. She was going to stay out there by herself and sleep in the open, living off of game. I had a hell of a time making her see reason."

"Goddamned, if you aren't right, Cap'n! She as much as said so, 'cept I clean fergot. And if that don't sound jest like Danny. She thinks that old ranch is heaven on earth."

"While we're speaking of Danny's financial situation, do you know if Pete had some money put away in a bank anywhere? She might not be as destitute as she thinks she is."

"Not Pete. He didn't trust banks." Rose glanced at Brant's glass, then asked, "You a teetotaller, Cap'n?"

Brant looked down at his glass and answered, "No, I guess I just forgot it was there." He raised the glass and took a cautious sip. A surprised expression came over his face. "Why, this is pure Kentucky bourbon."

"You're doggone right it is!" Rose said with a little laugh. "You don't think I'm gonna drink any of that watered-down rotgut I sell these cowhands, do you? Nope, this is one luxury I give myself."

Rose sat back in her chair and gazed off, drumming her fingers on the table. Then, just as Brant was taking another drink from his glass, she leaned forward and said, "I reckon you're jest gonna have to take Danny with you to Fort Davis."

Brant was so shocked at Rose's unexpected announcement that he choked on the liquor, throwing him into a violent coughing spasm. When he had recovered, he asked in a hoarse voice, "Take her with *me?*"

"Yep. She can't stay any place 'round here."

"Fort Davis is in the heart of Apache territory!"

"Hell, half of Texas is Injun country. Her brother got killed by Apaches near here, didn't he? Seems a fort would be the safest place for her, unless you can take her back to San Antone, or Fredricksberg. I've heard that's a nice little town."

"I'm supposed to report to Fort Davis in ten days. That's almost three hundred miles from here. And San Antonio is two hundred in the opposite direction. I can't drag Danny all the way back to San Antonio and double back in that time."

"I heard you calvary boys could ride sixty miles a day."

"Yes, if we have to, but that's stripped saddle and riding like hell nonstop. Danny couldn't keep up with that pace. Besides, even at that rate, I couldn't make it. Not eight hundred miles in ten days."

"Then take her with you," Rose said, not in the least perplexed by Brant's arguments. "She probably wouldn't like San Antone anyway. It'd be too tame fer her. I've heard there're settlements around those army forts. Maybe she could find a job there with room and board."

"You wouldn't want Danny in one of those fort towns. They attract the scum of the earth. Gamblers, cutthroats, thieves, gunfighters, whiskey peddlers. Why, San Angela, outside of Fort Concho, where I was just assigned, is the roughest town in Texas."

"What about the sutler's store? Since it's there with the army's permission, it must be run by decent folks."

"Well, yes, but—"

"Or why can't Danny work for the army?" Rose asked as another thought came to her and cut across Brant's objection. "I heard they hire washerwomen to keep up the soldiers' uniforms. Why, I've even heard the army provides 'em with their own rations and quarters."

"Out here, those quarters consist of a line of leaky tents set at the very back of the post, and those women are nothing but camp followers, for the better part. Oh, a few are the wives of enlisted men and respectable, but most are foul-mouthed whores who haven't even got the guts to admit to what they are. And they're rough. The majority carry knives strapped to their thighs. Some of the worst fights I've ever seen have been among those women. The place is filled with undisciplined, unkept illegitimate children—who'll pick your pockets at the drop of a hat—mangy curs, and scratching chickens, with garbage laying all around. Soapsuds Row is even worse than those Scabtowns, as the troopers call the fort towns. Danny would be better off here than a place like that."

"Well, it can't be all that bad, not if the officers take their wives and families with 'em," Rose argued. Then her eyes lit up as a sudden solution came to her. "Say, that's an idea! I heard the officers' families in those remote forts have a hell of a time trying to find servants."

That was true, Brant admitted silently. Some were so desperate for domestic help that they had even paid the servant's passage from the east, and at twelve-and-a-half cents a mile for stage fare, that was a considerable expense. Then, unless the woman was old and decrepit, or as ugly as sin, she was courted by one of the women-hungry troopers and the officer lost her anyway, unless her husband was willing to let her continue to work. But . . . "Somehow, I can't see Danny as a servant."

"Nope, it won't be easy for her, as independent as she is," Rose agreed. "But she's gotta work, and she's practical enough to realize that. She'd sure be better off in one of those officer's homes, with his wife looking out for her, than out on her own. Why, those folks would be good for her. Maybe they can smooth some of the rough edges off her. She ain't never been exposed to a gentlewoman, and she's got a soft heart in her, despite her tough exterior. She jest ain't never been taught to act like a woman." Rose leaned over the table, asking, "Have you seen that pet snake of hers?"

"Yes."

"Well, she croons to it and pets it jest like it's a baby. Now, anyone who can treat a snake that way has got to have an awful soft spot in her heart."

"Why didn't her brother get her a more appropriate pet, like a dog? There certainly seems to be enough strays around. Hell, I've never seen as many dogs as they have here in Texas."

"Yep, we Texans are big dog lovers," Rose admitted readily. "And she did have a hound, but it got bit by a mad skunk, and Pete had to shoot it. Jest about broke Danny's heart, and watching her mourn that old dog tore Pete up so bad that he flat refused to let her have another four-legged critter. Said he couldn't go through that again. So she took up with that snake."

"What did she mean when she asked if Charlie was the reason she couldn't stay with you?"

Rose laughed, then answered, "She thinks I'm mad at Charlie fer what happened one day when she was visiting. He crawled out of his bag and slipped into the saloon here. Those silly girls of mine started carrying on something awful. I tell you, the racket they made would have woke up the dead. There were a couple of cowhands here that were pretty likkered up. They started shooting at Charlie. Thank God, they was so drunk that they couldn't have hit the broad side of a barn if their lives had depended on it. Danny heard all the commotion and the girls screaming 'snake,' and figured it was Charlie. She tore in here and fired a few warning shots that flat put a shine on those boys' boots and left a couple of holes in my floor, then told them if they took another shot at her snake, she'd blow them to hell and back. Danny still swears to this day that Charlie was so scared he was trembling when she picked him up, but it was Danny's hand shaking, and not Charlie. She was fighting mad." Rose laughed again in remembrance, then said, "I'm telling you, that Danny is something else."

Suddenly, Rose sobered, and tears came to her eyes. "I shore am going to miss her." She looked Brant directly in the eye and said, "You take good care of her, Cap'n. She's . . . well, she's special."

Brant smiled, then said, "Yes, I've discovered that for myself."

Rose felt an immense wave of relief. She was an excellent judge of character, particularly men's. She could read them like a book. She knew the man sitting across from her was strong and as steady as a rock, but knowing that he appreciated Danny's uniqueness made her feel a lot better about placing her in his capable hands. She wished something would come between the two, besides a friendship. She'd sure like to see Danny hitched up with a fine man of his caliber, but she knew she was just being a silly romantic. He was a gentleman to the bone. He might like Danny, might even come to love her, but he wouldn't never marry a wild little thing like her. Nope, his kind never married out of their class, particularly these army officers. It seemed to be some kind of iron-clad rule.

Rose pushed herself up from the table, feeling as if the weight of the world was on her shoulders, and said in a voice filled with dread, "Well, I reckon I'd better go tell Danny that she can't stay."

"What reason are you going to give her?" Brant asked, coming to his feet.

"Damned if I know."

"Why don't you tell her you can't afford to keep her here. You said she thinks that you just work here."

Rose's face brightened at the suggestion. "Well, danged if that ain't a good idea. Thanks, Cap'n. I'm much obliged."

"I'm glad I could be of help."

Rose turned and walked to a door that sat at the back of the building. Brant followed. Stopping with her hand on the door, she looked over her shoulder and said, "You know, I ain't done many decent things in my life. Turning Danny down for her own good is one of them. But how can doing something good make you feel so damn rotten?" But before Brant could offer a response, Rose pushed open the door and stepped into the kitchen.

As they walked into the small room, Brant glanced around, seeing that Danny was the only occupant. She jumped from the kitchen chair she had been sitting in and asked anxiously, "Well, Rose? What did you decide? Can I stay with you fer a spell?"

"I'm afraid not, honey. I thought it through real good, but . . . well, it jest won't work out."

The wounded expression that came over Danny's face tore at Rose's heart. Tears swam in the prostitute's eyes. In a choked voice, she said, "It ain't that I wouldn't like to have you, but I jest can't afford it. I jest work here, and the owner is the meanest old skinflint you ever saw. If you stayed here with me, he'd charge me an arm and a leg for yer room and board, and as much as I hate to admit it, honey, I'm flat broke."

A wave of relief washed over Danny. She'd thought Rose had turned her down because she didn't like her, and that had hurt. "Well, why didn't you jest say so in the first place?" Danny asked, her self-confidence bounding back.

"I was too ashamed to admit it. Nobody likes to admit they're broke, particularly when it means they have to turn down a good friend."

"Shucks, there ain't no reason fer you to be ashamed to tell me. I understand. I'm flat busted myself. And I know you'd help me out, if you could."

Rose smiled broadly, feeling vastly relieved that Danny had believed her tale. "I sure would, honey, and that's jest what the Cap'n, here, said. That you'd understand and not hold it against me. And we've been talking about yer future too. As yer two best friends, we've decided that you should go to Fort Davis with him."

"Fort Davis?" Danny asked in a shocked voice. "What would I want to go there fer?"

"Danny, you're gonna have to git a job," Rose said in a patient, but firm voice. "That's the only way you're gonna be able to save up any money to go back to yer ranch. Now, you've never worked fer someone else before, but I have, so let me give you some advice. Unless you can find a job with room and board, you ain't gonna be able to save enough to feed a mosquito. The married officers at the forts are always looking for live-in servants. I'm shore you won't have any trouble gitting a job at Fort Davis, particularly if the Cap'n can vouch for yer good character."

Danny looked at Brant, saying, "Well, I'm much obliged fer that, but I ain't interested in a-being no servant. I'm a waddy."

"We've already been through that, Danny," Brant reminded her. "You admitted yourself that it wouldn't work."

"But I don't know nothing about a-being a servant," Danny objected. "And I purely hate a-cleaning house."

"Then what about hiring on as a cook?" Brant suggested. "Anyone who can mix cornmeal and water and make it taste as good as those ash cakes you made last night must know something about cooking."

"You shore do," Rose said enthusiastically. "Pete told me you were almost as good a cook as he was, and you've been helping Cook out with the meals here. If I ain't mistaken, he gave you some of his secret recipes."

Danny gazed off thoughtfully for a minute, then said, "Well, maybe that wouldn't be so bad." She turned to Brant and asked, "Do they pay cooks good wages?"

"Good cooks are in such demand that some of the officers' wives would kill for one." Seeing a shocked expression come over Danny's face, he modified his statement by adding, "Well, almost."

A big grin spread over Danny's face. "Well, I reckon that's jest what I'll do, then," she said in a decisive voice.

"I'll tag along with you and get me a job as a cook at Fort Davis."

"Good. I'm glad that's settled," Brant said with all sincerity. He'd been afraid Danny might not be agreeable to the suggestion, and he hadn't the slightest notion of what to do with her if she had. Damn, he sure got himself into a hell of a mess when he'd seen that smoke and gone riding off to help some poor settler. But despite all the problems it had presented him, he couldn't regret it. If he hadn't gone, he wouldn't have met Danny and would have missed out on something special. Rose was right. She was like a breath of fresh air in his stuffy life. Just being around her was an experience. And she certainly kept him on his toes, trying to keep one jump ahead of her.

Chapter 4

After saying goodbye to Rose, Brant and Danny walked to the general store to buy provisions for their long trip to Fort Davis.

As soon as they stepped into the dim, musty interior of the building, Brant said to Danny, "You're going to need a change of clothing and a saddlebag to carry them in. Why don't you shop for them while I put in our order for supplies?"

"But I ain't got no money to buy clothes with," Danny objected.

Brant knew better than to offer to buy them for Danny. She would never stand still for that, not as independent as she was. "I'll buy them, and you can pay me back out of your first paycheck."

Danny didn't like the idea of being in debt, but she liked the idea of having to wear the clothing she had on all the way to Fort Davis even less. She didn't worry about what she wore as long as it was reasonably clean and didn't smell bad, and as far as her personal habits went, she was meticulous, bathing every day. "Do you mind if I add a towel, a bar of soap, and a box of clips for my Spencer to the tab?"

Brant was pleased to hear about the towel and soap, but not the ammunition for her rifle. "You're not going to run out on me, are you, Danny?" he asked suspiciously.

"Consarn it," Danny said angrily, "anyone who knows me will tell you that I'll do to tie to! I said I was going to Fort Davis with you, and I'm a man of my word!"

"All right, Danny, I'll take your word," Brant answered, his lips twitching at her calling herself a man when she was so obviously female. He suspected much of what she said was in imitation of her brother. "I just wanted to be sure you weren't having second thoughts. No, I don't mind. Put anything you like on the tab."

"How about a hair brush?"

"Yes, but why don't you get yourself a ladies' brush, and a new pair of drawers while you're at it. You'll need a change of them too."

"You can buy drawers already made?" Danny asked in astonishment.

"I'm sure you can."

"I ain't never seen 'em in here. Long johns, but not drawers."

"Have you ever looked in the ladies' section?"

"Well, no," Danny admitted.

"Well, I'm sure you'll find something in the way of underwear there."

As Danny started to walk away, Brant said, "Wait a minute. I just thought of something."

"What?" Danny asked irritably. If he kept adding things to her list, she'd never get out of debt to him.

"While you're buying new clothes, why don't you get them in a larger size?" Brant's eyes swept over her shapely, provocative figure. "You're about to burst out of those."

Danny looked down at herself, seeing her shirt straining across her breasts. "Yeah, I reckon I am," she admitted, totally unabashed. "Reckon I've grown some since I got 'em."

Danny turned, making a beeline for the men's section of the store. She didn't have any trouble picking out a pair of pants from the stock sitting on a table there. They only came in two colors, dark blue and a drab brown, and Danny didn't like brown. She shook the pants out and placed them up against her to judge the size. Deciding they were bigger than the ones she had on, she tossed them over her arm and turned to the table with the shirts on it. She had a terrible time choosing between all the colors and whether to pick a striped one, a plaid one, a checked one, or a solid-colored one. Consarn it, she wished she could at least pick two, Danny thought. Then her dark eyes lit up. Why not? She would be paying for them with her own money. She finally picked a blue checked shirt and a red and blue plaid, after much lip-chewing indecision.

Her next stop was the counter with the towels on it. She picked one up, flung it over her arm with her clothes, and fished in a box sitting there until she found a bar of White Rose soap, her favorite.

She turned and headed for the women's section, picking up a pair of saddlebags as she passed the leather goods on her way and shoving aside dresses and sun bonnets hanging on racks and cluttering up the aisles. Spying a table with small garments laying on it, she stepped up to it and saw a stack of petticoats, a stack of drawers, and a stack of some strange-looking garments with tiny straps on them. Curious, she put down her selections and picked one up, holding it up in the air by its straps. Since it was so short, she decided it must be something the women wore on the top, but she'd be danged if she'd waste her money on it. It was bad enough that she had to wear drawers.

Danny tossed the garment aside and picked up a pair of drawers. Placing it against her, she decided it would fit, then noticed the eyelet ruffle that was sewed at the bottom of both legs. Now what would those silly females be putting ruffles on their drawers for? she wondered. Why, no one could even see them.

Spying a box that held brushes, combs, and hair nets, she grabbed a brush at random, picked up her selections, and headed for the checkout counter, then came to a dead halt, her eyes wide with puzzlement.

This was how Brant found her, staring at a corset hanging from a pole. "I was wondering what was keeping you," Brant said as he stepped up beside her.

"I've been a-trying to figure out what that gol-durn contraption is."

Trying very hard to keep a straight face, Brant said, "It's called a corset. Women wrap them around their middles and pull those strings tight and tie them."

"They cinch themselves up in a harness?" Danny asked in a horrified voice. "What in tarnation fer?"

"So that their waists will look small."

"Well, that's jest about the silliest thing I ever heard. How in tarnation do they breathe?"

"You've got a good point there," Brant admitted.

Danny turned to Brant and asked, "You suppose Rose wears one of those contraptions?"

"I would imagine so."

71

"Well, no wonder her tits look like they're about to pop right outta her dress. They ain't got no where else to go."

At the shocked expression on Brant's face, Danny asked, "What's the matter? Did I say something wrong?"

"It's not important," Brant said, trying to gloss over the awkward situation.

"No, tell me. I told you I don't want to be tacky."

"All right. In polite society, they don't call that part of a woman's body . . ." Brant found he couldn't look Danny directly in the eye while saying such a crude word. He directed his gaze directly over her shoulder. ". . . tits."

"Then what do they call 'em?"

"They call them bosoms, but the subject is never mentioned in mixed company."

"What's mixed company?"

"Men and women."

"You mean we ain't supposed to be a-talking about this?"

"A lady and gentleman would never discuss corsets, or bosoms, unless they were married."

A flush of mortification rose on Danny's pretty face. Seeing it, Brant felt somewhat like a murderer. She was an innocent, and he had taught her shame. Hoping to undo the damage he had done, he quickly said, "But friends can discuss anything."

An immense look of relief spread over Danny's face. "I shore am glad to hear you say that. I'd hate to ride all the way to Fort Davis and be scared to open my mouth fer fear I'd say something wrong."

"And I most certainly wouldn't want you to feel that way," Brant answered with all sincerity. He took her arm and led her towards the checkout counter, saying, "As a matter of fact, you're teaching me a thing or two. Maybe, I won't be such a greenhorn by the time we reach Fort Davis."

Danny was glad to hear Brant admit it wasn't all one-sided. Then the full realization hit her. She'd be in his company all the way to Fort Davis, and even after they had arrived there, she'd get to see him. He'd said they were friends. A thrill ran through her. As much as she liked Rose, she had been dreading having to part with Brant. He was the most beautiful and wonderful man in the whole world. And the most exciting. She didn't even care anymore that he was a greenhorn. She'd look out for him. She wouldn't let nobody or nothing harm him, just like she did Charlie. She'd see that they got to Fort Davis safe and sound.

Brant came to a dead halt, breaking into Danny's thoughts and saying, "I almost forgot. You'll need a dress."

"A dress?" Danny asked with a horrified expression on her face. "What tarnation fer?"

"You can't apply for a job with one of the officer's families dressed the way you are."

"What's wrong with the way I'm dressed?" Danny asked resentfully.

"Your attire may be appropriate for wearing on a ranch, but not in polite society. You're wearing men's clothing, something a lady would never do. You'd shock the officer's wife."

Danny's eyes narrowed. "Now you jest back up there. You ain't said nothing about me a-having to wear a dress. I ain't never worn one of those sissy things in my life, and I ain't gonna start now. Why, I wouldn't have one of the

73

consarn things! I'd probably break my fool neck a-tripping on the skirt. If they won't hire me dressed the way I am, then I jest won't go."

Brant didn't doubt her words, and he wasn't going to jeopardize all of his and Rose's manipulations to force the issue. His job was to get Danny to Fort Davis and to a potential employer. If the officer's wife who hired her didn't approve of her attire, then *she* could tackle the problem of getting Danny into a dress, and Brant fervently wished the poor woman luck. "I didn't realize you felt so strongly about it."

"I shore do!"

"In that case, we'll just forget about the dress," Brant conceded. "I'm sure your future employers would be willing to overlook the matter, in view of how difficult it is to obtain servants."

Danny gave an undignified snort and said, "Consarn it, I should hope so! Lessen they ain't got the sense a hog's born with. How I'm dressed ain't got nothing to do with the job I'm gonna do."

"I agree," Brant said in a soothing voice, wishing he had never brought up the subject. He'd had no idea he was going to get such a violent, negative reaction.

As they stepped up to the counter, Danny placed her selections on it beside the provisions that Brant had ordered, seeing that he had added a tin plate, cup, and set of eating utensils for her. She sighed deeply, thinking that her debt was going higher and higher. Then as a sudden thought occurred to her, she said, "We'll go halves on the grub, since we're partners."

Brant knew better than to argue. "In that case, perhaps you'd like to add something."

Danny eyed the provisions, noting that Brant had

74

ordered another sack of coffee. She was vastly relieved. She'd hate to have to travel all the way to Fort Davis without a cup of coffee, and she sure wasn't going to drink any of that army poison. She turned around and glanced at the barrels and sacks sitting on the floor there, then asked, "How about some of those gubbers? They taste mighty good roasted in the ashes of a fire."

Brant turned and looked about. He hadn't the slightest idea of what a gubber might be, and he hated to out-and-out ask Danny, for fear she would think him stupid again, and he very much disliked playing the role of a greenhorn before her. Then seeing Danny's gaze locked on one large gunny-sack, he smiled and said, "I presume you're talking about those peanuts."

"Shore am."

"I'll ask the clerk to add a few pounds of them. Anything else?"

"Jest my box of ammunition. Don't ferget that."

"I won't," Brant answered in exasperation, wishing she'd forget about her guns and ammunition. He was certainly capable of protecting her. He turned back to the counter, saying, "I wonder what happened to the clerk?"

"Mr. Perkins? He's probably in the storeroom having a snort."

"Doesn't the owner object to his drinking on the job?"

"Nope, 'cause he's the owner. He takes a swig from his jug every time he goes back there to carry something to the front. He don't think folks are wise to him, but you can smell him 'fore you see him. Pete said he ain't nothing but an old souse."

The object of Danny's scorn walked from the doorway that led to the storeroom. To Brant, he didn't look like a typical drunkard. The man was pale and thin, gaunt-faced

75

and stoop-shouldered, his thinning hair plastered to his head with a thick coating of hair oil.

Spying Danny, Mr. Perkins smiled, showing yellowed, broken teeth. "Well, hello, Danny," he said in a silky voice. "I didn't see you come in."

"Hello, Mr. Perkins," Danny answered, her nose wrinkling at the strong odor of whiskey coming from the man.

Mr. Perkins looked around the store, then asked, "Where's Pete?"

"He's dead. 'Paches hit the ranch yesterday and killed him. Burnt everything to the ground and stole our herd."

A shocked expression came across the man's face, to be quickly replaced with a sly one. He stroked Danny's hand where it was laying on the counter, his gaze locked on her breasts, saying, "Oh, you poor little thing. Why you're all alone now, aren't you? But don't you worry. You can stay here with me. I'd be glad to have you."

Danny pulled her arm away and placed it at her side, saying, "Thanks jest the same, Mr. Perkins, but I'm a-going to Fort Davis with my new friend here."

Mr. Perkins startled. He hadn't realized the stranger was with Danny. He gave Brant a hard look, then said, "And who might you be, young fella? And let me warn you, if your thinking of taking advantage of this girl, I'll have the law on you."

It had been all Brant could do to keep from slugging the man when he had seen him caressing Danny's hand and staring at her breasts, and now, with the man accusing *him* of making improper advances, Brant was livid. But before Brant could speak, Danny said, "This is Cap'n Brant Holden, Mr. Perkins. He's on his way to Fort Davis. He helped me bury Pete, and he's gonna help me git a job with one of the officer's families out there."

Mr. Perkins found his hopes for eliminating any competition for seducing Danny going out the window at her words. He couldn't challenge an army officer's authority, anymore than he could a lawman's, for the cavalry officers often served in the capacity of a marshall when federal law was broken, and undoubtedly the captain considered it his duty to see to the settlement of the homeless young woman. He flushed in a mixture of embarrassment and mortification at being caught in the act, wondering if trying to seduce someone who had been placed under the protection of the United States Army was a federal offense. "Forgive me if I seemed to be unjustly accusing you, Captain," he said nervously, "but I was only concerned for Danny's welfare. After all, I've known her all her life."

Like hell you were concerned for her welfare, Brant thought angrily. "Explanations aren't necessary, Mr. Perkins," he answered in a hard voice. "I'm well aware of what your intentions were. Now, if you'll add a box of Spencer clips and a few pounds of peanuts to my order, I'd like to pay and be on my way."

Mr. Perkins was so relieved that he wasn't going to be arrested that he quickly added the two items to the order and tallied the bill. He wanted to be rid of the officer as soon as possible. Considering the angry way the young man was glaring at him, he was lucky to get off so lightly. The captain looked as if he could gladly murder him with his bare hands.

As Danny and Brant walked from the store, she with her purchases in her new saddlebags and he carrying a gunnysack with their provisions, Danny asked, "How much do I owe you?"

Brant hadn't paid any attention to the bill. "We'll figure that out later, Danny. What I want to know is, has that man made improper advances to you before?"

"What's that mean, improper advances?"

"Has he ever touched you?"

"Oh, he's always pawing me when he thinks Pete ain't looking."

"And you let him?" Brant asked in an outraged voice.

"Heck, no, I don't let him!" A shiver ran over Danny. "I can't stand fer him to put his clammy hands on me. Makes me feel dirty. I shove 'em away."

"Did you ever tell your brother?"

"Nope."

"Why not?"

Danny stopped and gazed off thoughtfully. It was hard to explain, but she had sensed Mr. Perkins was doing something wrong, something that would make Pete very angry if he knew. "I was scared Pete might get mad, so mad he might kill the old souse. And I didn't want Pete to hang. 'Sides, Mr. Perkins didn't hurt me. If he had, I'd a-blown him to pieces."

Brant was forced to admit that Danny was more capable than most women in protecting herself, as long as she had her gun strapped to her hip. And it appeared that, while she hadn't been educated in the ways of lecherous men, some intuition had warned her away from danger. Knowing that she wasn't totally defenseless made Brant feel easier from that standpoint, but it didn't temper his anger. Once more, he knew it wasn't just his indignation at the man attempting to seduce a young, innocent woman that had enraged him. It was something much more elemental than his gentleman's code to protect a woman from men bent on taking advantage of them. No, when he had seen the old lecher eyeing Danny's breasts and touching her, he had experienced jealousy, an emotion that Brant had never felt about anyone or anything.

As he and Danny rode away, Brant was deeply disturbed. She did bring out the worst in him, but he felt helpless against the emotions that were surfacing. Despite his good breeding, despite the gentleman's code he lived by his entire life, he wanted her, desired her as he had never begun to desire another woman. It was as simple as that. Fort Davis looked a long way off. The next ten days were going to be sheer hell.

Chapter 5

It wasn't until Brant and Danny had traveled several miles from "town" that Brant tore himself from his dark brooding and turned his attention to more immediate problems. He reined in and pulled a piece of paper from his shirt pocket.

As he unfolded it and looked down at the paper, Danny asked, "What's that you're a-reading?"

"A map. I thought I'd better check to see how far I've strayed from my planned course."

"What do you need a map fer? All you gotta do is travel directly west. You're bound to hit the Davis Mountains."

"And what are we going to do for water between here and there? We'll be traveling through some of the most arid territory in the west."

"Does it really tell you where the water holes are?" Danny asked, amazed that a piece of paper with strange markings and lettering could tell you how to find water.

"Yes."

"Where'd you git it?"

"From the army. It was our engineers who drew up this map. Back in the forties, when gold was discovered in California and everyone was heading west for the gold fields, the army was ordered to find a water route through west Texas and the Davis mountains. They followed an old Indian trail and mapped out each water hole and how many miles between them. It later became the Overland Trail, and was used by both wagon trains and the old Butterfield Stage Line. That's why Fort Davis was founded, to protect the Overland and all of those using it, and to protect the Chihuahua Trail that veers off to Mexico south of it."

Danny was impressed. She hadn't realized that Fort Davis protected so much. "If it's such an important fort, how come the army pulled out of it during the war?"

"Are you talking about the Union Army, or the Confederate?" Brant asked.

Danny frowned. Pete hadn't been specific. She just remembered he had been angry when the army had pulled out of the forts in west Texas and left the settlers totally unprotected.

Guessing she didn't know which, Brant answered, "The Federal troops were ordered out when Texas withdrew from the Union. The general that made that order was later dismissed from the army for abandoning such a strategic fort in enemy territory. The Confederate Army took over the fort, but when traffic on the great trails dwindled down to almost nothing and the settlers started leaving because of renewed Indian hostilities, there was nothing left to protect, and they pulled out too. From then, until it was reoccupied by Union soldiers, back in '67, it was used by renegade Indians and outlaw bands, who tore down the wooden buildings for firewood and all but destroyed it. I understand they're still rebuilding it."

While Brant had been talking, he had been studying the map. He refolded it and placed it back in his pocket, saying, "We're about twenty miles to the north of the trail. If we ride hard, we can reach it by nightfall. Do you think you're up to it?"

Danny felt highly insulted. Why, she could outride anyone, and certainly some dad-blasted greenhorn. "I shore am. In fact, I'll race you to it." She tore off, calling over her shoulder, "See you tonight, partner."

Brant put his spurs to his horse, but he knew he wouldn't be able to catch up with Danny, not with her riding that little mustang pony. He'd already found that out with the Indians. Army mounts simply couldn't match the undersized, scrubby-looking mustangs for speed, which was why the cavalry did more chasing Indians than fighting them, and was precisely why the army was finally beginning to buy mustang mounts. Not only were they swifter, but they had better endurance than the thoroughbreds that the cavalry had been riding for years. And they could eat the native grasses, while the thoroughbreds had to be grain fed, feed that the troopers had to carry with them. But the army finally realizing its mistake wasn't going to help Brant win this race. His mount was a Saddlebred, a Kentucky breed known for its smooth gait, intelligence, courage, and adaptability to drills, but not its speed. Throughout the long, hard ride he was seething with frustration. It was bad enough to be bested by an Indian, but to be beaten by a girl was downright humiliating, particularly when he was a cavalryman who took particular pride in his riding skills.

Danny didn't have any trouble finding the Overland Trail several hours later. It was clearly marked by deep ruts made by thousands of wagons passing over it. She reined in and turned her mount, patting his sweaty neck fondly and saying smugly, "Well, Red, I reckon we showed him."

She gazed off into the distance. Brant and his mount were nowhere in sight. Had he gotten lost, despite his fancy map? Or what if his horse had stepped in a prairie dog hole and had thrown him? Why, he might be lying out there unconscious somewhere. A tingle of fear ran through her. She shouldn't have challenged him to a race. If anything happened to that beautiful, wonderful man, she'd never forgive herself.

Danny was just about to spur her horse and go back to look for Brant when she saw him and his mount coming, leaving a trail of dust in their wake that was rose-colored in the light of the setting sun. She took her hat off and waved it, then watched while he rode up to her, admiring his use of the rising trot that marked him as an accomplished cavalryman and wondering how he did it. He might not ride fast, but he sure could ride pretty, she admitted silently. Then she noticed the furious expression on his face. Another shiver of fear ran through her. When he was angry, Brant was a very dangerous-looking man, his blue eyes flashing like streaks of chain lightning. Yep, she'd made a mistake by challenging him to a race. He didn't like her beating him one damn bit. Funny, but she hadn't pegged him as a sore loser.

"Howdy," Danny said brightly, hoping if she didn't mention she had won the race that Brant wouldn't be so mad at her.

Brant reined in, asking angrily, "Why did you run off like that? You could have gotten lost!"

Another woman might have been pleased to know that

Brant was so angry because he had feared for her safety. His caring to such an extent would have told her volumes. But Danny didn't think like a woman. Again, she was insulted. "I ain't never gotten lost in my life! I found the trail, didn't I?"

Brant had never been so terrified as when he had completely lost sight of Danny. Visions of her getting lost and dying from lack of water had flitted through his head; then he had been tormented by fears that she might run into a band of Apaches. Her finding the trail did nothing to sooth his anger. Instead her self-reliance just irritated him all the further. "Come on," he said in a harsh voice, turning his lathered mount. "The water hole is another mile up the trail. And if you ever take off again on your own, you can damn well find your own way to Fort Davis."

As Brant rode off, Danny glared at his back resentfully. She could find Fort Davis by herself, without any silly old map, she thought hotly. All she had to do was follow the trail. Even a hog had that much sense. Imagine him saying she might get lost without him. She didn't need him. If anything, it was the other way around.

It wasn't until they had made camp and finished eating that Brant's anger finally abated. He was forced to admit that he had been judging Danny by the standards he used for the women he was accustomed to socializing with, women who not only needed protecting in this dangerous country but expected it. And he supposed he should be glad that Danny was so self-reliant and trail wise. It would certainly make his job of getting her to Fort Davis easier. But deep down, Brant wanted her to be like other women, dependent upon the strong male and appreciative for the protection he offered her. His ego struggled with his sense of fairness, until he grudgingly said across the fire, "I'm sorry I snapped at you this afternoon."

Danny had been angry, as evidenced by her silence and her black eyes shooting daggers at Brant all evening, but she had never been one to hold a grudge once an apology had been made. She smiled broadly and answered, "That's okay. You're used to a-traveling with those tenderfoot troopers of yers, and not a waddy that knows his way 'round these parts."

Brant could have pointed out that, while Danny might know her way around this area, she didn't know the mountains. More than likely, she had never seen mountains before. Brant had. There every trail looked alike, and often the paths meandered around in a hopeless, twisted maze that confused even the most accomplished frontiersman. But Brant knew better than to say as much to Danny. Her confidence in herself was nothing short of monumental, something that he both admired and was frustrated by, for despite her remarkable abilities in taking care of herself, she had a lot to learn about life and living, and Brant feared that, in that learning, she might be hurt. Dammit, he was doing it again. Wanting to protect her. Except it seemed to go deeper than just wanting. It had become a need deep within him.

"How far to the next water hole?" Danny asked, breaking into Brant's thoughts.

"Twenty miles. Why do you ask?"

"I was jest a-wondering how far we'd be a-traveling tomorrow."

"I think we'll try to make the one beyond that. It's just another twelve miles."

85

"Well, looks like we've got a good day's ride ahead of us. Think I'll get some shut-eye."

Brant watched while Danny rolled up in her blanket, settling down flat on her back. He could tell she was shimmying out of her pants beneath the blanket. Just knowing she was twisting those curvaceous hips of hers and the provocative words printed on her drawers made Brant's heat rise. It was a relief when she finally lay still. Then as she placed her hat over her face, Brant frowned and asked, "Why do you sleep with your hat over your face?"

Danny lifted the hat with one hand and looked across the fire, the expression on her face clearly telling Brant that she thought his question was downright stupid. "Why, to keep the night dew off of my face. Every waddy knows it causes wrinkles."

Danny placed her hat over her face again, and Brant rolled up in his blanket on his side, shaking his head at Danny's illogical reasoning. She didn't worry about what the blazing sun did to her complexion, but she worried about the harmless night dew. She was the most unusual female he'd ever met, her beliefs in direct contradiction to those of the women back east.

When Brant woke up the next morning, the first thing he became aware of was the bright sunlight in his eyes. The second thing he noticed was much more unnerving. Charlie was curled up on his chest, and he was staring almost eyeball-to-eyeball with the reptile. Despite the fact that Brant knew the snake wasn't poisonous, his heartbeat accelerated and a shiver ran over him. Then the snake did something that Brant knew was impossible. Charlie actually seemed to be smiling at him.

Very careful not to move a muscle, Brant called, "For

God's sake, Danny! Will you get this damn snake off me?"

Danny turned from where she was building a fire. Seeing Charlie, she rose and hurried to the two. Picking the snake up, she said, "Shame on you, Charlie. A-making a pest out of yourself. You know better than that."

She picked up the canvas bag that Charlie resided in, shoved the twisting snake into it, and closed the flap, saying to Brant, "Sorry about that. I fergot to leave the flap open fer him. But I reckon he must have decided he likes you. I ain't never seen him do that to no one 'cept me before."

Brant could have done without Charlie's show of friendship. He still felt a little unnerved. After all, a man hardly expected to wake up and find himself face to face with a snake, even if it was a friendly one. He sat up and looked about him, then noticed that Danny had donned her new clothing. To his relief, the shirt and pants were much looser. Oh, the womanly curves were still there, but not near as blatant. Then Brant frowned. Danny's old clothes had been worn and faded and had done nothing to enhance her beauty, but the vibrant coloring of the red and blue plaid shirt brought out the golden tan on her face, the natural pink flush on her sun-kissed cheeks, and the red highlights in her thick mane of hair. She looked very beautiful, and very desirable.

Seeing Brant staring at her so intently made a peculiar tingle run through Danny, and she felt a warm curl form deep in her belly. His dark blue eyes seemed to sear her clean to her bones. "How do you like my new clothes?" she asked, feeling suddenly nervous.

Brant realized he was staring—again. He jerked his

eyes away and said, "They look very nice."

Danny felt a twinge of disappointment at his words. She wondered at the strange feeling. What had she expected him to say? That she looked pretty? How silly. Only a sissy girl would want a man to say something like that to her. She turned and focused her attention on the fire, saying over her shoulder, "I'll have a pot of coffee a-going in jest a minute."

"No hurry. I'd like to shave before breakfast," Brant answered, rubbing the day's growth of golden bristles on his chin.

Brant gathered his shaving paraphernalia, a towel, and a fresh change of clothing and headed in the direction of the small stream that lay in a grove of twisted mesquite trees a small distance away. As he passed several bushes on which Danny had laid out her washing, he wondered how long she had been up. For an army man, he would have thought he would have arisen much earlier than Danny. Apparently, ranchers were up with the birds too.

When the coffee was finished, Danny poured a cup, and without a moment's hesitation, sought out Brant. It never occurred to her that she might be invading on his privacy. She always took a cup of coffee to Pete while he was shaving.

When Brant came into view, she stopped dead in her tracks. He had stripped off his shirt and was standing with his back to her, peering into a small mirror that he had hung on one of the branches of the tree he stood beneath while he shaved. Danny stared at the muscles rippling in his broad back in mute fascination. Again, she felt that peculiar tingle of excitement and wondered at it. She had seen her brothers without their shirts, and other cowhands, too, but Brant's back seemed so much more masculine, the muscles so much more powerful.

Spying Danny in his mirror, Brant startled, nicking his chin on his upward stroke across it. Muttering a curse beneath his breath, he quickly turned, asking in an alarmed voice, "What's wrong? Did you see a band of Apaches riding towards us?"

"'Paches?" Danny asked in a bewildered voice. "Heck no! I jest thought you'd like a cup of coffee while you're a-shaving."

Brant felt a little foolish, but he had assumed that Danny wouldn't invade his privacy unless something drastic had happened. Again, he had been judging her by his standards, this time those of propriety. But Danny obviously saw nothing improper about interrupting a man during his morning ablutions. He supposed he should be thankful that she hadn't walked up while he was changing his trousers. Then he would have been completely nude, instead of half, and *that* would have been embarrassing. "Thank you," Brant responded graciously, taking the cup and placing it on the ground by his shaving mug.

Assuming that Danny had left, Brant resumed shaving. He was just making another swipe up his throat when Danny said, "That shore is a funny-looking knife." Again, Brant startled, this time nicking his throat. He turned his head to see Danny standing beside him. "It's not a knife!" he threw out irritably. "It's a straight razor. It's what you're supposed to shave with."

"Oh, well, I reckon I didn't know that. Pete always shaved with his knife." Danny looked at the bleeding places on Brant's chin and throat and said, "Maybe you ought to try a knife. Then maybe you won't nick yer-self up so bad. Seems to me that razor is downright dangerous. You're a-bleeding like a stuck pig."

Brant picked up his towel and dabbed at the cuts, saying in exasperation, "It's not the razor. You startled me when you walked up, and just now, I thought you had left. I've shaved with pieces of glass when I was out in the field and never nicked myself."

"Pieces of glass? How come you were a-shaving with that?"

"Because when we're traveling stripped saddle, we only carry the bare essentials for survival, and that doesn't include our shaving gear."

"Then why don't you just grow a beard?" Danny suggested.

It was a good point. In this day and age, beards and mustaches were most definitely in vogue, in both the civilian population and in the military. Today's army was probably the hairiest in American military history, almost every trooper and officer alike sporting something on their face. Brant had never figured out if the men grew beards just to avoid the daily tedious ritual of having to shave, or because every one else was doing it, but he did know it wasn't for him. "Because I don't like the feel of hair on my face. It feels scratchy."

Danny studied Brant's face and decided she wouldn't like him with a beard either. It would hide that strong, masculine chin and detract from his well-shaped mouth. She stared at that sensuous mouth, wondering what those lips would feel like pressed against her skin. A shiver ran through her.

Brant decided that if Danny wasn't going to leave, he should at least put on his shirt. Maybe she didn't know any better, but he did. He laid down his razor and towel and reached for it. Instead of concealing his partial nudity, his action only served to draw Danny's attention to it. As he slipped his arms into his sleeves, flexing the muscles in his chest, Danny became acutely aware of that broad expanse of bare skin. There was a light smattering of golden hair that ran from his neckline down between the bulging muscles and tapered to a fine line at the waistband of his pants, seemingly pointing like an arrow to his manhood. Without even thinking, she glanced down, seeing the outline of the proof of his masculinity in bold relief against one thigh in his tight pants. Suddenly her knees felt weak, and she turned warm all over. Her heart raced, and her mouth felt as dry as fall leaves. Bewildered, and just a little frightened at the peculiar feelings he was arousing in her, she jerked her eyes away and muttered, "Well, I reckon I'd better be a-gitting breakfast."

She turned and hurried away, feeling strangely light-headed, and Brant wondered at her sudden departure.

By the time Brant returned to camp, Danny had recovered from her strange experience. They ate in silence and quickly packed up. While Brant was occupied with putting out the fire, Danny pulled out a plug of tobacco from her shirt pocket and bit off a bite. Brant rose and walked towards her, then noticing that she was chewing on something, asked, "What are you chewing?"

Danny spat a stream of tobacco juice on the ground, the brown liquid barely missing Brant's gleaming boots, and answered, "Tobacco. You want a chaw?"

Brant ignored the plug of tobacco that Danny was holding out to him and stared at her in absolute horror. He had become accustomed to seeing her in men's clothing, to her almost mannish mannerisms, to her frank speech because they didn't detract from her beauty

91

and her strong femininity. Not even the swaggering walk of the cowhands she imitated could hide her womanliness. If anything, the swinging of her hips only added to her sensuality. But Brant abhorred the idea of Danny chewing tobacco. Besides being an utterly masculine habit, it was a filthy one, one he barely tolerated from his troopers, and then only because he knew they couldn't afford to buy smoking tobacco or cigars that many of the officers used.

"I asked if you wanted a chaw?" Danny repeated, wondering why he was staring at her so strangely.

Suddenly, Brant was angry. Danny's chewing tobacco cheapened her, and Danny wasn't cheap. She was sweet and fresh and innocent. He grabbed the tobacco and tossed it away, saying, "No, I don't! And you won't chew it either. Not when you're around me."

Danny was too shocked at his surprising reaction to be angry. "Why not?"

"Because it's a filthy habit, spitting that foul stuff all over the place. It's bad enough that men do it, but it looks absolutely trashy in a woman. Besides that, it stains your teeth."

"My teeth ain't stained," Danny countered, flashing a mouthful of sparkling white teeth at him.

"It's just a matter of time before they will be."

Danny remembered seeing people with yellowed, half-rotten teeth. She wondered if tobacco had done it to them. But even if it hadn't, Brant had said it looked trashy, and that was even worse than being tacky. She hated to give up her tobacco. It seemed to soothe her nerves. But if Brant felt so strongly about it, she would. She'd do just about anything to please him. She wanted him to like her something fierce.

She gave a longing look at the plug of tobacco on the ground, then conceded grudgingly, "Okay, if that's the way you feel about it."

Brant was surprised. He had expected an argument, or another reminder that he couldn't tell her what to do. He wondered why she had bowed to his wishes. It wasn't at all like the independent Danny he had come to know.

They followed the old Overland Trail that day, weaving across the broad prairie that was studded here and there with scrubby mesquite, patches of cactus, and yucca plants. The trail was deserted except for one wagon, and they smelled it almost as soon as they saw it. They spurred their horses and galloped past, anxious to be away from the foul odor of uncured buffalo hides that the wagon carried and ignoring the greeting that the two buffalo hunters called to them.

When they had left the wagon behind them in a cloud of thick dust and slowed their mounts to a trot, Danny said, "I purely can't stand buffalo hunters."

"Why? Because of the stench that reeks from them?"

"Nope. Because of what they do for a living. It jest ain't right, a-killing all those buffalo and a-leaving the meat to rot in the sun. That's waste, and a-wasting anything, particularly something to eat, is dead wrong."

Brant could have pointed out that the only people who ate buffalo were the Indians, but he had never thought about it from Danny's viewpoint before. He supposed the senseless waste of meat was a crime against nature, to say nothing of the red man. He wondered what the people back east would have to say to Danny's argument. Many of them, far removed from the dangers that the Indians posed for the white man on the frontier, championed the noble red man and made the army the villain for trying to bring them under control—the same people that put such a high value on the buffalo hides. Would they be willing to give up their fashionable coats and hats if they knew the Indians were slowly being starved to death by the disappearing buffalo? He doubted it. It was one thing for the people on the frontier to suffer from Indian deprecations, many caused by the Indians' anger at having their source of food needlessly wasted, but quite another for them to go without. People could be incredibly selfish. He gazed over at Danny, wondering if she was mimicking her brother again. "Is that one of your brother's beliefs?"

"Nope. It's mine," Danny replied with a determined set of her small chin.

Brant was impressed. Apparently there was more to Danny than met the eye.

Later that afternoon, Brant spied a line of angry thunderheads coming over the horizon. "It looks like we're going to be in for a storm."

"Yep. Should hit about sundown. I shore hope it ain't as bad as that storm we had last month. It turned as dark as a crooked tunnel a mile deep in the ground, and the wind was a-blowing great guns. There was flash lightning, then forked lightning, then chain lightning. Then the rain came. I'm a-telling you, it rained pitchforks, purple snakes, billy goats, and bobtailed calves. I ain't never seen such a frog strangler, dam buster, duck drencher as that one was. It was a regular gully washer. It stompeded our herd clear to Jericho and scattered them from hell to breakfast."

Leave it to Danny to give such a colorful description, Brant thought with amusement. Anyone else would have just said it rained hard and stampeded their cattle. But

Brant found he liked the way Danny said things. From her lips, the words seemed to come to life. Certainly a frog strangler was a much more impressive description than a cloudburst, and only God knew how far from hell to breakfast was.

"I reckon if we're gonna beat that storm to the next water hole, we'd better hightail it. It's moving as fast as a streak of greased lightning," Danny pointed out.

"Yes, it does seem to be coming down on us pretty fast," Brant agreed, then frowned, thinking how bland his words had sounded.

They spurred their horses to a gallop. Deliberately, Danny held her little mustang mount back, although Red was champing at the bit for a good hard run. She didn't want Brant to get angry at her again, regardless of the reason. It made her feel awful low. Besides, he looked so handsome riding on that big horse of his, with the wind whipping his shiny golden hair around his face and hat and his beautiful blue, blue eyes gleaming. She just couldn't get enough of watching him. And she couldn't look at him if she was riding miles ahead of him.

Chapter 6

Danny and Brant had barely had time to make camp and eat before the wind that preceded the storm hit, blowing sand and tumble weeds everywhere and extinguishing their small fire.

"We're in for a regular gully washer," Danny said in a loud voice so that she could be heard over the wind and the crashes of thunder. "I can smell that dad-blasted rain in the wind."

Brant caught his hat as a strong gust of wind almost blew it from his head. He looked about him, saying, "We're sure not going to get any protection from these scrubby mesquites. We'll have to sleep in my dog tent tonight."

He rushed to where he had piled up his things and picked up the rolled-up tent and blankets. He quickly spread the blankets out, then began putting up the small tent, but the wind seemed determined to tear it from his hands, the canvas snapping in the hard wind. "Come hold this thing in place," he instructed Danny, "while I hammer down the stakes and secure the poles that hold it upright."

Danny hurried to help, the wind whipping her long hair wildly around her face as Brant secured the small, triangle-shaped tent. Rising from hammering the last stake in the ground with a rock, Brant said, "We'll put our guns in our saddlebags, then take off your hat and boots and toss them in the back. It's almost impossible to remove your boots in that small tent, not without knocking the damn thing down."

They removed their guns and placed them in their saddlebags, placing the bags near the opening of the tent where they could be easily reached, then sat on the ground and yanked off their boots, the wind blowing swirling sand in their eyes and stinging their faces. Brant tossed the boots and their hats to the back of the tent, saying, "Better let me get in first. Then you can slide in beside me."

With a deftness born from practice, Brant maneuvered himself into the tent and lay on his side while Danny backed in awkwardly, bumping against Brant and then one of the poles of the tent, causing Brant to make a quick grab for it to keep the tent from collapsing. Once she was in, Brant said, "You'll have to lie on your side. These things aren't called dog tents for nothing. They're hardly big enough for a good sized dog, much less two people."

Danny stretched out on her side, facing Brant. "Well, now," she said with a bright smile on her face, "we're just as cozy as two bugs in a rug."

Too cozy for his comfort, Brant thought. He was acutely aware of Danny stretched out beside him. The heat from her body seemed to be searing him, and her sweet, feminine scent engulfed him. To make matters even worse, he was very conscious of Danny's soft breasts brushing his chest every time she took a breath, each touch seemingly burning like a branding iron. He should have known better than to put himself into such close proximity to Danny, as desirable as she was. He should have offered her the tent and slept outside.

"I shore am glad you had this tent with you. It's a-raining cats and dogs out there."

Brant hadn't even been aware that the rain was pounding down on the tent and making loud pattering noises on the canvas. A flash of lightning illuminated the tent. In that brief moment, Brant saw where Danny's hair had come undone and was laying around her shoulders in wild disarray. Almost as if his hand had a will of its own, he reached out and touched it. He had never felt anything as incredibly soft. He slid his hand up her shoulder and across her throat to bury it in the thick hair at the back of her head, his head descending as his mouth sought her lips.

When Brant's lips touched hers, Danny felt as if she had been hit by a bolt of lightning. She was stunned. Then as his warm lips moved softly over hers, coaxing, wooing, brushing back and forth, a warmth suffused her, and her heart raced. When the tip of his tongue traced her lips, she tingled all over, clear to the tips of her fingers. Without realizing she was doing it, she snuggled closer, pressing against him, wanting more of all these new sensations.

The tip of Brant's tongue pressed insistently at her small white teeth. Danny opened to him, instinctively knowing that was what he wanted. The feel of his warm tongue sliding down hers, then swirling around it, left her weak and breathless. She could almost feel her bones melting. As his tongue slid in and out of her mouth in a sensuous pattern, shivers of intense pleasure ran through her, and she strained closer to him, glorying in the feel of his hard, masculine body and all the wonderful, exciting things his kiss was doing to her.

Brant's senses were reeling. He had never tasted anything as sweet as Danny's mouth. His hand slipped from her neck down to her waist, his fingers slowly tracing her spine, then moved up and around the curve of her rib cage. Still kissing her deeply, he cupped one breast, his fingers sensuously stroking the soft flesh through her shirt. Danny whimpered and pressed closer, and Brant felt himself responding to her soft, womanly curves against his long length. His manhood hardened and rose in eager anticipation, straining against his tight pants in its urgent demand to be freed.

Brant came to his senses as if a bucket of cold water had been tossed on him. What in the hell was he doing? He jerked his mouth away, withdrew his arm as if he had been burned, and rolled to the opposite side, muttering in a hoarse voice, "Good night."

Danny was as stunned by Brant's sudden withdrawal as she was by his unexpected kiss. For a moment, her mind whirled dizzily. Then, as reason flooded back, she felt a keen disappointment, wondering if that was all it had been, a good night kiss. If so, she had never been kissed that way by her brothers. All they had ever given her was a quick peck on the cheek. But her intuition told her that a brother would never kiss that way, only another man. She wondered what it would have felt like if it had been one of the cowhands she had known that had kissed her. Danny knew it wouldn't have been the same. The kiss had been wonderful, special, terribly exciting because it had been Brant kissing her. Sudden tears came to her eyes. Dad-blasted, she sure wished he hadn't stopped. She felt even lower than she ever had, and she was aching everywhere, her lips, her breasts, between her legs. Yep, he sure did peculiar things to her.

It was a long, uncomfortable night for Brant. For hours, he lay on his side with his back to Danny, staring at the canvas and fighting down his desire. It took all of his willpower to keep from turning and taking Danny back into his arms, to finish what he had begun. To add to his dilemma was his guilt. She was an innocent, young girl who knew nothing of men and passion. He could only hope she believed him when he tried to pass off his kiss as a simple good night token. Christ, what in the hell had gotten into him? Danny had put her trust in him, and he had betrayed it. Well, he wouldn't do it again, he vowed. He'd keep his distance and his hands off her. He'd made himself her protector, and if that meant protecting her from himself, he would, even if it killed him.

Brant was just about to fall asleep when he felt Danny snuggling up to him, pressing her soft curves against his back and legs. He glanced over his shoulder to see that she was sound asleep. She's only seeking the heat of my body for warmth, he told himself. But Brant found that knowing Danny's actions were entirely innocent didn't help him cope with his desire. It flamed anew, until his loins were aching painfully and his guts were tied into a thousand knots. Careful not to wake her, he slipped from the tent, welcoming the cold rain on his heated body. He slept that night under a scrubby mesquite by the water hole, tossing and turning in a vain effort to get warm and cursing his baser nature that had forced him to such misery.

When Danny awoke the next morning, she was surprised to find that Brant had already left the tent. She rolled on her stomach and peeked outside, seeing that the rain had stopped and that Brant had a fire going. She reached for her boots and slipped them on, wondering why Brant hadn't taken his with him when he left. Then picking up her hat and the rawhide string that had slipped from her hair, she crawled from the tent.

She was pouring herself a cup of fresh coffee when Brant walked from mesquite brush that surrounded the water hole, dressed in fresh clothing and splashing through the mud puddles that still littered the ground with his bare feet. "Morning!" she said brightly; then noticing the clothing he was carrying, she asked, "How'd yer clothes get so muddy?"

Brant had hoped that he could hide his muddy clothing in his saddlebags before Danny arose. He certainly wasn't going to tell her he had slept outside. Then she would want to know why he had left the warm, dry tent. "I'm afraid I did something very stupid. I slipped on the mud and fell this morning."

"Well, you must have fallen in a good-sized water puddle. They're soaking wet."

"Yes, as a matter of fact, I did," Brant answered, wishing she wasn't so damned observant.

"How come you didn't take yer boots with you?"

The last thing Brant had been worrying about when he had made his exit the night before had been his boots.

"You had your foot across them, and I didn't want to disturb your sleep."

"Well, I'd rather you'd done that than go a-walking 'round here without them on. A gully washer like we had last night forces all the rattlers outta their holes. Might drown everything else, but not those ornery things."

Brant glanced around him apprehensively, then as a sudden thought occurred to him, asked, "What about Charlie? Would it drown a grass snake?"

"Oh, you don't have to worry about Charlie. He purely hates rain. As soon as it starts a-raining, he makes a beeline for his bag. That's where he's at right now, all rolled up in his bag and a-sleeping."

Brant turned and walked to the tent for his boots. He didn't know why he had worried about a stupid snake, and apparently, Charlie had spent a more comfortable night than he had.

They stopped early the next day because both had washing to do. As soon as they'd made camp, the two walked to the small stream with their dirty clothing. "I don't mind a-doing your washing along with mine," Danny offered.

"Thanks, anyway, but I'm used to doing my own washing when I'm out in the field."

A sudden, horrifying thought came to Danny. What if he was married? "And who does it fer you when you ain't in the field?" she asked, thinking she would just lay down and die if he said his wife.

"The army hires washerwomen for that purpose. They do both the officers' and the troopers' laundry."

Danny frowned. Brant's answer still hadn't answered her question. "What about yer meals? Who cooks them fer you?"

"I usually eat at the officers' club in the post store. They operate a mess for the bachelor officers. Of course, I could hire a Dog Robber to cook for me, as well as clean my quarters for an additional five dollars a month, but it just seems simpler to eat at the club."

Danny felt an immense relief to know Brant wasn't married. The word bachelor meant nothing to her, but surely if he was married, his wife would do the cooking and cleaning. After all, that's what wives were for, weren't they? "What in tarnation is a Dog Robber?"

Brant laughed. "I'm sorry. I was using army slang. He's a striker." Seeing the confused expression still on Danny's face, Brant explained, "That's an enlisted man who hires out to an officer for additional pay. At thirteen dollars a month, a trooper can always use an additional income, particularly if he's married. But I'm afraid the other troopers make it hard on the strikers. They were the ones that named them Dog Robbers."

"How come?"

"Because the troopers don't want any association between them and the officers that doesn't lay strictly within their duties as soldiers. I'm afraid the army has very strict social rules. The officers and enlisted men don't mix under any circumstances, and the enlisted men adhere to it just as rigidly as the officers, if not more so. They even have their separate club at the post store, where an officer is strictly forbidden, unless of course, there's a riot going on that has to be broken up and he's the officer of the day, the sheriff so to speak."

"Don't sound very neighborly to me," Danny commented. "Why can't you jest all be friends?"

"There's a good reason for it, Danny. Contrary to what most civilians think, we're not just being snobbish. It's

103

an officer's job to send his men into battle, to order them to do something that might cost them their lives. That's a difficult thing to do to a man. Can't you imagine how much more difficult it would be if he was your friend?"

Danny frowned. It didn't sound like Brant had an easy job, sending men to their deaths, even if it was necessary. She sure wouldn't want it, but someone had to do it. And those deaths must prey on his mind. He had admitted it was difficult. She had never thought much about officers before. All she knew about them was what her brother had said. But now she thought Joe was wrong. They weren't weak and lazy. They had a different kind of strength. Her respect for Brant rose a notch.

While they were washing their clothes in the stream, Danny's thoughts turned to what Brant had said about the Dog Robbers. "Jest what all does this Dog Robber do?"

"You mean besides keeping my house?"

"You have your own house?" Danny asked in surprise. "I thought you stayed with your troopers."

"No, they stay in barracks, and I'm assigned a house on the post. Just how big a house you get depends upon your rank. A captain, like me, gets a three-room house and a full colonel gets a six-room one. It goes up a room with each grade. But to get back to what the Dog Robber does, he cleans my quarters and weapons and takes care of my horses. Then, like I said, if I wanted to put out the additional five dollars a month, he'd cook for me."

"What'd you mean, takes care of yer horses? You ain't got but one."

"Every officer is assigned two horses. I'll get a second mount when I reach the fort." And by God, it will be a mustang, if they have any, Brant vowed. He was tired of eating the Indians' dust.

Danny mulled over what Brant had said. She knew how to clean weapons and take care of horses. Cleaning house didn't much appeal to her, but the thought of being in a three-room house with Brant sounded real cozy. She supposed, since she'd be with him, she could tolerate it. She looked up from her washing, saying, "I jest had a great idea. I can be yer Dog Robber!"

Brant was so shocked by Danny's suggestion that he automatically clenched his fist, and the bar of lye soap he had been using to wash his clothes went flying through the air and would have hit Danny in the face, if she hadn't ducked. "Watch what yer doing!" Danny snapped. "You danged near hit me in the eye with that dad-burned soap."

"I'm sorry. It just slipped from my hand. But what you're proposing is impossible."

"You mean me being yer Dog Robber?"

"Yes."

"Why not? I can clean house and guns. And I know how to take care of horses. And you won't regret a-paying me that extra five dollars fer a-cooking fer you, either. I bet my grub is a heap tastier than anything they can give you at that officers' club. 'Sides, I'd rather work fer you than some stranger."

"I'm not saying you aren't capable of doing the job, Danny. Undoubtedly, you'd be a top-notch striker, if you were a man."

"What's that got to do with it?"

"Everything. You're a woman and I'm a man, and we're not married. It would be totally improper for us to

105

be alone in a house, even for a few hours, or anywhere for that matter."

"We've been alone on the trail," Danny pointed out.

"Our traveling together has been out of necessity. We didn't have any other choice. That's different."

"Well, I can't see why it's any different. That's jest about the silliest thing I ever heard. You need a Dog Robber and I need a job. It's as simple as that."

"Danny, women simply don't work for an unmarried officer, or even a married one, if his wife isn't with him. It isn't considered respectable. And the army is very strict about such things."

"Are you saying they wouldn't let me?"

"Yes."

"Well, why in tarnation not?" Danny tossed back in exasperation.

"Because something might happen!" Brant threw back, feeling just as frustrated.

"Like what?"

Like what almost happened last night, Brant thought. He took a deep breath to calm himself and evaded Danny's question. "It doesn't matter what. The point is, it's simply not done on an army post. You'll have to work for one of the officer's families."

Danny still didn't understand, but if it was the army's rule, stupid or not, she supposed she'd have to go by it. Otherwise they might not let her stay at the fort, and then she wouldn't get to see Brant again. And she'd rather die than have that happen.

That night, Danny kept hoping Brant would kiss her good night again. She'd been thinking about it all day, and every time she did, a little thrill had run through her.

She felt a keen disappointment when she saw him roll up his blanket.

Feeling very let down, Danny pulled her own blanket around her, wiggled out of her duckins, and then lay thinking. She wondered if Brant was angry with her because she'd asked him about being his Dog Robber. Seemed like he'd been avoiding her all evening. And when their fingers had brushed when she had handed him his plate, he'd jerked back like she was poison. Danny pondered a few more minutes over Brant's strange behavior, then asked, "Are you mad at me 'cause I asked if I could be yer Dog Robber?"

Brant stiffened. For God's sake, she wasn't going to get off on that again, was she? Why in the hell hadn't her brother told her about the facts of life? But he supposed if Pete was as shy as Rose had said he was, he was too embarrassed. But it sure wasn't his responsibility. "No, Danny, I'm not mad."

"You've been kinda . . . quiet all evening."

Brant had been fighting a continuous struggle with himself. He had found that keeping from touching Danny had taken all his concentration, and the memory of kissing her tormented him. "I'm just tired. I didn't sleep well last night, because of the storm, you know," he quickly added.

Danny was vastly relieved. Thank God, it wasn't personal. "Then I reckon I oughta stop a-yapping and let you sleep." She rolled to her side, muttering, "Good night."

"Good night, Danny."

Brant shook his head in self-disgust. He'd never told as many lies as he had to Danny the past few days. In fact, he could probably count up the falsehoods he'd told in his entire life on one hand, up to that point. He didn't like lying to her, but it seemed the only way he could get her to do what he wanted, or the most graceful way out of an awkward situation. Yes, she certainly brought out the worst in him.

The next day, Danny and Brant stopped to eat their noon meal beside an outcrop of boulders. As they were walking back to their horses, they heard a sudden rattling noise. Both went for their guns at once, but Danny's draw was much faster. The rattlesnake that lay directly in Brant's path was dead before Brant could even get his gun from its holster.

"Why in the hell didn't you let me shoot it?" Brant asked irritably.

Danny had never been so frightened in her life as when she had seen the rattler in Brant's path. Her one and only thought had been to protect him. "Well, I didn't want it to bite you," she answered, stunned by his unexpected reaction.

"For your information, I could have shot it just as well. I'm not as helpless as you think I am!"

Danny had no idea that Brant's male pride was smarting because she had protected him, and not vice versa. "Well, you don't have to git all riled up over it!" she threw back hotly. "It's dead! What difference does it make who shot it?"

Danny turned and walked angrily to her horse, then flew in the saddle. Brant watched as she raced away, thinking he'd be eating her dust again. Frustrated, he mounted and followed.

Danny didn't relinquish her anger at Brant until the

next day. Out of the clear blue, she started talking to him again. Brant had thought that he'd reached the epitome of misery in trying to keep his desire for Danny at bay, but he found that her angry silence made even him feel even more wretched. He had thought to apologize at least a score of times, but found he couldn't. She had humiliated him. Dammit, didn't she think he was capable of at least protecting himself? After all, he was a battle-seasoned soldier. But now that she was talking to him again, he found that he was ridiculously happy. He'd never known a woman who could make mincemeat out of his emotions like Danny could.

"How far is it to the Pecos?" Danny asked later that day.

"We should reach it in an hour or two."

"I ain't never seen a real river before," Danny informed him, her black eyes sparkling at the prospect.

"Well, don't get your hopes up too high. From what I've heard, the Pecos isn't much of a river, at least not in width. And for the better part, it's almost inaccessible, flowing through deep canyons that go straight up in the air. There are only a couple of places where you can actually ford it. Horsehead Crossing, where we're heading, is one of them."

They rode over an area of rolling sand hills covered with a sparse grass and studded with Spanish daggers, creosote bushes, gray sage, and dusty mesquite trees, occasionally passing through wild breaks of thorn bushes and heaps of rocks and huge boulders that looked like some irate giant had tossed them there. It was a vast, sweeping, lonely land, the only visible living creature beside them a lone buzzard that circled overhead. Then, suddenly, there was a great fissure in the hard, red earth. They reined in and looked down at the river far below them.

"That's the Pecos?" Danny asked in a disappointed voice. "Why, it ain't no bigger than a creek."

"It looks smaller than it actually is from this height."

It did look an awfully long way down, Danny thought, a tremble of fear passing through her. "How are we gonna get down there?"

"According to my map, there's an Indian trail we can follow." Brant looked around, then said, "Looks like that's it over there. Come on."

They followed the old trail that twisted and turned as it ran down the steep canyon wall. Danny was terrified. The path seemed so narrow and the drop to the bottom so far. Every time she glanced down, her heart did a crazy flip-flop in her chest, and she felt dizzy. Glancing over his shoulder and seeing her ashen face, Brant said, "Don't look down. Just keep your eyes on the trail. Nothing more."

Concentrating on the trail helped, but it still seemed to take an eternity to reach the bottom to Danny. Then as the ground leveled out and they passed under a few trees that lined the bank, she saw the river. It did look wider, and it had also changed color. "Why, it's reddish colored! It looked silver from up there."

"That's because it was reflecting the sunlight."

Brant studied the river. It was about sixty-five feet wide, and he had been told that it was only seven feet deep at this crossing, but its current was much swifter than he had anticipated, particularly in mid-channel.

While Brant was looking at the river, Danny was

110

pondering the canyon wall they had just descended. "How in tarnation do they git those wagons and stages down that steep trail?"

"We veered off of the Overland Trail yesterday. It crosses the Pecos about thirty miles south of here, where the banks aren't quite as steep and the army has built a pontoon bridge. I thought we could save time by crossing here, since we're riding horses and there might be a pileup of wagons at that crossing. But now I'm wondering. That current looks pretty swift."

Danny looked at the river. "Don't look no swifter than some of the creeks do when they're a-flooding. I've forded them."

"Can you swim?"

"'Course I can swim!" Danny answered in a highly affronted voice. "You don't think I'd be dim-witted enough to cross a flooded creek, lessen I could, do you?"

Brant supposed it was a stupid question, and God, she was feisty, particularly when she thought her skills were being questioned. "All right. We'll cross here."

The two swung down from their horses and removed their gun belts, hats, and boots, placing them in their saddlebags. As Danny slipped the canvas bag that housed Charlie, placed it squarely into the middle of her saddle, and tied the strap securely to her saddle horn, Brant said, "You and Red go first," thinking if Danny got into trouble that he could swim out and help her. "I'll follow."

Danny was thinking the same thing. "Why don't you go first?"

Brant had a sneaky suspicion of what Danny was up to, and he wasn't about to be protected again. He said in a hard voice, "Danny, we army officers have an ironclad rule, and I'm not going to break it, even for you." He made a small bow and sweeping motion with his hand, saying, "Ladies first."

Another one of their dumb-fool rules, Danny thought in frustration. Besides, she wasn't a sissy lady. But this time she was wise enough not to argue. Brant had a mighty determined look on his face, and his blue eyes were flashing warning signals. She led Red into the river, then slapped his rump. As soon as the water got deep enough for the horse to swim, Danny caught hold of his tail and let him tow her across. When they reached the center of the river, Danny was shocked at how swift and turbulent it was. The river twisted and turned her body wildly, jerking her this way and that, then pulled her down into its murky, reddish depths. She came up spitting water and muttering curses, her hair hanging in long wet strands across her face.

"Are you all right?" Brant called.

"Dad-blasted! 'Course I'm all right!" Danny yelled back, irritated at both Brant's unnecessary concern and herself for having let the river temporarily get the best of her.

When Red reached shallow water, Danny released his tail, stood, and glanced over her shoulder, seeing Brant and his horse entering the water. She watched anxiously until they had passed the dangerous swift water, then turned and walked to the bank where her horse was shaking the water from his coat. Then, spying the canvas bag hanging from the side of her saddle, she cried out and ran to it.

A moment later, Brant waded through the water and

112

up to her, asking, "What's wrong? I heard you cry out."

"My bag slipped off my saddle, and I was scared Charlie had got drowned," Danny replied, peering into the bag. "But he's all right. Mad as blue blazes at gitting soaked, though."

Danny pulled the snake from the bag, and Brant had to admit that the glistening reptile did look mad as hell. Danny set him on the bank, saying to the snake, "Go see if you can't find a rock to dry out on."

At the mention of drying out, Brant glanced at Danny. She was soaking wet, her garments clinging to her curves like a second skin, and he could clearly see the outline of her nipples. Feeling his heat rise, he averted his gaze, saying, "You'd better get dry yourself."

Danny glanced down at her wet clothes, answering, "Yeah, I reckon so. We gonna make camp here?"

"We might as well. The next water hole is thirty miles away," Brant answered, busying himself with unsaddling his horse and not daring to look in Danny's direction.

Then she'd have a leisurely bath while she was at it, Danny thought. That gol-durn river ought to be good for something more than getting dunked in. Then, as a sudden thought occurred to her, she said, "I thought river water would taste better than that consarn stuff. It's got a bitter taste to it. I ain't never tasted anything so awful, lessen it was that army coffee of yers."

"It's the alkali in it. I've been told the Pecos is so full of it during dry spells that you can't even drink it," Brant answered, still keeping his gaze averted and wishing that Danny would hurry and leave. She was too much of a temptation with her wet clothing plastered to her luscious curves.

As Danny began unsaddling her horse, Brant glanced up and said testily, "I thought you were going to change your clothes."

"I am, as soon as I git this wet saddle and blanket off of Red. No sense in him a-standing around and a-being miserable, while I'm a-gitting comfortable."

"I'll unsaddle him for you."

"Heck, no! Ain't nobody gonna say I don't pull my load on the trail."

Brant clenched his teeth, thinking she was the most exasperating woman he had ever met, and the most dense. Didn't she have any idea of what the sight of her was doing to him?

A few moments later, Danny took her saddlebags and walked around a bend in the river. Brant breathed a sigh of relief. Now if he could just make the next eight days without touching her.

It sounded like an eternity to him.

Chapter 7

Brant had changed his clothes, set up camp, had a fire going, and even laid out his and Danny's blankets, and still there was no sign of Danny. Again he glanced at the bend in the river where she had disappeared, wondering what was taking her so long. Finally, growing more apprehensive by the minute, he rose and went looking for her.

He found her just around the bend, sitting on the bank naked and toweling her hair dry. He came to a dead halt at the arresting sight.

Spying him from the corner of her eye, Danny jumped to her feet, holding her towel in front of her instinctively.

"I'm sorry," Brant blurted, recovering his senses. "When you didn't come back for so long I was worried about you."

"I took a bath and washed my hair. It always takes a long time fer the dad-blasted stuff to dry. If I'd put my clothes on, they'd have been sopping wet too."

Brant glanced at Danny's hair. It hung around her in wild disarray, and the settling sun behind her picked up its glorious red highlights. He'd never seen anything so beautiful. His eyes swept over her body. The towel covered the essentials, but he could see the indentation of her small waist, the graceful curve of her hips, and almost the entire length of her shapely legs. And holding the towel grasped tightly to her chest pushed her breasts up, so that the ivory globes looked as if they would spill out over it any minute.

His desire rose, fierce and urgent, a throbbing in his blood and temples and loins. As if in a daze, he walked up to her, threaded his fingers through the hair at the back of her head and lifted it, his eyes slowly roving over her face. "You're beautiful, Danny," he said in a husky voice. "Did you know that?"

Stunned, Danny shook her head slightly. She stared into Brant's eyes. She had never seen them look so intense, the blue so vivid, his gaze so searing. Suddenly she found it hard to breathe, and her heart raced.

He kissed her then, softly on the mouth, then the tip of her nose, then each cheek. As his mouth closed over hers, his lips brushing back and forth, Danny leaned into him, shivers of pleasure running over her as his tongue slowly traced her lips, then slid over her teeth. Without hesitation, she opened her mouth, the feel of his tongue sliding the length of hers making her weak with longing. His kiss grew more urgent, kissing her as if he were reaching for her soul and leaving her feeling giddy and her stomach fluttering wildly.

Brant raised his head and gazed down at her, his blue eyes smoldering with desire. "Help me, Danny," he said in an agonized voice. "Stop me. Because God knows that I can't stop myself."

But stopping Brant was the last thing Danny wanted.

She had been aching for his kiss and touch. She wanted him to go on kissing her forever, for the wonderful, exciting feelings he was arousing in her to never end. She dropped the towel between them and slipped her arms around his shoulders, standing on her tiptoes as she offered him her mouth.

It was an invitation that Brant didn't have the strength to turn down. It had taken all of his willpower to break the last kiss and ask for Danny's help in bringing his passion to heel. He knew it was madness, but every muscle and nerve in his powerful body was clamoring with need. He had to have her.

With a groan that sounded as if it were wrenched from the depths of his soul, he dropped his hands to her back and molded her soft body to his long length, his mouth crashing down on hers in hot, fierce demand, a kiss that seemed to sear Danny's lungs and melt her bones. The world spun dizzily around her as his tongue ravaged her mouth, on and on and on, until the bones in Danny's knees dissolved and she slumped in his arms.

Brant broke the torrid kiss and swept Danny up in his arms, carrying her back to their camp, his legs feeling incredibly weak. He knelt beside his spread blanket and placed her on it, then sat back on his heels and devoured her loveliness hungrily. Her skin was the color of warm ivory, every curve and hollow perfection. He lingered at her proud, full breasts, the nipples looking like tiny pink rosebuds that were begging to be kissed. His eyes swept down to stare at the tight curls at the junction of her rounded thighs, the hair the same glorious color as her thick, unruly mane. His mouth turned dry, and his manhood, already straining at his trousers, lengthened another inch.

Danny's senses were still spinning from Brant's passionate kiss, but even so, she was aware of him taking in her nakedness. She might have felt shamed if it had not been for the obvious admiration on his face, a look that told her he found her pleasing to the eye. For the first time in her life, Danny was glad she was a woman. A warmth filled her, making her skin take on a rosy glow.

Brant raised his eyes and looked directly into Danny's. Her breath caught at the intensity she saw there. His eyes were almost black with the heat of his desire, his gaze burning. Suddenly, she wanted to feel his lips on hers again, to be pressed to his hard male body. She lifted her arms in silent invitation.

Brant stretched out beside her, leaning halfway over her, and Danny slid her arms around his neck. He placed soft, feathery kisses over her face, his hand sweeping down her side, lingering to stroke her thigh sensuously, then moving back up in a long caress that took her breath away. His mouth slid over her cheek, kissing her temple, then her ear before nibbling at the delicate lobe, sending shivers of pleasure through her.

Brant's mouth descended ever so slowly, following the pounding pulse beat in her throat, then supping at the crook of her neck, the silky softness of her skin awing him and her taste and scent intoxicating him. Danny's breath caught as he cupped one breast in his hand, his thumb brushing back and forth over the crest and making the nipple spring to life.

As Brant's head slipped lower, dropping kisses over her breasts, then licking the soft mounds, Danny felt the flesh swell, the tip feeling as if it would burst. When Brant's mouth closed over one aching peak, rolling the tender nipple between his lips, his tongue flicking in and

118

out, Danny cried out softly, feeling as if a bolt of fire had rushed to her lower belly, leaving her throbbing and aching between her legs.

Her hands tangled in his golden hair, holding him against her as Brant performed his magic there, each tug sending waves of delicious pleasure through her, until she didn't think she could stand any more of this exquisite torment. As Brant relinquished her breast, she whimpered in disappointment, then gasped with renewed delight when he took its twin in his mouth.

Her hands slipped down to his back, clutching his shirt and pulling harder as each shudder ran through her. Brant felt the constriction on his chest, the buttons biting into his skin through his dulled senses. He lifted his head, muttering, "Let me take off my shirt."

He sat up and slipped off the garment while Danny stared at his magnificent chest, the sight exciting her even more. When he leaned back over her, kissing her mouth softly, Danny gasped as his heated flesh met hers, the crisp hairs on his chest tickling her swollen, aching nipples. She trailed her hands over the broad expanse of his back, delighting in the feel of the smooth skin and the powerful muscles there, enjoying touching him as much as his touching her.

Brant renewed his assault on her senses, stroking her breasts, her hips, her thighs, while his mouth played havoc at her throat and shoulders. When his hand slid upward and touched her between her legs, Danny startled and squeezed her thighs instinctively.

"No, don't close your legs," Brant whispered thickly in her ear. "Let me touch you there."

It was the feel of his tongue tracing her ear, rather than his impassioned plea, that made Danny relax her legs.

119

Her entire concentration was focused on Brant's tongue flicking in and out of her ear, until Brant's slender fingers slipped through her warm, velvety dewiness, searching and finding the core of her womanhood, then teasing and tantalizing it. Then all thought fled. Danny was consumed in a scorching heat as wave after wave of delicious tremors flowed over her, inside her, growing more and more intense until her breaths were coming in tiny gasps and a powerful tremor shook her, curling her toes and burning the soles of her feet.

Brant knew that Danny was as ready for him as she would ever be. Her womanly essence bathed his fingers, and her spasms of joy had excited him unbearably. He sat up, jerking off his boots and socks, then laying down, slipped off his pants and kicked them away.

He rolled on his side and took Danny in his arms in a tight embrace, thrilling to the feel of her incredible softness against his feverish skin full length. Danny's dark eyes widened with wonder. She could feel his powerful heart pounding against hers, his warm breath fanning her ear, the slight smattering of hair on his thighs where they were pressed against hers, his erection, hard, hot, and throbbing where it was trapped between their bellies. Her concentration zeroed in on the latter, and a brief tingle of fear ran through her. It seemed immense and very threatening. Then as an answering throb began between her legs, her fear fled like the wind, to be replaced with an unbelievable excitement. She pressed closer, rubbing her belly against his rigid length and bringing a groan of pleasure from Brant.

He kissed her, deeply, thoroughly, passionately, his hands caressing her everywhere and leaving Danny's nerves strung tight and burning. When he rolled her on her back and reared over her, looking powerful and magnificent, her heart leapt for joy, for she sensed she was on the brink of discovering even more exciting, wondrous things. She felt his hands slipping beneath her and cupping her buttocks, lifting her, then the hot tip of his manhood parting the tender, pulsating moistness between her legs, slowly moving deeper, kissing the core of her womanhood and rubbing against it. Waves of quivering heat ran through her.

Brant eased inside Danny slowly, the muscles on his big body trembling in protest at his caution. He felt the barrier he had been searching for and paused, torn between his raging need and his reluctance to cause her pain. He leaned forward and whispered against her swollen lips, "I'm going to have to hurt you. But it will only be for a moment."

Danny heard his words as if they had come from a great distance. All she could think of was Brant's throbbing, rigid heat inside her and his warm, muscular thighs pressed against hers. She nodded her head slightly, and then as Brant gave a powerful, swift thrust, bit her lips to keep from crying out as a sharp, searing pain tore through her lower belly. As quick as it came, the pain was gone, to be replaced by a dull ache. She looked up at Brant and, seeing the almost anguished expression on his face, lifted her hand and stroked his cheek, saying softly, "That wasn't so bad."

Brant felt an immense wave of relief. The worst was behind them, but he was shocked by how tight she was. Her velvety heat seemed to be squeezing him, pushing him dangerously close to release. He struggled for control, wanting to give Danny time to adjust to him, his body breaking out in a fine sheen of perspiration from his supreme effort.

Danny was acutely aware of Brant filling her. Then as the realization hit her that they were actually one, she was filled with the wonder of it, the beauty of it. But she sensed it wasn't over. There was an aching pressure building down there. She moved her hips tentatively. A bolt of electricity ran through her. Thrilled at her discovery, she moved again, gasping in delight.

All too aware of her experimentation and the smile on her face, Brant began his movements, slow, incredibly sensuous movements that awakened nerve endings Danny had never dreamed existed. When his mouth covered hers, his tongue thrusting in unison, Danny felt a pulsating sweetness lifting her, higher and higher as Brant quickened his movements, driving harder and deeper. Danny's body was on fire, every nerve ending tingling. She wrapped her legs around him, bringing a gasp of pleasure from Brant as he slid deeper, rocking her hips against his in total abandon and urging him on, muttering over and over, "Yes, yes, oh, yes."

Danny heard a roaring in her ears and felt a terrible pressure building in her. A wild turbulence seized her, sweeping her up in a maelstrom of swirling colors, before she exploded with a violent shattering force that hurled her to the ends of the universe.

With her cry of joy ringing in his ears, Brant followed her with his own shattering, white-hot release, then collapsed weakly over her.

It was a long time before Brant's strength returned and reason flooded back. He lifted his head from where it lay pillowed on Danny's long hair and propped himself up on his elbows, looking down at her with horror as the full impact of his actions hit him.

Danny opened her eyes, the long lashes sweeping upward to reveal twin lipid pools as dark as coal. Then she smiled radiantly and breathed, "That was wonderful! Can we do it again sometime?"

"No!" Brant said harshly, then jerked away from her as if he had been burned.

As he reached for his trousers and jerked them on, Danny sat up with a bewildered look on her face, then asked, "Why not?"

Brant glanced over his shoulder as he was rapidly buttoning his pants and, seeing Danny's tempting nakedness, snapped, "For God's sake, cover yourself!"

"Why? You've already seen everything."

"Please, Danny, just do as I asked."

Danny pulled the blanket up over her shoulders, wondering what was ailing him. She'd never seen him act nervous and jumpy.

Looking over his shoulder, Brant saw that Danny was covered. He also saw the baffled expression on her face. He turned and dropped to his knees beside her, saying, "We can't do that again, Danny, because it should have never happened in the first place. It was wrong. I know you didn't know any better, but I did. I accept full blame."

"Blame? Why would I blame you?"

"Because it was wrong. You're a young, innocent girl. I took advantage of that innocence."

"Now you jest back off there," Danny said, her dark eyes flashing. "I ain't no child. I'm full grown, and I can

123

make my own decisions. I wanted you to kiss me."

"There was a lot more that happened than a kiss, Danny," Brant reminded her.

"Yep, and I reckon I wanted that, too, 'cept I didn't know what I was a-aching fer."

"You don't know what you're saying."

"I do too know what I'm a-saying!" Danny flared out. "I told you, I ain't no child. And I don't believe it was wrong, either. Otherwise, I'd a-known it, deep down inside. No, it was right. Why, it was downright beautiful." Danny dropped her head and averted her eyes, adding, "At least, to me it was."

Brant had to admit that it had been a beautiful experience for him too. It had been much more than just a physical release. It had been a sharing, a giving and taking that he had never known with any other woman.

Danny peeked at Brant between her long lashes, then asked in a hesitant voice, "Don't you like me?"

Brant cupped the side of her face in one hand and lifted it. "Of course, I like you, Danny. Very much. If I didn't like you, it would have never happened."

In Danny's estimation, Brant's admitting that he liked her very much was as good as an avowal of love. And she loved him, too, something fierce. So much it made her ache inside.

Danny's eyes sparkled with happiness. "And I like you a heap too. So it couldn't be wrong. We was jest a-showing each other how much."

Had it been an expression of a deeper emotion, Brant wondered. He honestly didn't know. His emotions were in such a turmoil that he didn't know if he was coming or going. But he did know that he had never felt this way about any other woman.

Danny pushed the blanket away and slid her arms around Brant's neck. At the sight of her creamy breasts and their impudent little nipples puckering in invitation, Brant's desire flamed anew. "Don't do this to me, Danny," he said in a husky voice. "When it comes to you, I'm as helpless as a newborn kitten."

"Then I'll be strong enough for the two of us," Danny answered, pulling him down over her and placing her lips against his.

"No, we can't!" Brant muttered in a desperate effort to retain his sanity.

"Shore we can," Danny answered in a sultry voice, kissing his lips with tantalizing purpose. "And don't tell me you don't want to, 'cause I won't believe you." She reached down and placed her hand on his rapidly growing and hardening manhood, her touch seemingly searing him right through the material. "Yer lips may tell me one thing, but yer body says another."

Brant couldn't deny it. He wanted her as much, if not more so, than before. Helpless against the onslaught of their mutual desire, he surrendered, giving both him and Danny another taste of heaven.

Chapter 8

Over the next two days, Brant discovered that Danny was an even more determined woman than he'd thought. She had decided that they were lovers, and nothing short of Brant riding off and leaving her would change her mind. He might have seduced her in the beginning, but both nights, Danny seduced him, crawling into his bedroll naked and pressing her soft tempting body against him. It seemed he had roused a sleeping tiger when he had awakened her passion, and he was no more immune to her unique charms than he had ever been. To the contrary. Making love to Danny only made him want her more, for Danny was an enthusiastic, exciting lover who gave freely of herself, holding nothing back. Brant had never known such nights of wild abandon and soul-shattering release. He finally gave up struggling against it on the third day. He might be able to fight off his own desire, but not her's too. She was as she had said, a woman full grown and capable of making her own decisions. He might be a gentleman, but he was just as human as the next man, and it would take a saint not to succumb to Danny's strong sensuality and her ardent advances.

Later that morning, they veered back onto the main trail. Before them they saw a wagon train making its way tediously across the high, open plateau and leaving a thick cloud of alkali dust behind it. Danny frowned, then said, "I thought the wagons on wagon trains had canvas over them."

"The American wagon trains do, but that's a Mexican train, hauling freight to Chihuahua."

"That's right," Danny said, remembering what Brant had told her. "This is the Chihuahua Trail too."

"Yes, it is. Before I came to Texas, I had never heard of the Chihuahua Trail. It came as quite a surprise to me to learn that more gold, lead, copper, and silver goes over this trail than the Santa Fe, and that it's at least equal to that well-known trail in the amount of freight that passes over it. Dollar for dollar, the Chihuahua Trail has by far the richest traffic." The dull gray, volcanic dust stirred up by the train was beginning to make Brant's eyes water. "Come on. Let's go around it, before we choke to death on all this dust."

The train consisted of twenty wagons that were twenty-four feet long, with no sides. But that didn't seem to stop the Mexicans from piling as much as they possibly could on them, the freight stacked so high that Danny marveled that it didn't fall off. "How many pounds you reckon they got on those wagons?" she asked Brant.

"I understand that they can carry 120,000 pounds of freight."

Danny looked at the fourteen little mules that were pulling one of the wagons and said, "Don't seem possible that those mules could pull that much weight."

127

"Those are Mexican mules, Danny. Not only are they stronger than American mules, but superior in every way. And they're much better trained. In fact, it looks like they're fixing to stop right now. Maybe you can see for yourself just how well trained they are."

Brant and Danny reined in and watched as the first six wagons veered off to the left forming a half-moon and the second six went to the right. When the circle was completed the mules were unharnessed on the outside, then trotted through the rear opening behind each wagon into the interior of the circle.

"How come they ain't heading fer grass?"

"Mexican mules don't eat grass. The train carries its own corn with them. They're fed from long, canvas troughs that are stretched across the sides of the wagons inside the corral."

A few moments later, the mules ran back out and down to a nearby pool to water. "Why don't we take our break now?" Brant suggested.

"But it ain't even noon."

"I know, but they'll rest the mules for a while before they take them back in to re-harness them, and that's the part I'd like you to see, providing the wagon master doesn't mind. Why don't you wait under that cedar over there while I ride over and ask him?"

"Ask him?" Danny asked in surprise. "But you're a Yankee. Where'd you learn to speak Meskin?"

"I learned Spanish in college. Of course, the Mexicans have their own dialect, but I manage to get by, even if my accent is atrocious."

Brant and Danny parted ways, and by the time Brant rode up to the dusty cedar he had directed Danny to, she had spread her blanket and laid out a few ash cakes and some of the roasted antelope that was left over from their meal the night before. As he sat on the blanket beside her, he said, "The wagon master said he didn't mind if we watched when they hitch the mules back up. He said he'd give me a call."

"What's so danged special about a-seeing a bunch of mules a-being hitched up?" Danny asked.

"If I tell you, I'd ruin the surprise."

They had just finished eating when a loud crack of the whip made Danny jump in surprise. She turned to see the mules heading for the wagons at the same time a Mexican standing by the train waved his hat and yelled to Brant, "Senor!"

"Come on," Brant said, rising to his feet and bringing Danny with him.

Brant rushed her to the wagons, Danny practically having to run to keep up with his long, quick strides. When they walked into the circle of wagons, the entire enclosure was filled with milling mules, many of whose mouths were still dripping water. Brant pointed to a slim Mexican standing in the center of the mules, saying, "Watch that man. He's the *caporal*, the second most important man on this train."

The *caporal* raised his long whip and cracked it in the air. The mules came to a complete standstill, raising their heads with their ears standing up alertly. At the second crack of the whip, the mules started trotting to the wagons, many crossing the entire width of the enclosure and brushing against others going the opposite direction. Then, unbelievably, they lined up in front of the wagons with such precision that the Mexicans merely had to pick up the harnesses where they had dropped them earlier and place them on the animals.

"Why, I ain't never seen nothing like it," Danny said. "All he did was crack that whip."

"That's what I mean when I said they're well trained. Each and every mule has taken its place before its wagon. Now, I can see training a few animals to obey your orders, but over a hundred and sixty? That took a lot of time and patience. Why, they're better trained than my troopers are. You never saw so much shoving around and trading places as when they're lining up for inspection."

Brant and Danny headed back to their horses. They were mounted and ready to leave just as the wagon train pulled out, the little mules trudging along with grim resignation. As they passed the lead wagon, Brant waved his hand and called to the wagon master, *"Gracias!"* The Mexican grinned broadly and waved his *sombrero* in return.

A mile down the trail, Danny was still marveling at the way the mules had performed. "That's the only trained critters I've ever seen," she admitted. "Once, when a medicine show was a-coming to town, they sent out flyers a-claiming they had a lion that could do tricks. Pete and I went to see it, but it turned out that it wasn't nothing but a dad-blasted worn-out bobcat that didn't do nothing but sleep."

"You've never been to a circus?"

"Nope. Have you?"

"Yes. They have lions that jump through fiery hoops, dogs that dance on their hind legs, and bears that juggle balls and do acrobatics. And then there's the sideshows, where a man eats fire and swallows a sword, and another man sleeps on a bed of nails and walks across red-hot coals, and the strong man lifts a thousand pounds. And then there's the elephant man and the bearded lady—"

Danny's eyes had gotten wider and wider as Brant talked, but when he said the last, they narrowed suspiciously, and she asked, "Are you a-pulling a sandy on me?"

"A what?"

"Are you a-pulling my leg?"

"No, Danny, it's true. That's the kind of things you see at a circus and the carnivals that usually settle down beside them. Inside the big circus tent, they have all kinds of animal acts, acrobats, and tumblers. But in my estimation, the most exciting acts are performed by the aerialists, who walk a tightrope hundreds of feet in the air, or ride a cycle across it, or fly from one trapeze to the other, doing somersaults in midair."

"Gol-durn, I shore wish I could see all of that."

Brant did, too, and he wished he could be the one to show her. He'd like to show her all the things he'd seen, watch the expressions on her face and listen to her comments. Seeing them with Danny would be a whole new experience. He'd like to take her to the circus, to the theater, to a concert, to an opera. Brant chuckled. Oh, he could just imagine what she'd have to say about the latter. Something to the effect of, "They was a-hollering like a bunch of lickered up Injuns and a-shrieking like a couple of tomcats in a dad-blasted cat fight."

It was later that afternoon that Brant did get to experience seeing Danny's reaction to something exotic. As they passed a large pile of boulders, an animal darted from behind them and ran away across the dull gray plateau, kicking up dust in its wake. Danny brought her mustang to a dead halt, stared in openmouthed disbelief, then asked, "What in blue blazes was that dad-blasted thing? I ain't never seen such a ugly-looking, long-legged,

131

knock-kneed critter in my whole life."

Brant chuckled. "It was a camel."

"Now jest a gol-durn minute. I've lived in Texas all my life, and I ain't never heard of no camel."

"That's because they aren't native to this country, or this continent, for that matter. They come from Africa, a place half the world away."

"Then what in tarnation is it a-doing here in Texas?"

"Back in the fifties, when Jefferson Davis was Secretary of the War, he decided to experiment with camels as possible mounts for the calvary in the west, since they were desert animals that could carry much heavier loads, go with less food, and go without water for four days at a time. He had them shipped over from Africa, along with their Moslem driver, Hadji Ali, who the troopers called Hi-Jolly, a colorful character with his red fez and rainbow robes. The camels were landed here in Texas and sent on a trial journey to California that passed through west Texas and the Davis Mountains. Some of the camels escaped on that trip. The animal we just saw must be one of them."

"Well, if that ain't jest about the most dumb-fool thing I ever heard of. How in tarnation did that Davis feller think the cavalry was a-going to ride 'em, with that big hump on their backs?"

"The army had special saddles made for them. Actually, it wasn't such a bad idea. In several trial runs between them and regular mounts, the camels outdistanced the horses and mules every time. I understand the troopers assigned to the camels even got over their humiliation at having to ride such an ungainly, rough-gaited, ugly animal and became proud of their performance, even though camels are even worse about biting

132

than mules. The plan only had one flaw in it. The camels did fine on the deserts, with all its sand, but when they got into the mountains, with all its rocks and pebbles, they couldn't hold up. Camels don't have hooves like horses and mules do, but grizzly pads on the bottom of their feet that can't be shod. The army had to abandon the experiment."

Danny veered her horse from the trail to avoid an ocotillo, a plant that had long leaves on it that looked like whips stuck into the ground. She admired the brilliant cluster of red flowers on the top as she passed it, then asked, "That Davis feller you was a-talking about ain't by any chance the same feller Fort Davis was named after?"

"Yes, as a matter of fact, he is. He ordered the fort built. He later became the South's president."

Danny frowned. She vaguely remembered Joe saying something about President Davis. Danny snorted and said in disgust, "Well, no wonder the South lost the war, if they had some dad-blasted fool like him a-leading them. Anyone who thinks those knock-kneed camels would make better mounts than horses ain't got the sense a hog does."

Brant chuckled. Apparently Danny hadn't heard anything he'd said about it not being such a bad plan, other than its one flaw. She was behaving like a typical Texan, who thought horses superior to any animal in the world for riding. Time and time again, the Texans had bet on the horses in the trial runs, and lost, while many a camel-riding trooper had raked in a small fortune.

They camped that night at Comanche Springs, within viewing distance of the tall stockade of Fort Stockton. The spring was one of the major water holes on both the Chihuahua Trail and the Overland and was crowded with both freight and passenger trains, the huge, conestoga wagons—known more popularly as prairie schooners—parked in circles here and there.

That night, from where they had made their camp in a more isolated area, they could hear the sounds of fiddle music floating in the air. Noticing Danny listening intently to the music, Brant said, "It sounds like they're having a dance over there. Have you ever been to one?"

"Nope."

Brant frowned. "Not even a barn dance?"

"Nope. But Joe said he went to a dance hall once. Said it was more a-kicking their feet and a-stomping and a-clapping their hands than anything."

Brant had the sudden urge to dance with Danny. He rose, saying, "Come on, let's go over there. I'm sure they won't mind us joining in. That's one thing I've found out from riding escort to a few trains. The people are always friendly."

"But I can't dance!"

"There's nothing to it. I'll teach you." He glanced down at her hip, adding, "But we'll leave our guns here. With all these people about, there's no danger of us being attacked by Indians."

After removing their guns and dousing their fire, Brant hurried Danny through the darkness to the wagon train where the music was coming from. They passed the train's corral of mules and then as they walked through the open passageway between two wagons, Danny looked up at them in awe. They towered over her, the wheels alone almost six feet high. She had never seen such huge wagons. Then as they stopped just inside the circle, her breath caught. A big bonfire was going in the center, casting dancing shadows over the wagons, and all around

134

it couples were dancing to the lively fiddle music, the men whirling the women around and making their long, colorful calico skirts swirl around their legs. A tingle of excitement ran through Danny.

A heavily bearded man standing by the wagon Brant and Danny had just passed, turned to Brant, saying, "Howdy."

"Hello," Brant replied. "We're camped about half a mile from here and heard your music. Do you mind if we join in the dancing?"

The man glanced at Danny, a little taken aback by her male attire, then quickly hid his reaction and answered, "Of course not. The more, the merrier. We got folks dropping in from all the trains around."

"Thanks," Brant answered, then led Danny off to the side, before he turned to her and asked, "Shall we dance?"

It looked like an awful lot of fun, but it also looked very complicated to Danny. She didn't want to embarrass Brant, tripping all over his feet. "Jest let me watch fer a spell."

Danny turned her attention back to the dancers, noting that many of the couples were just taking two steps one way, then two in the opposite, with an occasional whirl now and then. It couldn't be too hard. Why, even the children were dancing. Then her eyes widened in disbelief. She turned to Brant, saying, "I didn't know men danced together."

Brant chuckled, answering, "Neither did I, until I came to Texas. I understand it's a custom all over the west, where there's a decided shortage of women. The man with the white scarf tied around his arm is called the lady fair. That means he's taking the woman's role."

"You mean he's a man a-acting like a woman?" Danny asked in a shocked voice.

"Only for the dance. You see, one person has to lead, and the other follow. Apparently, they're so anxious to get in on the fun, that they're willing to accept the role of following."

Danny noticed that several of the men who had pegged themselves as a lady fair weren't doing such a good job of following. There was a lot of stepping on their partner's feet going on. But, strangely, their partners didn't seem to mind. Except for a grimace of pain on the injured party's face, they kept right on dancing. Surely, she could do as well.

She turned to Brant and said, "Well, I reckon we can try it."

Brant smiled, a smile that made Danny's heart melt. He slipped one arm around her waist, saying, "Put your right hand on my shoulder and give me the other."

Danny did as directed. "We'll start out with a simple two-step," Brant said. "Just follow me."

Brant found out that Danny was as light as a feather on her feet, and soon they were twirling and whirling all around the other couples. As the dance went on and on, the music got louder, as did the clapping in unison from the spectators on the sidelines, for the noise was part of the fun. Brant had never enjoyed dancing as much as he did with Danny. With her black eyes sparkling with excitement, her face flushed to a rosy color from their exertions, and the firelight picking up the red highlights in her hair, she looked incredibly beautiful. And every time he twirled her, she laughed, the spontaneous, joyous sound washing over him like a sensuous caress.

Then, when another couple bumped into them,

pushing Danny's body flush up against his, Brant's desire rose, hot and urgent. He dropped his arm from around Danny's waist, and led her from the circle of dancers.

"We ain't a-leaving?" Danny asked in a disappointed voice.

"Yes, we are," Brant answered tightly, pulling her through the opening between two wagons.

"But why? The dance ain't over."

Brant turned, and Danny's breath caught at the burning look in his eyes. "Because I can think of something we could be doing that's a lot more exciting."

Danny wasn't about to object. Compared to Brant's lovemaking, dancing was downright dull. Her heart raced in anticipation, and her mouth turned as dry as ashes. She nodded her head.

Brant rushed her twice as fast back to their camp as he did to the dance, Danny running to keep up with him. Then, when they were about a hundred feet from it, he suddenly whirled and took her in his arms in a tight embrace, kissing her fiercely, one hand slipping through the opening of her shirt to cup one breast possessively. His urgency only excited Danny more. She kissed him back, her small tongue twining around his.

He jerked back his head, saying in a thick voice, "Jesus! Don't do that!"

"Why not?"

"Because we'll never make it back to camp. I'll take you right here on the ground."

"Then I reckon we'd better hurry . . ." She glanced down at the bulge in his pants. ". . . 'fore you bust your duckins." She turned, running for the camp, calling over her shoulder, "I'll race you!"

Brant ran after her or, rather, tried to. It wasn't easy in

137

his aroused condition. When he reached the camp, he stopped and looked around him, seeing no sign of Danny. Then suddenly she jumped from behind a tree and threw herself in his arms, saying in a breathless voice, "What took you so long? I didn't think you was gonna ever git here."

Brant chuckled, answering, "You know damn right well what took me so long."

Danny grinned and rubbed herself against Brant's erection, bringing a groan of pleasure from him, saying, "Well, I reckon that big thing would drag you down."

She was a shameless little creature, Brant thought, but only because she had never been taught shame. And he certainly wasn't going to teach her. Her total honesty was a big part of her appeal. There would be no more lectures from him on what was right and wrong, and what ladies and gentlemen did or didn't do. Danny did what came natural to her, and that was a part of her appeal too. No, he wasn't going to fight their strong attraction to one another any longer, he thought, reaffirming the decision he had made that morning, not because he wasn't strong enough to resist Danny's sensuality, but because it was too beautiful, too natural to destroy. Danny was right. Deep down, it didn't feel wrong. He had never known anything that felt so right.

Later, much later, when they were lying on Brant's blanket after having made love, Danny snuggled closer in his arms, thinking she was glad that Brant had taken the initiative in their lovemaking that night. It seemed more natural for the man to be more aggressive that way and get things started than a woman. A woman. It sure did seem funny thinking of herself like that, but she did now.

"What are you thinking?" Brant asked. "I can almost

hear the wheels turning in that pretty little head of yours."

Danny smiled at Brant calling her pretty, then stroked his damp chest, answering without the slightest hesitancy, "I was just a-thinking that I'm glad I'm a woman." She laughed softly, saying, "Gol-durn! I didn't think I'd ever see the day when I'd say that. 'Course that don't mean I hafta act like one of those sissy women." She paused, then raised up and looked down at Brant, an intense expression on her face. "I jest want you to know that no matter what happens, I ain't gonna regret us a-being lovers. Not ever! I ain't never been as happy as I've been these past few days."

Brant was forced to admit that he had never been as happy, either, and knowing that he had helped Danny come to appreciate and accept her womanhood brought him a tremendous amount of satisfaction. He stroked her long hair that cascaded around them like a waterfall, saying in a voice husky with emotion, "I won't ever regret it either."

The smile that came over Danny's face caused an odd, twisting pain in Brant's chest; an immense tenderness for her welled up in him. He softly kissed her forehead, and lay her head back down on his shoulder, absently caressing her soft tresses while he wondered what the future held in store for them.

Chapter 9

When Danny and Brant rode out from Comanche Springs the next day, Danny got her first sight of the lofty mountains in the distance. Danny had never even seen a good-sized hill, much less mountains. She stared at them in amazement, then asked in a voice tinged with disappointment, "Is that the Davis Mountains jest ahead of us?"

"Yes, but they're not just ahead of us. They're still forty miles off."

"That ain't far. We could reach the fort by tomorrow."

"No, once we reach the foothills, our going will be much slower. We can't travel in a straight line, like we have been. The trail twists and turns. And Fort Davis doesn't sit on the edge of the mountains, but in the center. We still have some traveling ahead of us."

Danny was vastly relieved. When she had seen the mountains up ahead, she had thought her time with Brant was almost over. Oh, she knew she'd see him at the fort, but she realized that they'd never have the privacy there that they had been enjoying. Out here, she had Brant to herself. Yes, this was a special time, one that she might never have again with the man she loved. And she fully intended to make the most of it, to enjoy it to the fullest.

Later in the morning, a stagecoach passed them, the coach rocking back and forth and bouncing on the rutted road as the four half-wild Spanish mules pulling it raced along, while the two passengers on the top held on for dear life. Danny looked at the coach with wonder, then asked, "Have you ever ridden in one of those things?"

"Yes, I have," Brant answered in disgust, "and believe me, I've never had a rougher ride. They bounce you around so bad that you're black and blue, to say nothing of the jarring they give your teeth. That's one reason I decided to ride to Fort Davis, instead of taking a stage, even if it is faster."

"What were the other reasons?"

"There was just one. I wanted to get a closer look at the land."

"What'd you want to look at the land fer?"

Brant wondered if he should tell Danny of his decision to settle in Texas, then decided against it. As much as a greenhorn as she thought he was, she'd probably laugh at him. He shrugged his broad shoulders, answering, "Just curious."

Danny sensed that Brant's answer had been evasive. She stared at him, making Brant feel as if she were peering into his soul. Hoping to distract her, he said, "According to my map, there's a stage stand further up the trail. We could stop there and have a hot meal this noon."

"They serve meals?" Danny asked in surprise.

"Yes, they furnish meals for the passengers for an additional fifty cents apiece."

"You mean they ain't included in the fare?"

"No, the stage lines have a captive clientele, and you'd better believe they milk the passengers for every cent they can get from them. And let me warn you, the station tender cooks the meals, and for the most part, they're lousy cooks. We'll be taking a chance."

"It don't make no never mind to me," Danny answered with a shrug. "It's up to you."

"We'll give it a try. If the food looks too bad, we'll just get up and leave. But if we're going to eat there, we'd better catch up with that coach. Otherwise, they might not let us in."

Danny wondered what Brant meant about them not letting them in as they galloped after the coach. About thirty minutes later, the stand came into view, a lone adobe building sitting right out in the open. As they rode closer, Danny saw the heavy gate in the thick walls being opened for the coach. "They're gonna drive that dad-blasted coach right into the middle of the station?" she asked in shocked disbelief.

"That walled-in area is the corral. The station is right behind it. Now, hurry, before they close the gate on us."

The little Spanish mules dashed through the gate and came to a skidding halt, making the coach dip forward and almost unseating the two passengers on top. Brant and Danny slipped in right behind it. And not a minute too soon. They had barely reined in before the heavy gate was slammed shut.

Danny looked up, seeing that the thick walls around the corral were a good fifteen feet high. Noticing the

142

puzzled expression on her face, Brant said, "They're built that high to keep the Indians out. Otherwise, they'd steal all of their mules."

"What are they shutting the gate fer in the daytime?"

"Stage stands are a favorite target for Indian attacks, Danny. They can't be built too strong, and the tenders can't be too careful. From what I've heard, Apaches are more daytime raiders, than nighttime, and this is Apache country, you know."

A shiver ran through Danny at the reminder. Then, remembering what they had done to her brother and their ranch, she said, "I jest wish some of those red devils would come a-sneaking 'round so I could get a few of 'em. I'd blast them to hell and back."

Brant chuckled, then said, "We didn't stop here to fight Indians, but to eat, remember?"

The man who had slammed the gate shut walked up to them, asking, "Who in the hell are you?"

"We're just passing through on our way to Fort Davis and thought we'd drop in for the noon meal," Brant explained. "Have you got enough for two extra?"

The man scratched his shaggy beard and answered, "Well, I reckon so. With business so bad because of these damned Apaches, the stage line has gotta make every extra dollar it can." He nodded his head briskly towards the station, saying, "Go on in with the passengers and have a seat."

Brant and Danny dismounted, but before they could follow the passengers in, their way was blocked by the stage being turned around to face the gate in preparation for the next run. Danny wondered how the tender and old man helping him managed the chore all by themselves. The stage looked awful heavy. She glanced across the corral, seeing the driver leading the dusty, sweaty mules that had been pulling the stage away, while the guard brought a fresh team forward.

Once the stage had been turned, they walked into the adobe building, stopping to let their eyes adjust to the sudden dimness after the bright sunlight. Danny looked around her, seeing a large rectangular room with a stone fireplace sitting on the back wall to one side of her. Two long tables were covered with grimy red and white checked tablecloths, and strips of dusty, limp calico dangled on the windows at both ends. A smoky coal oil lantern hung from the ceiling, adding its dim light to that coming through the windows. There was a door that led to the outside at one side, heavily barred, and another on the wall facing them that Danny assumed led to the sleeping quarters and storeroom.

"Let's go sit with our backs to that wall over there," Brant said. "It's closer to the window and the light and away from the heat of the fireplace."

As they walked around the table at the back wall, Danny noted that the adobe walls were covered with old magazines, newspapers, and posters of buxom actresses and acrobats with fierce-looking, waxed mustaches.

One colorful poster caught Danny's eye. In the center of it was a picture of a man flying through the air with a pair of skin-tight, knee-length pants on, reaching for a bar suspended by red ropes. "That's a picture of one of the aerialists I was telling you about yesterday, advertising a circus," Brant informed her.

Danny's heart accelerated with excitement. "Where's it gonna be, and when?"

"At San Antonio, three years ago," Brant answered wryly.

"Three years ago?" Danny asked in a disappointed voice. "What in tarnation is it still doing a-hanging there?"

"All the posters are outdated, Danny. They leave them there because they add a little color to this gloomy place."

Brant turned and glanced over to one of the tables where the passengers were being served by the tender. "Looks like it's stew of some kind."

Danny craned her neck, asking, "What's it got in it?"

"God only knows."

Danny sniffed the air, saying, "Smells like venison to me. Maybe it won't be so bad."

"I hope not."

They sat down on the bench between the wall and table and waited to be served. While they waited, Brant studied the passengers seated at the other table. There was a middle-aged couple, a younger one with a small child, and three other men, two of whom Brant assumed must be cowhands, since they were wearing six-shooters. The third Brant figured was a gambler, judging from his natty dress and perfectly manicured hands. All looked dusty and bone-tired, and Brant didn't envy them having to crawl back into that coach for another twenty or thirty miles.

Two men walked in from the corral, and Brant recognized them as the driver and the guard. The guard set his rifle down by the door, and two men walked to the table where Brant and Danny sat, taking a seat at the other end.

Just as the tender was laying Danny and Brant's plates before them, a loud knock sounded at the side door. The tender jumped in surprise, almost dropping the plates, while the guard sprang to his feet, grabbed his gun, and walked to the door, calling out, "Who's there?"

"Just a few waddies looking for a hot meal!"

"Goddammit, what's gotten into everybody today?" the tender asked in disgust. "This ain't no damned restaurant!"

The guard slipped over to the window and cautiously peeked out, then said, "They look like cowhands."

"How many of them are there?" the driver asked.

"Three." The guard looked back at the tender and asked, "What'd you think?"

"Aw, hell, let 'em in. I'll just throw some more water in the pot."

The guard set his rifle down by the door, then slid the heavy bar across it back, placed it on the floor, and opened the door, the rusty hinges squeaking in protest. As soon as the three, heavily bearded men walked in, dusting themselves off with their hats, he closed it and put the bar back in place, picking up his rifle and walking back to the table where he had been sitting, then leaning the rifle against the end of the table.

The tallest and biggest of the three men, glanced around, then spying the tender, said, "Thanks, partner. We ran out of grub yesterday and were getting a might hungry."

"You could have shot some game," the tender pointed out testily.

"Yeah, but it tastes like hell without salt on it, and that stew of yours smells mighty good," he added in a smooth voice. "We could smell it all the way down the road."

The tender wasn't gullible enough to believe the man. He knew the stranger was just trying to butter him up. He gave a snort and said, "Take a seat. I'll serve you when

146

I'm finished with these other people."

The three men walked to the end of the table where the passengers sat and took a seat, facing the table where Brant, Danny, the driver, and the guard sat. Danny didn't like the looks of the three. They had a shifty-eyed, mean look about them, despite the smiles pasted on their faces.

The tender dumped a wedge of corn bread from a big cast iron skillet onto their plates, splattering gravy on the tablecloth as he asked Brant, "What'll you have to drink? Coffee or water?"

Brant knew better than to ask for coffee. It had probably been boiling for well over twenty-four hours. "Water, please."

After the tender walked away, Brant picked up his fork, saying, "Well, I guess I'll give it a try." He took a bite, then said with surprise, "It's not too bad." He glanced across, seeing Danny staring at the three men. "What's wrong?"

"I don't like the looks of those three," she whispered.

Brant glanced at the three men the tender was serving. They didn't look anything out of the ordinary to him. He looked down the table at the driver and guard, seeing that they were wolfing down their food. Surely if there were anything suspicious about the drop-ins, those two would sense it. "I think you're seeing ghosts where there aren't any," Brant said. "Now, eat up, before your food gets cold."

Danny glanced around to see that everyone was eating, including the three men, and from the way they were shoveling the food into their mouths, they did act as hungry as bears. Maybe she was just seeing spooks, she decided. Nobody else seemed to think they looked mean.

She picked up her corn bread. It felt as heavy as lead. She started crumbling it into her stew, watching the three from the corner of her eye. She tensed when one of the shorter men rose and walked to the back door, wondering why he would be going into the corral. Then realizing that the privy must be out there, she laughed at herself, and picked up her fork.

But still a niggardly little feeling of unease gnawed at her. She strained her ears for any strange noises coming from the corral, but heard absolutely nothing. It seemed to her that the man was taking an awfully long time. Then he walked back in and paused at the doorway, nodding slightly to the taller of his companions, who had glanced over his shoulder as the man stepped back inside. Danny knew in a flash that it was a signal of some sort.

Before she could even react, the two men sitting at the table slammed to their feet, their guns drawn and covering every one in the room. A split second later, the man at the door drew his six-shooter. "Don't anybody move, or we'll put a bullet clean through you!" the tall man called out.

The young woman screamed in fright, while the tender whirled from the fire, then seeing the guns, cried out, "What in the hell do you think you're doing?"

"Shut up!" the tall man spat.

"I knew it!" Danny muttered. "Dad-blasted, I knew it!"

"You shut up over there, too!" the man said, pointing his gun at Danny. "I'd just as soon kill a woman as a man."

The guard made a leap for his rifle. The tall man fired his gun, the deafening sound reverberating through the room, while the guard spun around from the impact of the bullet that hit his shoulder and the rifle flew through the air to land in the aisle between the two tables. The young woman screamed again.

"Stop that goddamned shrieking, you bitch!" the tall man yelled. The child beside her started sobbing in fear. "And shut up that snotty-nosed kid of yours."

Terrified for her child, she clutched the small boy tightly to her bosom, her face ashen as she tried to quiet him, her husband sitting rigidly beside her and glaring at the gunman with unmitigated fury.

"Everyone put their hands flat on the table, where we can see them," the tall gunman directed. "Fred," he said to the man standing next to him, "get that guard off the floor and back in his seat." As Fred moved over to the guard, the tall man motioned with his gun, saying to the tender, "You sit down too. I want everyone where I can keep an eye on 'em."

Shooting daggers at the man, the tender moved to the table and took a seat, placing his hands flat on the table like everyone else was doing.

Brant placed his hands on the table, furious with himself for not having listened to Danny. Then, seeing her hesitancy in obeying the outlaw, he nudged her hard with his shoulder and hissed from the corner of his mouth, "Dammit, don't even think about going for your gun."

That was exactly what Danny had been contemplating, but Brant's whisper drew the tall gunman's attention to them. "That goes for you, too, little lady," he said to Danny with an ugly snarl. "I want to see your hands."

Grudgingly, Danny placed her hands flat on both sides of her plate. Dad-blasted, she could kick herself for not listening to her instincts, she thought in self-disgust.

Now they were in a hell of a mess.

The gunman called Fred jerked the guard from the floor with one arm and shoved him back on the bench. The driver glared at him and said in an angry voice, "You don't have to be so rough with him. He's wounded!"

"He's lucky he ain't dead, the way Luke shoots. He could have jest as soon put a bullet through his head as his shoulder."

As the guard started to lift his hand from the table, Fred centered his gun on him and asked, "What in the hell do you think you're doing?"

"I'm going to get my handkerchief out of my pocket and bandage his shoulder."

"Like hell you are. Put your hands back on that table!"

"But he's bleeding like a stuck pig!"

"That's too bad," the outlaw said with an ugly snarl. "That's what he gets for being stupid and going for his gun." He reached down and jerked the six-shooter from the guard's holster, then elbowed him roughly in the back, saying, "Put your hands on the table too!"

"I can't," the guard muttered, his face as white as a sheet as he clutched his wounded shoulder with his free hand, the blood flowing freely through his spread fingers. "I think that bullet busted my shoulder socket. I can't move my arm."

"You don't say?" Fred said with a sneer. "Then you're in a hell of a fix, ain't you? Ain't nobody gonna hire a one-armed guard." Then, as quick as a flash of lightning, he reached for the guard's limp arm and jerked it from his grasp, dropping it on the table.

The guard cried out in pain, and the driver spat, "You dirty son of a bitch!"

Fred poked his six-shooter in the driver's face and said,

"One more word out of you, mister, and you're gonna be knocking at the pearl gates!"

The driver stared at the gun, his face draining of all color. "Leave 'em alone, Fred," Luke said in a hard voice. "They ain't gonna try nothing else." He glanced over his shoulder, asking the outlaw standing behind him, "Joe, did you take care of that old man out in the corral?"

"Shore did, Luke. He's knocked out cold and tied up tighter than a drum."

"What about the strongbox? Did you find it?"

"Yeah. Got it sitting right outside the doorway. You were right. This is a lot easier than holding up a stage in the wide open. We should have tried it before."

"I told you boys it would be like taking candy from a baby," Luke answered in a smug voice. "Now pick up the dishpan over there and start collecting their guns, before another one of 'em gets some bright idea in his head."

Joe picked up the dishpan and walked to the first cowhand sitting rigidly at the table, pointing his gun at the man's head and saying, "Ease your gun out real slow and put it in this pan. Try anything cute, and you're a dead man."

The cowhand drew his gun from its holster and dropped it in the pan, the six-shooter making a loud clattering noise as it hit the bottom. "Now you," Joe said to the second cowhand. Another six-shooter hit the bottom of the pan. Joe walked around the table and held the washbasin before the nattily dressed man.

"I'm not carrying a gun," the man said in a tight voice.

"Like hell you ain't! You goddamned card sharks always got one of them Boudoir Cannons in your pocket. Now cough it up, before I lose my temper and blast you to kingdom come."

151

Pale-faced, the gambler reached into his pants pocket, then placed the derringer in the pan, the small, but deadly gun looking like a toy against the two large six-shooters. "Now give me that knife you've got shoved up your sleeve," Joe said in a hard voice.

Knowing it was useless to deny it, the gambler withdrew the long switchblade and dropped it in the pan too.

Joe turned to the middle-aged man. "I'm not armed," the man said in a trembling voice.

"Yeah, that's what they all say," Luke drawled. "Frisk him, Joe."

"Stand up!" Joe said, poking his gun in the terrified man's back. The man stood, shaking so hard his pot belly was quivering like a bowl of jelly. Joe reached around the man and quickly patted his chest, then down both of his sides. "He's clean."

"Sit back down," Luke instructed the man, and the frightened man almost collapsed in relief.

Joe walked back around the table and held the dishpan before the younger man. His eyes glittering with anger, the man reached into his inside coat pocket and dropped another derringer into the pan. "My, my," Joe said with a grin, "we shore are getting a collection of those little cannons today."

"Stop your yapping, Joe," Luke said in an irritable voice, "and get over there and get that big, blond-headed man's gun. We ain't got all day."

Joe walked to the table where Danny and Brant were seated. He leaned across it, holding the pan before Brant. Brant's eyes flashed angrily, and a muscle twitched in his jaw. Joe felt a tingle of fear running through him, thinking, this one is dangerous. When Brant placed his

152

Colt in the pan, Joe sighed in relief, then glancing down at the gun, said, "Hey, that's army issue. Where'd you get it?"

"It's probably stolen, just like that hat sitting on the table beside him," Fred said from where he was standing at the end of the table.

Joe looked down at the hat, then said, "I don't see no patch on it."

"He probably ripped it off, but those yellow silk cords ending in acorns laying across the brim is a dead give-away. That's an officer's hat."

"Well, I reckon you ought to know, being a deserter," Joe replied. Brant jerked his head around and glared with fury at Fred, for there was nothing an officer hated worse than a deserter. Assuming he was angry because Fred had pegged him as a thief, Joe laughed and said, "Well, now, you ain't nothing but a low-down thief like us. How does it feel to be on the other end, for a change?"

"Dammit, Joe, I told you to get a move on!" Luke said from across the room. "Dump that pan of guns someplace and start collecting their valuables."

Resentfully, Joe did as he was ordered, turning from the table and walking towards the rear door. Danny was stunned when he walked away without demanding her gun, too, then glanced down and saw the long tablecloth was lying across her lap and concealing the butt of her six-shooter. He must have assumed, because she was a woman, she wasn't carrying a gun, she realized. And none of them could see her boots under the table from where they were standing. She glanced at Brant and saw the expression on his face was just as surprised, before he quickly hid it.

153

Joe passed the dishpan around the second time, saying, "Put all your watches, rings, stickpins, and money in the pot."

"Not my wedding ring!" the older woman objected. "Surely you don't want that."

"I shore as hell do, you old sow. And I'll take that brooch you're wearing too."

While the passengers dug into their various pockets for their valuables, Luke said to Fred, "Go drag that strongbox in. I want to get out of here as soon as Joe has collected their valuables."

Fred glanced down at the guard, who had fainted and was laying sprawled across the table in a pool of blood. "You think you two can keep them covered?"

"We've disarmed them, ain't we? Now go on!"

As soon as Fred walked outside, Brant whispered to Danny, "Slip your hand off the table, take your gun out, and slide it down the bench next to me."

Danny slipped her hand off the table and carefully removed the gun from its holster, but instead of sliding it down the bench to Brant, she held it close to her thigh, staring straight ahead.

From the corner of his eye, Brant had seen Danny slip the gun out, and he knew by the stubborn look on her face that she wasn't going to give it to him. He could have throttled her. "Give it to me!" he hissed from the side of his mouth.

"No!" Danny whispered back.

By then it was too late. Joe was walking towards them with the dishpan. Holding it out over the table to Brant, he said, "You know, I've been wondering about something. Did you kill that officer you stole that stuff from?

154

If so, you're in a heap of trouble, mister. Killing an army officer is a federal offense."

Brant glared at the man. "So is robbing the United States mail."

"Hell, we ain't interested in the mail. We just want the money in that strongbox."

"Tampering with the mail in any way is a federal offense. Anyone unauthorized to touch that strongbox is tampering with it."

There was a note of authority in Brant's deep voice, and Fred resented authority. "You know, mister, I'm beginning to like you less and less. You're a real smart-mouth," Joe said in an angry voice, shoving his gun in Brant's face. "Just for the hell of it, I think I'll blow your brains out."

Danny was terrified that the man was going to follow through with his threat and shoot Brant then and there. She fired her gun. The bullet ripped through the table and tore through Fred's chest, splattering blood everywhere as he and his gun flew backwards. It was only because Luke was stunned to discover everyone hadn't been disarmed after all, that Danny had the split second to pull her gun from beneath the table, leap to her feet, and fire at him. Their shots left their guns almost simultaneously, Danny's hitting the man square between the eyes, while his shot whizzed between Danny and Brant and hit the wall behind them with a dull thud. Hearing the gunshots, Fred ran back into the station, then spied the smoking gun in Danny's hand. As he aimed his six-shooter at her, Danny fired the third time, and the third outlaw went spinning from the impact, his gun discharging a bullet harmlessly into the ceiling before he fell to the floor.

Within seconds, it was over, and the room was filled with gun smoke, everyone so stunned by the sudden shoot-out that there wasn't a sound to be heard. Danny looked about her, seeing the shocked expressions on everyone's faces, then glanced at Brant. A shiver ran over her at the absolute fury she saw on his face.

Then everyone reacted at once. The women started sobbing hysterically, and the men started clamoring to their feet and running to investigate the bodies laying on the floor. "This one is dead," one of the cowhands squatting by Luke's lifeless body said. "Shot clean through the eyes," he added in amazement.

"So is this one," the other cowhand said, rolling over the man by the door. "Got him through the temple."

"This one is on his way out," the tender said, examining the body of the first man Danny had shot.

Instead of feeling proud, Danny felt sick to her stomach. All her life, she had bragged about her shooting, claimed she would blast someone to hell, but she had never killed a man. Then she remembered that if she hadn't done what she had, the man would have killed Brant in cold blood. She had reacted out of sheer protectiveness for him. But she still wished it hadn't ended the way it had, even if those dad-blasted outlaws did deserve killing.

The tender rose to his feet, asking the driver, "How's Bill?"

"He's okay," the driver answered from where he was pressing a pressure bandage on the guard's shoulder. "Lost a lot of blood though. Probably would have bled to death within a few more minutes if she hadn't killed those goddamned bastards. He owes his life to her."

156

"We may all owe our lives to her," one of the men at the table muttered.

"Never saw such straight shooting in my life," one of the cowhands remarked.

The tender turned to Brant, saying, "We shore are obliged to your wife and—"

"She's not my wife," Brant said in an angry voice, slamming his hat on his head. "If you have anything to say, say it to her!"

Danny flinched at his hard words, then risked a quick glance at him, seeing that he was walking away. She slipped her gun in her holster, picked up her hat, and hurried to follow. As she was rounding the corner of the table, the tender stepped before her saying, "That was mighty fine shooting, little lady."

"Thank you," Danny said absently, watching Brant from the corner of her eye as he picked up his gun from the pile of weapons the outlaw had dumped in one corner and slipped it back into his holster.

The younger married man stepped forward and said to Danny, "I want to thank you for what you did."

"Yes," his wife said with a little sob from where she was sitting and holding their terrified son, "we're so grateful to you. There's no telling what those horrible men might have done to all of us."

"You're welcome," Danny replied, then seeing Brant stepping out of the back door said, "Sorry folks. I gotta go."

As she rushed off, the tender called, "Wait a minute. There might be a reward out for these men. What's your name?"

"Danny," she called over her shoulder as she hurried out the door.

Stepping outside, Danny glanced around her, seeing Brant was untying the dazed-looking old man laying on the ground.

"Danny what?" the tender called from inside.

"Jest Danny!" she called back, wishing the man would leave her be.

Seeing Brant heading for the gate, Danny started forward, but was stopped dead in her tracks as the old man sat up, grabbed one leg of her pants, and asked, "What in the hell's going on 'round here? Who slugged me? And what were all those shots I heard?"

"There was an attempted hold up inside," Danny answered, trying to jerk free from the man's grasp. "But it's all over now. The outlaws are all dead."

"All of 'em?" the old man asked. "How many of 'em were there?"

Danny saw Brant mounting his horse. Then he and the animal flew through the gate. "Please, mister, let go of my duckins. I gotta go."

"You with that young fella that jest tore out of here?"

"Yep."

"He shore looked mad as hell about something."

"Yep, he's as mad as a cat that got his tail caught in a meat grinder, and if you don't let me go, I ain't never gonna catch up with him."

The old man released his hold on her, and Danny ran to her horse and leaped into the saddle, digging her spurs into the animal. She raced after Brant, wishing with all her heart that they hadn't stopped at the dad-blasted station. Now she purely had a skunk by the tail. She was in a heap of trouble.

Chapter 10

Brant saw Danny from the corner of his eye as she pulled her horse up beside his a short while later. He wasn't surprised. He had been aware of her mustang's hooves pounding on the road behind him ever since he had left the station. He didn't dare look at her directly, not as furious as he was. He didn't trust himself not to yank her from her horse and throttle her. She had refused to give him her gun, and he knew damn well why. Because she considered him a helpless greenhorn, not man enough to take care of himself, much less her. Rather than put her trust in him, she had put herself into danger in that wild shoot-out. He had never been so terrified in his life. He should have been the one to do it, not her. Dammit, he was the man! She undermined his masculinity every time he turned around, making him feel like a goddamned fool.

The entire afternoon, Brant never said a word to Danny, or even glanced in her direction, making her feel miserable. To add to her misery was her confusion. She couldn't understand his anger. She knew she was the better shot. It just made sense for her to do the shooting. And she sure couldn't stand by and watch someone kill him, no more than she could Charlie. She'd only protected him. What was so dad-blasted wrong with that?

By nightfall, Danny's own anger was coming to the rise. Everyone else at the station had seemed to think that she'd done the right thing, thanking her and even complimenting her on her excellent shooting. And Pete had always praised her when she did good. Brant didn't have any right to treat her so unjustly. After all, it was her gun. What she did with it was her business.

Finally Danny could no longer contain her seething anger. She whirled on Brant and spat, "I don't know what you're so gol-durned riled up about! It was my gun, and I'm a better shot than you."

Deep down, Brant knew Danny probably was the better shot, but her saying so was like rubbing salt in an open wound. As a calvary officer, he prided himself on his marksmanship as well as his riding skills. He glared at her, saying in a tight voice vibrating with anger, "I'm well aware of your low opinion of me, but for your information, I'm just as good a shot as you. Granted, my draw might not be as fast, but my aim is just as true. I didn't get through three years of war and manage to survive these past five fighting Comanches without having some shooting skill myself. I could have brought those three down just as well as you. And it was my place to do it. I'm a soldier. It's my job to protect people." Brant paused, then remembering his fear for her, thundered, "It was too damn dangerous for you! You could have been killed!"

Danny winced at his loud voice, then said, "Well, it would have been jest as dangerous fer you."

Brant's face was a thundercloud. "You still don't get the point! I'm used to facing danger, to being shot at. That's a man's place in this world."

For the life of her, Danny couldn't understand. She knew nothing of men and their pride, nor did she realize that men like Brant expected women to place themselves under their protection, to play the passive, defenseless role. She wanted to please him, but it seemed no matter what she did, it was wrong, and she feared he wasn't going to forgive her this time.

Brant saw the hurt and confusion on Danny's face and knew that she couldn't help what she'd done. She'd simply been doing what came natural to her. He was back facing the same dilemma, wanting Danny to behave like the women he had known back east, expecting something from her that she couldn't give. Not only had Danny been raised differently, but he knew the same rules didn't apply here in Texas. Oh, the women in the eastern, more civilized part of the state and those who lived in towns stood back and let the man take the protective role, but not on the Texas frontier. There, women were often as tough and self-sufficient as their husbands, and their men took pride in their strength and bravery, often bragging outrageously to others about them. Over the years, Brant had heard frontier men boast to one another that their wives could ride a panther bareback, sing a wolf to sleep and scratch his eyes out, scalp an Injun one-handed, swim straight up a waterfall, gouge out an alligator's eye, or shoot the feeler off a grasshopper's head twenty paces away. Overhearing them, Brant had been appalled at their boasting, thinking it terribly unflattering to the women. While he had come to appreciate Danny's uniqueness, her strengths, her total honesty, Danny's refusal to let him protect her was something he couldn't come to terms with. It was too deeply ingrained in him.

"I reckon we ain't friends no more," Danny said, breaking into Brant's thoughts.

The miserable expression on her face caused that strange twisting pain in Brant's chest again, and the remnants of his anger that remained disappeared like a puff of smoke in the wind. He couldn't stay mad at her, no matter what she did. Briefly he wondered why, then shook his head in frustration and folded her in his arms tightly against his chest, muttering in her hair, "Oh, Danny, what am I going to do with you?"

For the time being, just holding her, just not being angry with her was enough for Danny. It put her fears that it was over between them at rest.

The next morning, they reached the foothills of the Davis Mountains. As they traveled deeper into the mountains, Danny was surprised. She had always imagined that the hills would get progressively higher and higher until they formed a continuous ridge of mountains, but the Davis Mountains rose irregularly, hill upon hill, and peak upon peak, interspersed with sudden small valleys or deep canyons. By noon they had twisted and turned, gone up and down and around so much that she no longer knew which direction they were traveling, and the soil was so rocky in places that the deep ruts of the Overland Trail they had been following completely disappeared. When they reached yet another canyon where several trails converged, Danny was forced to admit that she was lost. She had no idea which way Fort Davis lay.

"Are you shore we're a-going on the right trail?" she asked Brant doubtfully, as she glanced back over her shoulder at another trail that had veered off to a side canyon behind them.

"According to the map, this is the trail."

"How do you know? You ain't looked at it since this morning."

"I memorized what we'll be covering today." Brant glanced over and saw the apprehensive expression on Danny's face. "Stop worrying. I know what I'm doing."

Danny hoped so, because she sure didn't. It was the first time in her adult life that she'd had to depend upon someone else for anything, and it was unsettling.

She glanced up one of the canyon walls, blinked her eyes, then stared real hard. "Well, gol-durn, if it ain't a burro after all."

"Where?" Brant asked, looking about him.

"Up there, on that ledge right over us. It was a-standing so still I couldn't be shore I saw it, with it the same color as the rocks behind it. What do you reckon it's a-doing out here?"

"I understand there are whole herds of wild burros in these mountains. If we looked real close, we might spy a few others."

"We had a burro once," Danny informed him. "That was the orneriest critter I've ever seen. You could beat him, kick him, gouge him with yer elbow, twist him into kinks, pull his ears off, or even build a fire smack-dab under him and he wouldn't move if he didn't want to.

163

Pete said burros are so dad-gum smart they act dumb jest to get outta work."

Brant chuckled, answering, "Army mules use the same tactics when the notion hits them."

"No, burros are really smart," Danny persisted. "Have you ever seen one when it's attacked by a lobo?"

"No, I'll have to admit I haven't."

"Horses and mules will rear up to protect themselves, but when they do, they can't see nothing. They're a-hitting out blind with their hooves. A burro will roll over on its back and kick something awful. I'm telling you, you ain't never seen legs kick and twist and lash out like theirs do, jest a-moving like greased lightning. With those legs going lickety-split like that, you'd swear on a stack of Bibles that they had more legs than a dad-blasted centipede. No matter how much a-snapping that lobo does, he can't get a hold on one of those legs, and if he tries to go for the neck, he'd git plumb cut to ribbons by that danged burro's hooves. Poor old lobo finally gets so gol-durned tuckered out, it jest gives up and sneaks away with its tail 'tween its legs."

Brant smiled. It had been a while since he'd heard one of Danny's long, colorful narratives. Over the past few days, he'd discovered that she could be very quiet as well as long-winded, often riding beside him for hours at a time without saying a word. But, strangely, the silences never seemed awkward between them. It was a quiet companionship that Brant had only experienced with his best friends, and most certainly never with a woman.

The next day they entered a canyon that was so wide it could almost be termed a small valley. A swift-running stream weaved back and forth across it, the water crystal clear and sparkling in the sunlight. In the distance the mountains were clothed with green grass and trees.

Danny looked around at the picturesque canyon appreciatively. In some places the grass was knee-high, and scattered among the patches of lush green were pink and red phlox, Hesper mustard with their showy lavender flowers, and Apache plume with their rose-like white ones. Even some of the prickly pear cactus were blooming, adding dashes of bright yellow to the scene. Holm oaks, junipers, maples, and pinon pines dotted the area.

"This sure is a purty place," she commented to Brant. "It even smells good."

"That's the pines you're smelling. I understand the Apaches roast the cones and eat the seeds."

Danny looked about her in confusion, then asked, "Which ones are they? We don't have any of these trees back where I came from."

"The pines are the ones with the long, thin, needle-like leaves."

Danny looked around her again, then asked, "You reckon there are any bears 'round here?"

"I would imagine so. You usually find them in mountainous areas."

Well, Danny thought, if they got lost out here, it might not be so bad, for she still didn't trust Brant's map. It was just about the prettiest place she'd ever laid eyes on, and she had seen turkeys, doves, rabbits, and deer over the past two days. Along with the bears, they'd certainly have enough to eat, and there was fresh water, the sweetest she had ever tasted, and wood for fires. In fact, she wouldn't mind staying out here forever, as long as she was with Brant.

They camped early that night in Limpia Canyon under

a stand of pines and made love with the trees' fragrance scenting the air and their boughs sighing softly in the breeze. Then they lay snuggled together under Brant's blanket and listened to the crackle and pop of the fire and the croak of a tree frog. They were just dozing off to sleep when a sudden, shrill shriek rent the peaceful night air.

Brant sat bolt upright and looked about him. "What in the hell was that?"

Danny had recognized the scream as that of a panther's. She grinned, then quickly hid it and answered in a deadly serious voice, "I reckon it must have been a gwinder."

Brant frowned. "What kind of animal is a gwinder? I've never even heard of one."

"It's the ugliest, meanest critter on earth, with long, sharp teeth that almost drag the ground and a short leg in front and one behind, so it can circle around a mountain as quick as blue blazes and catch a man and tear him to pieces."

Brant's eyes twinkled with amusement. "Danny, you're not pulling a sandy on me, are you?"

A look of disappointment came over Danny's face. "Yeah, I reckon I was," she admitted.

They lay back down, and Danny snuggled closer in Brant's arms. She wondered why her gwinder tale hadn't worked. It was the waddies' favorite way to frighten a greenhorn. But Brant didn't act like any greenhorn she'd ever seen or heard about. He never made any silly mistakes, and he wasn't scared of nothing. And he was smart, too. Why, he'd told her all kinds of interesting things he'd read in books and about the fascinating places he'd been and things he'd seen. Sometimes she almost felt like she was the greenhorn, like she was the one who didn't know nothing. Gol-durn, she sure wished she had some book learning. Then they could talk about all kinds of exciting things. She sure wouldn't want Brant getting bored with her.

The thought that Brant might find her company boring depressed Danny. But Danny wasn't one to be defeated. She'd learn to read, she promised herself. If she could break a wild horse and rope a steer, she could learn to read. Somehow, someway, she'd manage it.

When Brant awoke the next morning, Danny had already left their simple bed on the ground. He sat up and looked groggily around him, then, spying Danny, was instantly alert. She was bathing in the shallow stream beside their camp, her wet, nude body glistening in the bright sunlight and her thick mane of reddish-brown hair tumbling down around her as she bent to wash one shapely leg.

Surprisingly, the unexpected scene didn't arouse Brant. It was one of innocence and beauty, and not seductiveness. He sat and drank in the vision, thinking he had never seen anything so lovely.

Feeling Brant's eyes on her, Danny rose to her full height and said cheerfully, "Morning!"

Brant sucked in his breath sharply as Danny revealed her nakedness to him in a full frontal view. His eyes swept over her creamy breasts with their pert, rosy tips, her incredibly small waist and curving hips, lingering at the triangle of reddish-brown curls at the juncture of her legs. If Danny was aware of his scrutiny, she showed no signs of it. She stood before him totally unabashed, and had it been any other woman but Danny standing there in all her naked glory in broad daylight, Brant would have been shocked at her lack of modesty. But again, Danny was only doing what came natural to her. To have covered herself after their intimacies would have been hypocritical, or coy, and Danny didn't know the meaning of either.

"Ain't this jest about the most beautiful morning you ever seen?" Danny asked in an exuberant voice as she looked all about her.

Brant was totally unaware of the birds singing joyfully, of the dew drops on the long needles of the pine trees glistening in the bright sunlight, of the sparkling water of the stream or the lush green of the mountains towering all around them. He didn't smell the sweet scent of the wildflowers, or notice the nip in the crisp mountain air. His total concentration was on Danny. "Yes, it is the most beautiful sight I've ever seen."

Danny finally became aware of Brant's intent gaze on her and realized that he had been referring to her, and not the scenery. His compliment and the blatant admiration she saw in his eyes filled her with pride in her femininity, and a warm glow spread through her. She had never been as glad that she was a woman as she was at that moment.

But Danny wasn't the kind to wallow in her female pride, even if it was a new emotion for her. Her practical side came to the fore, and she turned her attention back to her bath. As he watched her, Brant asked, "Isn't the water a little cold for bathing? That stream is spring fed."

Danny laughed, the spontaneous burst tinkling in the crystal clear morning air. "It shore is. Cold enough to freeze the tail off a rattler. I was a-shivering so bad when I first got in, I thought I'd shake every tooth outta my head, but I got used to it."

Brant thought the sparkling water did look inviting and was tempted to join Danny. He hesitated, torn between the rigid social rules that had governed his behavior since his birth and his desire to act as natural and uninhibited as Danny. A gentleman simply does not bathe with a woman, regardless of the intimacies they had shared in bed, a part of him sternly told him. Another part argued that those rules didn't apply to Danny and himself in this mountain paradise. Why couldn't he act the Adam to her Eve? Shame and false modesty had no part in their relationship. Feeling as if a heavy burden had been lifted from him, he tossed back the blanket covering his lower body, slipped his bar of soap and towel from his saddlebags, and rose.

From the corner of her eye, Danny watched while Brant walked to the small stream to join her. With his height, his superb male physique, his graceful, princely walk, and his thick, wavy hair shining in the sunlight, he looked absolutely magnificent. Even the light sprinkling of hair on his body shone in the sunlight, making him look as if he had been dusted with gold. Yes, he was a golden god, tall, powerfully built, incredibly male, and so beautiful it made her ache inside just to look at him.

They bathed in silence, each acutely aware of the other, until Danny said, "I'll make a swap with you. I'll wash yer back fer you, if you'll wash mine fer me."

"Agreed," Brant said, with a little one-sided smile that made Danny's heart do crazy flip-flops in her chest.

He turned his back to her, and Danny stepped up to him, admiring the powerful muscles on his back and his tight, steely buttocks as she lathered his skin, again amazed at how firm and smooth it felt. For good measure, she washed the back of his corded horseman's thighs and, when she had finished, felt a twinge of disappointment that the chore was done. Touching him was such a pleasure. With a little sigh of regret, she cupped her hands and bent to the stream, then poured the water over his broad shoulders and back, over and over, rinsing off the soapsuds and assuming that the shivers running over his powerful body were from the cold water.

The tremors had nothing to do with the temperature of the water. Danny's washing his backside had been one of the most sensuous experiences Brant had ever had, the slow circular movements of her hands over his buttocks and down the backs of his thighs arousing him.

"Now, it's my turn," Danny said.

Brant turned to see Danny standing with her back to him, the tips of her long wild mane brushing the crest of her buttocks before she parted it with her hands and pulled it over her shoulders to give him access to her back. Brant stared at the creamy skin, the indenture of her spine, the rounded curves of her buttocks. The bar of soap that he was holding slipped from his hand as he stepped forward, his eyes glued to a small curl at the nape of Danny's neck that seemed to be begging to be kissed.

Danny jumped in surprise when she felt his warm lips there, then shivered in pleasure as the palm of one hand ran over her back, across her buttocks, to caress the back of one rounded thigh. When his other hand slipped around her to cup one breast, his thumb brushing back and forth over the rosy tip and bringing it to throbbing life, she knew the bath was over for the time being. As he pulled her back against him and she felt his manhood rising and brushing against her leg, then her buttocks, her heart raced in anticipation. She squirmed closer, thrilling at Brant's gasp of pleasure and his hot breath

170

against her throat, the feel of rigid flesh pressing into her scorching her with its heat. Her passion for him rose like a skyrocket.

Holding her against him tightly with one hand possessively cupping her breast, Brant slipped his other arm around her hips, his palm trailing fire as it traveled across the softness of her belly before his fingers tangled in the tight curls between her legs. There he dallied, twirling the curls around his fingers, then stroking her groin and caressing her thighs. Danny gasped in pleasure as his fingers moved between her legs, stroking the swollen, throbbing flesh that was bathed with the moisture of her longing. When two long fingers slipped inside her, moving in and out with sensuous purpose, while his thumb circled the bud of her womanhood, Danny saw sparks behind her eyes as she suddenly climaxed, the tremor of intense pleasure that engulfed her turning her legs rubbery. She sagged against him weakly, but Brant held her tightly to him, bringing her over and over again to that shuddering brink, glorying in her spasms of joy and her breathless whimpers, his bringing her pleasure exciting him unbearably.

Danny was as limp as a rag doll when Brant swept her up in his strong arms and carried her to the bank of the stream, then lay her down on the soft, spring grass that grew there. Through dazed eyes she looked up at him where he knelt between her sprawled legs, feeling completely drained of all passion. Then, seeing his eyes dark and blazing with the heat of his desire, hers flared anew. She glanced down and saw his manhood jutting from the golden nest of curls at his groin, standing long, full, and proud, the moist tip glistening in the sunlight.

Danny's heart pounded erratically as she reached for

171

him and wrapped her hand around his hot, throbbing flesh, feeling once again amazed at the velvety texture of his feverish skin over the steely rigidness of his erection. At her touch, Brant felt as if he had been struck by a bolt of lightning. Hot waves of electricity danced up his spine and exploded in his brain. "Don't!" he whispered in a hoarse, urgent voice, pulling her hand away.

"Why not?" Danny objected with a little frustrated sob. "I like a-touching you."

"Because I'm about to explode already," Brant answered in a ragged voice. "I don't want this to end too soon. It should be savored, enjoyed to the fullest."

He leaned over her, the crisp hairs on his chest brushing against her swollen nipples and bringing a gasp of pleasure from her. Then he was kissing her, his mouth hot, hungry, and fierce with passion, sending her senses swimming and spreading fire through her. His hard male lips bruised hers as his tongue pillaged the heady nectar of her mouth, kissing her as if he was reaching for her very soul in his sweet-savage possession.

While Danny was still gasping for breath, Brant's devouring mouth slowly moved over her shoulders and breasts, nipping, then licking the tiny stings away. He traced her ribs with his tongue and dropped fiery kisses over the softness of her belly, before he stopped to pay homage to her tiny navel, playing havoc on her already reeling senses.

When Danny felt Brant's hands slipping beneath her buttocks and lifting her, she gave a sob of relief and lifted her hips in anticipation of his thrust. She was glad it was almost over. She didn't think she could stand anymore of this delicious torment. Then, when she realized that it was his tongue, and not his manhood touching her there,

172

she stiffened. Not even in her wildest imagination had she expected Brant to do such a shocking thing to her. It was too personal, too intimate.

But before Danny could voice her doubts and stop him, Brant was working his erotic magic, his warm tongue swirling around and flicking out like a flame of fire at the core of her womanhood, his lips nipping and tongue wildly licking at her softness as if he meant to devour her. Danny felt a warm languor invading her and spreading through her like wildfire before the exquisite spasms of delight once again rocked her small body, her heart beating so fast and hard she feared it would burst from her chest. She twisted her hips, wanting more, yet fearing if she felt anymore sensation she would die from sheer pleasure. It was heaven; it was hell. It was wonderful!

Brant's loving her with his mouth was exciting him wildly too. When the urge to kiss her there had suddenly struck him, he had been momentarily shocked that he would even consider something that surely must be wicked. But her intoxicating womanly scent had been too much for him. He was seized with the overpowering desire to know what she tasted like there, forbidden or not. After drinking of her sweet nectar, he was lost in the throes of passion, her uninhibited response to his bold lovemaking spurring him on and exciting him like nothing he had ever known. He ached for her, exalted in his power to bring her pleasure, wanting everything possible for her and more.

Then, when he felt as if his skin could no longer contain him, as if he would burst if he didn't bury himself in her, his mouth left her softness, and he plunged into her, his breath catching in his throat at the feel of

173

her tight, searing heat surrounding him. Danny felt Brant's powerful, deep entry like a bolt of fire. She cried out in joy, her legs folding around his slim hips as she clasped him tightly to her, reveling in the sensation of his feverish naked flesh pressed against hers and his immense maleness filling her. Then, as he began his movements in a sweet-savage loving of giving and taking, all she could think of was Brant and the wonderful, exquisite things he was making her feel. His power flowed over her, through her, sinking into every pore and filling every inch of her with an incredible sense of strength. She felt invincible, immortal in this golden god's arms, every stroke of his rigid manhood filling her with the warmth of life and an overpowering happiness that brought tears to her eyes.

As his deep thrusts quickened, then became frenzied, Danny clung to him for dear life, feeling as if every nerve ending in her body was on fire, while an unbearable pressure rose and swelled inside her like a monstrous tidal wave, higher and higher and higher. Suddenly the world spun away as an uncontrollable force seized them both, and they climaxed in a blinding flash of exploding stars that hurled them out of their bodies and sent their souls careening through space.

Slowly, Brant floated down from those lofty heights of ecstasy, feeling strangely disembodied and yet reborn. His first awareness was the sound of a bee droning in search of the nectar of the wildflowers nearby, then that of the warm sun on his back. He felt blissfully relaxed and utterly contented. He could stay here forever with Danny in this enchanted canyon, making love to her, or just enjoying her company. And then cold, hard reason returned. His dream was impossible. He was a soldier, with a job to do.

His thoughts focused on the future. What part would Danny play in his life, if any? No one had ever made him feel as happy as she did. Was he falling in love with her, or was the strange emotion he felt for her just infatuation because she was so different from anyone he had ever known. Would her appeal eventually wear off? Would he tire of her in time? They were from such totally different backgrounds.

Brant pondered over these perplexing thoughts, but his mind seemed to be chasing in circles. It was impossible to think clearly around Danny. Maybe it was a good thing that they'd be arriving at their destination today. He needed distance from her intoxicating sensuality and time to sort out his feelings. He wasn't a man to act rashly.

Brant lifted himself to his elbows and said, "We'd better finish our baths and eat. I'd like to reach the fort by this afternoon."

Danny had been floating on a warm, rosy cloud in the aftermath of their lovemaking. Brant's words hit her like a dash of ice water. "We'll reach the fort today?" she asked in a shocked voice.

"Yes, Fort Davis sits at the end of this canyon." Brant sat up and pointed to where the canyon narrowed just beyond their camp, saying, "That's Wild Rose Pass. It's just a little over eighteen miles from there to Fort Davis."

Brant rose and walked to the stream. Danny didn't notice his reluctance to leave her. She was too wrapped up in the disappointment that surrounded her like a heavy shroud. Her special time with Brant was suddenly

175

over. That it had ended with such a beautiful, spontaneous lovemaking made her feel all the more let down. She blinked back tears and bit back a sob, feeling absolutely miserable. Then, remembering that she'd still get to see him, she forced her depression down, telling herself firmly that all that mattered was being in the same place with him. Bravely, she rose and followed him to the stream, but deep down inside her, she feared things would never be the same between them.

Chapter 11

Danny and Brant bathed and dressed in silence, each occupied with their own thoughts. It wasn't until Brant slipped on his coat that Danny became aware that he had donned his cavalry uniform. She stared at him in absolute awe, thinking that the dark blue brought out the intense color of his eyes and the gold of his hair, making him look even more striking and handsome.

Seeing Danny gawking at him, Brant laughed and asked, "What's the matter? I told you that I was an officer. Didn't you believe me?"

"I believed you. It's jest . . . it's jest that you look so . . . so gol-durn purty," Danny stammered.

Brant might have laughed at Danny calling him pretty, except, at that moment, her heart was in her eyes, and he could clearly read her feelings for him. She loves me, he thought, feeling a joyous thrill run through him. Then, remembering that he was unsure of his feelings for her, he felt suddenly confused and torn. A part of him wanted to shout out that he loved her, while another, more reserved part, cautioned him against it. He struggled with

177

the conflicting emotions, then, hoping to gloss over an awkward situation, said, "You look very pretty yourself. Isn't that a new shirt?"

Danny glanced down at the blue-checked shirt, then answered, "Yep. I saved it for when we got to Fort Davis. I wanted to look nice, even if I wasn't a-wearing one of those fool sissy dresses."

Brant wondered what the people at the fort would think of Danny in her male attire. Personally, he thought she looked lovely, but he realized that he was prejudiced in her behalf. Would they laugh at her, or scorn her? The thought infuriated Brant, his strong protectiveness for her once again coming to the surface.

Seeing the thunderous look coming over his face, Danny asked, "What's the matter? What are you a-looking so mad about?"

Brant wasn't about to tell Danny what he had been thinking, for fear it would lower her self-confidence, and she was going to need every bit of that if she was going to get a position with one of the officers' families. Some of the wives were such pompous snobs, thinking themselves much above everyone else, and then on the other hand, others were warm, friendly women. He could only hope that Danny would find herself in the service of one of the latter. Otherwise, she was going to be hurt, and Brant didn't think he could stand by and watch that happen. "I'm not mad," Brant lied smoothly. "I was just thinking that maybe I ought to coach you a little on how to act when you're applying for a position with an army family. For example, you never call an officer mister, but either sir, or preferably, by his rank."

Danny didn't object to Brant giving her a few helpful hints. After all, she had never worked for someone before, and she was a little nervous about it. "And their wives? What do you call them?"

"Ma'am, just like any other married woman. They don't hold the rank. Their husbands do, although many of them act like they do."

"What do you mean by that?"

"I mean that some of the women lord their husband's rank over the other wives, trying to order the junior officers' wives around just like their husbands do the men under them. However, that shouldn't affect you. You'll be hired out to one family. Pleasing them will be your only concern."

"Anything else I should know?"

Brant wondered if he should give Danny a crash course in army etiquette, then decided against it. At this point it would only confuse her. She'd do better behaving naturally and letting her warmth and unique personality carry her. As Rose had said, you couldn't help but like her, despite her rough exterior. Hopefully, her employers would come to appreciate her too. "No, I think that's the main thing. Just be friendly and polite."

Danny didn't have any trouble being friendly. As a general rule, she liked other people and made no effort to hide her feelings. Her warmth bubbled as freely from her as a spring from the ground. And her brother had taught her the rudiments of politeness. "I reckon I can manage that."

While they were eating their breakfast, Danny allowed herself a more leisurely look at Brant's cavalry uniform. The dark blue, single-breasted coat fit his impressive shoulders to a tee and hung halfway to his thighs. His sky-blue trousers were stuffed into his high black boots, with a yellow stripe, one and a half inches

179

wide, running down the length of the outer seam. The same color of yellow piping decorated the front of his coat and the cuffs of his sleeves, while a gold embroidered patch sat on each wide shoulder, the two silver bars at the end of each strap gleaming in the sunlight. Five gold eagle buttons with a *C* on the bird's chest held the coat closed, and the glittering metal, combined with the gold oval buckle on his belt, gave the uniform a final touch of elegance. Danny thought he looked incredibly handsome, and the uniform looked as if it had been designed just for him, the blue and gold complimenting the searing color of his eyes and golden glints of his thick, wavy hair. She could sit and gaze at him forever. Then, becoming aware that Brant was aware of her staring so avidly, she flushed and said, "I was jest a-wondering why you ain't a-wearing yer sword."

"We don't wear sabers with our field uniforms anymore, and thank God for that. The damn things were absolutely useless against the Comanches with their long lances, and didn't do anything but clatter and get in the way."

Brant set his plate aside and picked up a black velvet patch with the cavalry insignia embroidered in gold on it from the ground where he had laid it. "What are you gonna do with that?" Danny asked.

"Sew it back on my hat. I can't ride into Fort Davis without it. Otherwise, I'd be out of uniform."

"I can sew it on for you," Danny offered.

"Thanks, but I'm pretty handy with a needle and thread. Every soldier has to learn a little basic sewing with all the patches and buttons on our uniforms. Why don't you wash the dishes while I'm doing this?"

By the time Danny returned from washing the dishes

in the stream, Brant had finished sewing the patch on his hat and had tucked a pair of fawn-colored buckskin gauntlets with huge flared cuffs into his belt. As he started saddling his horse, Danny stared in surprise at the dark blue blanket fringed with gold that he threw on the back of his mount, then commented, "I ain't seen that before."

"I had it in my saddlebags, along with my uniform. It's my cavalry saddle blanket. All officers' mounts wear them. They're as much a part of my uniform as my hat or coat."

Danny shook her head in amazement, thinking that the cavalry certainly went all-out in dressing their officers. "Are you a-carrying all yer uniforms with you?"

Brant laughed, answering, "No, I could hardly get them all into a pair of saddlebags. I had the rest of my field uniforms and my dress uniform shipped ahead by stage." He frowned, then said, "I hope to hell that trunk got through. At the outrageous prices those stage companies charge for freight, it better had."

It suddenly occurred to Danny that Brant might be a little short on cash himself. She had no idea how much a captain made, and he had loaned her money. A tingle of guilt ran through her. "You never did tell me how much I owe you."

Brant realized that when he had complained about the freight costs, Danny had assumed he was tight on cash himself. Nothing could be further from the truth. With the money he had inherited from his maternal grandfather, he was quite well situated. But if he had to live on his army pay, like the other officers and their families, he would be struggling to make ends meet. Which was why the exorbitant rate the stage companies charged the army personnel irritated him so badly. In his opinion, the stage companies should ship their personal belongings for free, as a complimentary service. After all, one of the cavalry's biggest jobs was to protect those stages. But as it was, the officers' families had to auction off practically everything they owned every time they were transferred, which meant that they never had much in personal possessions or household goods.

Becoming aware that Danny was awaiting an answer, Brant said, "Forget what you owe me, Danny."

"Heck no, I ain't gonna fergit it. I pay my debts."

Brant realized he should have known better. Despite how well they had come to know one another, Danny had her pride. "All right, if you insist, you owe me five dollars," Brant said, splitting Danny's debt to him in half.

"Does that include the grub?"

"Yes."

It didn't exactly sound on the up-and-up to Danny. Hellfire, she sure wished she had paid closer attention that day. She could do a little figuring. Seems to her that box of ammunition would cost almost that much alone. She gave Brant a suspicious look and asked, "You're shore about that?"

"I'm positive."

Because Brant had such an innocent look on his face, Danny dismissed the issue and quickly saddled her horse. Finishing that chore, she tossed her saddlebags over the animal's back and reached down for the canvas bag that housed Charlie. Realizing that it was empty, she looked about her in exasperation, then began searching for the tardy snake.

Brant stopped to put out the fire before stuffing his

personal belongings into his saddlebags. He rose from smothering it with dirt to see Danny frantically running about the camp, lifting bushes, and peering beneath them. "What are you looking for?"

"I can't find Charlie anywhere. I looked under every bush and rock. I found a lizard, a nest of scorpions, even a dad-blasted tarantula, but no Charlie."

My God, Brant thought, they had been sleeping in the vicinity of all those creepy things? And he had even forgotten to shake out his boots this morning. But he heard the panic in Danny's voice. "Calm down," he said in a soothing voice. "He's bound to be around here someplace."

"But where? I done told you I looked everywhere. What if he's lost?"

"Has he ever gotten lost before?"

"No, but he ain't never been in the mountains either. Maybe he's like me, so turned around, he don't know which way is which no more."

Danny's words came as a surprise to Brant. He hadn't realized that she felt lost and confused. He took a moment to savor the knowledge that, for once, he had the advantage over her, then said, "I'll help you look for him."

As Danny ran off to look by the stream, Brant searched the camp, thinking Danny must have missed looking under some bush or rock. Charlie was nowhere to be found. Then, seeing his saddlebags lying open on the ground, he picked them up and peered into one pouch. There, where his uniform had been packed, lay Charlie, curled into a tight, cozy little coil. Then the snake had the audacity to look up and smile at him.

"Danny! Come here!" Brant called.

183

"Did you find him?" Danny asked anxiously, running back to him.

"Yes," Brant answered, holding out his saddlebags. "Look in there."

"Charlie! What in tarnation are you a-doing in there?"

While the look of immense relief that came over Danny's face brought a warm feeling to Brant, he didn't appreciate Danny's pet taking up residence in his bag. What if he had put his belongings back in without noticing the snake. The thought of reaching in and touching that cold, scaly creature sent a shiver of revulsion through Brant. "Would you mind removing him?" he asked in a terse voice.

Without the slightest hesitation, Danny reached in and lifted the snake from the leather pouch. She held Charlie up by his neck and scolded, "Shame on you, Charlie, a-scaring me like that. Why, I oughta plow your field."

Brant had bent to put his belongings in the saddlebags. He looked up and asked, "Do what?"

"Give him a whipping," Danny explained.

Brant rose, asking, "You mean a spanking?"

"Yep."

Brant briefly wondered how one went about spanking a snake when the creatures didn't have a rump. Shaking his head in disgust at his ridiculous speculation, he turned and walked to his horse.

After he had left, Danny held Charlie before her and whispered, "I ain't really mad at you. I reckon that was yer way of a-saying how much you like him, a-crawling into his bag that way. Iffen I could, I'd do the same thing, 'cept I'd crawl right inside him. Then I could stay with him forever."

Danny slipped Charlie back into his canvas bag and placed its strap over her shoulder. She turned to see Brant sitting on his horse. Her breath caught at the splendid sight he presented, then noticing the dark scowl on his face, she hurried to mount.

As they rode away, Danny noticed that the scowl was still on Brant's face. She had assumed that he was irritated that their departure had been delayed. "You ain't mad at Charlie, are you? He didn't mean no harm, a-sneaking into yer bag."

Brant had been thinking about Charlie, but not about his irritation at finding the snake in his saddlebags. He had been wondering what Danny's future employers' reaction to her unusual pet might be. He would suggest that Danny turn Charlie loose, except he knew she wouldn't hear of it. She actually loved that stupid snake. But Charlie could create serious problems for her. "As a matter of fact, I was thinking about Charlie," Brant admitted. "In view of most people's fear of snakes, particularly women's, I think it's only fair that you warn the people who hire you about him. They may not want a snake, even a harmless one, in their homes."

Danny frowned. She supposed she could leave Charlie outside, but she hated to. Other than when she let him out to eat, Charlie was used to staying indoors, except when she took him for a ride, which he dearly loved. Working for other people was sure getting complicated.

As they entered the narrow pass at the end of the canyon, Danny looked about her in amazement. The high vertical walls around her went straight up in the air and were colored pink and white from the profusion of wild roses that the pass was named after. She had never seen so many roses in her entire life, and their sweet scent filled her nostrils.

While Danny was admiring the beauty of the pass, Brant was eyeing its upper reaches with suspicion. His soldier's instincts told him that it was a dangerous place, an excellent place for an ambush. If there were any Apaches up there, they would be sitting ducks, and he wouldn't have a ghost of a chance in protecting Danny. "Come on," he said in a voice made harsh by his fear for her, "let's get the hell out of this place."

As Brant tore off, Danny followed reluctantly. She would have liked to have enjoyed the breathtaking view a little longer. He sure was acting peculiar this morning.

An hour later, they left the pass and rode upon a wide, gently undulating tableland. Feeling more comfortable out in the open, Brant slowed his lathered horse to a walk. Reining in beside him, Danny pushed a strand of hair that had come loose from her face and asked, "What were you in such a dad-blasted hurry fer? You lit outta there like a bat outta hell."

"It looked like an excellent place for Mr. Lo to ambush us."

"Who in tarnation is that fella? One of your enemies?"

"I'm sorry. I was using army slang again. Mr. Lo is what the cavalry call Indians, whether singular or plural. But I think we're safe here. Fort Davis is just another four miles from here."

Danny felt the dread of their parting coming down on her like a heavy blanket. She paid no attention to where they were riding until Brant pointed to a box canyon, saying, "That's where the original Fort Davis used to sit, at the back of that canyon. If you look closely, you can still see some of the rubble from the stone buildings. I

186

don't know why they picked that place as the site for a fort. It was a poor location. The Indians fired down on them from the tops of the canyon so badly that they never did finish building the fort."

They crossed the same sparkling stream that they had camped beside in Limpia Canyon. Beside it lay a small Mexican village with crude adobe huts that Brant informed Danny the troopers called Chihuahua. Danny frowned at this information, then said, "I thought Chihuahua was the name of a city in Mexico."

"It is, but the troopers automatically call all these little Mexican villages that spring up beside the forts Chihuahua." As they passed another village that lay adjacent to the Mexican one, Brant said, "And this must be Fort Davis' Scabtown."

Danny looked about her. The place looked even dingier than the Mexican village, the buildings nothing but hovels made of an assortment of materials. The strong smell of sour liquor and stale sweat assaulted her nostrils, and Danny noted that the few inhabitants she saw had a mean, shifty-eyed look about them.

They followed the road that ran beside the stream, then passed through a magnificent grove of cottonwood trees. Danny looked about her in appreciation, thinking that it was a lovely spot, then said, "I wonder how all these cottonwoods got here. I ain't seen any of 'em fer days."

"If this is the same grove of trees I've heard about, I understand that the original corral was situated here, and the cottonwood posts they used to build it took root."

"Well, I'll be," Danny said in amazement. "Ain't that something? 'Course those cottonwoods really take to water. Don't hardly ever see 'em, 'cept 'round a creek.

187

They're jest about the thirstiest trees there are. I reckon that's why they rooted."

Just as they left the grove of trees, a cavalry patrol approached them, the swallow-tailed banner they carried snapping in the breeze. Brant and Danny led their horses off the road to let the soldiers pass. As they did so, the lieutenant at the head of the column saluted smartly, and Brant returned the official recognition of his rank. Danny's full attention was the guidon, noting that the top half was red with a white letter in it, and the bottom half was white with a red number on it. "What's those markings on that flag say?" she asked Brant.

"Every troop has its own guidon, and the top marking is a letter that designates the troop and the bottom marking is the number of the regiment they belong to. Every regiment has twelve troops that are lettered from A to M, with the letter J omitted. Four troops make a squadron, and the third is called the milk squadron, because that's what its troops spell."

Danny felt a little irritated at being given so much information and, yet, not having her question answered. "I didn't ask all that!" she snapped. "All I want to know is what letter and number that is."

"That's a B and a seven, for B Troop, 7th Cavalry," Brant answered, wondering why she was so insistent on knowing which letter and numeral the standard carried.

Danny stared at the number and letter until she had memorized them, then directed her attention to the troopers riding past her, their saddles creaking and their harnesses jingling. Her eyes widened as she said, "Why, they're all a-riding black horses."

"Yes, every troop has its own color of horseflesh. All whites, all blacks, all chestnuts, all sorrels, all bays, and so forth. Except for grays. Only buglers ride them. What's left over goes to M troop, the calico troop as we call it. Thank God, I've never had to command that troop."

"How come you don't want the calico troop?"

"Because the whole purpose of making each troop ride one color of horse is that it makes it easier for the commanding officer to keep up with his men in the confusion of battle. When the troops all mingle together, even at the speed they're riding, he can easily pick out one of his men. The same holds for the trooper, if he's gotten separated from his group. But if you've got the calico troop, with every color of horseflesh imaginable, you don't know where in the hell your men are."

"How many men do you have in yer troop?"

"It varies from regiment to regiment. In the Fourth, a troop commander has a first and second lieutenant, one first sergeant, five regular sergeants, four corporals, two trumpeters, two farriers, one saddler, one wagoner, and eighty-four privates."

Danny struggled to keep count as Brant listed the men in one troop, but couldn't. Her arithmetic simply didn't go that far. "Well, how many is that in all?" she asked in a sharp voice, irritated at her own stupidity.

"Roughly a hundred men."

"A hundred men?" she asked in astonishment. "Well, no wonder you can't keep up with 'em, a hundred men a-going lickety-split in every which direction."

"It was even worse during the war, when I was a squadron commander. Then I had four times that many."

As Brant kneed his mount and the horse moved back to the road, Danny pulled her horse up beside him, asking,

"How come you ain't a squadron commander now?"

"I left the army for a few years after the war. When I re-enlisted, the highest rank they could offer me was a captain. You see, after the war, the army found themselves with too many officers. Most of them were downgraded at least one rank. Of course, they offered to give me my former rank back as a brevet major, but since that was only an honorary title, I turned them down. If I'm going to get the captain's pay and am assigned a captain's duties, then I might as well be called a captain. Besides all those brevet titles only confuse the troopers."

Danny could understand that. She was confused herself. Somehow or another, Brant started out as a major, then landed up as a captain. Well, it didn't make no never mind to her. As long as he was satisfied with what he had.

They passed an army wagon that was hauling water barrels from the stream to the fort, the mules pulling it looking disgruntled and one snapped at Red as they rode by. Danny shot the offender a murderous look, then catching her first sight of the fort, reined in and gazed at it in wonder.

Fort Davis sat in a wide, open recess between the towering mountains and was walled in on three sides with perpendicular rock formations of great height that looked like huge towers of stone, and Danny had never seen so many buildings in her life. To her left was the commissary, and sitting next to it were four long adobe barracks, each surrounded by a wide covered porch. When she craned her neck, she could see the quartermaster's storehouse at the opposite end of the line of barracks and just barely get a glimpse of the stables and small cabins that sat to the back of the enlisted men's quarters. To her right was the guardhouse, the executive offices and the hospital, and sitting across from the line of barracks and separated by the wide parade ground were the officer's quarters, a neat line of twelve little houses made of either whitewashed adobe or native limestone, and behind them, Danny could see that even more were in the process of being built, as was a large building at the very back of the fort.

"I didn't know it was so big," Danny said in an astonished voice. "Why, it's a regular city!"

Brant chuckled. The fort could hardly be compared to a city, but by Texas standards, it could qualify as a good-sized town.

They stopped at the guardhouse, and Brant gave their names and purpose for being at the fort to the sentry standing there. After they had ridden into the fort proper, Brant reined in and sat patiently on his horse while Danny took in the sights and sounds of Fort Davis. Just as she had never seen so many buildings, she had never seen so many people and so much activity. Two troops of cavalrymen drilled in the middle of the huge parade ground, turning their mounts this way and that and raising a huge cloud of dust. Another troop rode past them on their way out of the fort, their horses' hooves pounding on the ground and harnesses jingling. Along the main street, wagons loaded with salted beef, grain, and sacks of flour lumbered, their wheels creaking and the teamsters' whips snapping in the air. Added to these sounds were that of the ring of the blacksmith's hammer, the neigh of a horse, the bark of a dog, the cry of a baby, and the lusty swearing of a first sergeant as he called orders to his drilling troopers.

Besides those mounted and riding on the wagons, there

were people on foot everywhere. Blue-coated officers rushed from building to building; women strolled leisurely at the edge of the parade ground with parasols flung over their shoulders, their children darting here and there; prisoners, guarded by a trooper with a rifle, loaded garbage on a wagon; and mingled among all the military personnel were civilians employed by the meat, grain, and building contractors hurrying about, to say nothing of the hunters come down from the mountains, the cowhands and travelers passing through, and a few horse thieves, whiskey peddlers, and scalawags that had come to the fort for nefarious reasons. Danny took it all in, and then her eyes widened in disbelief.

She leaned from her saddle and whispered to Brant, "What's that Injun a-doing here?"

"He's one of our Seminole scouts."

"Seminole? I ain't never heard of no Seminoles."

"They're an eastern tribe. Many of them were slaves of the Kickapoo Indians, who moved to Mexico at the outbreak of the war to keep their slaves from being taken away from them. After the war, many of the Seminoles left their old masters, crossed the border, and signed up as army scouts."

"How can you trust 'em?" Danny asked, shooting the scout a suspicious glance. "They're Injuns too."

"We've never had any instances of them betraying us."

Danny gave the Indian a closer look, then said, "Well, maybe they are different from the Injuns out here. I ain't never seen an Injun with kinky hair."

"He's a half-breed. When the Seminoles were still living in Florida, many of the runaway slaves from the South found refuge with them and joined their tribe.

Then their children were captured by the Kickapoos and made slaves again. It seemed the poor bastards couldn't win. Maybe that's why they make such faithful scouts. They figure the Union Army has given them their first taste of real freedom."

Danny had never seen anyone with Negro blood before, but she remembered what her brother Joe had said about them. "So that's why they call them burrheads," she said in amazement.

Brant frowned, then said, "Let me warn you, Danny. In the cavalry, they're called Negroes, or if you want to use the troopers' expression, Brunettes. To call one a burrhead is just as insulting as a nigger."

"I didn't mean no harm," Danny said defensively. "I jest didn't know no better. That's the only thing I've ever heard 'em called. Hellfire, I ain't got nothing against 'em. Why, I ain't never even seen one, 'til today."

"I suspected as much, but we in the cavalry are rather touchy about it. We have two Negro regiments that are doing an outstanding job. Besides, part of the 24th Infantry is stationed here, and they're a Negro regiment. Just remember, if the occasion happens to arise again."

Brant glanced at the building across the parade ground that held the executive offices, then said, "Come on. I'm supposed to be reporting in, you know."

They rode up to the office building, dismounted, and tied their horses to a hitching post. As they walked up the stone steps and passed two troopers on the wide porch, the men gave Danny's male attire a startled look before they remembered, a little late, to salute Brant. Danny didn't notice the men's expressions, but Brant was acutely aware of them. He gave the two men a hard, warning look that quickly sent them on their way.

As they stepped into the building that housed the executive offices, Brant glanced around them, then said, "Danny, why don't you have a seat on that bench over there by the wall. I have to report to the executive officer and then see the commanding officer. After I've finished reporting in, I'll talk to Colonel Shafter about helping us find an employer for you. I'm sure he knows who among his officers are in need of a cook."

This time Danny was aware of the lieutenant sitting behind a big desk and the two clerks standing before their file cabinets staring at her. It never occurred to her that they were gaping at her clothing. "Maybe they don't allow no women in here. I can wait outside."

Brant was seething with anger. It was just as he had feared. Everyone was looking at Danny as if she were a freak, and he was getting defensive. He longed to smash his fists in their faces but knew he couldn't really blame them. He had been just as shocked when he had first seen her. He struggled to subdue his anger and said, "No, it's not against the rules for a woman to come in here, but it doesn't happen very often. Just ignore them, and I'll be back as soon as I can."

Danny accepted Brant's explanation. If women weren't frequent visitors, then she supposed they were surprised to see her. She turned and walked to the bench Brant had directed her to and sat down.

Brant turned and stepped up to the adjutant's desk, noting that the lieutenant had finally remembered his good manners and directed his gaze away from Danny. He also remembered his rank and shot to his feet, giving Brant a smart salute.

Brant returned the salute and said, "Captain Brant Holden, 4th Calvary, reporting for duty."

The adjutant bent and shuffled through the big pile of papers on his desk, saying, "Yes, sir. I believe your transfer papers are here someplace. I saw them just this morning."

Brant waited patiently, feeling a little sorry for the harassed lieutenant. He had put in his time as an adjutant when he was a lieutenant. It was perhaps the worst job in the army. The adjutant not only did all the monumental outgoing paper work for the company, but issued all orders, assigned all quarters, kept guard and fatigue rosters, approved all hunting and fishing trips for overnight absences, and had to listen to all the complaints; and army people were perhaps the biggest complainers in the world. They griped about the quality or quantity of the products they found, or didn't find, in the commissary, the quartermaster, their housing; the condition of their officers' club, their neighbors' children and dogs— anything and everything. It was a job that not only took organization, but a great deal of finesse and tact, and Brant had been vastly relieved to be rid of it.

"Here it is, sir," the lieutenant said, pulling a file from the bottom of a stack of papers. "It got placed in the stack with the 24th Infantry by mistake. You are aware that Colonel Shafter is at the present time commanding both it and a part of the 4th?"

Brant nodded. The 4th went back and forth between Fort Concho and Fort Davis and was often split between the two posts.

The lieutenant flipped through the file, then said, "Yes, everything seems to be in order. I'll see if the Colonel will receive you now."

The adjutant walked to a door behind his desk, rapped on it, then opened it. Brant waited while he walked into the colonel's office and closed the door behind him. A moment later, the lieutenant returned, saying, "You may go in, sir."

Brant glanced over at Danny, shot her a reassuring smile, and walked into the office, saying over his shoulder, "Thank you."

As the door closed behind Brant, Danny swallowed nervously. It wasn't the two clerks still gawking at her, however, that made her feel so edgy. That stopped when the lieutenant loudly cleared his voice. It was the realization that from here on, she was really and truly on her own. She was in a strange place, among strange people. That alone was enough to make her apprehensive, but what if Brant had been wrong, and there wasn't a job for her here? Then what would she do? But even worse, what if they made her leave, and she never saw Brant again? She'd die if that happened.

She sat and stared at the closed door anxiously, feeling dangerously close to doing something she couldn't recall ever doing. She felt like breaking down and bawling like a baby.

Chapter 12

When Brant stepped into the office, he found himself facing Lt. Colonel William Shafter, a tough, battle-seasoned officer who had distinguished himself during the war and was fondly called "Pecos Bill" by his senior officers and peers. The junior officers referred to him as the "Old Man," as they did the commander at every fort in the west, but never to his face, of course.

After the military greetings had been completed, Colonel Shafter said, "I'm pleased to have you, Captain. I trust you had a pleasant trip from Fort Concho."

Brant remembered just how pleasant the trip had been, smiled, and answered, "Yes, sir."

The colonel wondered at the smile. It hadn't been the usual perfunctory smile that he usually saw when one was observing the social amenities. "No trouble when you rode through Wild Rose Pass?"

Brant frowned, remembering the uneasy feeling he had riding through the pass. He could have almost sworn that there was someone's eyes on him. "No, sir."

"That's where the captain you're replacing was killed,

you know," the colonel informed him. "His patrol was ambushed there by Mescaleros. That pass is the most dangerous stretch of ground between San Antonio and the Pacific Ocean."

"I sensed as much, sir, but did you say Mescaleros? I thought Lipans were the only Apaches in Texas."

"No, the Davis Mountains are the heart of Mescalero country. As a matter of fact, the original fort was built on one of their main *rancherias*. Those damned Apaches are firmly entrenched in these mountains, and the Chisos Mountains, to the south of us. I'm beginning to wonder if we'll ever clear this area of them, short of blasting these damn mountains to kingdom come."

"Mescalero," Brant said thoughtfully. "That's Spanish for mescal makers, isn't it?"

"Yes, they're called that because of their custom of roasting and fermenting the hearts of sotal, a type of cactus. You'll find their mescal pits all over these mountains. Huge, circular-shaped piles of rock, fifteen to twenty feet in diameter."

Brant frowned, then asked, "Did you say fermenting, sir? Do you mean it's intoxicating?"

"Very much so, but only the warriors drink the juice squeezed from the fermented sotal, and not solely for the purpose of becoming intoxicated. As I understand it, it has something to do with their religion. Under its influence, they have dreams and visions which they use to guide their future decisions in life. I wouldn't want you to get the mistaken impression that they're a bunch of weak-minded drunkards. That's the farthest thing from the truth. They're tough, vital, and extremely dangerous."

"I'm sorry if I seem to be asking some pretty stupid

questions," Brant apologized. "I'm afraid I don't know very much about Apaches."

"None of us do, Captain, certainly not as much as we'd like to know. I'm afraid that you're going to find fighting Apaches much more difficult than fighting Comanches. They aren't flamboyant, like the Comanches. They care nothing for show and have none of the noisy exhibitionism of the plains Indians. You won't see the Apaches making grand, sweeping charges with massed groups of warriors. You probably won't see them at all. An Apache hides behind rocks, blends into the desert, ambushes you where you least expect it, strikes with a startling swiftness. For that reason, some people mistakenly call them cowards. Don't you believe it, Captain. He's just more clever and cunning, an expert at guerrilla warfare, his tactics masterpieces of skill, particularly the Mescalero. He's a fierce hit-and-run fighter that knows every nook and cranny of these mountains, and he travels extraordinary distances under incredibly harsh conditions. He picks the time and the place for the battle, not you, seemingly materializing out of the ground, then disappearing like a wraith. It's frustrating, Captain. Terribly frustrating."

"I imagine it is, sir," Brant replied with a scowl on his face.

"I didn't mean to discourage you, Captain. I just feel you ought to know what you're up against. You'll be taking over Troop D. It's a good troop, mostly Irish."

Which goes without saying, Brant thought. Except for the Negro regiments, the majority of the troopers in the cavalry were Irish, and what wasn't, was German. Both were aggressive fighting men, the Irish more physically rugged with a natural affinity for horses and usually more resourceful in the field, while the Germans were more precision-minded and better disciplined, men who knew "The Book"—*Cooke's Cavalry Tactics*—and ate, drank, slept, fought, and breathed by their troopers' bible.

"Naturally, you can pick your own quarters on Officers' Row," Colonel Shafter said. "Ranking out of quarters applies here just as well as any other post."

Brant frowned. He had never really approved of the cavalry's custom of allowing an officer to inspect the quarters of all officers junior to him, then select the one he wanted and give twenty-four hour notice to vacate. Ranking out of quarters created havoc on a post. If one officer dispossessed another, it generally went down the line. Brant saw no reason to disturb two households, that of a first and second lieutenant below him. "That's not necessary sir. I'll take any house that's empty."

"I'm afraid there is only one vacancy at the present, a two-room house. We're still in the process of building, you know. As a captain, you're entitled to three rooms."

"I know, sir, but I'm a bachelor. I really don't need that much space."

The colonel wondered how much longer Brant planned to remain a bachelor—surely when he married, his wife would want larger quarters—but decided to face that problem when it presented itself. For the time being, he was relieved that the fort wouldn't be disrupted by "bricks falling," as ranking out of quarters was called on Officers' Row. Colonel Shafter smiled broadly and said, "Well, now that our official business is settled, I have—"

Thinking that the Colonel was about to tell him he had work to do and dismiss him, Brant quickly interjected,

"Excuse me, sir, for interrupting you, but I have something of importance to discuss with you. I brought a young woman to the post with me." Seeing the shocked expression on the colonel's face and suspecting that the man thought he meant a mistress, Brant quickly continued, saying, "No, sir, it's nothing like that. She was the victim of an Apache attack."

Brant told his commanding officer how he had found Danny, ending with, "So you see, sir, she was left without a home and family. The only other living relative is a brother who took off for California years ago, and she has no idea where he might be, or if he's even alive."

"Wasn't there any place you could take her?" the colonel asked. "A nearby town? Neighbors?"

Brant wondered if he should tell the colonel about the nearby "town" and decided against it. Then he would have to explain Rose, and he didn't want his commanding officer thinking badly of Danny for her selection of friends. While Brant had come to like Rose, himself, he didn't know how the colonel would feel about it. "No, sir. It was a very isolated place. According to Danny, the nearest neighbor was fifty miles away and—"

"Excuse me, but who is Danny?" the colonel asked. "I thought you said the victim was a young woman."

"She is. You see, her father wanted another son and named her Danny. She was raised out there on that isolated ranch by an older brother, and as I said, the nearest ranch was fifty miles away, and she didn't even know those people. It was either bring her with me, or take her back to San Antonio, and if I had done that, I wouldn't have been able to report here on time."

"You could have left her at Fort Stockton," the colonel pointed out, wondering where he was going to

201

house the young woman. He could hardly ask for one of his officers to take her into his household for free, and there wasn't room in his, not with a young woman visitor already residing there.

"Yes, sir, I could have," Brant admitted, "but she decided she wanted to get a job as a cook here at Fort Davis. She has to work, now that she's alone, and I thought I could be more help to her here in securing employment than at Fort Stockton."

The colonel could understand Brant feeling responsible for the young woman. He would have expected that from any officer and gentleman. And knowing that the woman was willing to work for a living put an entirely different light on everything. "Well, in view of everything you've told me, it's a good thing you happened along, Captain. Why the poor young lady would have probably starved to death, or been killed by wild animals, stranded out there like she was. She must have been terrified."

Brant wondered if he should tell the colonel that Danny was a very self-sufficient young woman and wasn't afraid of anything, that he'd had had a devil of a time convincing her to leave her ranch. Again, he decided against it. "No, sir. She wasn't terrified. She's a very brave young woman."

"Well, I'm glad to hear that. An army post is no place for a fearful woman, particularly one in Indian territory. And if she wants employment, she's certainly come to the right place. In fact, in view of the demand for servants here, I'd better assign her to one of the families. Otherwise, they'll be fighting over her."

"I'm relieved to hear you say that, sir. You see, Danny is rather unusual. As I said, she was raised out in the wilds by an older brother. She'll be a hard worker, but she

202

has some rough edges on her, but only because she's never been taught any different," Brant added quickly, coming to Danny's defense.

The colonel wasn't stupid. Obviously the young woman was of frontier stock, hardy but uneducated and unversed in the social arts. He knew what Brant was thinking. That some of the more snobbish ladies in the fort would look down on her and make things hard on her. She needed to be placed with one of the more kindly women. "I understand, Captain. And I think I know just the woman to offer her services to. Major Duncan's wife. She's a kind, practical woman, and they've been sorely pressed for a cook. In fact, Major Duncan has been frantically searching for one since the Mexican woman they previously had died in childbirth. You see, his wife was consumptive at one time. She's cured now, thanks to this dry, healthful climate, but she's still rather frail. I don't think she's quite as frail as Major Duncan believes, but he's been worried about her having to cook in the summer heat, for fear she'll have a relapse." The colonel paused, then asked, "Where is this young woman you brought with you?"

"Waiting in the outer office, sir," Brant answered, feeling immensely relieved that the colonel had read his thoughts and was an understanding man.

"Why don't you ask her in?"

"Yes, sir."

Brant walked to the door and opened it. Danny's head shot up, and the apprehensive look in her eyes tore at Brant's heart. He gave her a broad, reassuring smile and said, "Danny, come in. Colonel Shafter would like to meet you."

Danny knew by the smile on Brant's face that everything was going to be all right. The fear she had been living with evaporated, and her self-confidence came rushing back. She rose and walked to the door with her usual swagger, then as Brant closed it behind her, stood and smiled broadly at the man standing before her.

"Colonel Shafter, may I present Miss Danny Morgan," Brant said, making the introductions.

Without the slightest hesitation, Danny stepped forward, took the colonel's hand and started shaking it vigorously, saying, "Howdy, Colonel. I'm mighty pleased to meet you."

Brant rolled his eyes and groaned silently. He had told Danny to be friendly, but she was overdoing it. Her bold friendliness bordered on out-and-out disrespect. And she was pumping his hand so hard, Brant feared she would dislocate the colonel's shoulder.

To the colonel's credit, he wasn't at all insulted. Once he had recovered from his shock at seeing Danny in her male attire, with a gun strapped to her hip, no less, he was frankly amused, and just a little enchanted. He had expected her to be wearing a ragged calico dress and to be prematurely aged, as so many of the frontier women were, and he certainly hadn't been prepared for the beautiful young woman standing before him, much less her enthusiasm and warm, infectious smile. In her presence, he felt ten years younger and suddenly light-hearted.

"I'm pleased to meet you, too, young lady," Colonel Shafter replied with all sincerity. "Captain Holden tells me that you're looking for employment as a cook."

Danny dropped the colonel's hand, saying, "Yes, sir, I shore am. You don't by any chance know of someone who's a-looking fer one, do you? Iffen you do, I'd shore appreciate you pointing me in that direction. I need a job mighty bad. I'm flat busted. And I'm a good cook," Danny quickly assured the colonel. "They won't be sorry they hired me. Why, I reckon I could cook the horns off a billy goat, iffen I put my mind to it."

The colonel found Danny's country speech delightful and her honesty refreshing. Nor did he find her bragging on her abilities offensive. If anything her self-confidence was intriguing, and he had the strangest feeling this self-assured young woman could do anything she set her mind to. Now he knew why the captain had smiled when he'd asked if he had a pleasant trip. The girl was delightful, possessing an almost magical charm.

"As a matter of fact, I do know someone who's looking for a first-rate cook. Major Duncan and his wife. Why don't you and I walk over to their house right now, so I can introduce you."

Brant was stunned by the colonel's offer. "That's not necessary, sir. I'm sure you're much too busy. If you'll just tell me which house they live in, I'll escort Danny there and make the necessary introductions and explanations."

The colonel was a busy man, but he wanted to enjoy the company of this enchanting creature just a few more moments. Besides, the captain didn't know it yet, but he had certain social duties of his own to attend to. "I have nothing pressing at the moment. Besides, I have a little surprise for you, Captain. I was going to tell you when you interrupted me with the news about Miss Morgan. Your fiancée is here at the post."

Brant felt as if he'd been kicked by a mule. "Here? At Fort Davis?" he asked in shocked disbelief.

"Yes. It seems she arrived at Fort Concho the day after

you left. She took the stage and arrived here two days ago. She's been staying with me and my wife."

Damn Elizabeth, Brant thought angrily. What in the hell was she doing here in Texas? And how embarrassing. Did the colonel think he had run off, knowing that she was on her way? It made him look like an irresponsible fool in his commanding officer's eyes. "I'm sorry about the imposition, sir. I wasn't aware that she was even contemplating a visit. I planned on writing her about my transfer when I arrived here."

"She explained that. She said she meant to surprise you, since it had been some time since you've seen one another. And it was no imposition. As commanding officer, my wife and I are used to putting up young ladies visiting from the east, since we have the largest quarters on the post. Naturally, they're curious about the west. During my years as post commander at the various forts, it seems we always have some officer's sister or cousin or niece visiting us. But your fiancée is our first visitor at Fort Davis. She's a very brave young lady, to come this far, through such dangerous country."

Like hell she's brave, Brant thought. She's up to something, and he strongly suspected he knew what. Undoubtedly, she was here to pressure him into marrying her. He'd been putting her off for years. Now, she had finally tired at the delay and was brazenly chasing him across the country, just as she chased him back in Philadelphia.

Suddenly Brant was aware of Danny listening to the conversation. Did she think he had deliberately betrayed her? It was nothing like that. He didn't love Elizabeth. He didn't even like her. He shot Danny a quick glance, then, seeing the bland expression on her face, realized she didn't know who a "fiancée" was. It was an expression that wasn't used on the frontier. Thank God, he thought. Perhaps he'd get a chance to explain. But how was he going to explain his engagement to a woman he couldn't stand? He hated to tell Danny that he was so drunk at the time that he didn't even remember proposing. It would make him look like such a damn fool in her eyes.

The colonel saw Brant's worried glance at Danny and assumed he was just concerned for her welfare, since he had accepted responsibility for her. "Go along, now, Captain. I'll see to getting Miss Morgan settled. I know you must be anxious to spend some time with your fiancée. My residence is number seven, in the middle of Officers' Row."

Brant knew that he was being dismissed, but he hated to leave Danny, even if it was in such capable hands. He would have liked to have seen the couple the colonel was placing her with to assure himself that they would treat her kindly. "Would it be inappropriate for me to call at Major Duncan's home tomorrow, to see how Danny's faring in her new job?" Brant asked the colonel, thinking he might also have a chance to explain his awkward state of engagement.

The colonel wondered if Brant's fiancée wouldn't object to his calling on another young woman, particularly one as beautiful and utterly delightful as Danny. And was the young officer only proposing to follow through with what he felt was his responsibility, or was he a little smitten? He seemed unduly reluctant to part with her. While an engaged gentleman had no business calling on another young lady, the captain wasn't a married man, at least not yet. Then the colonel would have to strenuously object, for fear it would cause a scandal. Even then, it might cause talk, particularly with his fiancée present on the post. Army people were such gossips, living in such close proximity as they did.

Danny had no idea what the colonel was thinking, or why he was hesitating. To her, it seemed ridiculous for a grown man like Brant to have to get permission to visit her, but she chalked it up to one of the army's silly rules, like that one about not allowing her to be his Dog Robber.

"I shore would appreciate you letting Brant visit me," she said. "He's my best friend in the whole wide world, and I'd feel plumb awful if I couldn't see him no more."

The colonel had no way of knowing that Danny equated being best friends in the whole wide world with someone as loving them. He felt somewhat like a heel. While he suspected Brant's motives to be more of an amorous nature, he certainly couldn't deny Danny her friend, if that's what she considered him at the present time. She did seem to be attached to him, which he supposed wasn't unusual, given the circumstances. After all, the captain had rescued her, and the poor girl was all alone, in a strange place, among strangers. She needed the captain's continuing support and friendship, at least until she felt more comfortable in her new environment. And if the friendship developed into something more, it was beyond his control. Besides, he didn't particularly like the captain's fiancée. She was the most snobbish, conceited woman he'd ever met, despite her beauty and breeding. He couldn't imagine what the captain saw in her.

"I see no harm in his visiting," the colonel answered, "providing the visits aren't excessive."

Brant heard the warning tone in the colonel's voice, and knew he was reminding him that he was an engaged man and cautioning him not to create a scandal. Damn

Elizabeth! If she hadn't shown up, no one would have ever known he had a fiancée. He would have been free to see Danny as often as he liked. Now he'd have to watch every step he made, or risk ruining his reputation as a gentleman and causing a scandal. Christ, what a mess he was in, and all because he'd gotten stinking drunk one night. "Thank you, sir. I won't abuse the privilege."

"I'll tell Major Duncan that I've given my permission when I present Miss Morgan to him."

Brant knew he was being dismissed by his commanding officer once and for all. He saluted smartly, saying, "Good day, sir," then turned to Danny and said, "Good day, Danny. I'll see you tomorrow."

Danny frowned. "How are you gonna know where to find me in this big place?"

The colonel chuckled at Danny calling the fort big, then said, "Major Duncan's residence is number eleven, Captain."

"Thank you, sir," Brant replied, then putting his hat on, turned and walked from the room.

Just as he was stepping through the doorway, Danny called, "Bye, and tell Elizabeth hello for me."

Brant missed a step, and Colonel Shafter could well imagine his discomfiture. Apparently, Danny didn't have the slightest idea who Elizabeth was.

Danny proved exactly that when she turned and said, "I shore wish I could meet her. Is she his sister or cousin?"

"Why do you ask that?"

"You said you always had sisters and cousins of the officers a-visiting."

Danny had made her own assumption, that Elizabeth was a relative, the Colonel realized. Well, he certainly wasn't going to tell her who the young woman was. That information needed to come from the captain. "I can't remember just exactly what relationship she said she was," he lied smoothly.

Danny frowned. The colonel had said she was Brant's fiancée. Maybe it was just a fancy word for kinfolks in general.

Colonel Shafter held out his arm and said, "Well, young lady, shall we be going?"

"What're you a-holding yer arm out that way fer, like a duck with a broken wing?" Danny asked.

The colonel's lips twitched with amusement. "A gentleman always holds his arm out to a lady, Miss Morgan."

"Shucks, I ain't one those sissy ladies that needs help a-walking. And I wish you wouldn't call me Miss Morgan no more. My name's Danny."

Well, he guessed that was why the two had been on a first name basis. Even before they had become friends, Danny had probably insisted on it, wanting nothing to do with formalities. Why, she probably didn't know such things existed. "All right, Danny, if that's what you want. And you can call me Bill."

"Oh, no, sir, I couldn't do that," Danny objected. "Brant told me how to act. I'm supposed to call you sir, or by your rank, and I ain't gonna break no army rules."

"And what else did Captain Holden tell you?" the colonel asked curiously.

"Jest to be friendly and polite."

So the young man had tried to smooth a few of the rough edges from her, Colonel Shafter thought as the two walked from the room. Did her lack of manners and breeding disturb him? He had read over Captain Holden's

210

records that morning. He came from a very wealthy, prestigious Philadelphia family. Perhaps he had misjudged the captain. Maybe the young man wasn't romantically interested in Danny, after all. Maybe their relationship was nothing but a friendship. The two were a world apart. They had absolutely nothing in common. He felt a strange sense of disappointment. Then he smiled, remembering something he had learned in physics. Opposites attract one another, and the more extreme, the greater the attraction.

Chapter 13

When Danny and Colonel Shafter stepped outside, Danny quickly looked around for Brant, but could see him nowhere in the crowded fort. She already missed him.

"Is that your horse, Danny?" the colonel asked.

Danny looked at her mustang standing before the hitching rail. "Yes, sir, he shore is."

"I'll have one of my men take him to the stables."

"No, sir," Danny objected. "Iffen you don't mind, I'd like to do it myself. Red don't like no one but me a-fooling with him."

"All right, we'll walk him over to the stables."

Danny pulled Red's reins loose and led him across the edge of the big parade ground, the colonel walking beside her. She looked around her, saying, "This shore is a big place."

"It won't seem so big, once you know your way around. In fact, I think you must already know your way around a little, or are you just guessing that the stables are behind the barracks?"

"No, sir. I thought I saw something that might be stables back there when we rode in."

As they walked, the colonel nodded to a large building they were passing, saying, "That's the commissary, a general store run by the army for the officers. And those small cabins behind it are the married enlisted men's quarters."

Danny looked at the cabins. They looked terribly small, especially when you considered all of the children playing around them. "They ain't very big, are they? Why, I've seen outhouses that weren't much smaller," she commented bluntly. "They must be squeezed in there as tight as beans in a tin can."

The colonel chuckled at her outspoken observation, then said, "I'm afraid all of our living quarters are a little tight. The army doesn't believe in providing spacious quarters for its men, particularly the cavalry."

Danny remembered Brant telling her of the skimpy field rations that the cavalry fed its men. "Why not?" she asked testily, feeling defensive in his behalf. "The army got something against 'em?"

"No, it's just that the cavalry is the most expensive branch of service in the army, and we do have to live within a budget. When a trooper needs three remounts every three months, and every horse eats fourteen pounds of hay and twelve of grain a day, the cost of the horses and feed alone is staggering. It's much more expensive to keep a regiment of cavalry in the field than a regiment of infantry."

By this time, they had reached where the stables and corrals sat. Danny came to a dead halt. She had just gotten a glimpse of the stables when she and Brant had ridden in. She had no idea they were so large. The stalls were set against a long adobe wall and were covered with a tile roof. The horse's and trooper's name were printed above each stall, and there were hundreds and hundreds of them. Danny had never seen the rear ends of so many horses in her entire life.

Recovering from her astonishment, she spied an empty stall and started to lead her horse to it. "No, don't put him in there," the colonel told her. "These are the company stables. We'll take him down to the quartermaster stables. That's where we keep our personal mounts and those provided for the officers' wives to ride."

The second stables sat behind the quartermaster's warehouse and were smaller, but Danny still thought they were impressive. Big enough for both a man and a horse to stand, with room left over, it seemed to her that the horses were allotted more spacious quarters than the troopers' families, and there was even a built-in feeding stall and watering trough. As she led Red into one of the open stalls, she said, "I shore hope Red don't get spoiled here. He ain't used to having a roof over his head."

"Didn't you at least put him in a lean-to during the winter?"

"Nope, we jest kept our horses in a corral, like those mules of yers over there. But they were jest mustangs. They was used to a-being in the open. Cold and rain don't bother them none."

The colonel was well aware how hardy the little mustangs were. Heat didn't seem to bother them either. The extreme high temperatures of the Texas summer seemed to sap the energy from the thoroughbreds, while the little mustangs seemed to thrive on it. "There's some hay over there," he said, motioning to a haystack by the corral of mules. "Maybe you had better feed him that, since he's not used to grain. The grain might be too rich for him."

"Yeah, and I don't want him a-gitting used to a-eating grain either," Danny answered, hanging her saddle on a sturdy peg at the head of the stall. "If he can't eat grass, like a dad-blasted horse is supposed to, he can jest go hungry. I don't need no horse that's spoiled rotten."

Colonel Shafter chuckled. She was a plain-spoken little thing, and she made no pretense of hiding her scorn of the cavalry's treatment of their horses. He could have pointed out that the mounts were an investment that they needed to protect and that putting a trooper on a sickly horse might well endanger his life, but he didn't bother. He knew Danny would probably tell him her little mustang had never been sick a day in its life. No, the mustang was strong, like her. Neither had ever been pampered.

As the two walked away from the stables, Danny looked back over her shoulder and said, "I hope the Major don't mind me a-coming out here to take care of Red. And he's gonna have to be exercised too."

"The stable sergeant has a trooper that can do both, if you like. He feeds and exercises the other horses."

"Nope. I done told you Red don't like no one a-fooling with him but me. He might eat fer someone else, but he shore ain't gonna let no one git on his back. My brother tried that once. He bit the dust so fast he didn't know what hit him."

"Then who broke your mustang?"

"I did."

Seeing the look of disbelief on the colonel's face, Danny said hotly, "I did! I ain't a-pulling a sandy on you.

I'm the best dad-blasted broncobuster in west Texas."

It seemed impossible that such a small girl could break a wild mustang, but the colonel found himself believing Danny. He wondered if she could break that little sorrel mustang, the one that none of his troopers had yet to stay on. Even the most accomplished broncobuster on the post hadn't been able to keep his seat for more than a split second. Then he quickly changed his mind. Not only would it be too dangerous, but he had a strong suspicion if he let Danny try her skill against the sorrel, Captain Holden would ring his neck when he found out, commanding officer or not.

Just as they were crossing the parade ground to Officers' Row, the sudden sound of a blaring bugle surprised Danny, almost making her drop her saddlebags. Almost simultaneously, every dog on the post began to howl, creating a horrendous noise that echoed through the mountains around them. She held her hands over her ears until the sounds died down, then asked testily, "What in tarnation was that all about?"

"That was recall for dinner."

"Not that. I'm a-talking about all the dogs a-howling. I never heard such a dad-blasted racket. What in blue blazes is wrong with 'em?"

"Apparently the sound of the bugle hurts their ears."

Danny looked about her, seeing that the soldiers were rushing to their barracks for their noon meal. "Do you play that bugle for breakfast and supper too?"

"I'm afraid there's a few more bugle calls than that. First there's reveille at five-thirty in the morning, then stable call at six, then Boots and Saddle for mounted drill at eight, then recall for dinner, then stables at four, then

216

retreat for supper at five-fifteen, tattoo at nine, and taps at ten."

A horrified expression came over Danny's face. "And those dad-blasted dogs make all that racket every time?"

"Yes, I'm afraid so, except at taps, for some strange reason. But then, taps is such a sweet, soothing sound."

"How in tarnation do you stand it, all that a-howling a-going on? My ears are still a-ringing."

"You get used to it. It's the same at every post. The only other recourse would be to get rid of the dogs, and I'm afraid if I did that, I'd have a riot on my hands. Army people are very attached to their pets."

Danny could understand that, and she wouldn't want the people having to give up their pets. "You could stop a-blowing those bugles," Danny suggested.

The colonel chuckled, then answered, "I'm afraid not. They're army regulation."

By this time, they had reached Officers' Row. Danny noticed that some of the houses were larger than others and they all had wide, covered porches with inverted U-shaped trellises before them. Danny wondered why the trellises were there, for there was nothing growing on them, nor was there anything growing in the flower beds before the houses, other than an occasional spindly wild-flower. The only touches of green were the cactus plants sitting about in huge clay pots, and Danny wondered why anyone would take the time and trouble to pot such an ugly, common plant, having no idea that the Easterners considered them exotic.

They walked up the stairs of one of the cream-colored limestone houses, and the colonel knocked on the door. A moment later, a tall, slim, silver-haired officer opened the door, an astonished look coming over his face before he recovered and snapped a salute.

"No, John," the colonel said, waving his hand slightly, "there's no need for that. This isn't an official call. I have a pleasant surprise for you. I've found you a cook. May I present Miss Danny Morgan?"

Before the Major could even recover from the surprising news and the unexpected sight of a pretty young woman dressed in male clothing standing on his doorstep, Danny smiled brightly and stepped forward, pumping his hand and saying, "Howdy, Major. I'm shore pleased to meet you."

Major Duncan was no more immune to Danny's unique charm than the colonel had been. His blue eyes twinkled with mirth as he answered, "The pleasure is all mine, Miss Morgan."

Danny wrinkled her pert, little nose, then said, "Jest call me Danny. I ain't one fer all that fancy stuff. I'm just ordinary folk."

"John? Who is it?" a woman's voice asked from within the house.

Before the Major could answer, a frail-looking, middle-aged woman stepped up beside him, then noticing the colonel standing there, said, "Why, good day, Colonel."

The colonel swept off his hat, answering, "Good day, Julia."

"Gracious, John, what's wrong with you, leaving the colonel standing out here on the porch? Won't you come in, Colonel?" the woman asked graciously.

"No, thank you, Julia. My dinner is waiting for me, and my wife will be furious if I don't show up for it, particularly since we have a house guest. I just wanted to deliver Miss Morgan to you. She's looking for employment as a cook, and since I knew you had lost yours, I thought to give you first grabs at her."

Again Danny boldly took the initiative, taking the woman's dainty hand and shaking it, saying, "Howdy, ma'am. Jest call me Danny."

Julia was too well mannered and much too kind to let her shock at seeing Danny dressed in her atrocious male attire show. To her credit, she even endured Danny's almost painful, manly handshake. "How do you do, Danny," she replied sweetly.

Quickly Colonel Shafter explained the circumstances of Danny's sudden appearance at the fort. As he related the tale, the couple was filled with compassion for the small girl who had been left homeless and alone. Even if Danny hadn't been seeking employment, the kindly couple would have insisted upon taking her in. But both sensed that Danny was much too proud and independent to accept such an arrangement, something that they both respected and admired.

When the Colonel had finished, Julia smiled and said, "Well, we certainly are fortunate. Thank you, Colonel, for keeping us in mind." She turned to Danny, saying, "We'd be pleased to have you, Danny."

"Does that mean I'm hired?" Danny asked, a little shocked at how smooth things had gone. She had expected them to ask more questions, or maybe even ask for a demonstration of her cooking skills.

"It certainly does, if you're willing to accept the position," Julia answered. "We'll pay you fifty dollars a month, with room and board."

The colonel's bushy eyebrows rose in surprise. Julia was offering Danny top wages for a cook, and she wasn't even an experienced servant. He glanced at the major to see his reaction to the salary his wife was proposing and saw that the man was smiling in perfect accord. Yes, he had certainly made the right selection in placing Danny with these kind-hearted, generous people.

Danny was astonished at the salary Julia quoted. It sounded like a fortune to her. Why, she'd have her debt to Brant paid off in one month, with money to spare. Then she could start stashing her full salary away to save for a fresh start at her ranch, not that she was in any hurry to get away, not as long as Brant was at the fort. "Why, I'd be plumb tickled to work fer you, ma'am."

The colonel beamed, saying, "Well, now that's settled, I'd better be going on my way."

Danny turned to him, saying, "Thank you, Colonel, fer yer help."

"You're quite welcome, Danny. I hope you'll be happy here at Fort Davis."

Danny thought of Brant and answered, "I shore will be, Colonel. There ain't no place I'd rather be right now."

The colonel smiled at her answer and nodded his head to Julia, saying, "Good day, Julia."

"Good day, Colonel, and thank you again for remembering us."

As the colonel turned to walk away, Major Duncan said, "Wait a minute, Colonel. I'll get my hat and walk across the parade ground with you."

"What about your dinner?"

"We ate a little early today," the major explained. He stepped into the house, then reappeared with his hat in his hand. Dropping a kiss on his wife's cheek, he said, "Now, you be sure and take your nap. Remember what the doctor said? You need plenty of rest."

"I will, dear," Julia answered patiently.

As the two men walked off, Danny asked, "You been a-feeling poorly, ma'am?"

"I had consumption, but I'm cured now. However, John still worries about me. I'm not really as frail as I look, but I can't seem to convince him of it. I'm afraid he's a little overprotective, but then that's the way men are. Sometimes we women just have to endure being pampered, otherwise we hurt their feelings. They have to feel manly and protective."

Danny frowned. Why should a woman act weak, just because it makes a man feel stronger? It sounded like a bunch of hog wash to her. But she was curious to know what had ailed the woman. "What's consumption?"

"It's a lung disease."

So she was a lunger, Danny thought, or used to be. Danny had heard that the disease was quite deadly. Maybe her husband wasn't being so silly after all.

As they walked into the house, Danny looked about her. The small parlor had a threadbare rug on the floor, and there were several cowhide chairs sitting about and two crude end tables with oil lamps sitting on them. What caught Danny's attention were the crocheted doilies and small figurines that graced the tables. She walked to one, ran her fingers over the doily, then picked up one of the figurines, saying "This shore is purty. And so is that lacy-looking thing."

"Thank you, Danny. I'm afraid it was a rather pitiful effort to try and make the place look more homey. We do have nice furniture and some really lovely things, but at the cost of shipping and the way things get broken by the stage lines handling them so roughly, we just leave our personal household articles in storage. The furniture you see was made by the post carpenters, and they're

221

certainly not skilled cabinet makers. We just have to make do with what we've got."

Danny had no idea of the gracious living Julia was lamenting, or the sacrifices she had made in comfort by following her husband to the remote western outposts, or the frustrations of just getting settled and making new friends only to be transferred to yet another place. Nor did she realize that it was only the army wives of remarkable courage and endurance who did so, while the others stayed back East with their families. Danny was used to harsh living conditions and loneliness, dust and heat, danger and fear of Indian attacks. And to her, the parlor looked a danged sight better than theirs had back at the ranch.

Julia led Danny to one of the small bedrooms that flanked the parlor, saying, "This will be your room."

Danny looked at the iron army cot, covered with a gingham spread, the straight chair, then at the window with its matching gingham curtains. Her eyes widened in disbelief. The windowpane was made of glass, and not the clarified rawhide that had covered the windows back at her ranch, and only let the light in. Why, she could actually see out, and the view of the mountains in the distance was absolutely breathtaking.

"I'm sorry it's so plain," Julia apologized, "and that there's no bureau for you to put your things in. I'm afraid we have to live out of our trunks. However, there are a few pegs for you to hang your clothes on, and there's a mirror over on that wall."

"Shucks, I don't need no bureau. I ain't got but two changes of clothing. And who cares how plain it looks? With that purty view out there, I ain't gonna be a-looking at the room nohow."

222

Two changes of clothing, Julia thought in shock. Immediately she felt ashamed of herself. Why, that was all the poor child had to her name, and she was regretting how pitiful her home looked. Then as a sudden thought occurred to her, she said, "My gracious! I completely forgot. You haven't had dinner yet. You must be starved."

"Well, my belly is a-rubbing against my backbone a mite," Danny admitted.

Julia laughed at Danny's frank admission and said, "Come into the kitchen. There's some stew left from dinner that we can warm up for you."

Danny put her saddlebags on the iron cot, then started to slip the strap from her shoulder when she suddenly remembered Charlie. Recalling what Brant had told her, she turned and said, "There's something I oughta tell you, ma'am. I would have said something sooner, but I plumb fergot. I brung a pet with me. You may not want Charlie in the house. Iffen that's so, I can leave him outside."

"A dog?"

"No, ma'am."

"A cat?"

"No, ma'am. Charlie's a grass snake. I keep him in this bag a-hanging on my shoulder. But he can't get out, not with the flap strapped down," Danny added quickly, afraid Julia would get hysterical and start screaming. "You don't have nothing to be scared of."

To Danny's utter surprise, Julia started laughing and said, "I stopped being frightened of grass snakes years ago, Danny. As a matter of fact, in my childhood. I grew up in a little town in Ohio, and my brothers delighted in trying to frighten me with all kinds of harmless snakes, to

223

say nothing of frogs and spiders. I found them in my bed, my bureau, stuffed into my shoes and hats. I had to get used to them out of self-defense. It was either that, or live in constant fear. No, you can keep your pet in the house. I don't think he'd be too safe outside, not with all of the dogs around. But I would prefer you keep him here in your bedroom. I wouldn't want any of the other women visiting me to have a stroke at finding a snake in my parlor."

There was nothing that Julia could have done that would have earned Danny's undying gratitude as much as allowing her to keep Charlie with her. "I shore do thank you, ma'am, and I promise he won't get out this room, 'cept when I take him outside fer him to rustle up some grub."

"Can't you find something to feed him here in the house? As I said, it might not be too safe for him outside, with all of those dogs."

"No, ma'am. All Charlie eats is bugs and crickets and ants, and I shore ain't gonna go crawling 'round on the ground a-looking fer 'em fer him. I don't want him a-gitting spoiled no more than my horse. But I won't let those hounds bother Charlie. I'll beat 'em off with a stick, iffen I have to."

Julia could have pointed out that there were probably enough bugs, spiders, and ants right here in the house to feed Charlie for a month, but said instead, "Well, you can do whatever you like, but for now, let's get some food into you. While you're eating, we can plan the bill of fare for the next few days."

Danny placed her canvas bag on the bed, unstrapped it so Charlie could get some fresh air, and followed Julia from the room, carefully closing the door behind her, wondering all the while what in tarnation a bill of fare was.

Danny's question was answered while she was eating. She was amazed to find out that people actually planned meals. She just cooked what was available, and if all she had to cook was beans, then that's all they ate. But Julia made sure there were two vegetables and a meat for every main meal, and insisted they had to have a dessert for Sunday's dinner. Why, they even had meat for breakfast every morning. Gol-durn, they must be rich, Danny thought, paying her fifty dollars a month just to cook for them and eating all that food.

Even more amazing to Danny was that Julia wrote everything down, then made what she called a shopping list. Danny watched as Julia wrote on a piece of paper with her neat penmanship, wishing she could write and make such pretty curlicues. She'd learn that, too, someday, she vowed, along with reading.

Julia rose from the table, saying, "You can wash the dishes later. Let's walk over to the commissary and shop for these things you'll be needing."

"I thought you were supposed to take a nap," Danny reminded her.

Julia laughed. "Danny, I don't nap in the afternoons, but don't you dare tell John. I'm not sleepy, or tired either. Oh, I usually sit in the bedroom and do some hand sewing, or write a few letters, or read a book, and none of those are strenuous. And neither is shopping, particularly if there are two of us to carry back our purchases."

"The major might see you out there," Danny warned.

"No, he won't. Not today. Today he'll be at the target range until three-thirty. That gives us plenty of time."

Danny took a closer look at Julia. She appeared frail,

but that was mostly because she was so tiny and small-boned. Her face looked a little pale, but then, all those sissy ladies' faces did. But she certainly didn't look tired, not with her pretty gray eyes sparkling the way they were. No, there was a vitality about Julia that put any notion about her being sickly to lie.

Danny remembered Julia telling her that she endured her husband pampering her to keep from hurting his feelings. And now she was sneaking around behind his back, not napping like he thought she was, but doing all kinds of things. Seemed to her that it would be a lot more honest and simpler to just tell him she wasn't gonna take a nap and be done with it. That's what she'd do.

Danny waited while Julia donned her bonnet and tied the ribbon in a neat little bow to the side of her face. Then as she slipped on her white gloves, Danny asked, "How come you're a-wearing those mittens? It ain't cold outside."

"A lady never goes out in the sun without her bonnet, and she never steps out of the house without her gloves." Seeing the disgusted look coming over Danny's face, Julia laughed and said, "I know it seems ridiculous to you. Sometimes, I think it's a little silly myself, particularly the gloves, but rules are rules, even on an army post. In fact, I think we army women are even more sticklers for etiquette than some of our sisters back East. We're just as regimental as our husbands."

When the two stepped out of the house, Danny noticed that the parade ground was practically deserted. "Where'd everybody go?"

"Oh, after dinner, they don't drill on the parade ground. It's much too hot. They attend class, or clean their weapons and repair their equipment, or practice their shooting at the target range, like John and his troopers are doing right now."

"It ain't hot at this time of the year," Danny pointed out. "Why, it's jest the end of April."

"Yes, I know, but the army never veers from its well-ordered regime. They have a time for everything, and they stick to it regardless of the season. And I'm afraid some of us Yankees would beg to differ with you about the heat, Danny. April in Texas can sometimes be as warm as mid-summer up north. We're simply not accustomed to heat like you Texans are."

"Yeah, well, I reckon I'll have to admit it does git a little hot sometimes, particularly in August. Then it's hot enough to melt snakes."

As they walked across the parade ground, Danny could hear the faint sound of gunshots being fired in the distance. "How often do the soldiers have to practice their shooting?" Danny asked, thinking it rather odd. She hadn't practiced shooting since she'd first learned. Oh, she practiced her draw every now and then, but standing around and shooting at a target seemed like a waste of ammunition to her.

"More often than you might think. Every man is required to put in a certain number of hours at the target range. Even we women are expected to do so."

"I didn't know ladies shot guns," Danny said in surprise.

"Ordinarily a lady wouldn't touch one, but you're going to find that we army women aren't ordinary ladies, Danny, despite our clinging to the rigid social rules that governed our lives back East. On these remote posts in Indian territory, we all must qualify with both a carbine and a pistol, and keep brushed up on our shooting skills.

227

We never leave the post without being armed. In fact, most of us carry derringers in our reticules," Julia said, patting the long, slim purse hanging from her arm, "in case of sudden attack."

"You mean you fight Injuns too?"

"We certainly do, and if we're threatened with imminent capture, we have orders to kill ourselves, after we've shot the children, of course."

Danny was momentarily speechless with shock. Then she said, "Kill yerself? Why in tarnation would you do that?"

"It would be better than being subjected to the horrible tortures that the Indians can devise."

Danny had heard of some of the tortures that the Apaches used: skinning a man alive, staking him naked and spread-eagled over a bed of voracious ants, torturing him over a slow fire, or burying him up to his neck to face a burning sun with peeled eyelids. No, she wouldn't want to be tortured either, but she didn't think she'd have the guts to kill herself. "Could you actually do that, kill yerself?"

"To be honest, Danny, I don't know if I would have the courage to do so. I just hope the occasion never arises to find out."

So did Danny, and she found she had a new respect for army women, even if they were ladies and did some pretty silly things.

When they entered the commissary, Danny looked about her, her eyes widening as they swept over the boxes scattered about among the usual barrels and sacks. "I ain't never seen so many cans of beans in my life," she blurted.

Julia laughed, then said, "They're not all beans."

"Then what's in all those tins?"

"Oh, potted hams, Bombay Duck—which in reality is tinned fish—Corned Willie, actually corned beef, Gold Fish—which is an utterly ridiculous name for salmon—green beans, peas, peaches, and a few other fruits and vegetables. The commissary even carries tinned butter, but take my word for it, Danny, you wouldn't want to eat it. Besides being an unnatural pink color, it tastes suspiciously like axle grease, or what one would imagine axle grease would taste like. It's horrible!"

"Well, I'll be danged," Danny said in amazement. "I didn't even know they canned all those things." She looked about her, then said, "Where did all those fresh vegetables come from?"

"We have a post garden down by Limpia Creek, but it doesn't produce near enough to supply the fort. The vegetables are terribly expensive. But then, everything out here is. I still haven't gotten used to a pound of butter and a dozen eggs costing two dollars each, or paying twenty-five cents for a quart of watered-down milk, and fifty cents a pound for bacon. However, that spinach looks good. It should be sweet and tender at this time of the year. Perhaps we'll buy some for a salad tonight."

"What's a salad?" Danny asked.

Julia was surprised at Danny's question, until she remembered that she had been brought up on an isolated ranch. "A dish of raw green vegetables, served with a dressing of some sort."

"You mean you're gonna eat yer greens without a-cooking them, like a horse does grass?"

"Yes. Raw greens can be quite tasty."

Danny wasn't about to eat any raw greens. Why, it might give her a bellyache. These army people sure had some weird ideas.

While Julia placed her order with the clerk standing behind the counter, Danny wandered around the commissary. She stopped at a display containing pipes, little muslin sacks of Bull Durham tobacco, cigarette papers, boxes of long, thin Mexican cigars, and Short Sixes, a fat, stubby version of the latter, eyeing the packages of chewing tobacco with longing.

Julia stepped up beside her and asked, "Do you smoke, Danny?"

"Shucks, no!" Danny said in a highly indignant voice. "I ain't no hick, a-puffing on a corncob pipe."

"I meant cigarettes."

"Cigarettes?" Danny asked in utter shock.

"I can tell by your reaction that you don't. Some of the women here do, even a few of the officer's wives. Of course, they do it in the privacy of their homes, but you know who does and who doesn't. You can smell the smoke on their breaths, just as you can sometimes smell the whiskey."

"Are you a-saying the ladies here drink hard liquor?"

"Unfortunately, yes, a few do nibble at their husbands' bottles. Many are bored and lonely, particularly when their husbands are gone on patrol for long stretches of time. They experiment with things that they would never dream of doing back East, including affairs with other men. With the excess of unattached, women-hungry men about, the temptation to get attention is very great. Unfortunately, the affairs aren't generally truly loving relationships, and the women end up feeling cheated and sordid, even if it doesn't destroy their

230

marriage. It's one of the sad things about army life."

Danny didn't know what an affair was, but she got the jest of what Julia was saying. She couldn't imagine a woman doing that with a man unless she loved him with her whole heart and soul, like she did Brant, and even though she hadn't had any formal religious training, had never even heard the word adultery, she knew marriage was a lifetime commitment and that the women's behavior was terribly wrong. But what amazed her was Julia had spoke of the women with compassion, and not condemned them, as she felt sure those of her class, as well as Julia's, would have. She realized that Julia was an extraordinary woman.

While they were waiting for the clerk to fill Julia's order, two other women walked in. They gave Danny's clothing a shocked scrutiny, then huddled together snickering and casting scornful looks in her direction. While Danny appeared to be unaware, Julia was acutely conscious of their rude behavior. Julia could show compassion for a woman turning to drink or other men out of loneliness, but she had absolutely no tolerance for snobbish women. Unfortunately, every post had them, and Fort Davis was no different. For two cents, she would go over and introduce Danny to them. The captain's wife and the lieutenant's wife would be forced to be polite, even if they did feel highly insulted at being introduced to someone they considered to be so far beneath them, if the introduction came from a major's wife. But Julia had never outranked any army wife, and she wasn't going to sink to such depths now. But she longed to scratch their eyes out, her gray eyes flashing with anger.

For once, Danny was aware of the scorn being shown her, and there was no doubt in her mind why. She pretended not to notice until the two women had made their small purchases and departed, then said to Julia, "Brant told me the ladies here were gonna be shocked at my clothing, but I'm gonna tell you jest like I told him. I ain't gonna wear no consarn dress. I ain't never worn one, and I ain't gonna start now. Iffen you don't want me fer yer cook 'cause of that, jest say so now."

"Why would you think I wouldn't want you for my cook because of the way you're dressed?" Julia asked in astonishment.

"'Cause you had a mad look on yer face when those women started a-gawking at me. I don't want to embarrass you, but I ain't gonna wear no sissy dress."

"I wasn't angry at you," Julia explained. "I was angry at them for being so rude. I don't care what you wear, Danny, as long as you're decently covered."

A look of relief passed over Danny's face. "Well, I shore am glad to hear you say that, ma'am, 'cause I like you. You're real friendly, and I think I'd be happy a-working fer you. But I do feel mighty strongly about my duckins and boots."

"Well, if you've never worn a dress in your life, I imagine you are more comfortable in those clothes. But, tell me, who is Brant?"

At the mention of Brant's name, Danny's black eyes sparkled, and a glow came to her face. "He's the fella who brought me here."

"The officer who rescued you?"

Danny frowned, then said, "Hellfire, he didn't rescue me! I didn't need rescuing! I jest tagged along to Fort Davis with him, 'cause I needed a job."

Julia chuckled at Danny's indignation. Yes, she thought, as independent as she was, she probably didn't

232

need rescuing. "But he did help you by bringing you here," she pointed out.

Danny still refused to admit that she couldn't have found her way by herself—eventually. "He helped me get this job," she answered. "I'm grateful fer that."

And apparently the captain had tried to smooth some of the rough edges off her, Julia thought, but had no success. In a way, Julia was glad. She liked Danny the way she was. She made her feel more youthful than she had felt in ages.

The clerk at the counter broke into Julia's thoughts, saying, "Your order is ready, Mrs. Duncan."

Julia turned and placed the basket she had been carrying on the counter, saying, "Put the smaller things in here, please." While Julia was signing the bill of sale, Danny eyed the basket and the other purchases that were wrapped in several large packages, then deciding that the packages looked the heaviest, swooped them up.

The lieutenant in charge of the commissary walked from a door behind the counter. "Oh, Lieutenant Rawls, I'm glad you happened by," Julia said to the officer. "This is Danny Morgan, my new cook. I may be sending her over to buy things every now and then. She has my permission to sign for them."

"Yes, ma'am. I'll make a note of that on your account."

When Julia and Danny stepped outside the store, Danny said, "Ma'am, I can't sign fer nothing. I can't write." Then as a sudden thought occurred to her, she quickly added, "Lessen you could teach me to write my name."

Julia could have kicked herself for not realizing that Danny probably couldn't read and write, and putting her in an embarrassing situation. But then, Danny acted more irritated at herself, than embarrassed by her lack of an education. "I don't know why I couldn't teach you. Over the years, my husband has certainly taught enough of his troopers to write their names."

Danny beamed with pleasure. She had said she was going to learn to read and write, and today she'd already learned a letter and a numeral, and now Julia was going to teach her how to write her very own name. Danny Morgan. She wondered how it would look on paper. She could hardly wait to find out.

Chapter 14

That night Danny lay on her iron cot, thinking over the events of her first day at Fort Davis. It had gone much better than she'd expected. Both the Major and Julia had been friendly to her, not in the least bit bossy as she had imagined an employer would be. Why, they'd even asked her to sit and eat with them, just like she was one of the family, and she knew they were pleased with her cooking. Julia had raved over how tender the beef was and marveled that Danny had managed to get the bitter taste of wild cattle from it, and the Major had wolfed down her sourdough biscuits, practically cleaning the platter all by himself. Their appreciation of her cooking skills had made Danny feel so good that she'd even let them talk her into trying a bite of the salad Julia had prepared. To her amazement, the raw spinach had actually tasted good, particularly with the bacon grease and bits of crumbled meat on it, and she hadn't got a bellyache, after all. At least not yet.

Danny's thoughts drifted to Brant. She wondered how his day had gone. He must have been awfully glad to see his kinfolk, whoever she was. They'd probably spent the whole afternoon visiting and telling each other what all had happened to them since they'd last met, but Danny hoped that Brant hadn't been so pleasantly occupied that he hadn't even thought of her. She sure had been thinking of him. She missed him something awful, especially now, laying on this cot all by herself, without his strong arms wrapped around her and his shoulder for her pillow. She had never felt so lonely in her entire life.

Danny would have been surprised to learn that Brant's day had been far from pleasant. He'd eaten dinner with the colonel, his wife, and Elizabeth, then spent a miserable afternoon in the two women's company, trying to behave charming and entertaining while he had been seething with anger deep down inside. He had managed to escape for a few hours, using the excuse that he had to get settled in his quarters. Then, much to his disgust, he had been forced to make a second appearance at supper time, since the colonel's wife had graciously invited him and he didn't dare refuse an invitation from that quarter. Fortunately, that visit hadn't been nearly as tedious, thanks to the colonel, who had kept them amused with some of the more humorous experiences of his army career. It wasn't until the meal was finished and they had retired to the front porch, that Brant had finally found a way to be alone with his fiancée, suggesting a walk around the parade ground before taps.

As soon as they were out of the older couple's vision, and far enough away that Brant was sure they couldn't be overheard, Brant turned to face Elizabeth and asked angrily, "What in the hell are you doing here?"

Elizabeth knew Brant was furious with her, had known from the minute she had laid eyes on him that he was far from pleased to see her. She pasted an innocent expression on her face and answered, "Why, I came to visit you. It's been over five years since I've seen you. After all, I am your fiancée."

"Is that why you came, to remind me?" Brant asked in a hard voice.

"Maybe I did," Elizabeth tossed back. "Five years is a long time to go without even seeing the man you're going to marry. Why, you haven't been home since you rejoined the army, not even on leave."

"I explained that in my letters. It's not easy to get leave in the cavalry."

"Yes, Mrs. Shafter said the same," Elizabeth admitted, "but that didn't stop me from wanting to see you. Besides, I was curious to see what the frontier looks like and how you live."

Like hell, Brant thought. She couldn't give a damn how he lived. She'd come to remind him of their engagement and to make him feel guilty for delaying their marriage for so long. Well, it wasn't going to work. He might be engaged to her, but hell would freeze over before she'd get him down the aisle. "All right. You've seen the frontier and how I live. Now, when do you intend to go back?"

Brant's curt question cut to the bone. It wasn't going at all like she had planned, Elizabeth thought. She had heard that the men on the frontier were so lonely and hungry for a woman that they would marry anything in skirts, and had hoped to lure Brant to the altar with her beauty and desirability. Damn him! Five years on the frontier hadn't made him any more susceptible to her feminine charms than he'd ever been, and there was no doubt in Elizabeth's mind that she had those charms.

With her lush breasts and tiny waist, her milk-white skin, her perfect features, her blue eyes, and raven hair that she fashioned into the most spectacular hairdos, she had been one of the most sought-after debutantes in Philadelphia. But Elizabeth hadn't wanted any of the men that had pursued her. From the moment she had laid eyes on Brant after he had returned from the war, she had wanted him. It wasn't just his golden good looks and the knowledge that he came from one of the most wealthy, influential families in Philadelphia that had made him so desirable. True, they had played a part in her attraction, but Brant seemed so much more experienced, more manly, more rugged than any of the others, and she had sensed a seething anger deep inside him that reminded her of a restless, caged tiger. The aura of a dangerous animal that hung over him had excited her, and she had set out to snare him, deliberately arranging to be seated beside him at every dinner party they had both attended, to appear on the same riding trail at the same time of the day, to be invited to the same balls and same house parties. For three years, she had relentlessly pursued him, but Brant had remained cool and aloof—until that fateful night.

Elizabeth smiled smugly as she recalled the events of that night. She had attended a ball at Brant's home and had anticipated seeing him, but Brant never made an appearance. Determined to seek him out, she had slipped away and found him in the library drinking himself into oblivion. With his shirt open halfway down revealing his broad muscular chest with its light sprinkling of golden hairs, and the wild look in his searing-blue eyes, he'd had a raw, primitive appeal that had made Elizabeth toss all reserve to the wind. She'd thrown herself into his arms, and for once, Brant hadn't been indifferent to her, kissing her with a brutal, animal savagery that had aroused her unbearably. Then, to her chagrin, he had passed out cold, collapsing limply on the leather couch behind him.

It was seeing him sprawled on the couch in such disarray that the idea had come to Elizabeth. With deliberate calculation, she ripped the bodice of her gown, pulled a few long strands of hair loose from its elaborate setting on top of her head, then stretched out beside him and wrapped his arms around her. Hours later, her parents and his father had found them, just as she had known they would. Brant had roused during her mother's hysterical screams and her father's loud, irate threats, confused and bewildered. Then, to everyone's stunned surprise—most of all Brant's—Elizabeth had explained that nothing really serious had happened and blissfully announced that Brant had proposed and she had accepted.

For a split second, Elizabeth had feared that her trap had failed, for a suspicious gleam had come into the elder Holden's eyes at her announcement. Even after her parents had taken her home, she had feared Brant's father would call her bluff. When no accusations came from that quarter, she'd relaxed and savored her victory. It wasn't until the night of their engagement ball that Brant's father had taken her aside and congratulated her on her cunning trap, telling her that he welcomed her as an ally to help bring Brant to heel. It seemed he wanted her aid in influencing Brant to accept the vice presidency of his business empire that he had been trying to force down his son's throat. Elizabeth had been more than agreeable, especially when Brant's father had promised her a hefty reward if she succeeded. Then, to both parties' fury, Brant had foiled their plans by suddenly rejoining the army. It had been Brant's father that had urged her to make the long, horrible trip to Texas in hopes of luring Brant to the altar and back to civilian life. He knew that Brant's enlistment would be up in the fall. Time was running out for both of them, for Elizabeth would rather die than be an army wife and live in some hellhole like this army post. She had to get Brant to the altar and back East. She had to!

"I asked you a question," Brant reminded her when Elizabeth was silent for so long. "How long are you planning on staying?"

Elizabeth resorted to her last line of defense when all else failed. At her bidding, tears welled in her blue eyes, and she said in a pitiful voice, "Why are you treating me so hatefully, Brant? I came all this way to see you, just because I love you and want to be near you, and you're asking me how soon I'm planning on leaving. How can you be so insensitive, so cruel?"

Brant hated it when Elizabeth cried, and she seemed to be able to do it at the drop of a hat. It made him feel so damn guilty. Every time he had questioned her about that night in the library, she had broken into tears, saying she didn't know why he couldn't remember, that he hadn't acted drunk to her, that he'd been so ardent and loving, that he'd made her so happy by proposing, that she loved him so much. Brant wished to hell he could remember what happened that night, but the more he tried, the more he drew a total blank. It was the only night in his life that he had drunk himself into a stupor, and it'd had disastrous results. It would have never happened if the tension that had been building between him and his domineering father ever since his return from the war hadn't reached the breaking point. He'd realized that his father would never acknowledge that he was a mature man, capable of making his own decisions and running his own life. Then, that day, the news that his best friend in the army had died of old war wounds had arrived. Combined with the stress he was already feeling, Brant had sought to drown his anger and depression in a bottle. The next thing he knew he was on the couch with Elizabeth in a very compromising position, in full view of her parents and his father. Had he proposed? If so, he was doing her an injustice. It wasn't her fault that he had made a damn fool out of himself. And if he had, he was honor bound to adhere to the engagement. Like it or not, he was a gentleman to the bone.

Thus, Brant went along with the engagement parties and the newspaper announcement, torn between his honor and his desire to be free from the oppressive commitment, but when Elizabeth and his father had started pressing to set a date for the marriage, Brant had grown progressively apprehensive. He realized that the time to object had passed, that to break the engagement would humiliate Elizabeth, insult her parents, and make him appear a total cad in everyone's eyes. Like a wary animal feeling the trap closing in, he had bolted and joined the army, deliberately requesting assignment on the frontier. He had hoped if he could put enough distance between him and Elizabeth and delay long enough that *she* would break the engagement. But now, here she was in Texas, making him feel guilty again. Dammit, why hadn't he told her right off he had no intentions of marrying her, that he didn't love her and never would? Instead, he had taken the cowards' way out and ran. Him, the same man who had been promoted twice for heroism in the field. Some hero he was. Hell, he wasn't even man enough to say no. He wished to hell he had never been born a gentleman. At that moment, the code of honor that had been instilled into him felt like a rock around his neck.

"I'm sorry to have been abrupt with you," Brant said, hating himself the whole time and not sounding at all contrite, "but it was quite a shock to arrive here and find you waiting for me. You could have at least warned me you were coming to Texas."

Elizabeth breathed a silent sigh of relief. Her tears had worked again. She dabbed at her eyes and answered, "But then it wouldn't have been a surprise."

"But don't you realize it put me in an awkward position with my commanding officer? My arriving here and knowing nothing of your planned visit made me look like a fool."

"I explained it was meant to be a surprise to him and his wife, and they were very understanding. As a matter of fact, Mrs. Shafter thought it was very romantic."

Brant grimaced at the word, romantic. "I should have had his permission for you to visit."

"I didn't know that, and they didn't seem to think that I was being rude. They've both been very gracious. In fact, Mrs. Shafter was the one who suggested I stay for a while, since it's such a long trip from Philadelphia."

Brant felt the trap closing in on him again. "You won't like it here, Elizabeth," he warned in an ominous tone of voice. "The living conditions are harsh, and there's not much in the way of social life."

"Oh, I admit the living conditions are a little rustic, but Mrs. Shafter assured me that I wouldn't get bored.

242

She said the ladies go riding together and that they have picnics, and hunting and fishing parties, and social get-togethers with the other officers and their wives. She even said they're planning a big ball for the Fourth of July."

The Fourth of July, Brant thought in absolute horror. My God, that was two months away! "Surely you're not planning on staying that long?" he asked in a harsh voice.

"Why not?"

"Think of the imposition it would be on the colonel and Mrs. Shafter."

"But she was the one who invited me to stay until then," Elizabeth objected.

At that moment, Brant could have throttled the colonel's wife, even though he knew she had extended the invitation out of graciousness. Army people were noted for their hospitality. He wondered if there was any way he could coerce Elizabeth into leaving earlier, then said, "It's too dangerous for you out here."

Elizabeth knew exactly what Brant was up to. She smiled sweetly and replied, "I'm not afraid with you here to protect me."

"I won't always be here to protect you," Brant answered curtly. "I'm a soldier. It's my job to fight Indians. I'll probably be out on patrol most of the time."

"I should be safe enough. After all, there are other women here. I'm sure the army wouldn't allow it if there was that much danger," Elizabeth countered.

Brant could see the determined gleam in Elizabeth's eyes, the same gleam that had been there when she had pursued him back East. "All right, Elizabeth," he said in a hard voice, "but don't expect me to entertain you. As I said, I have a job to do. I'll be too busy to escort you to all

243

those social get-togethers you were talking about. Just remember that I warned you."

"But you're my betrothed," Elizabeth objected. "Surely the Colonel won't send you off while I'm here on a visit."

"Dammit, Elizabeth, didn't you hear a word I said? This is an army fort, not a social club, despite what Mrs. Shafter might have told you. I have responsibilities, and even if the colonel were willing to relieve me of some of them, I wouldn't hear of it. I pull my weight just like any other man."

Damn him, Elizabeth thought angrily. He was still avoiding her, this time using his job as his means to get away from her. But surely, he couldn't be gone all the time. She'd just have to concentrate her efforts while he was around. "Well, I'll have to admit that I'm disappointed," Elizabeth said, then seeing the gleam coming in to Brant's eyes, added sweetly, "but I understand. Seeing you some of the time will be better than not at all."

Brant knew that he had been outmaneuvered—again. The urge to tell Elizabeth he didn't love her and had no intention of marrying her rose in him, but Brant couldn't bring himself to say them. If he broke his engagement at this point, particularly after his betrothed had come all this way to visit him, the Colonel and his wife would think his behavior unseemly for an officer and a gentleman, and he had yet to prove himself in his commanding officer's eyes. He couldn't afford that kind of a black mark. He was facing the same dilemma he had run from back in Philadelphia.

And what about Danny? Brant thought bleakly. How in the hell was he going to explain his engagement and

244

Elizabeth's presence, particularly if she drew her visit out? Brant was seething with frustration.

Elizabeth decided to make the most of her time with Brant. She stepped closer, pressing her lush breasts against his chest and saying in a petulant voice, "You didn't kiss me hello."

If Brant remembered correctly, he hadn't kissed her goodbye either. He stepped back, saying in a terse voice, "I didn't think it would be appropriate in front of Mrs. Shafter."

Boldly, Elizabeth stepped up to him again, this time dropping her voice to a seductive timbre and saying, "She's not here now."

Damn, she was like a dog with a bone, Brant thought in exasperation. She wasn't going to leave him alone until he had kissed her. He bent and pecked her cheek.

Elizabeth could have screamed in frustration. She could feel his anger, had hoped he would kiss her like he had that night in the library, wild and brutal. Instead, his kiss had felt like ice on her cheek.

Brant took Elizabeth's arm and turned her back towards the colonel's house, saying, "We'd better get back. It's getting late."

"Why, it isn't even ten o'clock," Elizabeth objected.

"The army goes to bed early, Elizabeth."

God, Elizabeth thought, she didn't know how she was going to stand it, living in this hot, dusty hellhole, sleeping on that hard cot, eating that bland, plain food, bathing in that little tub made from a vinegar barrel and associating with these common, middle-class officers and their wives, who pretended to be ladies and gentlemen, but had no real breeding at all. Why, Mrs. Shafter had told her she was a doctor's daughter. Elizabeth had never thought she'd see the day when she'd be brought so low. And to top it off, she'd be bored to tears. She hated riding and the smell of horses, and the thought of going on a hunting or fishing trip was absolutely repulsive. Even the prospect of a picnic didn't appeal to her, sitting on the hard ground in the heat, with all those bugs crawling around. She hated the outdoors and relished the comfort of her luxurious home. Her idea of a pleasant afternoon was shopping for new clothes, and she'd spent a small fortune on her wardrobe for her trip to Texas. A lot of good it did her. Brant hadn't even noticed the fashionable dress she was wearing.

When he and Elizabeth walked back up the steps of the Colonel's front porch, Brant was relieved to see the couple still sitting on the rocking chairs there. With them present, Elizabeth wouldn't dare ask him to kiss her again. He turned to the pair, thanking them for inviting him to share their evening meal.

"You're quite welcome, Captain," the colonel's wife answered. "We'd be pleased to have you tomorrow evening too."

Aware of Elizabeth's eyes on him like a hungry vulture's, Brant answered, "Thank you, Mrs. Shafter, but I'm afraid I'll have to decline your invitation. Tomorrow is my first day as commander of a new troop, and I imagine I'll be quite busy."

"I understand, but please feel free to visit any time you like," Mrs. Shafter answered.

"Thank you, and good evening," Brant replied, then turned to the colonel and said, "Good night, sir."

"Good night, Captain."

Brant turned to Elizabeth and said stiffly, "Good night."

"Good night, Brant," Elizabeth answered, infuriated by his aloof behavior.

As Brant walked off, Mrs. Shafter gazed at his broad back thoughtfully, thinking something didn't seem quite right with the young couple. The colonel, however, wasn't at all surprised at Brant's cool farewell to his betrothed. It only confirmed his earlier suspicions that Brant was smitten with Danny. He glanced at Elizabeth and saw the fury in her eyes, then wondered if Brant had told her about the enchanting creature he had brought to Fort Davis.

"Did you tell the Captain how long you intend to stay?" Mrs. Shafter asked Elizabeth.

Elizabeth quickly hid her anger and answered brightly, "Oh, yes, and he was thrilled. Thank you so very much for inviting me."

Then she doesn't know about Danny, the colonel thought, and Danny had yet to learn about her. He didn't envy the young captain his predicament.

The next morning, Brant was up before reveille. He walked to the barracks that housed his troop, and there in front of it, in the gray, pre-dawn light, he saw a burly first sergeant with a mop of bright red hair and a fierce sweeping mustache on his ruddy face dunking a trooper's head in the horse trough.

Spying him from the corner of his eye, the sergeant turned to face him and snapped a salute with one hand, while he held the struggling, half-submerged trooper with the other, saying, "Morning, sir. First Sergeant Daniel O'Bannon here."

"O'Bannon? Then you're my first sergeant?"

247

"Aye, sir."

Brant looked pointedly at the man the sergeant was half-drowning and asked, "And am I to assume that's one of my troopers?"

"Aye, sir. Corporal Riley. But don't you worry, sir. I'll have the little Mick sober before stable call, I promise ye."

Brant knew that every commanding officer had the option of declaring his post wet or dry. "I assume Fort Davis is a wet post, then."

"Aye, sir."

"How late does the enlisted men's bar stay open at the sutler's store?"

"I'm afraid the corporal wasn't at the sutler's store, sir. He snuck off to a nearby hog ranch."

A hog ranch was the army's term for a hastily thrown-up shack, located off the post and operated by crooked bootleggers, that offered the troopers whiskey, gambling, and the services of a few aging, degenerate women who more than likely were eaten up with venereal disease. That explained the corporal's "drinking jewelry," Brant thought, eyeing the rings made of horseshoe nails that surrounded the man's knuckles, for no trooper visited such a rough place without them. They were his only protection against the thieves and gamblers, and could rip a man's face to pieces. Brant was surprised to hear about the hog ranch, however. While the post commander couldn't touch them, a good deal of them disappeared mysteriously. "Does the Old Man know about this hog ranch?"

O'Bannon raised the trooper's head just long enough for him to get a gasp of air before answering, "Aye, sir. He found out about it the day before yesterday." The sergeant gave Brant a knowing look, then said, "It wouldn't surprise me none if it didn't catch on fire some night, with those flimsy coal oil lamps and all, ye know."

"Yes, I know," Brant answered, knowing full well what the sergeant was suggesting and thinking it would be good riddance. As O'Bannon lowered the corporal's head back into the horse trough, Brant spied the empty whiskey bottle lying on the ground. "Did you catch him with that in his hand?"

"Aye, sir, but don't you worry. I'll see that he buries it."

Brant shook his head in understanding, thinking that the corporal was going to be a very busy man once he sobered up. The hole he would have to dig to bury his bottle in would be ten feet wide and ten feet deep.

The corporal started struggling again, surfacing just long enough to sputter, "Goddammit, ye're drownin' me!"

Still standing at stiff attention, O'Bannon hissed, "Shut up, you dumb Mick," roughly shaking the trooper by the scuff of his neck like a terrier does a rag doll and sending drops of water flying everywhere, before dunking the man again, this time to mid-chest. He looked at Brant and asked, "Do you want me to bust him, sir?"

Brant squinted his eyes to see in the pre-dawn light, taking note that the corporal's chevrons were attached to his sleeves with hooks and eyes, instead of sewed on, which meant that the man had been busted and then regained his former rank so often that the hooks and eyes were simpler. It was the mark of a capable man, except when he was drunk. "I'll leave that up to you, O'Bannon, since you know the man much better than I."

"Aye, sir."

Brant looked down at the wildly thrashing trooper that the burly sergeant was holding down with one powerful hand, then said, "I think you better let him up for a breath of air now. A drowned trooper wouldn't do us any good."

With that, Brant turned and walked away.

Later, at stable call, Brant reviewed his troop for the first time. He knew they were typical troopers: tough, crude, hard-swearing, tobacco-chewing, battle-seasoned, devil may care men who devoted their paydays to whiskey, gambling, and fast women, if they could find them; but still they were the hardest riding, damnedest fighting, most courageous cavalry in the world, and he was proud to lead them. As his eyes swept down the line of men and horses, the troopers standing at attention and looking straight ahead—a fixed stare that made you swear they could see a fly a hundred miles away—Brant's gaze zeroed in on a man with one inverted stripe and several hooks sewed on his sleeves. He knew it was the corporal. Apparently, the sergeant had seen fit to bust him back to a private, and while the man was red-eyed and looked a little green around the gills, he was on his feet, just as the first sergeant had promised he would be. O'Bannon was tough, a man who controlled his men by fist and boot, and Brant was glad. Either the first sergeant or the captain had to be a first-rate son of a bitch, or you didn't have a troop worth a damn. O'Bannon playing the role just took the burden of being the bad guy from him. Now he could concentrate on leading his men, instead of disciplining them, a duty he much preferred.

He turned his attention from the troopers to their mounts, his second biggest responsibility. They were all bays, many with white-stockinged forelegs. Brant wasn't surprised at the latter. The Irish considered stockinged horses lucky and would trade off with the Dutchies for such prized mounts. But he was going to have to turn in his sorrel for a bay, Brant thought, since that was the color of horse for his new troop. He hated to give up the animal. He had become attached to him, even though such was discouraged by the cavalry, but it was hard for a man not to become fond of the animal he spent so much time with. He'd seen hardened troopers cry like a baby when their mount was killed in battle. But if he was going to have to turn in his horse, he'd see to it that he got two mustangs, even if he had to break the damn things himself. Danny wasn't going to win the next race between them.

At the thought of Danny, Brant frowned. Maybe when she found out who Elizabeth was, there wouldn't be a next race. He tried to push his personal problems from his mind and concentrate on his professional duties, but all day long, they were there at the back of his mind. That evening, when he walked to Major Duncan's house, he was determined that he would tell Danny the truth about how he had come to be engaged to Elizabeth, even if it did make him look more foolish in her eyes. Above all, he didn't want her to feel used or hurt. Where he would go from there, Brant didn't know. Danny might expect him to break the engagement, particularly in view of their intimacy and the fact that Brant knew Danny loved him, and that was something Brant couldn't do without losing the respect of his peers. A man who wasn't respected was no man at all. Dammit, he was in a hell of a mess, engaged to one woman and in love with another. Or was what he felt for Danny really love, or just infatuation? he asked himself once again. And if it was love, was he prepared to

251

offer marriage? He honestly didn't know. If Elizabeth hadn't shown up, he might have had time to sort out his feelings, to get to know Danny under more normal circumstances, to move cautiously about something as serious as marriage. But he did know this much. He couldn't wait to see Danny. Just thinking about seeing her made his spirits soar.

Julia opened the door when Brant knocked on it, then said, "Good evening. You must be Captain Holden. Colonel Shafter told us you might call. I'm Julia Duncan."

"I'm pleased to meet you, ma'am," Brant said, sweeping off his hat to reveal his thick golden hair.

Goodness, Julia thought, what a handsome young man. No wonder Danny was so impressed with him, for all Danny had talked about that day was Brant, so much so that Julia had suspected that the girl was infatuated with the man who had come to her aid. Julia couldn't blame her. Not only was he tall, rugged, and extremely good looking, but he vibrated his powerful masculinity like the sun did heat waves, the kind of man who made every woman's heart beat a little faster and a tingle of excitement run up her spine, regardless of her age.

John Duncan stepped forward, offering his hand to Brant and saying, "I'm Major Duncan. Won't you come in, Captain."

Julia took Brant's hat, saying, "Have a seat, Captain. I'll get Danny. She's just finishing up in the kitchen."

But Julia didn't have to summon Danny. She had been anxiously listening for Brant's knock on the door all afternoon. She didn't walk into the parlor; she burst into it, filling the small room with her amazing vitality and saying cheerfully, "Howdy!"

In her presence Brant felt as if he had stepped from a dark, gloomy place into the bright sunlight. A warmth spread through him, and he was acutely aware of a broad smile spreading across his face. He wondered if the Duncans saw it and thought it unseemly, but he couldn't seem to help himself. Then seeing the broad smiles appearing on the couple's face, he realized that Danny's exuberance had the same effect on them. Her cheerfulness and sunny smile were infectious. No one was immune to her enchanting charm.

"Hello, Danny," Brant replied warmly. "How are you?"

"I'm jest fine, but why don't you take a load off your feet and sit down?"

Brant sat in one cowhide chair, and Danny perched in another across from him. Then, as the Major and his wife seated themselves on the small sofa, Brant realized, with no small horror, that they intended to stay. Why, he asked himself, when he had clearly come to visit Danny? Then it occurred to him that they were chaperoning them. Brant had mixed emotions. He was glad to see that they felt protective over her, but how was he going to ask Danny how they were treating her with them sitting there, and he certainly couldn't broach the issue of Elizabeth in their presence. No, he'd have to catch Danny when she was alone sometime to make his explanations.

Hoping at least to feel out how the couple was treating Danny, Brant asked, "Well, Danny, how do you like it here at Fort Davis?"

Danny took Brant's question literally. "Well, I like the way it smells," Danny answered bluntly. "The odors of sagebrush, dust, gun oil, leather, and horse sweat makes me feel right at home, but—" Danny hesitated, not wanting the others to take offense.

"But what?" Brant prompted, fearing she had some objection to her new employers. Dammit, if they weren't treating her decently, they'd answer to him.

"But this is jest about the noisiest place I've ever seen," Danny answered. "Before the sun even came up, those dad-blasted mules started a-braying. A-hollering for their breakfast, I reckon. Then those bugles started a-blowing and that cannon went off. Jest about scared me plumb outta my skin. I thought we were a-being attacked by Injuns. Then all day, it's been bugles a-blaring and those consarn dogs a-howling, to say nothing of all the creaking wagons and the troopers a-riding their horses back and forth across the parade ground. Might not be so bad if I'd gotten any sleep last night, but those fellas a-hollering all night long kept me awake."

"What fellows hollering?" Brant asked.

"Those fellers a-hollering out what time it is, every hour on the hour. Dad-blast it, who cares what time it is in the middle of the night, and it seems to me, if all's well, they oughta kept their mouths shut and let a body sleep. Save their a-hollering fer when something's wrong. I got up more tired this morning than I was when I went to bed."

Julia laughed, saying, "You're not the first visitor I've heard complain about the night watch. I guess we army people are used to it. As a matter of fact, I find it reassuring to wake up at night and hear them. I listen until the last man at the last sentry post calls out, then go back to sleep, feeling safe and contented at knowing that all's well with our little world."

Danny wondered how Julia had even gotten to sleep in

the first place. She was used to being out on the wide open prairie, where the only night sounds were the gentle sigh of the wind, the cheep of crickets, or an occasional low of a cow and the mournful howl of the coyote calling to its mate. Those were soothing sounds that lulled her to sleep, natural sounds and not man-made. "Well, I reckon it's like you said, it's all what you're used to a-hearing," Danny conceded. "But other than all those consarn noises, I like it here jest fine, and the Major and Miz Duncan have been real nice to me. They made me feel so at home that I don't even feel like a servant," Danny informed Brant, telling what he had been wanting to know in the first place.

Brant shot the couple a grateful look and answered, "I'm glad to hear that."

The couple engaged Brant in a conversation about the various posts they had lived at, while Danny drank in the sight of Brant hungrily. She didn't mind if she didn't have anything to add, not as long as she could sit and gaze at him, but when he rose, saying, "I'd better be going," she felt a keen disappointment.

Brant felt just as disappointed. He would have asked her to take a walk with him, except he knew the couple would think it strange. He was supposed to be following through with the responsibility that he had assumed when he had found Danny, not courting her.

"When am I gonna see you again?" Danny asked, when they reached the door.

Acutely aware of the couple's eyes on him, Brant answered evasively, "Oh, I imagine we'll see each other every now and then here on the post."

"You ain't gonna come a-calling again?" Danny asked in disappointment.

Brant wanted to, desperately, but he couldn't think of a likely excuse. He had already assured himself that Danny was in good hands, and if the couple felt protective enough to chaperone Danny, they surely wouldn't allow an engaged man to visit her.

Julia had no idea what thoughts were running through Brant's head. She assumed he looked so miserable because he was being put in an awkward position by a young girl who clearly idolized him. "Feel free to visit anytime," she told Brant, thinking that would give him the freedom of choosing if he wanted to or not, and sooth Danny's disappointment at the same time.

"Thank you, Mrs. Duncan, and good night," Brant answered politely, then said to Danny, "Good night."

"'Night," Danny answered, feeling immensely relieved by Julia's invitation to Brant. She watched him until he disappeared in the night, then shut the door and announced to Julia and John, "Well, I reckon I'd better go finish the dishes."

A little later, Julia wondered what was taking Danny so long in the kitchen. She walked to the small room at the back of the house and found her washing out her clothes for the next day.

Danny looked up from what she was doing, saying, "I plumb fergot to wash these out this morning. I hope they dry overnight."

"Wouldn't it be easier to buy some more clothes? You're going to get awfully tired of having to do this every day."

"I reckon it would be easier," Danny admitted, "and I shore could afford it, with all the money you're a-paying me, but where am I gonna find shirts and duckins around here? I didn't see none at that commissary we went to yesterday."

"No, the commissary only sells food, but the post store carries civilian clothing, what with all the men working for the contractors here at the fort and the wagon trains passing through on their way west. I'm sure you could find something there to fit you."

Danny was pleased at the information Julia gave her. "Then maybe at the end of the month, when I git paid, I'll jest do that."

"There's no reason to wait until then, Danny. I can have them charged to our account and just deduct it from your first month's salary. If you like, we could walk over there Saturday afternoon. I would suggest tomorrow, but a wagon train arrived this afternoon, and I'm afraid the store will be much too crowded."

"Well, I shore appreciate that, Miz Duncan. That's mighty wide of you."

"You're quite welcome, Danny, and I wish you would call me Julia."

Danny frowned, then said, "I didn't know cooks called the people that hired them by their first names."

Ordinarily they didn't, Julia thought, but Danny didn't seem like a servant to her. She was becoming quite fond of the lively girl. "Well, it isn't usual for a servant to call the lady of the house by her first name," Julia admitted, "but I'd still like for you to call me Julia. I think it will make for a much more relaxed relationship between us."

"I'm shore glad you said that," Danny admitted. "You don't seem like someone I jest work fer. You seem more like a friend. But that don't mean I won't do my job, like I'm supposed to," Danny added quickly, not wanting Julia to think she was going to take advantage at her offer of friendship.

Julia followed Danny to the back door and watched as she hung the dripping wet clothes on the line that sat in the small back yard. Catching sight of something from the corner of her eye, Danny glanced up and saw the fire burning on the top of a low, flat mountain to the south of the fort. "What's that fire a-doing up there?" she asked.

Julia looked up at the glowing fire and smiled sadly, then said, "That's Dolores's fire."

"Who's she?"

"A beautiful, doe-eyed Mexican girl from Chihuahua. Her sweetheart, a goatherder, used to tend his flock a few miles away from town. Sometimes, he'd be gone for days at a time. They agreed to light signal fires each night as an assurance of their love and fidelity. She built her fire up there, and Jose built his on some peak near his flock. They were preparing for their marriage, the little adobe house they were to live in already built, and Dolores having put the last stitch in her wedding gown, when Jose was attacked by Apaches and killed. But she still goes up there and lights her fire every Thursday night, to commune with her dead lover. For years, in all kinds of weather, she has climbed that mountain with her faggots over her shoulder and kept her fire burning brightly for hours. I don't think I've ever seen such a touching testimony of everlasting love."

Had Julia told Danny the story a month before, she would have thought the girl silly to be lighting a signal fire for someone who was dead and gone. But Danny had come to know the deep love a woman could feel for a man,

258

and the sad, romantic tale brought tears to her eyes. She gazed at the fire burning brightly under an ebony sky filled with glittering stars, and her heart went out to Dolores in perfect understanding. If anything ever happened to Brant, she'd never stop loving him either. Her love was as much a part of her now as her heart and soul, and nothing, not even death, could change it.

Chapter 15

On Saturday afternoon, Danny and Julia walked to the post store to buy Danny's new clothes. Danny spied two buildings in the distance and asked, "Which one is the sutler's store?"

"The larger one with the big sign that reads Abbott and Davis on it," Julia answered, then frowned, remembering that Danny couldn't read. She turned her head to see Danny staring at the sign intently. Why, she's memorizing the words, Julia realized. A sudden thought occurred to her. "Danny, would you like for me to teach you to read, as well as write your name?"

Danny's black eyes sparkled with excitement. "I shore would."

"Well, I think that can be arranged. At least, enough so that you could read simple words. We have a library on the post that all the officers and their families contribute to. There ought to be a primary reader or two there, with all these children around. We'll walk over on Monday and see what we can find."

"Are you shore it won't be too much trouble?" Danny asked.

"Gracious, no. I taught my son, you know, until he was old enough to go back East to school."

"You've got a son?" Danny asked in surprise.

"Indeed I do, and he's a fine young man," Julia said proudly. "He's at West Point right now."

"Where's that?"

"Back East, and it's the best military school in the States. Why, half of the officers in the cavalry graduated from there."

"Then he's going to be a soldier too?"

"Yes. It's very rare for an army brat, as we call our children, not to follow in the footsteps of their fathers. Even the girls marry military men almost without exception. Our way of life is so firmly ingrained in us that we feel out of place in civilian life."

"Do you have any more young'uns?"

A sad expression came over Julia's face. "There was a daughter, but she died of cholera when she was ten."

"I'm shore sorry to hear that," Danny said with all sincerity.

Julia glanced over at the girl, wondering if that was why she had become so attached to Danny. Her feelings for the girl seemed to be growing stronger than just those of friendship. Was she beginning to think of her in terms of the daughter she had lost? Anne had been a tomboy too. Of course, she had never allowed her to wear men's clothing, for that simply wasn't done, even on an army post, but Anne had been just as sturdy and independent, as fine a rider and schooled in the use of fire arms as Danny, and if truth be known, even rougher talking.

261

Having grown up around the troopers, both she and her brother had known and freely used every profane, four-letter Anglo-Saxon word in existence, much to Julia's horror and utter exasperation. Of course, when she had reached high school age, Anne would have been sent back East to be educated in the ways of a lady, but Julia couldn't picture her in that role. Her son might be a gentleman now, but Anne would always remain a tomboy in Julia's memory, wild, full of life, independent to the point of exasperation, and totally lovable.

"What's that other store?" Danny asked, breaking into Julia's thoughts.

"It's another merchant store that belongs to Patrick Murphy. It's frequented mostly by single men, soldiers, hunters, trail drivers, and teamsters. I understand they meet there to drink and relate their stories of daring and bravery. There's yet another general store just a step away from the south walls of the post, owned by another Murphy. He and his wife are very social-minded. There's hardly an evening that goes by that they don't have a few of the officers and their wives over for dinner, followed by cards or a musical evening. John and I attend one of their social gatherings at least once a month."

As they stepped into the post store, Danny looked around her in amazement. She had never seen such a large store, or such a wide variety of articles for sale. There seemed to be everything conceivable in the world, from jewelry to firearms and evening gowns to wagon parts. As they passed a door at one side of the building, Danny peeked in, seeing a large room with a bar, a billiard table, and several tables with chairs. There were even a few overstuffed chairs, around which ragged, yellowed newspapers and magazines were laying.

"That's the enlisted men and civilians' club," Julia informed her.

"What's those wheelbarrows by the bar fer?" Danny asked with a puzzled frown on her face.

"They're provided so that those men too drunk to walk can be returned to the barracks by their friends," Julia answered with a little laugh.

"Well, that's mighty wide of 'em," Danny remarked.

"Yes, the post store owners usually bend over backwards to be accommodating. They don't want to lose their contract with the army. They serve as a local banker and post master, as well as operate an officer's club. Of course, it's much more attractive."

Danny remembered Brant telling her that he planned on taking his meals at the officer's club. It was a little late for dinner, but he might be here. "Where's the officer's club?" she asked, looking around her anxiously in hopes of getting a quick glance at him, for she had seen nothing of Brant since his visit.

"It's on the other side of the store."

Danny stood on her tiptoes and craned her neck to see, but to her disappointment, the only door on that side of the building was firmly closed.

Thinking that Danny was looking for the men's clothing, Julia said, "I think we'll find what you're looking for over there by the back wall. At least, the last time I was in here to just browse around, that's where I saw the shirts and pants."

When they reached the men's department, Danny had never seen such huge stacks of pants and shirts, or so many tables of them. As she shuffled through the stacks, pulling out shirt after shirt that caught her eye, Julia smiled in amusement. While Danny didn't care a fig for

263

women's clothing, she was just as attracted to pretty colors and patterns as any other female, and just as indecisive over her final selections. Seeing that Danny was going to take a while, Julia said, "While you're doing your shopping, I think I'll walk over to the dry goods section to pick up a package of needles. It's highway robbery to have to pay a dollar for something that would cost ten cents back East, but I really have no choice. I broke my last needle this morning."

"We need some ginger, too," Danny informed her. "I was a-looking over the spices this morning and couldn't find none. Lessen you want to fergit about that ginger-bread I was gonna bake tomorrow."

"Forget about it? Gracious, no! John has been looking forward to it. He said he hasn't had gingerbread since he was a boy. I never realized that he was so fond of it, or I would have learned to bake it myself. Yes, I'll pick up some ginger, too, and meet you at the counter."

Julia was at the counter before Danny, even though she had stopped to browse a time or two. She looked about, but could see no sign of Danny at the back of the store. Then turning she saw her coming from the women's department with several pairs of drawers laying on top of her other selections that she had thrown over one arm, her black eyes sparkling with excitement. Julia laughed to herself, thinking how out of place the lacy drawers looked against the men's clothing, but she was relieved that Danny had thought to buy more. Hopefully she'd throw away that homemade pair with those crude words printed across them. Julia had never been so mortified in her life as when she had found those drawers hanging on her clothesline in full view of the entire fort and realized what several troopers passing by were snickering at. As soon as the men were out of sight, Julia had snatched them off the line before her neighbors could see them. She knew Danny was totally innocent, had no idea how crude the words seemed on such an intimate garment, but she was determined to protect her from any more gossip that was going around the post about her.

"Did you find everything you need?" Julia asked Danny as she stepped up to her.

"Yep. Got me some new socks, too. The ones I've got have more holes in them than a tin can someone's been a-using fer target practice."

As Danny laid her new clothing on the counter, Julia said to the man standing behind it, "Just put everything on the Major's account, Mr. Abbott."

"Yes, ma'am."

At the sudden sound of loud curses, followed by the sounds of what was obviously a fistfight coming from the enlisted men's club, Julia glanced toward the club and said, "My gracious! What's going on in there, Mr. Abbott? It sounds like a brawl."

"No, ma'am, it's not a brawl," the storekeeper answered with a pleasant smile, acting as if he didn't even hear the sound of glass breaking that came from the room. "Some troopers came in while you were shopping. One was just promoted to a corporal."

Julia laughed, saying, "Oh, that explains it. I should have guessed."

Danny was acutely conscious of the grunts and groans coming from the bar. She jumped at the loud sound of a chair being broken over someone's head, then asked, "Guessed what?"

"It's army custom, when a trooper is promoted, that he has to whip any man who challenges him to a fistfight," Julia explained. "If he can't prove he's tougher than them, he's not worthy of the promotion."

Julia turned back to the counter, and she and the storekeeper calmly resumed their business, behaving as if they were totally unaware of the violent noises coming from the bar. Danny jumped as a trooper came flying through the door to land flat on his back with a loud crash. She knew the man had to be the newly promoted corporal, for the bright chevron on each sleeve was conspicuous against the other, faded-out stripe. She watched as he sat up and shook his head, his nose dripping blood all over his shirt, then struggled to his feet. Lowering his head like an enraged bull, he let out a bellow that shook the walls and charged back into the barroom.

Danny glanced at Julia and the storekeeper to see their reaction and saw that they were engrossed in a pleasant conversation about the weather. Danny could see the storekeeper not showing any particular concern—he was probably used to seeing bloody fistfights—but she couldn't understand Julia not being in the least perturbed. She was kindness and gentleness, a lady to the bone, someone Danny would expect to abhor violence of any kind. Danny found the fight very distressing. Why, that poor corporal was probably being beaten to a bloody pulp, and no one even cared. Well, dad-blasted, if the storekeeper or Julia wasn't going to stop it, she sure was. She'd go in there and fire a couple of warning shots, before they killed that poor trooper.

Danny was just fixing to follow through with her decision when a sudden quiet fell over the room next door. Julia and the storekeeper stopped talking in midsentence and turned their attention to the barroom door, waiting anxiously to see what the outcome of the fight had been. A moment later, the battered corporal staggered from the room, his uniform tattered and ripped in many places. One eye was swollen shut and already turning blue; his bloody nose sat peculiarly to one side of his face, and there were scrapes and contusions all over him, but he was grinning broadly, showing several missing teeth.

"Mr. Abbott, me friends and I will be havin' a bottle of that coffin varnish ye be sellin' now," the corporal announced in a boisterous voice, swaying dangerously from side to side.

"Of course, Corporal," the storekeeper answered, "and congratulations on your promotion."

"Thank ye," the corporal replied, then as a glazed look came over his eyes, pitched forward to land flat on his face on the floor, where he lay perfectly still.

"Well, it looks like he'll keep his promotion," the storekeeper commented to Julia with a big smile.

"Yes, indeed," Julia answered with a smile, handing Danny's packages to her and slipping the jar of ginger and package of needles into her reticule.

As Julia walked away, she said over her shoulder, "Good day, Mr. Abbott."

"Good day, Miz Duncan. Be careful not to trip over the corporal there."

"I will," Julia answered, lifting her skirt with one hand and daintily stepping over the unconscious man sprawled on the floor.

Danny followed, shaking her head in disbelief and thinking that the army sure had some peculiar customs.

As they walked towards the parade ground, several

women on horseback galloped passed them. Danny came to a dead halt, then said in alarm, "Why those dad-blasted horses are a-running away with 'em."

Julia shot a quick glance at the officer's wives, then asked, "What makes you think that?"

"Why, they ain't even in the saddle good. They jest got one foot in a stirrup."

Julia laughed, then said, "No, Danny, they're riding sidesaddle. No lady would ride a horse astride."

"You mean they're a-riding that way on purpose?" Danny asked in disbelief.

"Yes."

"How in tarnation do they keep from a-falling off?"

"They're riding a special saddle that's designed for ladies. It has a large horn in the front that they wrap their knee around to support them."

It sounded awfully uncomfortable to Danny, and not in the least bit safe. Hellfire, if you weren't supposed to sit flat on a horse's back, how come God made them with such broad ones and people with legs long enough to go around them? "Do you ride one of those silly things?" she asked Julia, her voice tinged with scorn.

"Yes, I do," Julia admitted freely. "If I rode astride in a dress, my lower limbs would show, and a lady never allows so much as her ankle to show in public."

"You could wear duckins, like I do," Danny pointed out.

"I'm afraid not, Danny. It just isn't done."

Danny frowned. Julia seemed so sensible in so many ways, and in others, she was just as silly as the other ladies. She sure hoped Julia didn't break her fool neck. She was becoming downright fond of the older woman. The admission came somewhat as a surprise to Danny.

268

She never thought she'd see the day when she'd like a sissy. But Julia didn't seem weak, despite her gentle ways and soft speech and frail appearance. She had a quiet strength about her. For the first time in her life, Danny wondered what her mother had been like. Had she been gentle, kind, and soft spoken? Oh, she knew her mother wouldn't have been a lady like Julia. They were country folk, hard-working people who didn't have time for all those fancy manners. But still, she hoped her mother had had some of Julia's qualities.

As they rounded the guardhouse, they suddenly came face to face with Brant. Danny stared at him, thinking he looked absolutely magnificent in his uniform. Why, he was even wearing a saber and had a red sash over his shoulder and across his broad chest.

"Hello, Danny," Brant said warmly, quickly drinking in the sight of her, before he turned to Julia and tipped his hat, saying, "Good day, ma'am."

"Good day, Captain," Julia answered, the sight of his golden hair shining in the sunlight momentarily taking her breath away.

As Danny opened her mouth, a trooper from across the parade ground called to Brant. "Excuse me, but I have to go," Brant said, cutting across Danny's words, then turned and rushed away.

Seeing the hurt expression on Danny's face, Julia said, "Captain Holden didn't mean to appear rude, my dear. He's officer of the day and a very busy man. He really doesn't have time to stop and say anything but hello. You see, until sunup tomorrow, he's the local chief of police, and Saturdays are by far the worst day to pull that duty. Of course, I suspect Colonel Shafter deliberately picked today for that reason, to see if the young man can cut the

mustard, as we army people say. He'll have to check each
sentry post at least once during each relief, day and night,
between settling any quarrels or disturbances, and by the
time this day is over, the captain will know every nook
and cranny on this post. He'll hardly have time for a
quick meal, and he'll have to sleep in a little room in the
guardhouse, not that he'll get much sleep. John dreads it
when he has to be officer of the day. He comes home
looking more exhausted than when he's been out on
patrol for weeks."

Danny was vastly relieved to hear Julia's explanation.
Brant's abrupt departure had hurt her. Combined with
his failure to stop by the day before, she had feared he
was deliberately avoiding her. Then, as Julia's words
sunk in and she realized that he wouldn't be visiting that
evening either, she was filled with a keen disappointment. Yes, it was just as she had thought it was going to
be. She wasn't going to get to see Brant very often. Their
time together on their trip to Fort Davis had been special.

The next day was Sunday, the day the post commander
reviewed his troops, and a full dress parade took place.
Everyone on the post attended, and the parade ground
was surrounded by civilians and the families of the men.
Danny watched the proceedings wide-eyed, impressed
with the pomp and pageantry, and thrilling to the rousing
marches the regimental band was playing, for she had
never heard a band before. She ignored the infantrymen
marching past her and Julia, her full attention on the
mounted men behind them, thinking they all looked very
handsome in their blue dress uniforms and parade
helmets, especially the officers with their snow-white
gloves and the gold stripes on their coat sleeves and the
epaulets on their shoulders glittering in the sunlight.

270

Even the horses were spruced up for the occasion, their freshly curried coats gleaming as they trotted smartly along.

It was an exciting experience, standards snapping in the wind, music playing, sabers rattling, saddles creaking, harnesses jingling, and bright colors everywhere. Then she spied Brant riding at the head of his troop. Despite the lines of fatigue etched on his face from his twenty-four-hour ordeal as officer of the day, he sat ramrod straight in his saddle, his startling blue eyes staring straight ahead, and Danny thought he looked absolutely magnificent in his finely tailored coat that fit his impressive shoulders and broad chest to a tee and his skin-tight pants that outlined his muscular thighs. She stared at him unabashed, thinking he was the most beautiful creature on earth.

Julia was very aware of Danny's admiring stare. She wished the child wouldn't be quite so obvious in her adoration. Then, as Julia glanced around her, she noticed that Danny wasn't the only woman staring at Brant in awe. Quite a few of the officer's wives were too. Yes, he was one of those rare men that stood out even in a crowd, a man who possessed such a powerful male magnetism that he made every woman present acutely conscious that he was male and they were female.

Spying a beautiful, dark-haired, young woman standing next to Mrs. Shafter, Julia noted that she, too, was staring at the young captain, her look absolutely ravenous. Julia knew she had to be a visitor, for she had never seen the young woman before. Was she single? If so, Julia feared Danny was going to have some stiff competition. In fact, Julia seriously doubted that rough, wild, tomboyish Danny could compete for the captain's attentions against the beauty. Why, even from this distance, and despite her almost embarrassing stare, she reeked of good breeding and money. Julia's heart went out to Danny. She feared the little tomboy was going to be in for a big disappointment.

The next day, Danny insisted upon helping Julia with her washing, even though Julia had reminded her that she'd been hired as a cook, and not as a servant. For hours, the two women worked in the hot sun, stirring the laundry in a big pot over a blazing fire, then rinsing and wringing it out, before hanging it on the lines that stretched across the tiny back yard.

Standing there, soaking wet, Julia looked at the other women still laboring over their pots, then laughed and said, "Well, I do believe I got my laundry out before any one else, for a change. Why, I even beat Mrs. Wagner, and I think that's something that's never been done before. Thank you, Danny, for your help."

There was no doubt in Danny's mind which of the women was Mrs. Wagner. She was glaring at Julia with something akin to fury. "You're welcome," Danny answered, "but how come everyone decided to wash today?"

Julia laughed and answered, "It wasn't a coincidence. Monday is always wash day in the army, Danny, on every post in the country, regardless of the weather, or what might be going on, Why, I do believe we could be under attack and would still do our washing religiously, with arrows flying all around us. It's an ironclad rule that no army wife would dream of breaking. As I said, in some ways, we're even more regimental than our husbands."

As the two walked up the back steps, Julia confided with a mischievous twinkle in her eyes, "You know, I've often been tempted to wash on Tuesdays, just to see the furor it would create, but I've never had the courage to follow through."

"Well, consarn it, why not? Seems to me you oughta be able to wash when you danged well want to."

"I was always afraid some terrible catastrophe would occur. I know it sounds silly, but I could no more do that than deliberately break one of the Lord's commandments."

Danny shook her head, once again thinking that army people sure had some peculiar customs.

That afternoon, while Julia was resting in her bedroom, Danny walked to the stables to feed and exercise her horse. Having finished the chore, her attention was drawn to a corral a short distance away that was surrounded by troopers yelling and cheering. Curious to see what all the excitement was about, she walked over and, through a crack between two men, saw several troopers wrestling a mustang down to the ground. Then they blindfolded the animal, roughly pried a bit into its mouth, saddled the horse and pulled the cinch until the poor animal's eyes almost popped out. As a trooper, carrying a stick big enough to fell a giant and wearing rowels the size of a tin plate on his spurs, jumped in the saddle and the blindfold was torn away, Danny pushed her way through the two men and yelled in outrage, "You dad-blasted fools, that ain't no way to break a mustang!"

As if to prove her words, the mustang sunfished and the trooper on his back went flying through the air to bite the dust.

A beefy, red-headed first sergeant, leaning on the rails, turned to Danny with a furious expression on his face. Then, seeing it was a girl dressed in men's clothing, he gaped at her for a moment before asking, "Who in the hell are ye?"

"I'm Danny, that's who!" Danny spat angrily. "And that ain't no way to break a mustang."

"Yeah, who says so?" Sergeant O'Bannon threw back with a sneer.

"I say so! There ain't no need to be that cruel. It only makes those mustangs madder and more determined to throw you."

The sergeant's eyes narrowed. "Now you look here, lass. We're Irishmen, and we know more about horses and breaking wild ones than anyone in the cavalry. Are ye trying to tell us our business?"

"You're darn tooting I am! You dad-blasted troopers don't know nothing about a-breaking wild horses. I know, 'cause I'm the best gol-durn broncobuster in Texas."

Several of the troopers standing behind Danny laughed outright at her outrageous boast, infuriating Danny all the more. She whirled on them, her black eyes shooting sparks. "You fellers think I'm a-telling you a sandy? Well, I'll jest show you!"

As Danny bent to climb through the rails, O'Bannon caught her arm, saying in an alarmed voice, "Here, now, lass, ye can't be going in there. 'Tis too dangerous. No one has ever stayed on that bastard's back."

Danny snorted in disgust and said, "Well, I shore ain't surprised, the way you gol-durn fools have been a-going at it. I'd buck you clear from hell to breakfast, too, if you put one those big rowels in me. It's a wonder that poor horse has any skin left on him."

With that, Danny jerked her arm away and ducked under the railing, saying to the astonished troopers standing in the corral, "Move back, fellers. I'm gonna show you the right way to break a mustang."

O'Bannon was right behind her, again catching her arm and saying, "Didn't ye hear what I said? He's dangerous!"

Danny looked him directly in the eye and asked, "Are you afraid I can break him? Is that why you don't want me a-riding him?"

"Jesus, Mary, and Joseph!" O'Bannon exploded. "Are ye deaf? He's dangerous, I'm a-tellin' ye."

"He ain't no more dangerous than any mustang is." Danny looked down at the hand curled around her arm and said, "Now, you let go of my arm, mister, 'fore I take offense at it. Then I'd have to pull my gun on you."

"Ye wouldn't?" the dumbfounded Irishman asked.

"I shore would," Danny drawled, her free hand dropping over the butt of her gun. "And I feel it's only fair to warn you that I'm a dead shot. I'm a-riding that mustang, and that's that. Ain't no one here gonna stop me."

Stunned by her threat and the determined glint in her eyes, O'Bannon dropped his hand and stepped back. Keeping her hand on her gun, Danny turned and walked up to the horse. As he shied away nervously, Danny crooned, "Easy, boy, easy. I ain't gonna hurt you. Here," she said raising her hand to his nostrils, "take a sniff of me."

The troopers held their breaths for fear the mustang would bite Danny's hand, then stared in amazement when the animal took a wary sniff.

"See, I don't smell near as bad as they do, do I?" Danny said with a smug smile. "And I ain't gonna mistreat you either."

For a moment, Danny gently stroked the mustang's

275

neck, crooning to the animal all the while. When she stepped to its side, it moved away, anticipating her trying to mount. "No, boy, don't go a-gitting goosey with me. I'm jest gonna take off this saddle."

Danny reached down and uncinched the saddle. As it slid from the horse's back, the animal looked down at it and then at Danny, a baffled expression on his face.

"I thought you said you was gonna ride him?" O'Bannon said from the rail where he had been watching Danny with a mixture of resentment and grudging admiration.

"I am. Mustangs don't like those heavy saddles on their back 'fore they're broke. That's why they keep a-bucking even after they've thrown you."

"Are ye saying ye're gonna ride him bareback?" someone in the crowd asked in disbelief.

"Shore am."

Then, before even the men, or the horse realized what she was up to, Danny flipped the reins over the horse's head and sprang on his back. As her weight came down on him, the horse bucked, but Danny had wrapped her legs around him in a tight vise. He bucked, twisted, and turned, kicked up his heels, then reared, bowed out his back, jumped straight up in the air, and came down on all four hooves, jarring Danny's bones and knocking the breath from her, but she hung on with the tenacity of a bulldog. The troopers watching went wild with excitement as the little mustang went through a series of frenzied gyrations in a futile effort to throw Danny from his back, cheering and hollering encouragement.

Brant heard them from where he was standing by the stables and talking to the quartermaster about finding him a second bay mustang. He turned and faced the corral, asking, "What's going on over there?"

"From all the commotion, I'd guess they've finally found someone who could stay on that mustang they've been having so much trouble trying to break. Come on, Captain. This should be a ride worth seeing."

By the time Brant and the quartermaster reached the corral, the troopers' excitement had reached a state of frenzy. They were jumping up and down, clapping one another on the back, and hollering so loud that the noise was deafening, and they were crowded so tightly around the corral that it was all Brant could do to shoulder two men aside so that he could see what was going on. Then, spying Danny on top of the crazed horse, he froze with fear, watching with horror through the cloud of dust as the sweaty mustang bucked and whirled and twisted dizzily, snorting and shaking his head in fury.

"Well, I'll be damned," the quartermaster muttered. "It's a girl!"

"Aye, sir," the trooper next to him said, his face flushed with excitement, "and I ain't never seen anyone who can ride like she does. Why, he's been a turning and whirling like a regular tornado, and she's stuck him like she'd glued there."

"He's tiring!" another trooper called out. "Goddammit, she's gonna do it! That little lass is gonna break him, just like she said she would."

It didn't look to Brant like the mustang was tiring. He was seven hundred pounds of animal fury, and Brant was terrified. But Brant hadn't seen the mustang in the beginning. The horse tried a few more teeth-rattling bucks, then tried to shake Danny off his back by kicking up his heels again, and suddenly, without warning, stood perfectly still with his head hanging, his chest heaving, and his muscles trembling.

Danny's head was still whirling dizzily and every bone in her body ached, but she knew she had won the battle. She smiled, savoring her victory for a moment, then leaned forward and stroked the trembling animal's sweat-slick neck and said softly, "It's all right, boy. There ain't no reason for you to feel ashamed. You put up the best dad-blasted battle I ever fought. You're gonna make some lucky trooper a fine mount. Wish I could keep you myself, but I got all I can do to take care of one horse right now. Now, I want to see you lift up that purty head of yers. Be as proud of yerself as I am of you."

As if he understood her words, the mustang raised his head and whinnied. While the Irish troopers watching were far from professionals, each and every one knew that Danny had broken the horse, but not his proud spirit. A ringing cheer rang out, bouncing from mountaintop to mountaintop, a tribute to the courage and determination of both the girl and the horse.

For a moment Brant was too stunned to react. Then, as a tremendous wave of relief washed over him, he was too weak to even move his legs. Then a slow fury filled him. He bent and slipped through the rails.

But it was Sergeant O'Bannon who reached Danny first, just as she was sliding from the mustang's back. Danny grinned at him and boasted, "I told you I was the best dad-blasted broncobuster in Texas."

"Aye, I'll have to admit ye did a fine job," he said grudgingly, then seeing Brant coming down on them, his face looking like a thundercloud, O'Bannon muttered,

"Jesus, Mary, and Joseph! Here comes the shoulder straps. Now I'm in for it."

O'Bannon snapped a salute, which Brant totally ignored. "What's the meaning of this, O'Bannon? What idiot let this girl in this corral?"

O'Bannon's ruddy face turned two shades redder at being called an idiot by his commanding officer. "I didn't let her in, sir. I tried to stop her, but—"

"Goddammit, she could have been killed!" Brant roared, making both the Irishman and Danny wince and every trooper around make a beeline for their barracks for fear the captain's anger would spill over on them.

"I know, sir. I told her 'twas too dangerous, but she insisted she could break the mustang. Believe me, sir, I tried to stop her."

"Are you standing there and telling me that you can control a troop of tough, hardened troopers, but you can't stop one small girl from satisfying some silly whim?"

"Now you jest back up there!" Danny said in an angry voice. "That wasn't no silly whim. I—"

"I'm not talking to you!" Brant said in a hard voice, cutting across Danny's words and stunning her with his furious glare. "I'm talking to the sergeant. He was in charge here. Stopping you was his responsibility."

At that moment, O'Bannon fervently wished he had never laid eyes on Danny. "Aye, sir, 'twas me fault, but, would ye believe it, sir? She threatened to pull a gun on me if I tried to stop her. And sir, she wasn't bluffing. I'd swear to that on me mother's grave."

That sounded just like Danny, Brant thought, feeling almost sorry for the flustered sergeant. He knew only too well that once Danny set her mind to something, nothing or no one was going to stop her. He struggled to calm himself, then said, "Very well, O'Bannon. But let me warn you. If this ever happens again, I'll personally see to it that the non-com officer present rots in the guardhouse, after I've beaten him to a bloody pulp. Do I make myself clear?"

O'Bannon didn't doubt Brant's threat for one minute, or his ability to follow through with it. The look on the captain's face when he walked up had been absolutely murderous, sending a tingle of fear up the tough sergeant's spine. "Aye, sir, very clear. And I'll spread the word around. She won't get anywhere near these corrals again. But, sir, even at the risk of losing me stripes, there's something I gotta say. I've always prided meself on being a fair man."

"What's that?"

O'Bannon's blue eyes glittered with remembered excitement as he answered, "I've never seen such a magnificent ride in me life. I'll remember it to me dying day."

Brant was a man who prided himself on his fairness, too, but he wished O'Bannon hadn't complimented Danny. She was wild and unpredictable enough without someone encouraging her, taking unnecessary risks that endangered her life and scaring the living hell out of him. Brant nodded curtly in recognition of the sergeant's tribute, then said, "You're dismissed, O'Bannon."

O'Bannon shot Brant a grateful look, saluted, and turned, walking rapidly away across the corral and thinking that he was lucky to have survived the ordeal in one piece, to say nothing of still retaining his chevrons.

Brant turned to face Danny and saw she was livid with

anger. "I'm sorry that I snapped at you earlier, but I won't tolerate you interrupting when I'm disciplining one of my troopers."

"Well, I ain't one of your troopers, and you ain't gonna tell me what I can and can't do. I told you that the first day I met you."

"Danny, when it comes to your safety, I can't stand back. Riding that mustang was too dangerous!"

"You're always a-telling me things are too dangerous, and I'm a-gitting sick and tired of a-hearing it! I know what I can and can't do—and I don't do nothing on a whim! They was about to kill that poor horse, a-trying to break him. I wasn't gonna stand back and watch that. I knew I could do it without a-hurting him. I don't care how mad it makes you, I ain't gonna stand 'round and watch some animal suffer when it ain't necessary."

Danny whirled and walked angrily away. Brant stared at her back and thought in despair, But I can't stand by and watch you get hurt, either. Why can't you understand that?

It wasn't until Danny was almost out of sight that Brant realized he'd had his chance to be alone with her and lost it. Maybe it was just as well, he consoled himself. As angry as she was, this wouldn't have been a good time to try to explain his engagement to Elizabeth. He just hoped, by the next time he ran into her, she would have gotten over her anger. Damn, she had his guts tied in knots again.

Chapter 16

By the next morning, Danny had forgiven Brant. No matter what he did, she couldn't stay mad at him. Besides, she didn't want to hold her anger. Being angry at Brant made her feel absolutely miserable.

After the breakfast dishes were washed, she and Julia sat at the kitchen table with a primary reader spread out before them. Danny was a little disappointed to find out that she was going to have to learn letters before words, but as the lesson progressed, she became fascinated with the alphabet, amazed at how different each letter looked. Why, there were nine of them in her name alone.

After dinner, Danny went to her room and practiced printing her name, laboriously copying the letters Julia had written out for her. It sure wasn't as easy as it looked, she thought. Her letters came out looking more like hen's scratches. She sure wished she could print as neat and straight as Julia. And she couldn't hardly wait to learn to write and make all those pretty curlicues.

When her hand began to get cramped, Danny put the slate and chalk aside. She was laying on her cot and staring out into space, daydreaming about Brant, when Julia knocked softly on the door, then peeked in, saying, "I hope I didn't wake you."

"Shucks, I ain't been a-sleeping," Danny answered, sitting up. "I ain't never napped in the daytime. Not even when I was knee-high to a grasshopper."

"I thought I would go for a walk over to the old pump house. Would you like to go along?"

"Might as well. If I lay here much longer a-doing nothing, the spiders are gonna start a-spinning cobwebs on me."

Julia glanced at a cobweb hanging from the ceiling in one corner and wryly thought Danny's words probably weren't too far from the truth. It seemed the spiders could spin their webs faster than she could brush them down. "Don't forget to bring your gun. We'll be going off the post."

"Shucks, I don't ever go no place without my gun. I'd feel downright naked without it." Danny glanced down at the canvas bag laying at the foot of her bed. "Do you mind if I bring Charlie along? He ain't been outside to rustle up any grub today."

"No, I don't mind, but the grass is rather tall in some places. You might lose sight of him."

"That don't make no never mind, even if he decides to play a game of hide-and-seek with me. If he ain't back by the time he's supposed to be, I jest go a-looking fer him. I always found him, too, 'cept for that time he hid in Brant's saddlebags. I never thought to look there."

"Then who found him?"

"Brant did, but I don't think he was too happy about Charlie a-sneaking in there. He tolerates Charlie, but I don't think he's any too fond of him."

Julia chuckled, thinking there weren't too many people who could become fond of a snake.

As they walked across the parade ground a few moments later, Danny spied Brant and a young woman strolling along the gravel walk that sat before the first row of officers' homes. She started to wave, then frowned in disappointment when the couple turned at the small walk that led to the colonel's home and put their backs to her. "Dad-blasted, I shore do wish I could meet her."

"Who?"

"That lady who was a-walking with Brant. She's his kinfolk, you know, come to visit him. She shore is purty. I reckon good looks just run in that family."

"Yes, she is a very beautiful girl," Julia admitted, surprised to learn that the young woman was a relative of the captain's. The way she had stared at him that day at the parade, and the way she was possessively clutching his arm right now, didn't seem at all like the way a relative would behave, unless she was a distant cousin. If that were true, she was just as much a threat to Danny as if she were no kin at all.

They walked from the post, and between it and Limpia creek, and at the foot of a towering mountain, they stopped at a lovely little spot that was shaded by a few cottonwood trees. Danny looked at the sparkling creek in the distance, the lush green grass, and the rustling leaves of the trees overhead and said, "This shore is a purty place."

"Yes, it is," Julia agreed. "That's why I come here ever so often, even though it is quite a walk. It's always so cool and restful."

Danny spied a crude, wooden headboard sitting in the

rocky soil at the foot of the mountain. "Is that a grave over there?"

"Yes, it is. Does that bother you?"

"You asking if I'm afraid of spooks? Shucks, I don't even believe in 'em." Danny squinted her eyes, then asked, "What's those words on the headboard say?"

Julia didn't have to strain her eyes to see. She had them memorized. Many times she had stood by the grave, looking down on it sadly. She'd even weeded it a few times. "It says, Indian squaw—killed by accident—saved garrison from massacre."

"There's a Injun buried over there?" Danny asked in surprise.

"Yes, but not just any Indian. A very special Indian to all who have served at this post. Let's sit down, and I'll tell you the story."

When Danny and Julia were seated beneath one of the trees, Julia said, "Shortly after Fort Davis was reoccupied by the Union forces, the Apaches attacked. They were repulsed, but they left many of their dead and wounded behind. One was a beautiful, young Indian girl. Mrs. Easton, the mother of Lieutenant Thomas Easton, found her in the hospital and insisted upon taking charge of her. She put her in a little adobe hut behind their house on Officers' Row and nursed her back to health. While the girl was recuperating from her wounds, Mrs. Easton became very fond of her, and the Indian girl eventually became her servant and constant companion. Mrs. Easton named her Emily.

"As time went by, Emily fell in love with Tom. Then the Nelsons moved to Fort Davis with their beautiful daughter, Mary, and Tom fell in love with her. The night

285

that Tom and Mary announced their engagement, Emily disappeared. I guess she just couldn't bear seeing the man she loved married to another woman. Mrs. Easton mourned her as if she had lost a daughter. A year passed, with no word from Emily, and the Apaches grew increasingly troublesome. One night, a sentry heard someone trying to slip past him. He called out, 'Halt or I'll fire,' but received no reply. He saw the intruder running towards the post buildings and fired, then heard a woman scream out in pain."

"You ain't gonna tell me it was Emily?" Danny asked in distress, having gotten caught up in the poor Indian girl's plight.

"I'm afraid it was," Julia answered sadly. "She was mortally wounded. They carried her to the colonel's house, where she called out for Mrs. Easton. When the kind woman arrived, she knelt down by the girl with tears in her eyes. Emily whispered to her, 'I hear talk. All my people coming to kill by light of morning. I tell you so Tom not get killed.' Then Emily said goodbye and died in Mrs. Easton's arms. The Apaches did attack in the morning, but because the fort had been forewarned, they were able to fight them off. Even then, there were heavy losses. It would have been a total massacre if they hadn't been prepared for the attack. They buried Emily out here, and a post carpenter built that headboard and carved those words into it. When I first heard the story and saw the headboard, I thought a nicer epithet could have been written in her memory. I resented her being called a squaw. She gave her life so that the man she loved could live, and saved countless other lives besides his. I understand that the Indians resent their women being called squaws, that it's a white man's term that they consider offensive and insulting. I thought 'maiden' would have been more appropriate, particularly in view of her saving the fort, but I came to realize that the man who wrote it was a simple man, that he was trying in his own way and his own words to honor her."

Danny blinked back tears and said, "You sure got some sad stories to tell about this place. First Dolores, and now Emily."

"Yes, my heart goes out to both of them. That's another reason I like to come out here every now and then. I like to think that Emily knows I'm here, and that she knows she hasn't been forgotten, and I keep hoping that I . ."

"Hoping what?" Danny prompted when Julia's voice trailed off.

Julia smiled sadly, then answered, "That someone visits Anne's grave, and that she knows she hasn't been forgotten."

A lump the size of a goose egg came to Danny's throat. "Where's your daughter buried?"

"At Fort Riley, in Kansas." Then, brushing her melancholy away, Julia said, "Now, let's talk about something more cheerful. Did I tell you that my son is going to come visit us when he graduates next year?"

"I bet you're excited about that."

"Gracious, yes. I've been counting the days. We're hoping that he'll be stationed here in Texas, so we can see him more often."

Later, as they walked back to the fort, Danny was glad to see that Julia was in good spirits. She wondered if there was something wrong with her? She hadn't been near as torn up over her father and brothers' deaths as Julia seemed to be over her daughter's. But maybe daughters and mothers were just closer, or a mother's love was just more powerful. Dad-blasted, she sure wished she'd known her mother. She had a feeling she'd missed out on something real special.

The next night, after Danny had retired and John and Julia were sitting in the parlor, John asked, "Well, how was the tea at the colonel's house this afternoon?"

Julia frowned, then answered, "Very nice. You know Mrs. Shafter gave it to introduce the officers' wives to her house guest."

"Yes, I know, but I wonder why she waited so long. That young lady has been here for almost two weeks."

"Mrs. Shafter was waiting for Mrs. Brantley to recover from her childbirth, so she could attend too. Gracious, that poor girl must have had a terrible time with her delivery. She's been bedridden for almost a month, instead of the usual two weeks, and she looked ghastly, as white as a sheet. I don't understand why the army doesn't allow the post medical officer to attend birthings. A woman can die from hemorrhage after childbirth just as easily as a man from a bullet wound. It infuriates me that the army can be so blind to the needs of their men's womenfolk. Why, that silly rule is almost as bad as their insistence upon listing us wives and daughters as camp followers. Camp followers, indeed! We're respectable women, not Spikes like those low-moraled women on Suds Row."

John chuckled. When Julia got on her soapbox about something, she could be a regular little spitfire. "Mrs. Brantley was probably better off without Pills at her birthing. He doesn't know as much about delivering babies as you women do."

Julia shook her head, saying, "Honestly, John, you talk more and more like your troopers every day. Pills? Now what kind of a name is that for the medical officer? Why it's almost as bad as calling the chaplain, Holy Joe."

John chuckled, then said, "We don't call the gentlemen that to their faces. Besides, is it any worse than calling one of the laundresses a Spike?"

Julia laughed, then admitted, "No, I'm afraid I'm just as bad as you are, throwing the troopers' slang around. Do you know I actually caught myself calling one of the cooks a slum-burner the other day?"

"Well, getting back to the tea, what did you find out about Mrs. Shafter's guest," John asked.

Julia frowned again, wondering where in the world Danny had gotten the idea that the young lady was Brant's relative, then answered, "She's Captain Holden's fiancée from Philadelphia. It seems they've been engaged to be married for some time now."

"Captain Holden? The same young man who brought Danny here?"

"Yes," Julia answered with a deep scowl on her face.

"Why are you frowning so?"

Julia didn't want to tell John that she thought Danny was infatuated with Brant and that she was worried about how the girl would take the news of his engagement. She felt it would be breaking Danny's confidence in some way. "Well, to be perfectly honest, I didn't like the girl. Oh, she's beautiful enough, and just dripping with good breeding, but she seemed such a snob, and every time someone even mentioned Mrs. Brantby's baby, she pouted like a child. I got the impression that she's very spoiled and very selfish."

"She's probably used to being the center of attention. All those high-classed women are that way. But considering that the captain comes from a very prestigious family himself, you'd hardly expect him to marry someone that wasn't as well-bred as he. Why, she probably attended one of the best finishing schools in the East."

"Oh, she did. You can be sure she was very quick to drop the name, just as she let everyone know her clothes came from Worth."

"Did she say anything about when the wedding is to take place?"

"No, apparently the date hasn't been set yet."

After a brief silence, Julia set aside her embroidery and said, "It's getting late."

"Yes, bedtime for us two old folks."

Julia laughed and said, "You may be getting old, but I'm not. I just need my beauty sleep."

"You don't need any beauty sleep, my dear. If you got any prettier, I'd have to fight the men away from my door."

Julia smiled fondly at her husband, then said, "You're a terrible flatterer, John, but I do love it."

Next door, Danny lay on her iron cot, feeling as if her world was coming apart. The beautiful young woman wasn't kinfolk. She was the woman Brant was going to marry. For a brief moment, Danny felt terribly betrayed. Then she remembered that Brant had never told her he loved her, only that he liked her a lot, and that he had tried to tell her making love to her was wrong, but she wouldn't listen to him. She had thrown herself at him, convinced that he loved her as much as she did him, and

Danny knew that no man would have turned her down, even if they hadn't cared a fig for her. She'd seen enough animals mating to know that. No, she couldn't blame Brant. She had only herself to blame. She'd been a fool to think he would fall in love with her. Why, she was nothing but a country hick—uneducated, rough-talking, and tacky-acting. Why, she didn't even dress and act like a woman. No, Brant wouldn't want to marry her. He'd be ashamed of her. He wanted a woman he could be proud to call his wife, one that was beautiful, had pretty manners, talked soft, and had just as much book learning as he had. She was just as bad as Emily, wanting someone that was far above her. Instead of keeping her feet on the ground, she'd been reaching for the stars and fell flat on her face. She was a dad-blasted fool!

The tears spilled over, and Danny rolled to her side. She had never felt so miserable or lonely in her life. She pulled the canvas bag that housed her pet to her chest, and sobbed, "Oh, Charlie, I should have known it was too good to be true."

The next day, Danny walked to the old pump house and sat beside Emily's grave. She could relate with the pain the Indian girl must have felt when she realized that she couldn't have Tom. She, too, had lost the man she loved. In that way, she and Emily and Dolores were all alike, except she and Emily had lost to another woman, a woman much above them, and not death. But Emily hadn't carried any bitterness in her heart. The Indian girl had given her life to save Tom's. She ought to be at least as brave. Step back and let the better woman have Brant, since it was for his own good. Above all, she wanted him to be happy, even if it did make her miserable.

Danny walked back to the fort, and just as she was passing the stables, ran into Brant. Brant came to a dead halt, expecting her to still be angry with him. But what he saw in Danny's eyes wasn't anger but pain. She knows about Elizabeth, he thought, and she's been deeply hurt. Dammit, he didn't want her hurt. That's why he had wanted to be the one to tell her.

Stepping up to her and catching her arms, Brant said, "Danny, let me explain about my engagement to Elizabeth."

Remembering that she had vowed to step back for Brant's own good, Danny quickly hid her pain and said brightly, "Oh, you don't have to explain about her. I understand."

Brant frowned, then asked, "How can you say that after what happened between us?"

"You mean on the trip out here? Oh, that wasn't nothing," Danny said, deliberately trying to make light of their love affair. "That was jest between good friends." Danny jerked her arm free and said, "Well, I gotta be a-going. Time for me to git supper started." She turned and rushed off, calling over her shoulder, "See you 'round."

Brant was stunned by Danny's blase words. Just between good friends, he thought. No! Goddammit, no! It was more than that. Much more! For both of them. "Danny, come back!" he called.

But Danny was out of hearing, and even if she hadn't been, she wouldn't have been able to face Brant. Tears were trickling down her cheeks. That was the biggest bluff she'd ever pulled in her life, she thought, and it plumb tore her up to lie that way. But she'd done it. Now he could be happy. Maybe she hadn't given her life, like

Emily, but she sure felt like she had. There was an emptiness in her, a big gaping hole that she didn't think no one or nothing could ever fill.

Over the next few days, Danny was unusually quiet and pensive. She also spent her free time alone in her room. Having no idea that Danny had overheard her and John talking and learned the truth about Elizabeth that night, Julia worried over her strange behavior.

One night, when she and her husband had retired to their bedroom, she asked, "Have you noticed anything about Danny?"

"Are you talking about how quiet she's been the past few days?"

"Yes, I'm worried about her. I hope she's not coming down with one of these strange fevers we've seen so much of here in Texas."

"No, I don't think what ails her is physical. She's much too healthy-looking."

"Then whatever could be wrong?"

"Perhaps she's going through a delayed mourning for the brother and home she lost. It hasn't been all that long, you know."

"Yes, now that you mention it, she does act like someone in mourning, so sad. But we can't let her continue like this. Sitting in her room all alone and grieving."

"Aren't you getting rather concerned for a servant?"

"She doesn't feel like a servant to me."

John gave Julia a penetrating look, then asked, "Like Anne, perhaps?"

"Oh, John," Julia said with a little laugh and a shake of the head, "you could always read me like a book. Yes, I admit that Danny reminds me of Anne. But there's more to it than just that. In many ways she's like Anne, but in so many other ways she's unique, like no one I've ever known. I've come to appreciate her for herself and have grown quite fond of her."

"Yes, I have too," John admitted. "You know, I find myself waiting breathlessly to hear what she's going to say. You never know what's going to pop out of her mouth." He paused, then said, "We'll just have to try to keep her mind occupied, so she can't dwell on her loss."

"I'm afraid that's not going to be easy," Julia replied with a deep sigh. "She hasn't shown the least interest in learning to read since she started acting so strangely, and she was doing so well. Why, I was absolutely flabbergasted at how quickly she learned." A fiercely determined expression came over Julia's face. "But I'm not going to let her give up on it. I'll make her sit there and learn, just like I did our children when they balked at their lessons."

The next day, that was exactly what Julia did. She forced Danny to sit at the table and drilled her on her letters and the words she had already learned, as tyrannical as the first sergeants putting their troopers through their "Monkey Drills" outside on the parade ground. It was only out of respect for Julia that Danny tolerated it, and when they finished, she said to the older woman, "Consarn it, how come you're so bossy all of a sudden? You're a-acting like a straw boss that's got a bee up his tail."

Julia laughed. It was the first natural thing she'd heard Danny say in days. "Because I firmly believe that everyone should know how to read and write. Without it, you're at the mercy of every crooked business man, lawyer, banker, and scalawag that comes along. If you sign anything, you can read it for yourself. You don't have to take anyone else's word for it. And you can keep abreast with what's going on around you, to say nothing of being able to keep in touch with distant friends. And you learn new things, by reading books and magazines. It opens up a whole new world for you."

Danny wasn't as enthusiastic about learning new things as she had been, and she didn't have any friends to write to, because Rose couldn't read either; however she didn't like the idea of anyone pulling the wool over her eyes just because she couldn't read. Dad-blasted, no pole-cat was going to cheat her. "Well, I reckon when you put it that way, I'd better learn."

"I'm glad to hear you say that," Julia said with obvious relief. "We'll have another lesson this afternoon."

Well, she didn't have to get that carried away, Danny thought. Her rump was already numb from sitting on this hard chair for so long.

That night, when John saw Danny coming from the kitchen and heading for her bedroom, he asked, "Danny, could I interest you in a game of checkers? Julia won't play with me."

"Indeed, I won't," Julia said from where she was sitting and doing some mending. "If you can't act like a gentleman, and let me win a game every now and then, I just won't play with you."

John laughed, saying, "No, my dear, I can't let you win, and being a gentleman has nothing to do with it. Checkers is a game of tactics and skill just as much as planning and executing a battle plan."

Danny knew they were teasing each other from the tone of their voices and the twinkle in their eyes. That was the reason she didn't want to be around them. They had so many ways of showing their love: teasing one another, smiling at one another across the room, exchanging warm glances, touching each other's hands. Seeing them and knowing she and Brant would never share such a deep love was like rubbing salt in an open wound. "I'm sorry, Major, but I don't reckon I know how to play checkers."

"I'd be more than happy to teach you."

"Well, maybe some other time."

"There's no time like the present," John said, jumping to his feet and removing the oil lamp from the table next to his chair. "We can play right here on this end table, and you can sit in my chair. I'll get another one from the kitchen and the checkers."

Out of courtesy, Danny was forced to sit and listen while John explained the game to her. She lost the first two games, but Danny had a strong sense of competition for a woman and paid much closer attention to John's moves on the third and fourth. She almost beat him on the fifth game, then did so soundly on the sixth.

John looked down at the checker board and said, "Well, I'll be damned! You beat me."

Danny grinned broadly and said, "I shore did."

"Well, I hope you'll give me a rematch tomorrow night."

"Shore will." Danny leaned forward over the checker board, her black eyes sparkling brightly, asking, "Would you be interested in a little gambling, say a penny a game?"

John wasn't about to tell Danny that the officers gambled for much higher stakes on their checker games at the club, for fear she'd fleece him. He chuckled and answered, "That ought to make the game even more interesting."

Later, as he and his wife were undressing for bed, Julia said, "That was very sweet of you, John, letting Danny win."

An embarrassed look came over the major's face. "Well, I shouldn't admit it to you, my dear, for fear I'll never hear the end of it, but I didn't let her win. She beat me fair and square. She does have a quick mind, and I'm going to have to play much more carefully from now on, or else lose my reputation as one of the sharpest checker players on the post."

Over the next week, Danny slowly emerged from her depression over losing Brant. Part was due to the determined efforts of Julia and John to keep her mind occupied, but mostly it was Danny's own indomitable spirit. She came from hardy stock, rugged frontiersmen that never gave up, no matter what man or nature threw at them. She simply wasn't the kind to mope over what had been lost and could never be regained, to wallow in self-pity. She was too full of life to bury herself in grief. She couldn't hold down her vitality and exuberance, for they were the wellspring of her soul. The old Danny came back, much to Julia and John's delight, and the only time Danny allowed herself a time to reflect on her loss was when she visited Emily's grave to commune with her soul sister. Otherwise, she kept her burden close to her heart.

Brant, however, wasn't coping well. Time and again, he had thought to go to Danny, to insist that she listen to his explanation. He knew he cared for her very deeply, but he still didn't know if he was prepared to offer her marriage. They came from such different backgrounds, and if it didn't work out, he would have done her a terrible injustice. Nor had he figured out how he was going to disentangle himself from his present commitment. And if truth be known, Danny's claim that what they had shared had been nothing but friendship, stung his male pride. He found it hard to believe her, surely he couldn't have misread what he saw in her eyes that day in Limpia Canyon, but if it were true, and he meant no more to her than a friend, then he'd make a damn fool out of himself by going and declaring his love for her. His emotions seemed to get more tangled every day.

But there was one area in which Brant had no doubts about how he felt. Elizabeth. His seething anger at being caught in a trap from which it seemed he couldn't escape, fed by his resentment at what her unexpected appearance had done to his and Danny's relationship, had reached the point of a volcano that was about to erupt. Her touch repulsed him so much that he cringed, and he feared if she whined one more time about his neglecting her, or said one more insipid thing, or fluttered her eyelashes at him again, he'd explode, regardless of who might be around. For that reason, he threw himself into his work and welcomed the first real assignment he was sent on, that of hunting down some deserters who had taken a herd of army mounts with them when they had gone over the hill.

Chapter 17

Brant and his troop rode out of Fort Davis the next morning just as the sun was rising, the bright light tinting the towering mountains around them a golden color and their swallow-tailed guidon snapping in the wind over their heads. Since they had no idea how long they would be gone, they were traveling packed saddle. Each man was carrying a saddlebag, hooked into a stud on his cantle and hanging down each side, in which he carried his curry comb and brush, a fourteen-inch picket pin, a spare horseshoe and nails, his mess gear, and extra ammunition. A blanket roll and cylindrical canvas feed bag were lashed at the rear of the cantle, a dog tent rolled across his pommel in which was a change of clothing, and dangling from rings on his saddle was his picket line, canteen, and tin cup. Every trooper wore a "thimble belt" in which he kept his cartridges, a revolver on his right hip, and a carbine slung across his back, muzzle down. Combined with his blanket and saddle, it was an awesome seventy-three pounds of gear.

As soon as they passed the sentry post, the troopers

broke out into their marching song, singing, "Forty miles a western day, on beans and hay, in the Regular Army O." Brant, riding at the front of the column, smiled, knowing they were in good spirits, despite the fact that their quarry wasn't Apaches, but deserters. Like him, they would prefer to be going into battle than tracking down one of their own. However, that wasn't to say the troopers didn't feel as strongly about the deserters as their officers did. They were cowards and traitors, running from their duty and deserving of the punishment they would receive.

"What are our orders, sir?" the first lieutenant riding beside Brant asked.

"To bring them back, dead or alive."

A shocked expression came over the lieutenant's face. "But, sir, the Indian War hasn't been declared an official war. The death penalty for desertion can't be enforced in this case."

Brant groaned silently. Now he knew why he was transferred to Fort Davis to take command of this troop, instead of the lieutenant being promoted and taking over command. The young officer was obviously a "shavetail," an army term originating from the practice of shaving the tails of cadet mules so that the mulewhacker could differentiate the new recruits from the old and be on the alert for trouble. The lieutenant was spouting off what he had learned at West Point and had yet to learn that what the army preached in theory and what the army practiced in the field were two entirely different things. "And what do you suggest we do, Mr. Gibbs, if they resist? Stand there and let them shoot us?"

The lieutenant wasn't insulted at Brant's calling him mister. All lieutenants were called that by their superior officers, unless the young man was being introduced to someone. It was the army's way of reminding them that they were at the bottom of their hierarchy. But the green officer was taken aback by Brant's direct question. "Well, no sir. Of course not."

"I should hope not," Brant said dryly, then added, "Besides, these men are horse thieves, as well as deserters, and the punishment for that in Texas *is* hanging."

Brant's words made the lieutenant feel a little more comfortable. He had yet to learn that all was not black and white in the law, that there were a lot of gray areas in which the officer in command had to use his own judgment. "Which way do you think they went, sir?"

"Which way do *you* think they went?"

The lieutenant frowned. How was he supposed to learn anything if he had to do the thinking? "Well, I would guess they'd head east, towards San Antonio, since it's the nearest large town and has a big horse market."

"Think again, Mr. Gibbs."

"What . . . what do you mean, sir?"

"Do you think they'll really want to take the risk of trying to sell those horses in a large town where there's a marshall, a federal officer that's on the lookout for stolen government property? No, they'll head south to Mexico or west. My guess is west, to New Mexico."

"Why, sir?"

"Because they'll get the better price there, and the ranchers don't have any qualms about buying stolen stock."

"But there are federal marshalls there, too, sir, and those horses are branded."

Brant smiled. The young man was finally beginning to

301

think. "Yes, but he can't patrol all those isolated ranches. Besides, brands can be altered or totally obliterated."

The lieutenant flushed, then said, "I'm sorry, sir, if I seem stupid. I'm afraid I've got a lot to learn."

"How long have you been out west?"

"Seven months, sir."

"Well, don't feel bad, Mr. Gibbs. I've been in Texas for five years, and I'm still learning."

The lieutenant shot Brant a grateful smile and said, "Thank you, sir."

Brant turned in his saddle and said to Sergeant O'Bannon, who was riding beside an even greener second lieutenant behind him, "O'Bannon, get that scout out to see if he can pick up their trail."

O'Bannon didn't have to ask which direction to send the scout. He had overheard the conversation between Brant and the lieutenant. "Aye, sir!" he snapped, turning his horse.

A moment later the scout tore off from the column, wearing a pair of trooper's trousers, a calico shirt, and a pair of leather, knee-high moccasins, his long black hair flying out behind him as he crouched low in the saddle.

As O'Bannon rode back up the line, Brant motioned for him to come forward. As the Irishman pulled up beside him, Brant asked, "Do you know any of those deserters?"

"Aye, sir. They're from Troop K. Mueller, the Dutchie among 'em, is a Coffee Cooler, the laziest man I ever saw, but otherwise harmless. The other six are a bunch of mean bastards that spent more time in the guardhouse than not. O'Neal attacked a young Mexican girl over at

302

Chihuahua, but he was never convicted. Her parents were so mortified that they wouldn't let her testify. McMullen, the big bastard in the lot, beat up a trooper so bad that the man was in the hospital for two months, and everyone suspected that O'Hara was the man who robbed and killed that trooper they found behind the barracks one night, but the provost marshall could never get enough evidence on him to bring him to trial. They're a bad lot, sir."

"Thank you, Sergeant."

O'Bannon fell back to his place behind Brant. Brant turned to the lieutenant, asking, "Do you still have reservations, Mr. Gibbs?"

"No, sir, I certainly don't," the young officer said in an emphatic voice. "It sounds like they're men long overdue for punishment."

"That's the way it usually is with deserters. Oh, a few desert from boredom, or cowardice, or because they feel some injustice has been done them, but the greater majority are troublemakers to start with. That's one reason we bring them back, even though the army is better off without them. Left loose, most turn to a life of crime and prey off the settlers. We wash our own dirty laundry."

The scout found the deserters' trail to the west of Fort Davis, just as Brant had suspected he would. For a while, they followed the Overland Trail, passing by Van Horn Wells; then at Eagle Springs, the Seminole scout lost their trail.

"He says he can't find any sign of their trail ahead, sir," O'Bannon reported to Brant.

"I'm not surprised. Fort Quitman lies in that

direction. Tell the scout to look to the north."

"What about south, sir?" O'Bannon suggested. "The border's not far from here."

"No, I still think they're heading for New Mexico."

The scout found the trail to the north, but following it was tedious and time-consuming. The deserters seemed to be following an old Indian trail, and in some places, where the ground was rocky, there was no sign of the horses' tracks for miles, and Brant and his troop spent a lot of time sitting in the hot sun and waiting until the scout picked up the trail again.

For two weeks, they twisted and turned in the mountains and rode over scroching deserts, but Brant was determined not to give up the chase. During the daytime, he could keep his mind on his business, but the nights were sheer torture. Then, while his troopers lay all around him snoring and the coyotes in the mountains around them howled mournfully, he was tormented by memories of Danny and their trip to Fort Davis. All he could think of was Danny with her sparkling black eyes, her wide, warm smile, her infectious laughter, her pert, freckle-sprinkled nose, her wild mane of hair that couldn't seem to make up its mind whether it was brown or red. He remembered how light she was on her feet that night they had danced within the circle of wagons, how beautiful she had looked standing naked in the stream with the mountains as a backdrop, how sweet she smelled and how incredibly soft her skin felt when he made love to her. Each night was an agony of hell, for invariably he became aroused, and he was left to twist and turn the rest of the night, throbbing and burning for her, his unfulfilled desire leaving a lingering ache the next morning that made riding uncomfortable.

Fifteen days after they had ridden out of Fort Davis, they found the herd of stolen horses in a box canyon. The deserter left to guard them saw them coming and rode away like a horde of Indians were behind him. Leaving a few men to guard the horses, Brant and the rest of his troops rode off in hot pursuit. They lost the man, but Brant had no doubt where he had gone when he saw the ranch house in the distance. Sending half of his troop to cover the rear, Brant and his men rode boldly up to the ranch house.

The owner of the ranch walked from the sprawled, adobe building and stood on his porch asking, "What can I do for you, boys?"

"We're looking for some deserters," Brant answered, not at all fooled by the man's innocent act, "and I have reason to believe that they're hiding in your house."

An ugly expression came over the rancher's face. "Now, wait a minute, Captain. You ain't got no call to make an accusation like that."

"Don't I? I found the herd of horses they took with them when they deserted in a box canyon a few miles away."

A surprised expression came over the rancher's rugged face before he quickly hid it and said, "I don't know nothing about no herd and no deserters."

Brant turned in his saddle and said to O'Bannon, "Have the troopers dismount and search the house."

"Back off, Captain!" the rancher said angrily. "You can't do that. This is private property. You can't search my house without a warrant. I'll have the law on you!"

Brant's eyes narrowed dangerously. "Mister, my

305

troopers are searching that house, warrant or no warrant. Go ahead and call the law on me, and see if I give a goddamn!"

While the two lieutenants' faces blanched at Brant's blatant disrespect of the law, O'Bannon's eyes sparkled with approval. By damn, the Irishman thought, the captain was a man after his own heart. Aye, the Old Man had known what he was doing when he sent Holden after those deserters. He'd told him to bring them back, and by God, the Captain was, come hell or high water. O'Bannon turned in his saddle and yelled, "Dismount and search the house! If any of those deserting bastards pull a gun on ye, don't hesitate to kill 'em."

The troopers flew from the saddle and, with O'Bannon in the lead, ran into the house, their carbines held before them. The rancher, livid with anger, glared at Brant, who glared back, while the sounds of doors being slammed, men yelling back and forth, and troopers' boots on stairs drifted out to them. A woman screamed, and a Mexican servant ran from the house, her face pale with fright, followed by several gunshots. Then silence prevailed, the minutes ticking by before five cursing deserters were wrestled roughly from the house, flanked on each side by a very angry-looking trooper and covered by another in the rear with a carbine pointed at their backs.

Behind them, O'Bannon walked down the steps, a pleased smile on his face. He stopped before Brant, saluted, and said smugly, "Ye're deserters, sir."

"The other two?" Brant asked.

"Dead, sir. They both pulled guns on us."

"Anyone wounded?"

"Aye, sir. Private Donovan took a bullet in the

shoulder. Passed right through. Some of the boys are bandaging him up right now. He'll be able to ride."

"Then get those deserters mounted and handcuffed to their saddles, and those dead men wrapped in blankets and lashed across their saddles," Brant instructed. "Better wrap them in dog tents, too, Sergeant. Otherwise they'll be stinking to high heaven. It's a long way back to Fort Davis."

A week later, Brant and his troop rode back into Fort Davis. As soon as they had entered the fort's perimeters, the troopers driving the stolen horses veered off, taking the weary animals back to the stables. The rest of the troop, with Brant at the head, rode directly for headquarters, looking and smelling like a bunch of wild Bohemian raiders.

Brant didn't have to dismount to report to Colonel Shafter. The commanding officer was waiting on the porch when he reined in.

Colonel Shafter looked down the line of dusty, weary troopers, some so exhausted they were swaying in their saddles, his eyes coming to rest on one deserter handcuffed to his saddle. Before he could ask where the other six were, Brant raised his arm and motioned for the troopers at the back to come forward. They trotted their horses to the front of the column, each leading a horse upon which a canvas-wrapped body was lashed, face down, over the saddle.

"Two were killed when they were captured, sir," Brant reported in a grim voice. "The other four were shot while trying to escape one night. One trooper was wounded during the capture, but his shoulder is healing well. However, all the horses have been recovered, safe and sound."

"Where did you find them?"

"In New Mexico, about fifty miles from the border."

He had trailed them that far, Colonel Shafter thought in amazement. Why, many an officer would have given up and turned back. He was impressed.

"I feel it only fair to warn you, there may be some repercussions, sir," Brant continued. "The rancher hiding them objected strongly. He threatened to have charges filed on me for illegal entry and search."

"He can take his charges and shove them up his ass!" the colonel said angrily, shocking the two green lieutenants with both his crude words and his apparent approval of what Brant had done. "Don't worry, Captain. The army will handle any complaints. You were following my orders. You can give me a complete report tomorrow, when you're rested."

"Thank you, Colonel."

As Brant started to turn his horse, Colonel Shafter said, "One moment, Captain. I'd like to commend you on a job well done."

"Thank you, Colonel, but I can't take all the credit. This is a good troop, one I'm proud to serve with."

As Brant turned his troop and started to lead them to the stables, Sergeant O'Bannon rode forward and said to Brant, "I'll take yer horse to the stables, sir."

"That's not necessary, O'Bannon."

"I know, sir. But I'd consider it an honor."

Brant was more touched by O'Bannon's tribute than the public commendation the colonel had given him. He knew that he had passed the test as the troop's new commanding officer and that from now on his men would give him their full support. "In that case, I'd much appreciate it," Brant replied graciously, reining in, dismounting, and handing his reins to the Irishman.

As his troop trotted away, Brant walked wearily to his quarters, so exhausted that he could hardly put one foot before the other. When he came abreast of the colonel's home, Elizabeth ran down the steps, calling out, "You're finally back!" Then, stopping short, a horrified look came over her face, and her nose wrinkled with distaste.

"That's how a man smells when he's been in the field for three weeks, Elizabeth," Brant said bluntly.

"I . . . I—"

"I'm really not in the mood to pass the time of day," Brant said, cutting across what might have been an apology, or might not have. "I'll see you tomorrow."

For a brief moment, Brant savored the look of outrage that came over Elizabeth's face at his curt dismissal, then turned and walked away. Deciding to take a shortcut to his cabin on the second row, he walked between two officers' homes. As he rounded the corner, he ran right into Danny, her arms filled with the laundry she had just removed from the clothesline.

Brant drank in the sight of her hungrily, then said, softly, "Hello, Danny."

"Howdy!" Danny answered brightly.

Aware of her eyes sweeping down him, Brant said, "I'm sorry. I'm afraid I look and smell like hell."

"Well, you do look like something the cat drug in and then decided it didn't want," Danny said in all honesty, "but I ain't surprised. You've been gone an awful long time. I shore am glad you got back safe and sound, but you look dead on yer feet. You must be plumb tuckered out."

That was the difference between Elizabeth and Danny, Brant thought. One was shocked by his appearance, and the other showed concern for him. A warm feeling filled him. Suddenly he wasn't nearly as exhausted. "I am a little tired," he admitted.

Julia, who had been removing clothes from the other line, stepped up, saying, "Welcome back, Captain."

"Thank you ma'am, and forgive my appearance."

"Oh, you don't have to apologize to me. Believe me, I've seen John looking much worse." She turned to Danny and said, "Why don't you go inside and bring Captain Holden one of those apple pies you baked today?"

"Thank you, ma'am, but I'm not hungry," Brant said wearily. "All I want to do is bathe and fall into bed."

"Yes, I know, but you're going to wake up ravenous. John always does. Why, there have been times when I feared he'd eat the kitchen table."

Danny hadn't hesitated for a second when Julia had told her to get a pie for Brant. She was in and out of the house like a flash, then standing there holding it out to him and saying, "It's still warm."

Brant accepted the pie, saying, "Thank you, Danny. If it's anything near as good as your ash cakes, I know I'm in for a treat." Then, knowing that he had no excuse to linger longer, he said regretfully, "Good day."

As he walked away, Julia frowned. She should have invited him to dinner sometime, but she knew if she did, she would have to extend the invitation to his fiancée, and Julia wouldn't have the girl in her house. She glanced across at Danny, but saw none of the adoration in her eyes that she had seen when she first arrived. She wondered if she had simply gotten over her infatuation

310

with the handsome captain, or if she had heard of his engagement and realized she had lost even before she had begun to fight.

Having no idea that Danny had carefully schooled herself not to let her feelings show, Julia turned and walked into the house. But if she could have seen Danny's face then, she would have known. It was filled with naked longing.

Several nights later, after Danny had retired, John and Julia sat in their parlor. John looked at his wife, frowned, then asked, "Is something bothering you, my dear?"

Julia startled. "What?"

"I asked if something was bothering you. You've been sitting there with your needle poised over your embroidery and staring out in space for a good ten minutes."

"Goodness, I didn't realize I was that distracted," Julia said, placing her embroidery to the side. "Yes, I am disturbed over something. Mrs. Shafter had another small tea today and I attended. Every time I'm around her house guest, I dislike the girl even more. I sense something devious about her. Well anyway, I was the last guest to leave. Apparently the other wives don't like her any better than I do. Mrs. Shafter walked home with me. She said she just had to get out of the house and away from that awful girl for a few moments, or she thought she would scream."

"Mrs. Shafter said that?" John asked in surprise. "Why, she always struck me as one of the most composed women I've ever seen."

"She is. Usually nothing upsets her. But she said

Elizabeth complains constantly about everything and treats her servants terrible. She said Lee, the Chinese cook she and the colonel have had for years, has even threatened to quit if the girl insulted him one more time, and that the colonel has been taking quite a few of his meals at the officer's club to avoid being around the girl. She even caught Elizabeth kicking her dog, and you know how fond Mrs. Shafter and the colonel are of that old dog. Why, it's like a child to them. The girl is simply disrupting their entire household.''

"Well, if this Elizabeth is such a terror, why did Mrs. Shafter invite her to stay?''

"Mrs. Shafter said she wasn't that way at first, and that she has certainly regretted her invitation. But what upsets me the most is Mrs. Shafter said Elizabeth was going to make that nice Captain Holden's life sheer hell.''

"Well, I am sorry to hear that. He strikes me as a very likable and down-to-earth young man, despite the fact that he comes from a prestigious family. And he's a top-rate officer. We both know what a bad marriage can do to an officer's career. Why, it can ruin it.''

"Yes, I know. An officer needs a strong woman beside him, someone who's a helpmate, and not a pampered, spoiled little child. I just feel so sorry for him.''

"Well, he's not married yet, my dear. It's a little soon to be burying him.'' Seeing his wife about to object, John shook his head and held up his hand, saying, "No, no, my dear, don't you give me any of that foolishness about how serious an official engagement is. The only commitment for life is marriage.''

"I suppose you're right, John. It would be much better to break the engagement than be in misery the rest of your life. I only hope the young man realizes that Elizabeth is a poor choice for a wife before it's too late."

Next door, Danny heard everything. She might have been willing to step aside for Brant's own good, but she had vowed long ago not to let anything or anyone harm him. He couldn't marry Elizabeth, not if she was going to make his life sheer hell, not if she was going to make him miserable, not if she was going to ruin his career. Dadblasted, she wouldn't let Elizabeth do that to Brant!

But how was she going to stop her, Danny wondered. They were already engaged. Unless . . . unless she could take Brant away from Elizabeth, make him fall in love with her. She'd make Brant a better wife than Elizabeth would. She was strong, and she wouldn't make his life miserable by whining and complaining all the time. She'd make him a good helpmate.

Then Danny remembered how far above her Brant was. There she goes again, she thought in self-disgust, reaching for the stars. Elizabeth might not make Brant a good wife, but neither would a country hick like her.

Tears glittered in her eyes. She turned her head and gazed out the window, seeing a falling star streak through the night sky. She wished it was Brant, come down to earth so she could have him for her own. Then a sudden thought occurred to her. If he couldn't come down, then she'd just have to go up.

Her spirits soared. Yes, that's what she'd do, Danny vowed with firm resolve. She'd go right up there and snag herself that golden star.

Chapter 18

The next day, when Julia was laying out their books for Danny's daily lesson, Danny turned from the kitchen sink and said, "Can I ask a real big favor of you, Julia?"

"Why, of course, Danny."

"Would you teach me to be a lady?"

Julia was stunned. It was the last thing she would have expected from Danny. John was right. You never knew what was going to pop out of her mouth. She wondered what could have possibly prompted Danny to ask such a favor. "Why do you want to become a lady?"

Danny wasn't about to tell Julia the real reason, that she hoped to snag Brant, but she told her the truth in part, answering, "So I can better myself."

Perhaps it wouldn't be such a bad idea, Julia thought. She knew Danny had become friends with quite a few of the troopers, stopping on the parade ground to pass the time of day with them when she was on her way to the post store, or greeting them down at the stables when she and Julia were preparing to go for a ride. Julia knew by the glow and wide smile that came over the men's faces in

Danny's presence that they couldn't resist her charm either. Why, even a few of her lady friends had fallen under Danny's almost magical spell, one saying that she was like a little puppy, friendly and overflowing with energy, exasperatingly naughty but totally lovable. But it was the attention the troopers were giving Danny that worried Julia. She feared it wouldn't be long before they would be beating their door down trying to court her, and Julia wanted much better than that for Danny. The troopers' wives had a hard life, scrimping to get by all their lives, living in those terrible little houses on Hungry Hill, following their men from post to post with nothing to ever call their own, except a horde of rowdy children. Julia had noticed several of the single officers casting glances in Danny's direction. She knew they were attracted to her, but reluctant to show their attentions to such a wild tomboy. Maybe if she smoothed out some of Danny's rough edges, she'd be more acceptable to them.

"I'd be happy to, Danny. But learning to become a lady won't be easy. You'll have to learn how to talk like a lady, how to act, how to walk, how to dress. You will *have* to wear a dress, you know."

"I know. I already thought of that. I'll wear dresses and bonnets and even those silly gloves, iffen I have to, but I ain't gonna wear one of those corsets. I ain't about to get cinched up in one of those consarn things and have the daylights squeezed outta my middle for nobody."

Julia couldn't blame her. She hated the constrictive garments herself. She laughed, saying, "Well, with your small waist, I don't think you'll really need one."

"Well, I shore am glad to hear you say that," Danny answered with obvious relief. She paused, then said, "I reckon I'll go over to the post store this afternoon and

315

buy me some dresses, since I got money of my own now."

"Gracious, Danny, you can't afford that. Why, you won't be able to find a dress there for under twenty-five dollars, and you're going to need other things, like hose and shoes. I have a trunk full of dresses and things that I can't wear any longer, since I lost all that weight when I was ill. They ought to fit you, with a few alterations. Why, I even have a bonnet, a reticule, and some gloves you can have."

"But maybe you'll gain that weight back," Danny objected.

"No, it's been over two years. I think if I was going to gain it back, I would have by now. I was considering taking them over and giving them to one of the troopers' wives before they rot, but I'd much rather you have them. Of course, they aren't the latest style, but we can remedy that. We'll go over to the post store and look at the mail-order catalogs from Altman's that Mrs. Shafter donates when she's through placing her order. I'm sure we'll get some ideas from them. A ribbon here, a dab of lace there, some new braid can do wonders for an old dress."

Over the next two weeks, Danny worked very hard at learning to be a lady. Not only did she suffer through wearing the shoes that pinched her toes, the dresses that felt much too confining over her breasts, the petticoats that tangled around her legs, the bonnets whose ribbons scratched her neck, and the gloves that made her palms sweat, but she allowed—no, welcomed—Julia's drilling her on her walk, her manners, the correct way to sit down, the way to hold a tea cup with her little finger held out, and, the hardest thing for Danny, how to talk like a lady. She seemed at a loss for anything to say if she couldn't put a "dad-blasted," "consarn," or "tarnation" in someplace, and she had a terrible time remembering not to say "ain't" and "shore." She even learned to ride sidesaddle, terrified the whole time that she would fall off, but not because she was afraid of hurting herself, but because she didn't think she could bear the humiliation. But Danny endured, always keeping her goal in mind. No sacrifice, no amount of work, no discomfort, no amount of frustration was too big a price to pay for Brant. She'd become a lady if it killed her!

It was after a Sunday parade that Brant saw the new Danny for the first time. As he hurried from the parade ground, she walked up to him with her new dainty, graceful walk, smiling prettily, instead of grinning broadly, her magnificent mane of hair piled on the top of her head and hidden by her bonnet. He came to a dead halt and stared at her in disbelief.

"Hello, Brant. How are you?" Danny said in her new soft, well-modulated voice.

"I'm . . . I'm fine. And you?"

"I'm fine, thank you. It certainly has been hot this past week, hasn't it?"

"Yes, it has."

"Well, of course, it's to be expected. After all, it's almost July."

"Yes, it is."

Danny glanced over her shoulder, then said, "Well, I'd better be going. Julia is waiting for me. I just wanted to say hello. It's been a pleasure talking to you. Good day."

"Good day."

Danny turned and walked away, looking every inch the lady. It was all she could do to keep a smug smile from her face. Why, Brant was so flabbergasted he was speechless.

Brant's speech had been so stilted because he had felt uncomfortable in Danny's presence. The beautiful young lady standing before him wasn't the Danny he knew and had come to love. Oh, Danny, he thought, feeling sick at heart. What have you done to yourself, and why did you do it? You were special. What happened to the wonderful, spirited, natural, exasperating woman I fell in love with?

Julia knew the moment Danny turned and walked away from Brant why Danny had asked her to teach her to become a lady by the sparkle in her black eyes. She hadn't gotten over her infatuation, Julia realized. The captain was the reason she had wanted to better herself. Julia wondered if Danny had a ghost of a chance for nabbing Brant. He hadn't appeared very friendly from where she stood. But if Danny's heart was set on the young captain, Julia wanted her to have every possible chance. She'd give Danny the moon if she could.

As they walked back to the house, Julia said, "There's going to be a big hop on the Fourth of July. Would you like to attend with John and I?"

"A hop?" Danny asked with a frown. "What in the world is that?"

"That's what we army people call a dance."

Danny knew Brant would be there. Oh, to be held in his arms and dance again would be sheer heaven, she thought. Her heart beat a wild tattoo against her chest. "Can I? I mean, isn't it just for the officers and their wives?"

Ordinarily, an officer wouldn't dream of bringing a

318

servant as their guest, but Julia dared anyone to try and stop her. "No, we're allowed to bring guests."

"Do . . . do you think I'm ready for something that big?" Danny asked, having second thoughts.

"I certainly do. Why, you're as much a lady now as any woman on this post. I've been absolutely amazed at how fast you've learned. The Fourth of July hop will be your introduction into Fort Davis society. But you're going to have to have a ball gown, a special, very pretty gown. And not one of those ready-made ones, either. Tomorrow, we'll go to the post store and look through that catalog again, this time at the ball gowns. When we find just what we're looking for, we'll see if we can't copy it. You mark my words, Danny. You're going to be the most beautiful young lady at that ball."

They were heady words, and Danny's old self-confidence came bounding back. That's when it would happen, she told herself. The night of the hop. Brant would dance every dance with her and fall as hopelessly in love with her as she was with him. Oh, she could hardly wait. The next ten days were going to be an eternity.

The next day, after their washing was on the line, Danny and Julia walked to the post store and looked through the mail-order catalog at the ball gowns. As she flipped the pages, Julia said, "Well, it looks like ruffles are in vogue right now. Every gown seems to have one some place." Then, stopping at a page, she said in an excited voice, "Oh, Danny look at that gown! Isn't it beautiful?"

Danny looked down at the drawing. The skirt of the gown was fashioned with tiers of wide ruffles, and another wide ruffle formed the low cut neckline and sleeves. "How does she keep it from falling off her?" Danny asked, thinking that the woman in the drawing was about to lose her bodice, her big bosom looking as if it were about to pop right out.

Julia laughed. "I'm sure it's not near as low as it looks. These drawings always exaggerate everything. Goodness, if any woman had a bust that big and a waist that small, she'd be a freak." Julia read the description at the bottom of the page, then said, "It says the gown is made of watered silk, but I'm afraid we won't find any of that here. Let's walk over to the dry goods area and see what they have."

When they reached the dry goods, Danny looked about at the bolts of cloth stacked on the counters all around her in amazement, saying, "I ain't . . . I mean, I've never seen so much cloth in my life."

"Yes, it never ceases to amaze me what you can find in one of these post stores. Here's a bolt of satin, but that purple is the most hideous color I've ever seen." Then spying something, Julia said in excitement, "There it is! Why, it's perfect."

Danny looked about her, asking, "What's perfect?"

"That lace. Oh, Danny, that gown would look absolutely beautiful made from that."

"But it's white," Danny objected, thinking she wanted a pretty colored gown if she was going to have to wear one of the consarn things.

"Precisely. A coming-out gown should be white. That's what all the debutantes back East wear."

"But you can see right through that lace."

"No, you won't be able to see through it when I've finished. I'll make an underskirt out of another material and line the bodice."

"Ain't that gonna be a lot of work?" Danny asked, her speech momentarily slipping. "All those ruffles and things?"

"Isn't it going to be," Julia corrected gently, "and, yes, it will be a little work. But if I do say so myself, I'm an excellent seamstress."

Danny chewed her lower lip nervously, then said, "Maybe we ought to find something else. All those ruffles are going to take an awful lot of material. I ain't . . ." Danny winced, then corrected herself, ". . . haven't got that much money. And if I borrowed it from you, I'd be in debt to you for months."

"No, Danny, this gown is going to be a gift to you from John and I."

"A gift?" Danny asked in astonishment. "But my birthday isn't until February."

"You don't have to wait for special occasions to give gifts. Besides, this *is* a special occasion, your coming-out ball, and it's something John and I want to do. It's been such a pleasure having you with us."

Danny was deeply touched. Tears shimmered in her eyes. "I . . . I don't know what to say . . . except, thank you."

"That's quite sufficient, my dear. 'Thank you' are the two most meaningful words in the English language, if they're said with sincerity." Julia picked up the bolt of lace, saying, "Now, let's see if we can find some wide ribbon for your sash, and a narrower one for your hair,. and some white slippers. Satin would be nice, but we'll probably have to settle for white kid. And you're going to need some long dress gloves." Julia rushed off, calling over her shoulder, "Hurry, dear. We have a lot of shopping to do."

Danny stared at Julia's back, a horrified expression on her face. She was going to need all those things just to go to a hop? And, dad-blast it, she'd just got the shoes she was wearing broken in. Why, her feet would probably be covered with blisters by the time she'd danced all night in those new slippers. She longed for her wide, roomy boots, then groaned in resignation and followed Julia, thinking that being a lady was the hardest thing she'd ever done.

Two days before the dance, Julia sat at the kitchen table, putting the last stitches into Danny's ball gown while she tutored the girl in her reading. As a sudden thought occurred to Julia, she said, "My gracious! I completely forgot to ask. Do you know how to dance?"

Danny looked up from the reader and answered, "I suppose so. Brant took me to a dance a wagon train was having one night on our trip here."

He had taken her to a dance? Julia thought in surprise. Well, that sounded encouraging. "What did you dance?"

"Brant called it a two-step."

"Yes, we dance those, but we also dance schottisches, waltzes, even quadrilles. You'll have to learn those, too, and practice. But I'm afraid I can't help you there. We'll have to enlist John's aid."

That night John cleared the furniture from the middle of the parlor so that he could teach Danny how to dance. "But how can we dance without music?" Danny objected.

"I'll hum the tunes while you and John dance," Julia explained.

Danny was reluctant. She felt silly. Besides, she might step on the major's feet.

"Don't he hesitant, dear," Julia said. "John is an excellent dancer."

John grinned, saying, "You never told me you thought that."

"Well, I didn't want you to get swell-headed," Julia tossed back pertly.

John stepped up to Danny and slipped his hand behind her waist. As Danny took his outstretched hand, Julia said, "No, Danny, don't hold his hand. Let him hold yours. And remember to keep your gloves on tomorrow night. A gentleman and a lady never touch bare hands at a formal ball."

For hours, John and Danny practiced dancing. It was not until taps that Julia called a halt. Danny said good night and walked to her bedroom, wondering how she'd ever remember all the intricate steps of the various dances. Ladies and gentlemen sure made everything complicated.

As Julia pulled the bedroom door shut behind her and John, she said in a pleased voice, "She did so well. It's just amazing how fast she learns."

John sat the coal oil lamp he was carrying down on the small table beside their bed, answering, "She's a natural, born dancer, as light as a feather on her feet."

"Yes, I could see that. Oh, John, I've grown so fond of that girl."

John sat on the bed, looked at Julia for a long moment, than asked in a solemn voice, "Then why did you do it to her?"

"Do what?" Julia asked, stunned by his almost accusing tone of voice.

"Change her."

Seeing the stricken look come over his wife's face,

John said, "I'm sorry, Julia, but I have to say it. I don't approve of what you've done to Danny. There are thousands of beautiful young ladies in this world, so much so that they're commonplace. But there was only one Danny. She was never meant to live under a set of stifling rules that smothered her wild, free spirit, her remarkable vitality, and overflowing enthusiasm for life. You've destroyed something wonderfully natural and beautiful, and it saddens me."

Tears glittered in Julia's eyes. She rushed to the bed and sat beside her husband, saying in a distressed voice, "Oh, John, I fear you're right. I should have never done it."

"Then why did you?"

"Danny's becoming a lady wasn't my idea. It was hers. She asked me to help her, said she wanted to better herself. I only thought to smooth out a few of her rough edges. I had no idea that she'd throw herself into it the way she did. It wasn't until last Sunday that I realized why she was so determined. She's in love with Captain Holden. She has her heart set on him, and John, I'd give that girl anything she wanted, if I could. I just can't help myself!"

As Julia broke into tears, John took her into his arms, saying gently, "Don't cry, love. I understand now. I've come to love Danny just as much. But if Captain Holden couldn't appreciate Danny the way she was, he doesn't deserve her. No man would."

"Yes, as usual, you're right. Oh, John," Julia wailed softly, "what have I done?"

"Sssh, my dear. You can't blame yourself. If our little Danny has her heart set on that young man, nothing in the world will change her mind. Changing herself was her decision, and I suppose, her right. We'll just have to hope for the best."

"But I don't even know what's best for her anymore."

"Neither do I, my dear," John admitted, patting Julia's back consolingly, "but I'm afraid it's out of our hands. It's Danny's life. She has to live it as she sees fit."

The evening of the hop, Danny stood in the middle of her little bedroom as Julia gave her a last minute inspection before they left for the ball. "Do I . . . do I look all right?" Danny asked nervously.

Danny looked beautiful in her ball gown with the glittering silver sash around her tiny waist and the matching ribbon around the mass of reddish-brown curls piled on the top of her head. Julia hid the sadness in her heart and answered brightly, "You look absolutely ravishing, my dear."

Danny frowned. "Does that mean pretty?"

"Much more than pretty, my dear. Beautiful!"

A flush rose on Danny's face at Julia's compliment, making her complexion turn a delightful rosy color. In part, it was embarrassment, and in part excitement. This was the big night, the night she had been waiting for so anxiously. Oh, God, she prayed silently, please let Brant think she was beautiful too.

Julia pursed her lips and said thoughtfully, "However, there does seem to be something missing."

"What?" Danny asked in alarm.

"You look much too bare around the neck and shoulders."

Danny looked down at the broad expanse of creamy bare skin on her upper chest and cried in distress, "I was afraid it was going to be too low."

"No, that's not what I mean, dear. I mean it needs some jewelry." Julia whirled, saying over her shoulder as she rushed from the room, "Wait here. I'll be right back."

Julia returned with a long strand of pearls. Seeing them, Danny said, "I can't wear those."

"Why not?"

"Why, they must have cost a fortune. What if I lost them?"

Julia laughed, saying, "They're not real. Gracious, a real string of pearls like this *would* cost a fortune, something that you can be sure no officer could ever afford on his salary. No, every woman on the post has a string of these, and they're all imitations. But we don't care, as long as they're pretty. Now, duck your head, so I can slip them around your neck without messing up your hairdo."

Danny was still reluctant, but she complied. She raised her head and looked down at the creamy beads dangling over her breasts. Danny had never worn any jewelry, and she thought they looked awfully pretty, even if they weren't real. She fingered them, saying, "I'll take good care of them. I promise."

"I know you will, my dear, but even if you lost them, it wouldn't be any big loss. Now, slip on your gloves, and let's go. It's almost time for the hop to start."

When Danny and Julia walked from the bedroom, Julia stepped to the side, saying proudly to John, "Doesn't she look beautiful?"

While John much preferred the old Danny in shirt and pants and scuffed-up boots, the young woman standing before him was beautiful. "Yes, indeed she does. I've only seen one other woman who could compare with her stunning beauty."

Julia felt a twinge of jealousy. "Oh?" she asked in an icy voice, "and who was she?"

John smiled warmly, answering, "You, my dear."

A blush rose on Julia's face, then she said, "Oh, John, you're such a terrible tease!"

"I'm not teasing." The major stepped forward, and held out an arm to each lady, saying, "Shall we go? I can hardly wait to get to the ball and see the other officers' faces when I walk in with the two loveliest women on the post."

As they walked across the parade ground to the mess hall that had been cleared for the dance, Danny was so excited that her legs were trembling, and she feared her heart was going to jump right out of her chest if it beat any faster. The long wooden steps going up to the hall were decorated with red, white, and blue banners for the occasion, as was the interior of the hall, Danny discovered when they stepped into it. Then glancing at the other end of the long building, she said in surprise, "Why, the troopers are here too."

"They certainly are," John said, "This is as much their holiday as ours. They'll dance at that end, with their wives and guests, and the officers and their ladies at this."

Julia laughed, adding, "With the band in the middle so we can all dance to the same music."

"They don't seem to have many women to dance with," Danny observed.

"Oh, that won't stop them from joining in the festivities," Julia said. "They'll dance with each other." She laughed, saying, "Believe me, Danny, you've never seen anything as humorous as two tough Irishmen dancing with each other and tripping all over the other's feet. They curse and threaten to bash in the other's head if they step on their foot one more time, but they don't stop dancing. I've often feared it was going to turn into a brawl at that end of the hall with all the threats being flung about, but it never has. Apparently, insulting and threatening one another is part of the fun."

Danny laughed and turned her attention to the band. Then her eyes widened in surprise when she saw a fierce-looking bulldog sitting on the wooden dais with the musicians. "What's that dog doing in here?"

"That's King, the band's mascot," Julia informed her. "I'm surprised you haven't noticed him before during the parades. He always trots in front of the band, acting like he owns them, instead of vice versa."

Danny had never noticed the dog because her eyes had always been glued to the mounted men, hoping to get a glimpse of Brant. At the thought of him, Danny quickly glanced around her, but Brant was nowhere to be seen.

"Good evening, Danny," a deep male voice said. Danny turned, then said, "Good evening, Colonel Shafter."

"I'm so glad you came," the colonel said warmly. "You will save a dance for me, won't you?"

"I certainly will," Danny replied.

The colonel greeted John and Julia, then turned and walked away. The couple watched the commanding officer as he threaded his way through the crowd back to his wife with gratitude in their eyes. By making a point of personally welcoming Danny, the colonel had left no doubts in the others' mind that she belonged on this end of the hall, and not on the opposite end with the other female servants that the troopers had invited.

The ball started with the band playing the national anthem, as was befitting the holiday, the soldiers at both ends of the hall standing rigidly at attention and saluting the dais, although there was no raising of the flag. Mimicking the other women, Danny held her right hand over her heart, although she had no earthly idea what it was supposed to mean.

When the music died down and the hall was filled with a murmur of excited anticipation, John whispered to Julia, "Well, it looks like the boilermakers are in fine fiddle tonight."

"Shame on you, John," Julia scolded. "Why do you persist in calling the musicians that terrible name?"

"For the same reason the troopers do," John answered with a twinkle in his eyes, "because of all the noise they make."

"They don't make noise, they make music."

As if to prove Julia's point the band began playing a lovely waltz. When John stepped forward to take Julia in his arms, she whispered, "No, dear, dance the first dance with Danny."

"My dear, if you'd care to turn around and see for yourself, I don't think I could get anywhere near her right now. And if you think I'm going to wrestle all those young men aside at my age, you're sadly mistaken."

Julia turned and saw Danny was surrounded by a group of excited young officers, all asking to dance with her. She laughed and slipped into her husband's arms, saying, "We might not see her the rest of the night."

"Indeed, we might not," John answered, swinging his wife onto the dance floor.

Danny danced every dance, being very careful to

watch her manners and speech. All the young gentlemen were very polite, and the admiration she saw in their eyes was almost embarrassing. She might have been flattered by their attentions, except she had come to this dance for one purpose, to dance with one special man, and Brant had yet to show up. As the dance continued, she got more and more alarmed. What if he didn't come at all?

Then, during a break in the music, while she was standing and sipping a glass of punch in her circle of swains, Brant and Elizabeth stepped through the door. Danny stared at him hungrily, thinking he looked absolutely beautiful in his dark-blue dress uniform, with his golden hair shining under the lamplight and his blue, blue eyes. Then she frowned, becoming aware of how stormy those eyes looked. She knew he was angry.

Brant was more than angry. He was livid. Elizabeth had insisted that they wait outside until there was a break in the music so she could make a grand entrance. That in itself was bad enough, but Elizabeth had dressed to the hilt, wearing an expensive frock that looked like it was made of spun gold and her ears and throat and wrists dripping with diamonds. Christ, she even had a diamond tiara on her head, like she thought she was some goddamned queen. Brant despised her pretentiousness. In fact, he had come to the point where he despised everything about Elizabeth, and he didn't know how he was going to make it through the night. He felt like a total ass standing here with everyone staring at them.

Mrs. Shafter sensed his discomfiture and stepped forward, saying graciously, "I'm so glad you could make it." She glanced at Elizabeth, saying, "I was afraid you had changed your mind."

"No, I hadn't changed my mind," Elizabeth said in a haughty voice, smoothing the hair at the back of her ears in place to draw Mrs. Shafter's attention to her glittering necklace and dangling earrings. "I just couldn't decide which jewels to wear."

Brant clenched his fists to keep from throttling Elizabeth, then almost choked trying to hold a burst of laughter when Mrs. Shafter replied in a sickeningly sweet tone of voice, "Oh, those look very pretty, my dear. I always did like rhinestones."

As Elizabeth gasped in outrage, Mrs. Shafter turned and said over her shoulder, "Enjoy the dance."

The band struck up a waltz. "Did you hear what she called my jewels?" Elizabeth whispered to Brant in a furious voice. "Rhinestones! I've never been so insulted in my entire life."

Brant was saved from having to answer as an officer walked up and asked Elizabeth to dance. Elizabeth pasted a sweet smile on her face and said, "Oh, I really shouldn't. The first dance should go to my betrothed."

"Nonsense, Elizabeth, we don't stand on ceremony here," Brant said, thinking if he didn't get out of her presence soon, he'd kill her. "Be my guest, Lieutenant."

"Thank you, sir," the lieutenant replied, sweeping a startled Elizabeth out on the dance floor.

Relieved to be rid of her, Brant glanced over the couples whirling about the dance floor. Then, seeing Danny, his breath caught. The young lady did look incredibly beautiful, but she wasn't his Danny. It appeared that wonderful, delightful girl that he had come to love was gone for good, and so were any dreams he might have had for them. An unbearable sadness filled him, and he turned, wondering where the punch table was and if anyone had a bottle stashed away that he could borrow.

Danny had seen Brant looking at her, had wanted desperately for him to come and break in on the officer that was dancing with her. Then, when he turned and walked away, without so much as a smile, she was stunned. What had gone wrong?

As the ball progressed and Brant didn't ask Danny for one dance, she became increasingly more upset. She saw him dancing with Julia, with Mrs. Shafter, even once with Elizabeth, a wooden look on his face as he whirled the beautiful, dark-haired girl around the dance floor, but not once did he even glance in her direction.

Danny was dancing with a young lieutenant who had made a pest of himself in his ardent pursuit, trying very hard to remain polite and poised, although secretly she wanted to scream at him to leave her alone. Besides being obnoxiously persistent, he was a terrible dancer and kept stepping on her feet. She suddenly realized that the lieutenant was holding her much too close, and jerked away. When she did, the string of pearls Julia had loaned her caught in his coat button and broke. Pearls went flying everywhere.

Danny looked down at the pearls laying on the floor, the beads she had promised Julia she would be very careful with, and her composure broke. "You dad-blasted jackass!" she yelled at the startled lieutenant. "Now look what you've done! It was bad enough yer a-stomping on my poor aching feet all night, but now you've gone and made me bust Julia's purty string of pearls. They're scattered all over the floor from hell to breakfast. I ain't never gonna find 'em all."

"I'm . . . I'm sorry," the lieutenant stammered, his face white with shock.

Suddenly Danny was acutely aware that the music had stopped and that everyone was staring at her. She realized that her thin ladylike veneer had slipped, and that she had made a complete fool of herself, and fast on its heels came another, more profound realization. She had lost all hope of making Brant fall in love with her. Feeling the tears stinging at the back of her eyes, she pushed the lieutenant aside and raced from the hall.

Before she was even out the door, the band began to play a lively polka in hopes of covering what had been an awkward situation for everyone. As the couples began to dance, Julia said in a stricken voice, "Oh, John, go after her. Our poor little Danny."

"I'm going, my dear," he answered, patting her hand consolingly before he hurried off.

But as John weaved his way through the dancing couples, he saw another man shouldering his way to the door. Brant. As the captain stepped through the door, there was no doubt in John's mind that he was going to comfort Danny. He turned and walked back to his wife with a big smile on his face.

Seeing him, Julia asked in exasperation, "What are you doing back here? Why aren't you out there with Danny?"

"Calm down, dear. Let's step over there where we can talk more privately." John pulled his wife off to the side, ignoring the absolutely furious look on her face, then when they were out of hearing distance from anyone else, said, "Stop worrying, my dear. Danny's in good hands. Captain Holden went after her. Julia, that young man is in love with her. I saw it on his face as plain as day when he followed her. And I don't think it's something that recently happened. I think he fell in love with her on their trip here."

"Oh, John, that's wonderful!" Julia cried out joyously. Then as a sudden thought occurred to her, she said, "But, they shouldn't be out there alone, particularly if they're in love."

"They were alone for a long time on their trip here, Julia," John reminded her.

Julia's eyes widened at John's implication. "Oh, my goodness, they certainly were! Do you think—"

"I think it's time we leave the young lovers to themselves and concentrate on us two old ones," John said in a firm voice, cutting across Julia's words. He smiled warmly and said, "Did I tell you that you're the loveliest woman here?"

"Oh, John," Julia sighed, her love for her husband shining in her eyes, "you're such a terrible flatterer."

Chapter 19

When Brant stepped from the mess hall, he saw Danny running down the side of the parade ground in front of the barracks. He vaulted over the porch railing and ran after her, calling out, "Danny, come back!"

Danny was a white streak as she rounded the corner of the last barracks and raced towards the main gate, holding up the skirt of her lovely ball gown much too high for any lady and tears streaming down her cheeks. As she had done before in her pain, she was heading for Emily's grave, hoping to find consolation from the Indian girl who had also loved and lost.

As she tore past the sentry post at the gate, the startled trooper standing guard there stared at her in disbelief, then called out belatedly, "Halt!"

Danny didn't hear him, just as she hadn't heard Brant's call. Her total concentration was on her overwhelming pain. The flustered guard didn't know what to do. He certainly wasn't going to shoot the young woman, but if he left his post and went after her, the Sergeant of the Guard would skin him alive.

Hearing the sound of boots pounding on the packed dirt, he turned and saw Brant running towards him. "Thank God, you came along, sir," he said as Brant came abreast of him. "Some woman just ran past here like all the devils in hell were after her. She shouldn't be out there alone in the dark. It's too dangerous. Why, there might be wild animals out there, or Apaches. Do you want me to go after her?"

"No, I'll take care of it," Brant answered, looking about in the darkness, but seeing no sign of Danny. "Which way did she go?"

"Towards the old pump house."

Brant took off at a dead run. For a big man, he was a fast runner, but Danny was faster. She flew like the wind, despite her tight shoes. She heard Brant calling her. The sound of his voice only spurred her on. She couldn't face him now, not after the way she had humiliated herself. She was too ashamed, too mortified.

Her breath was rasping in her throat, her lungs feeling as if they would burst, and her arms were unbearably hot. She dropped her skirt, yanked off the long gloves as she ran, tossing them over her shoulder, then tripped on her skirt and almost fell flat on her face before she regained her footing. Cursing the hated female garment, she yanked it up to her waist, speeding through the night, the lacy skirt billowing out around her like white wings.

Danny would have run right past the old pump house, ran to the very ends of the earth to flee from Brant if she'd had to, but when she reached the grove of cottonwoods, the blisters on her feet were too painful to run any farther. She stopped to pull the offending slippers from her feet, jerking one off and tossing it aside angrily. Just as she was reaching for the second, Brant raced into the clearing. Spying him over her shoulder, Danny muttered, "Dad-blast it!" and made a leap for flight.

But Danny's stopping to take off her shoes had been her undoing. Brant caught her shoulders in mid-leap, pulling her back to him.

Danny struggled, crying out in a distraught voice, "Go away! I don't want you here! Dad-blast you, let me go!"

"No, I won't let you go, and I won't go away," Brant said in a firm but gentle voice, turning her to face him. "You need me."

"No, I don't need you! I don't need nobody!"

When Brant had seen the stricken expression on Danny's face when she had realized what she had done at the ball, his heart had gone out to her. Now, seeing her so anguished, with tears streaming down her face, his need to comfort her was even greater, a physical ache deep inside him. He wanted to take on the pain of her humiliation, to carry the burden for her, to hold her in his arms and keep her safe from all harm forever.

As Brant pulled her into his embrace, holding her tightly and muttering in his own anguish for her, "Oh, Danny," the pain within Danny welled up and spilled over as she started crying, heart-wrenching sobs that shook Brant to the depths of his soul.

And with the sobs came a flood of words, words that Danny would have never said had she not been so distraught and needing comforting so badly. "I made a dad-blasted fool of myself, and after all that hard work a-learning to be a lady. I ain't nothing but a tacky, country hick, and that's all I'm ever gonna be—an old sow's ear! I shamed myself, and Julia and the major, all because I wanted to make you proud of me, so you'd fall in love with me. I'm a silly fool, a-dreaming and a-wanting what

I couldn't have. A dad-blasted fool!"

She'd changed herself for him, Brant realized, his low spirits suddenly soaring to the limits of the sky. It hadn't been because she had wanted to be different, but because she thought he wanted it. Brant was deeply touched by her sacrifice, for he knew learning to become a lady had been sheer hell for Danny, but it had been totally unnecessary. "No, Danny, you didn't have to do that for me. I liked you the way you were. I told you that."

Brant slipped his hand under Danny's chin and raised her head. With his other hand, he smoothed back a long strand of hair that had come loose during her wild flight and was laying across her face. Then framing her tear-stained face with both hands, he looked deeply into her glistening eyes and said softly, "Danny, I love you, just the way you are."

Because Danny had waited so long to hear those words, because she wanted so desperately for them to be true, she believed. She stood, relishing his caring attentions while he pulled a handkerchief from his inside coat pocket and gently dabbed her tears away, then as he handed her the handkerchief and said, "Now, blow your nose," complied in typical Danny fashion by giving a loud, hardy snort that would have put a longhorn bull to shame, bringing a smile of warm amusement to Brant's lips.

As she handed the handkerchief back to Brant, he ignored it, his gaze on the glittering teardrops on her long, thick eyelashes. He bent and kissed them away, taking the salty drops from her as he longed to do to Danny's every pain. It was an incredibly loving act, and Danny knew she had died and gone to heaven, that she was drifting amongst the glittering stars. Her whole being was bathed with the soft glow of starlight, infusing her with warmth and filling her with an unbearable happiness. Yes, this was her night, the night she had promised herself, and nothing or no one was going to take it from her.

As Brant's lips closed over hers, warm and searching, brushing back and forth as if he was trying to memorize the texture of her lips, the handkerchief in Danny's hand fell to the ground between them. She folded her arms around his broad shoulders, her fingers seeking the soft golden hair that curled behind his ears as she leaned into him. It was heaven being held in his arms, feeling his strength surrounding her like a protective cocoon, being kissed so tenderly. As his tongue slipped into her mouth, tasting her sweetness as she tasted his, a moan of sheer ecstasy escaped her throat, her breath mingling with his.

Brant left a trail of soft kisses across her cheek and temple, then whispered in her ear, "I want to love you, Danny. Right here, right now."

Danny wanted it too, so badly she could taste it. "Oh, yes," she breathed.

He kissed her face, her throat, her shoulders, holding her to him with one arm, while his fingers on the other hand unbuttoned the tiny buttons at the back of her gown. When the gown fell away in a soft, frothy puddle of lace between their feet, Brant buried his face in the valley of her high, proud breasts, breathing deeply of her essence through her sheer chemise, then kissing her softness and saying in a husky voice, "You smell so sweet, so incredibly sweet."

He swept her up in his arms, lifting her from the puddle of her ball gown and her remaining shoe, and carried her beneath one of the cottonwoods. Over his shoulder, Danny saw a full moon rising over the mountains, tinting the jagged peaks in glittering silver and throwing a soft light over everything. She glanced up and saw Brant's hair was shining like a halo as it reflected the moonlight. She was filled to overflowing with beauty; the beauty of the moonlit summer night, the beauty of being carried in her lover's arms, the beauty of being loved by this golden god.

Brant sat her down on her feet beneath the tree, removed her petticoats, and spread them out on a moon-dabbled patch of ground for their bed. His immaculate, white gloves, dress sword, and coat followed. Then as he removed his shirt, Danny watched breathlessly as he bared his magnificent chest to her, the powerful muscles there and on his forearms flexing. Oh, God, she loved him so much it made her hurt inside.

Brant tossed his shirt aside, and then removed his boots and socks, his eyes never once leaving Danny. Then he undressed her, slipping off her chemise and drawers and kissing each inch of skin he exposed, adoring her with his eyes and lips, and cherishing her in his heart. His hands were trembling with an emotion much deeper than desire as he slipped down her hose, once again amazed at how silky soft her skin was.

He stood and gazed at her, drinking his fill of her beauty, then muttering in awe, "God, you're beautiful. Even more beautiful than I remembered."

Danny reveled in his blatant admiration and his heady words. Then boldly, she stepped forward and reached for his belt, thrilling at the shudder of excitement that ran over him at her touch and acutely aware of the huge bulge straining at his pants. As her fingers brushed his heated skin, moving lower and lower, Brant wished she would hurry. The suddenly too-tight pants were an agony, and he grew longer and harder at every tantalizing touch. Then, before undoing the last button that would release him from his confinement, Danny bathed his chest in torrid kisses. When her tongue flicked out across his hard male nipple, Brant sucked in his breath sharply, feeling as if a bolt of fire had shot to his loins. At that moment, Danny undid the last button and his erection leaped into her hand, hot, throbbing, and magnificent.

They both moaned, and a shudder of intense anticipation ran through them. Then Brant brushed her hand aside, and slid the pants past his slim hips, stepping out of them and drawing Danny to the ground with him, kissing her with fierce urgency.

Danny's blood sang at the feel of Brant's naked, feverish skin against hers, of his hard male body pressed against her softness. She kissed him back with wild abandon, her hands running over the powerful muscles on his back as his ran over hers. She matched him, kiss for kiss, deep and drugging one moment, then fierce and feverish the next, caress for caress, as they hungrily explored and rediscovered one another's secrets. As his hand slipped between her thighs, hers reached for him, both shuddering as waves of pleasure washed over them as they sensuously stroked one another.

When Brant felt as if he was being consumed by a flaming torch, he stilled her hand, drowning her objection in a deep kiss that left her breathless and her senses whirling, seemingly draining her soul and then pouring it back in. He dropped his golden head, his warm tongue swirling about the soft, silken flesh of her breasts before his teeth gently raked the throbbing peak. Danny

341

moaned, arching her back to him, then gasped as he took the nipple in his mouth, his tongue dancing and flicking, sending sparks racing up her spine.

"Now, Brant," Danny begged, the throbbing between her thighs having become unbearable and knowing only he could ease that pain. "Come into me, now."

But Brant ignored her as he slid down her body, dropping kisses as he went. He wanted to give her more pleasure before he buried himself in her warm, silken sheath, and give and give and give. And that's exactly what he did as his lips supped at her sweet moisture and his artful tongue worked its magic, stroking, swirling, flicking like a fiery dart, dipping in and out of the fount of her femininity. Over and over he brought her to that shuddering peak, holding her thrashing hips firmly in his hands so she couldn't escape him.

While she was still convulsing, he lifted his head, took her in his arms, and slipped into her velvety warmth, filling her slowly, deeply, completely with himself. Danny's eyes flew open, and their gaze locked. For a long moment, they stared into each other's eyes as they savored the exquisite feel of their bodies joined, throbbing in unison as if they shared the same heart. Then, unable to bear the tension, they moved simultaneously, the electric sensation of that movement taking their breaths away. Brant's mouth swooped down on hers, kissing her long, deeply, and lovingly. His thrusts, slow and sensuous at first, became harder, deeper, swifter as his kiss grew wilder and more and more passionate, reaching for her soul, determined to brand her as his for life. Steadily, they climbed those thundering heights until they reached that rapturous peak, trembling in intense anticipation as they hovered there, then crying out in joyous exhilaration as they soared to edges of the universe amongst showers of sparkles, the sweet sound of angels singing in their ears as they drifted back down.

When Danny emerged she was sobbing at the beauty of it, the wonder of it, the glory of it. Tenderly, Brant held her close, kissing her tears away. When she had regained her composure, he said softly. "We'd better go. The dance will be ending soon. If Major Duncan and his wife come home and don't find you there, they'll be worried about you."

Danny hated to give up her special night with Brant, but she knew what he said was true, and she had already caused the kindly couple enough heartbreak. They rose and dressed in silence.

As they started to walk away, Brant took her hand in his, then noticing she was limping, asked, "Is there a rock in your slipper?"

"Nope. These dad-blasted shoes are so tight they rubbed blisters on my heels. Reckon I'd better take 'em off."

As Danny bent to remove her slippers, Brant swooped her up in his arms, saying, "I'll carry you."

"All the way back to the fort?" Danny asked in disbelief.

Brant felt it was the least he could do after all the suffering Danny had gone through for him. "Yes, all the way back to the fort."

Danny didn't object. It meant she could be in his arms a little longer.

When Brant walked up to the sentry post, the guard standing there said, "I'm sure glad you found her, sir. You've been gone so long I was beginning to get worried."

343

"It took me a while to find her," Brant lied smoothly.

"How come you're carrying her? Is she hurt?"

"She twisted her ankle." Brant gave the trooper a hard, warning look and said, "I'd appreciate it if you won't say anything about this to anyone."

The guard was no fool. He knew it was an order, and not a request. He snapped a salute and answered, "Yes, sir."

Brant turned, saying over his shoulder. "Good night, Trooper."

"Good night, sir," the guard answered stiffly.

When they reached the parade ground, Brant stopped and looked about the wide-open area. Bathed in moonlight as it was, he could see almost as well as if it were broad daylight. No one was in sight, but he could hear the sounds of music coming from the mess hall where the hop was still going on. If someone should come out for a breath of air and see him carrying Danny across the parade ground, it would cause even more talk about her, and he wanted to protect her from any further embarrassment. That's why he had told the sentry to keep his mouth shut. No one had to know where Danny fled when she ran to the old pump house, or that he and she were out there for much too long.

Brant ducked his head, trying to see Danny's face. Laying with her head on his shoulder, she had been so still and quiet that he wondered if she had fallen asleep. "Danny, are you awake?"

"Yep."

"Do you think you can walk from here?"

"I can if I go barefooted."

Brant dropped Danny to her feet and supported her while she slipped off her shoes. Taking the slippers from her, Brant offered her his arm, and they strolled across the parade ground, looking like any other couple who might be on their way home from the dance.

When they reached John and Julia's home, the house was dark. Standing on the front porch, Brant said, "Let me light the lamp in the parlor first, so you won't trip on anything."

Danny waited outside while Brant found and lit the lamp, then seeing the flare of light, stepped across the threshold. Carrying the lamp with him, Brant quickly checked all the rooms, although he realized it really wasn't necessary. A trooper might rob another in the barracks, or lie in wait in the dark outside to attack someone, but no one would ever dream of entering someone's home. Homes were considered sacred on these lonely, remote outposts.

Placing the lamp on the table, Brant turned to Danny. He had noticed that she had been unusually quiet, and now she had a sad look on her face. Assuming that she was mulling over her humiliating experience at the dance, he said, "Don't worry about what happened at the dance. It wasn't that important. A few people may talk about it for a day or so, but then it will be forgotten."

Danny nodded.

Brant bent and kissed her lips softly, then said, "I'll see you tomorrow. You'll feel much better after a good night's rest."

Brant turned and said, "Good night," then stepped outside, pulling the door shut behind him.

How could he say what had happened at the dance wasn't important, Danny thought, feeling as if her heart would break. It was a catastrophe to her, and now, because she failed so miserably at becoming a lady, she had lost him for good. Oh, he had told her he loved her, but that was only after she had blurted out her feelings for him. He didn't love her. He just pitied her. But Danny had wanted it to be true so bad that she had allowed herself to believe, had reveled in his lovemaking. He had taken her to heaven, up to his world amongst the glittering stars, but Danny didn't belong there. Nothing had changed. If it had, if he truly loved her, he would have asked her to marry him.

The tears came then, in an anguished torrent. She ran to her room and threw herself on her bed, crying until she was so exhausted from the emotional upheaval of the evening's events that she fell asleep.

When Brant stepped into his small cabin after he had left Danny, he sensed someone was there. He looked about the darkness warily and asked, "Who's there?"

He heard the sound of a match being struck, then as the lamp flared, saw Elizabeth. "What in the hell are you doing here?"

"Don't use that tone of voice to me!" Elizabeth threw back angrily. "How dare you humiliate me by leaving me at the dance and running off after that . . . that—"

"Don't say it, Elizabeth," Brant said in a hard, warning voice. "Don't call Danny any ugly names, because if you do, I can't be responsible for what I might do to you."

Elizabeth was stunned by the fury she saw in his blazing blue eyes. For once, she wasn't excited by his anger. She was terrified. He looked as if he could kill her with his bare hands.

"Why . . . why not?" she stammered.

"Because Danny is the woman I love, the woman I'm

going to marry, and I won't stand by and have her insulted by anyone."

"The woman you're going to marry?" Elizabeth asked in a shocked voice. "But you're engaged to me!"

"Not anymore, I'm not. As of this minute, we are no longer engaged. I'm breaking it."

"You wouldn't dare! Think of what people will say."

"I don't give a damn what people say! Not anymore. All I care about is Danny. She's the only person who's important to me."

"You'd sacrifice your honor for her?"

"I'd give up my life for her, and be proud to do it. Honor without honesty is nothing but a sham. And that's what our engagement has been. A sham! I never loved you, and I never had any intention of marrying you."

Elizabeth realized that she was losing Brant and was desperate to hold on to him. "Your father will be furious! He'll—"

"My father doesn't run my life!" Brant threw back angrily. "He never did, and he never will. When are you and he finally going to learn that? How long is it going to take to sink into your thick skulls that I'm my own man?"

"And you're actually going to marry that..." Elizabeth hesitated. She had been about to say slut, but seeing the warning glitter in Brant's eyes, quickly revised her words. "... that girl? Take her back East with you?"

"I'm not going back East, unless for a visit sometime," Brant answered, thinking that someday he'd like to show Danny all of the things he had seen. Seeing them through her eyes would be a totally new experience. "I'm planning on settling here in Texas when my enlistment is up this fall."

347

Elizabeth was even more shocked by Brant's announcement than she had been by his telling her he was in love with that crude, backward tomboy. "You'd live in this hellhole by choice?"

"I know there are some people who consider Texas a hellhole, but I don't. I think it's a beautiful land, particularly the western part, with its wide-open spaces and stark beauty. It's a harsh, untamed land that challenges a man to conquer it and stirs his imagination, a land where a man can become a giant, if he sets his mind to it."

Elizabeth thought Brant had gone insane. She knew nothing of dreams and visions of greatness that could stir a man's soul. Her whole little world had revolved around herself. And it was herself she was thinking of at that moment. She couldn't bear the shame of being jilted. "I wish you had told me that sooner. If I'd had any idea of your ridiculous plans for settling here in Texas, I would have broken the engagement long ago. After all, I should have some choice where I'm going to live the rest of my life."

Brant knew what Elizabeth was suggesting. If she wanted to save face by claiming she had broken the engagement, instead of him, that was fine with him. He just wanted her permanently out of his life. "If you prefer to tell people that you were the one who broke the engagement, I'm agreeable."

A look of profound relief came over Elizabeth's face. Then she remembered Mrs. Shafter's insulting remark about her jewels. What in the world had gotten into the woman to treat her in such a disrespectful manner? Yes, she'd be glad to see the last of this dusty, hot, backward settlement and this rude man and that insolent woman. She couldn't wait to go back East. "I'll be leaving on the stage tomorrow, instead of waiting for the one later in the week."

"That's fine with me, Elizabeth. The sooner you're out of my life, the better."

He didn't have to be so damn happy about it, Elizabeth thought. Why, he was almost gloating. A furious expression came over Elizabeth's face. "You're hateful, Brant! I don't know what I ever saw in you! I hope I never lay eyes on you again in my life!"

Elizabeth flew from the cabin, slamming the door angrily behind her. Brant smiled in satisfaction. He was free! He had finally thrown off the shackles of convention that had held him bound to her and felt as if a tremendous burden had been taken from him. She had been like a millstone around his neck for over five years. He wondered why it had taken him so long to get up the courage. It had been much easier than he thought. All he'd had to do was stand his ground. Now, he could get on with his life with Danny. Tomorrow, he'd ask her to marry him. An immense happiness filled him.

Shortly after the call of "Boots and Saddles" rang out over Fort Davis the next morning, Brant was summoned to Colonel Shafter's office. As he crossed the parade ground, he wondered why the colonel wanted to see him. Had Elizabeth reconsidered and decided she wouldn't release him from their engagement after all? Had she enlisted the colonel's aid to remind him of his duty as a gentleman. If that were the case, they could both go to hell!

Brant entered the colonel's office with his face set with fierce determination. When he stepped into the room,

349

the colonel had his back to him and was studying a large map of west Texas that was pinned to the wall behind his desk. Without even turning around to acknowledge him, the colonel pointed to an area about sixty-five miles southeast of the fort and said, "That's where you're to take the gun, Captain Holden. To Pena Colorado."

Brant frowned, then asked, "What gun, sir?"

The colonel turned from the map and said, "I'm sorry. I'm getting ahead of myself. I want you to pick up a Gatling gun at Fort Stockton and deliver it to Pena Colorado."

"A Gatling gun?" Brant asked in disbelief.

"Yes. Word arrived before daylight that Chief Alsate and his warriors have been terrorizing the entire Chihuahua Trail for a good hundred miles north of Presidio. The garrison at Pena Colorado, who protects that area, has been expecting an attack for days now. They're pitifully undermanned. My superior officer believes a Gatling gun could help to even the odds between them and the Apaches. I've been ordered to send a troop to Fort Stockton to pick up the gun and deliver it to them. I've picked you for this assignment, but only take half of your men with you. With Troop A out on patrol already, I'm afraid that's all I can spare. We might well come under attack ourselves. The Apaches hit Musquez Ranch, six miles from here, yesterday."

"Yesterday?" Brant asked in surprise.

"Yes. I didn't want to spoil everyone's holiday, so I kept it quiet. Several people were killed and the cattle run off. That's the way the Apaches operate. They attack here one day, there another, then seemingly everywhere at once, spreading terror over the entire territory." The colonel paused, then said, "Because of the recent attack

350

in the vicinity, I'm sending you and your men as escort to the stage that leaves here this morning for Fort Stockton, since that's your first destination anyway."

That's the stage Elizabeth will be traveling on, Brant thought with a frown.

Seeing his expression, Colonel Shafter said, "I don't mean to put you in an awkward position, Captain. Elizabeth told my wife and I that she broke your engagement last night. But I really want you to lead this mission, since you did such an outstanding job on bringing back those deserters. This patrol might run into trouble with Apaches, and I want an aggressive, decisive office in charge."

"I can't see where riding escort to the stage my ex-fiancée is traveling on would pose any problem, sir," Brant answered, thinking there would be no reason for he and Elizabeth to even talk to one another. She'd stay in the coach and sleep at the stage stands, and he and his troopers would be outside.

The colonel wasn't particularly surprised at how well Brant was taking Elizabeth's breaking their engagement. If he were Brant, he would be jumping up and down for joy. But Elizabeth had told them some rather distressing news. "I understand you're planning on leaving the service in the fall and settling here in Texas."

"Yes, sir," Brant admitted readily. "My enlistment is up the middle of November. I planned on giving you a three month notice, so you could find a replacement for me."

"You won't change your mind?" the colonel asked hopefully. "I hate to lose a good officer like you."

"Thank you, sir, but I'm afraid not. I have definite plans for the future, and I'm anxious to get started on them."

351

"I understand," Colonel Shafter answered, wondering if Danny was included in the captain's future plans.

"Are me and my troopers to stay at Pena Colorado after we've delivered the gun, or return here?" Brant asked.

"You're to come back to Fort Davis at all possible speed. I may need your men to defend this post." The colonel pulled out his pocket watch, looked at it, and said, "I'm sorry I can't give you more time to make your preparations, but I just received my orders an hour ago myself. The stage leaves at nine o'clock. You'll have to hurry to pick the men you're taking with you and draw your field rations, ammunition, and feed from the quartermaster."

He certainly didn't have much time, Brant thought, and he was determined to see Danny before he left. He might be gone for several weeks, and he wanted her answer before he departed. "In that case, I'd better be going," Brant answered, snapping a salute.

As he walked to the door, Colonel Shafter said, "Good luck."

"Thank you, sir," Brant answered over his shoulder, already formulating his marriage proposal to Danny.

Fifteen minutes before the stage was due to depart, Brant rushed across the parade ground to the Duncan's home, leaving his men already mounted and waiting for him.

Julia answered his knock on the door, saying, "Why, good morning, Captain."

"Good morning, ma'am. May I see Danny for a moment?"

Julia frowned, then answered, "I'm afraid she's not here right now. I don't know where she went. She left the house right after we finished breakfast, but I'm sure she's somewhere here on the post. Perhaps you could come back a little later."

"I'm afraid that's impossible," Brant answered with a keen disappointment. "I'm leaving on patrol in a few minutes, and I may not be back for weeks."

"Oh, I'm sorry to hear that," Julia answered, knowing Brant was distressed at having missed Danny. His deep regret was clearly written on his face.

Brant glanced over the post, hoping to get a glimpse of Danny; then seeing Sgt. O'Bannon waving at him from the other side of the parade ground, Brant said in a resigned voice, "I'm afraid it's time to leave." He hesitated, then asked, "Would you do me a favor? Would you tell Danny we have something very important to discuss as soon as I've returned?"

He's going to propose, Julia thought in excitement. Her eyes shone with happiness for Danny as she said, "I most certainly will, Captain."

"Thank you, and good day," Brant answered, then turned and rushed off.

Danny had gone for an early morning ride on Red in hopes of relieving her depression over the disastrous results of the previous evening by spending some time with her old friend. She was riding back to the post when she spied Brant and his troop riding from the main gate. She veered her horse from the road and stopped behind some bushes, hiding there while Brant and his troop trotted past. She couldn't face him just yet.

353

As the stage passed, Danny saw Elizabeth in it, staring straight ahead. Danny saw nothing significant in her leaving. Everyone at the fort had known she had only come for a visit. What did impress Danny was that Brant was riding escort, going along to protect his fiancée. To Danny, it only confirmed what she had suspected. What Brant had shown her the night before had only been pity, and she could accept anything but that from him. Her fierce pride wouldn't allow it. She was glad that she had listened to her instincts and hid. She could never face him again.

Danny reverted to her old self, someone she much preferred being, or at least she thought she had. She relished the feel of her comfortable, old clothing, being able to take wide, swaggering strides and say what she thought, when she pleased, in her own inalienable way.

Julia and John were pleased to see the changes that took place, but Danny was still not the girl they had known from the beginning. She was just as energetic, just as entertaining in her speech, but that overflowing enthusiasm for life, that supreme self-confidence, that certain magical spark that had marked Danny as one of a kind seemed suppressed. The couple wondered if it was simply a hangover from the rigid control she had exercised over herself when she was learning to become a lady, or if Danny had undergone permanent changes in her personality.

One afternoon, a week after Brant had left the fort, Danny said to her pet snake, "Come on, Charlie. Let's go visit a spell with Emily. We ain't been to see her in a month of Sundays. I bet she thinks I've fergotten all

354

about her. 'Sides, I have a heap of a-thinking to do, and I always think better out there away from all these dad-blasted noises on this post."

Charlie didn't look like he was interested in going anywhere at the moment. He was perfectly content to lazily sun himself on Danny's windowsill. Nonetheless, Danny picked him up and shoved him into his canvas bag, her mind already preoccupied with her problems.

When they reached Emily's grave at the foot of the mountain, Danny sat down beside it and said, "Howdy, Emily. Sorry I ain't been to see you any sooner. I reckon you know all about me a-making a dad-blasted fool of myself over Brant. Plumb silly of me, wasn't it, a-thinking I could be a lady? I bet you was a-laughing yer head off. I reckon I should have come to talk it over with you first. You could have told me how hopeless it was."

The sound of delighted laughter caught Danny's attention. She looked out at the grove of cottonwoods in the distance, seeing a group of Mexican children playing tag there, darting from tree to tree as they chased each other. Then Danny frowned, noting a tow-headed boy playing with the Mexicans and recognizing him as an officer's son from the fort. "I bet his ma don't know he snuck out of the post and is out here with no grownups," Danny remarked to Emily. "She'd skin him alive if she did."

For a moment, Danny watched the children playing. Then her mind returned to her problems, so preoccupied with them that she wasn't even aware of Charlie squirming in his bag against her side, trying to tell her he wanted out. Danny knew Brant would be returning to the fort in a week or two. Julia had relayed his message to her, and while Julia seemed to think that Brant had been hinting at a marriage proposal when he had said he had something important to discuss with her when he returned, Danny scoffed at the idea. Julia was plumb loco if she thought Brant would marry her, but Danny hadn't wanted to hurt Julia's feelings, so she had just smiled. Danny still couldn't face Brant. She had to leave before he got back. She supposed she could get a job as a guard on the stage line, since she could outshoot just about anybody. All she'd have to do is remind them how she'd killed those outlaws, and they'd probably hire her right on the spot. But that would mean she would have to leave Julia and John, and she'd gotten real attached to them.

Dad-blasted, why did she go and get that silly idea about becoming a lady? Danny thought in self-disgust. She'd gotten used to the idea of knowing she could never have Brant, and could even face him. Now, she was gonna either have to swallow her pride, or leave, and she couldn't do the first and didn't want to do the latter.

The sounds of the children intruded on her thoughts. Suddenly she became aware that their squeals of delight had turned to screams of terror. She glanced quickly at the grove and saw, to her horror, that several Apache warriors had captured the children and were carrying them away. Danny sprang to her feet, her hand automatically going for the gun at her side. Then, a sick feeling came over her as she realized she had forgotten to bring it with her. She whirled, intending to race to the fort for help. Before she could even run a few steps, two Apaches leaped out at her, seemingly materializing out of nowhere.

"Let go of me, you dad-blasted Injuns!" Danny screamed, as the two grabbed her arms.

Danny fought with all her might. She kicked, twisted wildly, bucked, butted them with her head, cursing a blue streak all the while, but to no avail. The lean, sunbaked Apaches were unbelievably strong for men of such small stature, and apparently they were inured to pain, showing not the slightest reaction to her blows.

As they started to pull her away, Danny dug in her heels. That didn't work either. They simply dragged her to where they had hidden their horses amongst a pile of large boulders. She was as helpless against their brute strength and fierce determination as the children when they threw her astride a horse, tied her wrists together with rawhide, then tied her feet below the horse.

A second later, the Apaches were mounted. A bronzed warrior brushed past her, picking up the reins of her horse before he galloped off. As the animal Danny was on lurched forward, she held on its mane for dear life, knowing if she fell, she would be dragged beneath the horse. Why, her back and head would be a bloody pulp before the Indian could stop the racing horse—if he stopped it at all.

As they sped away, Danny knew there was no hope of help coming from the fort. It was too far away for anyone to hear the children's screams. But she wasn't afraid. She was much too angry at herself to feel that emotion. "You dad-blasted fool!" she muttered in furious self-disgust. "You were so danged busy a-mooning over a man that you plumb fergot your gun. Now look at the mess you're in. And all because you were a-acting like a stupid, silly female."

Chapter 20

Brant shifted his weight in the saddle and looked over his shoulder, seeing the double line of troopers riding behind him and the two mules pulling the heavy Gatling gun. Behind the clumsy gun, mounted on field gun carriage, rode the rest of his troopers, and bringing up the rear of the column was the supply and feed wagon. They had left Fort Stockton a week ago and had made tedious progress due to multiple breakdowns of the gun carriage. Every man was weary, frustrated from the delays, and covered with so much dust that their uniforms looked to be gray, instead of blue.

"I hope to God ye're not gonna tell me the wheel on that blasted carriage is wobbling again," Sgt. O'Bannon said from where he was riding beside Brant.

Brant turned in his saddle, answering, "No, it looks all right, at least for the time being. Let's face it, those carriages simply weren't made for the rocky, rugged terrain we've been traveling over."

"Well, this desert we're traveling over now 'tis sandy enough, providing the damn heavy thing doesn't sink in it." The sergeant paused, gazed up at the blazing sun for a short moment, then swept off his forage cap and wiped the sweat from his brow with his forearm, saying, "Jesus, Mary, and Joseph, 'tis hot enough to fry yer brains out here."

Brant was just as miserably hot, and like every one of his troopers, his lips were cracked, his throat was parched, and the back of his neck was sunburned. He looked around him. What he saw was a picture of barrenness and desolation. To one side of them was a long range of high hills, and to the opposite side and before them stretched out a desert on which only cactus, thorn bushes, and an occasional squatty desert olive grew, the flat terrain broken here and there by weathered buttes and towering spires of twisted rock that jutted from the landscape. Heat waves shimmered from everything as the desert and rocks reflected the scorching heat of the sun. It was a lonely, sunbaked, uninhabited, godforsaken world whose silence was as oppressive as its heat.

Spying a mountain range far to the south of them, Brant turned to the lanky, deeply tanned man riding on the opposite side of him and asked "What's the name of those mountains over there?"

"They're the Chisos Mountains. They look blue from this distance, but up close they have a copperish color, and when they're shrouded with mist in the wintertime, they look downright spooky. That's why some people call 'em the Ghost Mountains."

The words had been said with a lazy Texas drawl. Brant had been surprised when he'd discovered that this man had been assigned to him as his scout on this mission, instead of the usual Seminole. Sam Eaton was an ex-Texas Ranger temporarily employed as a scout for the army, and Brant was glad to have him along. He was a tough, old Indian fighter, as lean, as brown, as hard-muscled, as inured to hardships as the savages he sought. Having served in the Texas Rangers off and on for over a score of years, he had more experience in fighting Indians than all of Brant's troopers combined.

"Have you ever been to Pena Colorado?" Brant asked the scout.

Sam spit out a stream of tobacco juice before answering, "Yep. It's not much of a fort though. Just a few crumbling adobe buildings sitting in the middle of a heap of red rocks with a scorching desert all around it. Seems like a dumb-fool place to build a fort to me. There's not a damn thing within a hundred miles, other than one ranch. And you cavalry boys don't have to worry about protecting Milton Faver's ranch. Hell, his headquarters is built like a fortress. The Apaches could batter at those walls until doomsday and not break 'em down. Why, Faver even has a cannon."

"They're not there to protect the settlers in the area," Brant pointed out. "They're there to protect the Chihuahua Trail."

"Then why in the hell didn't they build that fort on the trail, instead of thirty miles south of its lowest fork?" Sam asked in disgust.

Pena Colorado had been built on the lower of the three old Comanche traces that led into Mexico, ancient trails by which the Indians made their annual raids into that country. But what Sam had said was true. The Chihuahua Trail split at Fort Stockton, half following the middle Comanche trace and the other half following the upper trail and passing south of Fort Davis. It did seem like Pena Colorado protected nothing. But Brant didn't comment. He'd learned a long time ago that the army didn't always do the logical thing. Like that Gatling gun back there. The rangy Texan scout had hit the truth square on the nose when he'd scoffed at the gun and said it would be useless against the Apaches. The machine gun was designed to be used against mass charges, a battle tactic that the Apaches scorned and never used. Brant feared taking the gun to the garrison at Pena Colorado would all be for nothing, a total waste of time, money, and energy. Besides, Brant had never been impressed with the gun. In theory, it sounded great. The ten barrels that rotated around a central shaft and were operated by a hand crank could be fired at the rapid rate of eight hundred shots a minute, but the guns were highly temperamental, apt to jam, break down, and prove unreliable in the clutch. In Brant's opinion the gun needed more perfecting and needed to be lightened. It was a heavy, awkward piece of equipment that needed several men just to turn it, to say nothing of bogging down in mud and sinking in deep sand.

Brant glanced over at the range of hills beside them, then tensed, seeing a puff of rolling smoke rising in the air from the highest peak. As a second puff followed, Brant looked quickly around him, expecting to see an answering smoke signal coming from one of the flat-topped buttes.

"They ain't signaling to other Injuns," Sam said in a lackadaisical tone of voice, having noticed the smoke signals even before Brant had. "They're talking to us. They want a parley with the war chief of this patrol. I reckon that's you, Captain."

"What do they want to talk to me about?" Brant asked in surprise. From all he had heard about Apaches, they

361

just attacked, suddenly and lethally, without any warning.

"They didn't say. They just said for you and your scout to ride out from your troop and meet with their spokesmen at the bottom of that big pile of boulders up ahead, and to warn your yellowlegs not to try anything. We're surrounded."

Brant looked all around him and saw absolutely nothing. The only sign of life was a lone hawk circling lazily in the azure sky high above them.

"You won't see 'em until they're ready for you to, Cap'n. Then they'll pop out of the desert all around you. Might as well save the strain on your eyes. But they're out there, all right. I can smell the stinking bastards."

Brant knew he had no choice but to obey the Apaches' summons. There was no telling how many Indians were concealed all around them. There could be fifty, or a thousand. Unlike the Comanches, who showed themselves and counted on the sight of their awesome numbers bringing terror to the hearts of their enemies, the Apaches hid behind every bush, boulder, and clump of cactus and lay in every gully, their brown bodies blending in with the landscape. Knowing they were there and not being able to see them was much more terrifying. You couldn't shoot an enemy you couldn't see.

Brant called his troop to a halt and turned to his second in command, Sgt. O'Bannon, since he had elected to leave his two green lieutenants behind at Fort Davis. "O'Bannon, if this is a trick and they kill us, head like hell for those rocks over there and load up that damn Gatling gun. I seriously doubt that it will do you much good, but it's unlikely that they've ever seen one. If nothing else, maybe it will scare the hell out of them. But whatever you do, don't let it fall into their hands. Those Apaches are lethal enough with their ambushes in mountain passes. Can't you just imagine how they could slaughter us if they had a machine gun up on one of those ridges with them?"

"Aye, we'd be so many sitting ducks fer 'em to mow down," O'Bannon answered in a grim voice. "Don't worry, sir. They won't get their hands on that gun, I promise ye. I'll personally blow it up, even if I have to do it with me last dying breath."

Brant nodded his head solemnly, then turned to his scout, saying, "Come on, Sam. Let's go see what those bastards are up to."

As Brant and his scout trotted their mounts to the pile of boulders, Brant saw two Apaches riding out from the hills where the smoke signal had come. He noticed that the warriors wore elaborate, fringed buckskin shirts that were painted with red, brown, and yellow symbols, breechcloths, moccasins, and turbans made of skins and decorated with amulets. "I thought Apaches didn't wear buckskins," Brant remarked, recalling what Danny had told him about the Indians that had attacked her home, "and that they wore cloth headbands."

"Ordinarily, they don't, even when they're raiding. Those skin shirts and turbans are their warpath clothes. See those strings of braided hide draped across their bodies? Those are their *izze-kloth*, their medicine cords. They have a bag of *ha-dintin*—cattail pollen—hanging on the end of 'em. The Apaches put a lot of faith in that pollen. They seem to think it's powerful medicine. They use it in almost all of their religious ceremonies."

"Are you trying to tell me that the Apaches differentiate between raiding and warring?"

"Yep, they sure do. To the Apaches, raiding is akin to hunting. It's a means of attaining food and plunder to buy the necessities of life. There are villages in Mexico that they allow to exist solely for that purpose, to raid. They leave just enough for the Mexicans to rebuild, so they can raid again. On the other hand, war is a matter of revenge and hate. Killing and total destruction are their prime objectives."

The Apaches reached the boulders first and reined in their horses and waited, the looks on their leathery, bronzed faces totally unreadable, making them look as if they were carved from stone, instead of flesh and blood. Brant and Sam brought their mounts to a halt a few feet away. For a long moment, the four men stared at each other, all taking silent measure of their enemy. Then one of the Indians introduced himself as Colorado, one of Chief Alsate's sub-chiefs, and started talking, directing his words to the lanky, tough scout.

Brant didn't have to wait for Sam to interpret for him. The Apache was speaking the *lingua franca* that the southwestern tribes used to communicate with one another, a mixture of several Indian dialects that was liberally sprinkled with Spanish. There was just enough of the latter that Brant got the gist of what the Mescalero was saying. The Apaches had hostages that they wanted to trade for the Gatling gun. If Brant refused to bow to their demands, the hostages would be killed.

Before Sam even turned to him to explain what the Apaches wanted, Brant asked the Apache sub-chief in Spanish, "Who are these hostages and where did you get them?"

A look of surprise crossed the Apache's dark,

weathered face. He had never met a yellowlegs chief who spoke Spanish. "Four children and a woman," Colorado answered in the Mexican tongue. "We captured them three days ago at Painted Camp."

Brant turned to Sam and asked, "Where is that?"

"Painted Camp is what the Mescaleros called their old *rancheria* where the original Fort Davis was built."

Brant's heart leaped to his throat, and his mouth turned dry with fear for Danny. He could hardly force his words to the Apache out. "You attacked the fort?"

"No. We went there to capture hostages. We took them from the grove of cottonwoods by the stream." The Apache's dark eyes glittered with unadulterated hatred, and a smirk crossed his thin lips. "We will attack the white-eyes after we have the big gun that rattles like a woodpecker on a tree. But you will not know where, or when."

Brant frowned. It was an excellent description of the rattle of Gatling gun. But how did this Apache know that?

"How do I know you aren't lying to me about these hostages, or that they're still alive?" Brant asked.

Colorado wasn't surprised by Brant's suspiciousness. It had been anticipated. "We will show them to you. Look up there and see for yourself."

Brant and Sam looked up at the flat-topped butte in the distance that the Mescalero pointed to. Brant could barely see the dozen or so people standing on it. Picking up his field glasses that were hanging around his neck, he lifted them to his eyes and peered through them. Four Apache warriors held a terrified child in front of them, three dark-headed children who Brant had never seen, and one tow-headed boy he recognized as Major Bentley's son. Then, as Brant turned his gaze to the fifth captive being held by two Apaches a little farther to the right, he sucked in his breath sharply. It was Danny!

Fear for the woman he loved came surging to the surface like a monumental tidal wave, but Brant knew better than to allow his feelings to show. If the Apaches knew he was emotionally involved with the woman captive, they would use it to strengthen their advantage. Why, they might even torture her before his eyes to force him to bow to their demands. No, he had to keep his fear and anger suppressed, to remain cool and calm, and not to let his emotions interfere with his thinking. He had to figure out someway to rescue Danny and those children, but he needed time.

Carefully schooling himself to betray no emotion, Brant said in a clipped voice, "Tell Chief Alsate that this is something I will have to think over very carefully. It's not just my decision. It involves many others. I will have to decide what my superiors would want me to do."

Colorado was well aware of the dilemma the yellow-legs chief was facing. If he didn't give the gun to them, five *pin-dah-lickoyee*—white-eyed enemies—would die. If he did, many more might die. But Chief Alsate was counting heavily on the yellowlegs chief's compassion. It would take a hard-hearted man to allow innocent children to die, particularly now that he had seen them and they were no longer faceless. That was why Chief Alsate had specifically ordered his warriors to bring back children. Because they were so helpless, they had more bargaining power. The woman they had found with them had only been an added bonus. White-eyes were as protective over their women as they were their children.

"Chief Alsate anticipated you would say this," the Mescalero answered Brant. "You have until tomorrow

366

morning to decide. At sunrise, you will return to these rocks and give us your answer. If your answer is yes, I will lead you to the spot in the mountains where the gun and hostages are to be exchanged. If your answer is no . . ." The Apache's voice trailed off and he shrugged, leaving Brant to come to his own gruesome conclusions.

"What are you talking about?" Brant asked in a hard voice. "Lead us into the mountains? Why can't we just make the exchange right here, if that's what I decide to do?"

"And have you try to rescue the hostages during the night?" Colorado asked with a sneer. "No! They are already being moved to a hidden place for safekeeping in the mountains, a place where you will never find them. That is where the exchange will be made."

Brant's eyes darted to the butte where he had seen Danny and the children. They and their Apache guards were gone. Damn, Brant thought in angry frustration. He had never credited the Apaches for having so much foresight. Apparently, this Chief Alsate planned his battle tactics as carefully and thoroughly as any general.

"Tomorrow, at sunrise," Colorado reminded Brant as he turned his horse, then galloped away with the second Apache, leaving a thick cloud of dust in their wake.

As Brant and Sam rode back to the waiting troopers, Sam leaned from his saddle, spat tobacco juice on the ground, and asked, "Who's the woman?"

Brant tensed. "What makes you think I know her personally?" he asked in alarm, fearing he had betrayed himself to the Apaches as well as the Texan.

"Those Apaches might not have noticed your gasp, but I did. I was sitting right next to you."

Brant knew there was no point in dissembling to the scout. The lanky Texan was much too perceptive. "Her name is Danny Morgan. She's the woman I intended to ask to become my wife."

Sam nodded, then said, "I sensed she was more than just an acquaintance. Does that mean you're gonna give 'em the gun?"

"Put a gun like that in the hands of Apaches?" Brant asked in a horrified voice.

"They ain't bluffing, Cap'n," Sam pointed out ominously. "They'll kill 'em."

"I know," Brant answered in an agonized voice. "That's why I need time to think."

Sgt. O'Bannon rode out from the troopers to meet Brant and his scout, asking, "What's up? Who were those people up on the top of that butte?"

"The Apaches are holding three Mexican children, Major Bentley's son, and Danny Morgan as hostages in exchange for the Gatling. They captured them at Fort Davis several days ago."

The Irishman's ruddy complexion blanched. "Jesus, Mary, and Joseph," he muttered, then suddenly remembering, asked, "Say, ain't that the lass that broke that blasted mustang?"

Sam's eyebrows rose at this surprising bit of information. He was consumed with curiosity. Who was this woman who went by a male name and broke wild horses?

"Yes," Brant answered grimly.

"Those red bastards!" O'Bannon cursed angrily. "If I could get me hands on 'em right now, I'd kill 'em!" Then, in a sudden turn about, he chuckled and said, "I bet she's giving 'em hell."

Brant feared that might be the case and fervently hoped not. From what he'd heard of the Apaches, they didn't put up with any foolishness. He said a silent prayer

368

that Danny would hold her tongue and behave herself. If she aggravated the Apaches, they might kill her before he could secure her and the children's release.

"Tell the men to go ahead and make camp," Brant said to O'Bannon, swinging to the ground from his saddle. "We're not going anywhere for the time being."

As the sergeant rode away, calling out to the column of troopers, "Dismount!" Brant asked Sam, "How much do you know about these Apaches?"

"Not as much as I do about the Comanches, that's for damn sure," the scout answered, swinging down from his mount. "The Apaches are more secretive about themselves and keep their villages hidden in isolated places. And they don't sell their captives back, like the Comanches will sometimes do. I don't think any man knows a hell of a lot about 'em, but I reckon I know about as much that's to be known."

"If this Chief Alsate wanted that gun so badly, then why didn't he just come and take it? Why go to all the trouble of taking hostages and making a trade for it?"

"Because if he'd attacked you, you would have fought back, and he would have lost many men. That's why the Apaches fight the way they do, by ambush and hit and run. They never lose a warrior unnecessarily, even if it means flight from a battle. This way he can get that gun without spilling any Apache blood."

"Just who is this Alsate? I'd never heard of him until my commanding officer mentioned him before I left Fort Davis to pick up that gun."

"He's one of the biggest, most powerful Apache chiefs in the Southwest. True, he hasn't gotten the notoriety in the papers back East like Mangus Coloradas, Cochise, or Victorio have, but he's just as shrewd, just as fierce and just as dangerous. White men might not recognize his name, but every Apache in the Southwest does. He's respected by all Apache tribes and revered by his own. He leads a large band of Mescaleros that make their home in those mountains you were asking me about. For that reason, they're called the Chisos Apaches. He and his Mescaleros terrorize this area as far west as New Mexico and a good part of old Mexico along the border." Sam paused for a long moment, then said, "If you want my opinion, he's probably the greatest Apache chief of them all. You know what they say, blood tells."

Brant frowned, then asked, "What do you mean by that?"

"He's a half-breed, the son of a Meskin who was stolen in his boyhood by the Apaches. But don't get the wrong idea. He may have white blood in his veins, but he's Apache to the bone. He grew up among them, knowing nothing but their way of living and warfare."

"I wasn't aware that half-breeds could become chiefs."

"The Injuns don't pick their chiefs by bloodlines. They're chosen because of their leadership abilities, and some of the greatest chiefs have been half white. Haven't you heard of Chief Quannah, who leads the Antelope band of the Comanches?"

"Yes, of course I've heard of him. He's the most elusive, most powerful, most dangerous Comanche chief the cavalry has had to contend with, but I didn't know he was half white."

"Yep, he sure is. His mother, Cynthia Ann Parker, was a white woman who was taken captive by the Comanches when she was nine years old. When she grew up, Chief Nacoma made her his wife. I was with Captain Ross and his company of Texas Rangers that day he found and attacked Nacoma's camp. It turned out the chief and his sons were gone, but Cynthia was among the squaws we caught who were trying to escape. The only reason we recognized her was because of her blue eyes. Otherwise, she looked just like the other squaws. She'd even forgotten how to speak English, but she did recognize her name. We took her back to her family with her infant daughter, but she never readjusted to the white man's life. After her daughter died, she kept wanting to go back to her husband and sons. Of course, her family wouldn't let her. They couldn't fathom her preferring to live with the Comanches. She starved herself to death. Quannah's her son. That's why we Texans call him Quannah Parker. So you see, the two most powerful chiefs in the Southwest are Quannah of the Comanches and Alsate of the Apaches—both half-breeds. That's what I meant when I said it's their blood telling. Maybe, because of it, they understand the white man better and can fight him more effectively, or maybe it just makes them better leaders, but no one in Texas has any doubts that their white blood has made them more fearsome enemies." Sam paused thoughtfully for a moment, then said, "But if I know my Injuns, Alsate is the most dangerous and the most fiercely determined of the two. You cavalry boys may eventually run Quannah down and put him on a reservation, keep him there by threat of starvation if he leaves, but you'll never keep Alsate on a reservation, even if you do manage to ever catch him. That damn Apache would eat rocks before he'd give up his freedom."

Brant frowned. It seemed he was up against a formidable foe. "All right, so he's a great chief, but can I trust him to keep his end of the bargain? What's to stop him from taking that gun, giving us the hostages in return, then turning around and ambushing us? I've heard Apaches are treacherous."

"Most of 'em are, but from what I've heard of Alsate, he's a man of his word. Like I said, he ain't no ordinary two-bit chief. He takes pride in his reputation as a fair man. Besides, what choice do you have? If you decide to trade that gun, you'll have to trust him."

It was a point that Brant couldn't dispute. As far as he was concerned, he only had one choice, to trade for the captives. Even if Danny hadn't been involved, he couldn't bear the burden of the deaths of innocent children on his soul. He could send men trained in the art of war to their deaths if necessary, but not innocent children. He would never be able to live with himself if he did.

As he and Sam walked to the roped-off corral where the troopers were putting their horses, Sam glanced over and saw the deep scowl on Brant's face. "Something else bothering you?" he asked.

"Yes, there is," Brant admitted. "I don't understand how the Apaches knew we were taking the Gatling to the post at Pena Colorado. They didn't just happen to run into us. They were waiting here for us, with hostages that were captured for the explicit purpose of making a trade. And how in the hell does that Apache know what a Gatling gun sounds like? We've never used Gatlings with any of our encounters with either the Apaches or the Comanches."

"That gun was tested outside of Fort Stockton when it arrived a couple of months ago," Sam informed him. "I heard it myself and went to investigate what was making all that racket. And I wasn't the only one who got curious and went to watch. So did practically every Meskin in

Chihuahua. That's probably how Alsate got wind of it. From his Meskin friends. Then he put a scout out to watch the fort, and as soon as he saw us riding out with that gun, heading straight for Pena Colorado, he rode off to tell Alsate."

"Are you saying the Mexicans spy on us, just because Alsate is half Mexican?" Brant asked in a furious voice.

"No, they don't spy, not in the literal sense. They've just got big mouths, particularly when they're all liquored up on mescal. Hell, every Meskin in Texas has a horde of relatives in Mexico. What probably happened was, one was visiting some of his relatives down there when Alsate and his warriors made one of their social trips to that village, and the news slipped out while they were drinking together. And Alsate being half Meskin don't have nothing to do with it. Practically every Apache band has a Meskin village they're friendly with, one that they trade with and socialize with during fiestas."

Brant didn't know whether to believe Sam's theory, or if the Apaches did have a spy at Fort Stockton. At this point it didn't matter how the Apaches had learned about the gun. His problem was how to keep it out of their hands without forfeiting Danny's and those children's lives. "Is there are possibility of finding the place they took those hostages and rescuing them before morning?"

"Hell, no. We'd never find them in those wild, rugged mountains. Why those Chisos Apaches have hiding places that even the other Apaches can't find. Besides, they're probably watching us from those hills over there. We couldn't sneak out of here, even under cover of darkness."

"That's what I was afraid you were going to say,"

373

Brant answered, having suspected as much.

Stopping beside the roped-in corral that the troopers had fashioned, Brant and Sam unsaddled their mounts and put them into the enclosure with the other horses. Then they walked to where a fire was burning and helped themselves to a cup of fresh coffee. While Sam and the troopers ate, Brant stood, sipping on his coffee and staring at the Gatling gun thoughtfully.

Placing his tin plate aside after he had finished eating, Sam said, "You've been staring at that gun for almost an hour, Cap'n. Mind letting me in on what you're thinking?"

"I've been wondering if there's some way we can sabotage it."

"Forget it, Cap'n. The first thing Alsate would do is test that gun to make sure it's in working order."

"But if there was some way we could arrange for it to work long enough to pass the test, but fail later."

O'Bannon, who was sitting next to Sam, asked, "How in the hell are you gonna arrange that, Cap'n?"

"Those guns are apt to jam, even under the best conditions."

"But how can you arrange for it to jam when you want it to, particularly if you ain't there?" O'Bannon asked.

Sam was beginning to get intrigued with what Brant was proposing. "Just how does that damn gun work, anyway?"

"As the crank is rotated, each barrel receives a brass cartridge from the bullet hopper on top of the gun by gravity feed. Then as the barrel moves around from station to station, the shell is pushed into the chamber, the breech is closed, the gun is cocked, the shell fired, then the breech opens again, and the case extracted and ejected."

Sam scowled, saying, "If you broke anything to foul up any of those mechanisms, you couldn't test fire it."

"You're right. That's why we'd have to sabotage the ammunition, which in turn would jam the gun." Brant tossed the dregs of coffee aside, walked to the two men, and hunkered down in front of them, saying, "This is what I have in mind. The bullets are stacked in that hopper. If we left several layers of bullets at the bottom, enough to get us through the test firing, then removed all but a small part of gunpowder from the next layer of bullets that would feed in consecutively, and replaced the gunpowder with primers—"

"Jesus, Mary, and Joseph!" O'Bannon exclaimed in a horrified voice, cutting across Brant's words. "Are you daft? Primers are made out of fulminate of mercury, highly explosive stuff. Why, when that powder ignites and those primers go off . . ." A sudden gleam came to the Irishman's eyes, and a big grin spread across his ruddy face as he realized what Brant had been thinking. ". . . it will blow the hell out that cartridge and fragments of twisted brass will go flying everywhere and jam the crank on the gun."

Sam was just as impressed with Brant's clever, inventive plan as the first sergeant. "But why a whole layer, Cap'n?" he asked Brant. "Sounds like all it would take would be one cartridge."

"If the first doesn't do it, maybe the second, or the third, or fourth would. It's bound to happen within a reasonable number of shots."

"And as fast as those barrels are being turned it might

get jammed in several places at once," Sam agreed, a slow grin stretching across his leathery face from ear to ear.

"You're a genius, Cap'n!" O'Bannon said in an expansive voice. "A goddamned genius! Why, not even the best gunsmith in the world would be able to repair it."

"Hell, Injuns don't know nothing about gunsmiths," Sam said in a scornful voice. "When a gun breaks, they just throw it away." He glanced over at the Gatling gun, then asked, "Where is that hopper, anyway?"

"We put it in the supply wagon with the extra box of ammunition," Brant answered. "We didn't want to take any chances of it getting dislodged by all that bumping while we were going over that rough terrain and falling off. A bent hopper won't feed correctly. Tonight, after it's dark, the three of us will sneak in there and unload it to the level we think will be about right for a test firing. Then, if there's not a box of extra primers in that case of ammunition that came with it, we'll just have to pry them out of the cartridges."

"That will take time," Sam remarked.

"Yes, it certainly will," Brant answered, "particularly since we're going to remove the primers on every shell that isn't used for the demonstration, except the top layer. I'll be damned if I'll give those Apaches bullets for their rifles, either, and those Gatling cartridges fit almost any standard rifle."

A horrified expression came over O'Bannon's face. "But, sir, that might take all night."

"Yes, I know," Brant replied calmly. "That's why it's a three man job, instead of one."

Shortly thereafter, the sun went down, bathing everything in a copperish color and tinting the sky with streaks of rose, mauve, and orange, the kind of spectacular sunset that Brant had only seen in west Texas. After darkness fell, Brant, O'Bannon, and Sam crept into the wagon that held the hopper, taking care not to silhouette themselves against the small campfire that the troopers had lit and carrying with them several blankets apiece. Not until the heavy army blankets were hung all around them did they light the small coal oil lamp in the wagon, fearing if the Indians from the hillside saw a light they might become suspicious.

Settling themselves on bags of feed, Brant placed the big circular hopper between them and lifted the lid. As they started removing the large supply of brass cartridges, O'Bannon asked, "How many bullets are we gonna leave in the bottom, Cap'n?"

"Several thousand. We don't want the gun to jam while it's being tested and we're around. The Apaches will suspect we tampered with it and probably kill us, as well as the hostages."

"But that will mean they can use it on somebody until those sabotaged bullets feed into it," O'Bannon objected.

"I know, but I'm afraid that's something I can't help. We'll just have to hope the Apaches' aim will be lousy, since they're not used to firing it. By the time they figure it out, hopefully it will be jammed. But I can't risk those hostages' lives by having it jam during the demonstration."

"Aye, ye're right," O'Bannon agreed.

"What are you going to do with that extra box of ammunition?" Sam asked Brant. "Surely you're not planning on prying the primers out of them too? Hell, we'll be here until doomsday."

"No, when we're through here, we'll distribute it among our saddlebags and bury the gunpowder we

377

emptied from the cartridges in the empty box. If the Apaches ask about ammunition, we'll just swear the loaded hopper was all the army sent."

Prying the primers from the cartridges with their knives was tedious work. After they had poured out most of the gunpowder, added the primers, and resealed the bullets on the sabotaged layer, Brant could see that removing the primers on the remaining bullets in the hopper would take much longer than he had anticipated. "I'm afraid we're not going to have time to remove the primers. Let's just bend the rest of these damn bullets, except for the top layer."

"Aye, they'd be just as useless," O'Bannon agreed. "Besides, working in this dim light is beginning to get to me eyes."

As the three men worked, Brant's thoughts turned to Danny. He wondered how she had been treated by the Apaches. He could see no signs of bruises on her, but he had only been able to see her face. Had they beaten her? Had they starved her? Had they raped her? The last thought filled Brant with despair. He couldn't bear the thought of her undergoing that degrading brutality. It preyed on his mind, a self-imposed mental torture that was anguishing.

As soon as the light had been extinguished and O'Bannon had left the wagon with the box of gunpowder, Brant stopped Sam before he could climb down and asked, "What do the Apaches do to their women captives?"

The scout didn't have to ask Brant if he meant did they rape them. It was the first question that decent white men always asked. They couldn't understand that the

Indian used rape as a means of forcing their female captives into submission, that it was a brutal and humiliating act calculated to break their spirits and leave them feeling dirty and worthless, and yet not physically maim them so that the women couldn't perform their duties as slaves. They carried their scars on their souls, not their bodies. Unfortunately, white men had difficulty accepting women back who had been raped by an Indian, a being considered lower than an animal. Many husbands whose wives had been captured and then returned to them had scorned the women and rejected them, only adding to the poor women's anguish. It wasn't unusual for these women to commit suicide as a means of escape from their shame. If Brant's woman had suffered rape, would he be like those men, unforgiving and scornful, blaming the victim, instead of the men who had perpetrated the crime. He hoped to God not.

"Well, to tell you the truth, I've heard all kinds of stories about that," Sam drawled. "Some say the Apaches rape 'em, string 'em up to trees, and slit their bellies open, so all their insides hang out, but I ain't never seen that. Some claim they use 'em as concubines to satisfy their lust. Others say they don't ravish them at all, because they don't like the white woman's smell. And still others claim that the Apache doesn't rape his female captives because he's too proud, that he thinks it's all right if the woman falls in love with him, but to force himself on her is unmanly and would make the other Apaches scorn him. Personally, I believe the last. It may come as a surprise to you, but Apaches are known for their fidelity to their women. They rarely take more than one wife, and they're real strict about protecting the virtue of their maidens. And they pride themselves on being good lovers. Don't seem to me that a man like that would sink to rape."

Sam's answer soothed Brant's tortured mind. He could only hope that the scout was correct and Danny had been spared. If not, he feared it would leave her with a permanent aversion to the act that was meant as an expression of love as much, if not more so, than the satisfaction of physical desire. And Brant both loved and desired her. Nothing could ever change that.

Chapter 21

The sun came up the next morning a red, blazing ball of fire that promised the day would be another scorcher. With it, Brant and his troopers were up, and before the men had even begun to light their fire to prepare their meager breakfast, Brant and Sam were in the saddle and on their way to their meeting with the Apaches.

Colorado was waiting for them, this time alone and looking just as stony faced as the day before. As soon as Sam and Brant reined in, he asked in Spanish "What is your decision?"

"We'll trade the gun for the captives," Brant answered.

A faint smile crossed the Apache's lips. The yellowlegs had bowed to their extortion, just as Chief Alsate had thought they would. Yes, their chief was a man worthy to lead their fierce band, wise in the ways of white men as well as brave and fearless. "You will leave all but four of your yellowlegs here. They can carry the children before them on their horses. Bring an extra horse for the woman. We will take the gun on its carriage and the wagon with us."

Brant wasn't surprised by the latter. The greedy Apaches wanted the supplies in the wagon as well as the gun. "If I bring the wagon with me, the troopers I leave behind will have nothing to eat while I'm gone. They might as well go back to Fort Stockton."

Colorado realized if the troopers rode back to the fort that they would alert them as to what had happened, but he wasn't worried. By the time the army had sent a large force back, they would be in the mountains and the yellowlegs would never find any of their hidden camps. If anything, they would get lost and wander helplessly until they died of thirst. Only the Chisos Apaches knew where the *tinajas*—the water holes—were in that huge pile of rocks that was their home. "As you wish, but make sure your yellowlegs understand your orders and obey them. We will have scouts following them, to make sure this is not a trick. After they have left, you will follow me to our camp where the exchange will take place."

"What about my scout here?" Brant asked. "I'll need him to find my way back out of those mountains."

Colorado gave Sam a look of pure, unadulterated hatred, then said grudgingly, "You can bring him with you."

Sam wasn't surprised by the Apache's look. Texans were hated by the Comanches and the Apaches alike, for it was them that had brought the tide of white men down on them. For almost forty years, the two Indian nations had fought to rid themselves of the hated interlopers, but the Texans had stubbornly held onto the land they had claimed, often rebuilding from nothing but ashes. And now, both nations stood on the threshold of destruction, all because of those tough, strong-willed, fiercely determined Texans.

Brant and Sam turned their horses and rode back to camp. After Brant had related what the Apaches said and picked four troopers to accompany him, O'Bannon stepped forward and said, "Sir, I request to stay with you, just in case we didn't correctly judge how many of those bullets were needed for a demonstration. If that gun jams before you planned on it, and you have to make a last-minute attempt to rescue those captives, I'm a good man to have around in a pinch."

Brant didn't doubt the first sergeant's words. He'd seen O'Bannon in action on the shooting range, and the man could ride like the wind. Any non-com could take the rest of the troop back to the fort. He needed his best men with him. He still didn't trust Alsate not to try and ambush them after they had made the trade. "All right, O'Bannon. You stay instead of Corporal Mullins. Sergeant McBride can take charge of the troop."

After the troopers had left for Fort Stockton, Brant and his remaining party pulled out. All day long, they followed the Apache sub-chief across the scorching desert, making camp that evening in the foothills of the Chisos, the copper-colored, jagged mountains rearing over them and looking like battered castle turrets.

As soon as the mules were unhitched from the wagon and the Gatling gun, they trotted off to a bare area and began to roll in the dirt, wiggling and tumbling about amongst gusty snorts, loud grunts, and disemboweled groans, while they raised a cloud of choking dust around them. "Would ye look at those stupid creatures," O'Bannon said in disgust. "And why do they have to have such volume with all their annoying noises? They never make quiet, soft sounds like a horse does. For the life of me, I can't figure out why God created such obnoxious animals."

Brant didn't particularly like the animals either, but for some strange reason he felt compelled to defend them. "They have more endurance and are stronger than horses."

"Yeah, and they're more stubborn and sneaky too. Have ye ever seen 'em ganging up right before they tear off to raid a feed train? I swear ye can see 'em plotting it. Then when it's all over and they've scattered hay and feed to kingdom come, and ye're ready to beat the hell out of 'em, they'll look at ye with that innocent, 'who me?' look on their faces. There ain't another animal in this world with as much pure devilry in 'em. The army would be better off without 'em."

"A team of horses would have never been able to pull that heavy gun over that rough terrain we passed through, and only a mule could pull one of those lightweight Hotchkiss cannons that you boys so prize through the mountains," Sam pointed out, entering the conversation. "Besides being stronger, mules are much more sure-footed than horses."

Brant started chuckling. Seeing the two men staring at him quizzically, he explained, "Sam mentioning a cannon and mules reminded me of a story I heard last year. It seems army brass has been on the lookout for lightweight cannons that can more easily be transported in the mountains, other than the Hotchkiss. An inventor approached the big brass at Fort Levenworth, Kansas, claiming that he had a cannon that was mounted on a platform that one mule could carry, and that the gun could be fired from the mule's back and aimed by merely turning the mule's rump in the direction he wanted to fire the cannon. It sounded good to the brass, so they asked for a demonstration. They all gathered on a high bluff overlooking the Missouri, and the inventor loaded his cannon on an army mule's back, with the muzzle pointing out over the animal's rump. Then positioning the mule's posterior so the shell would fall harmlessly on the opposite side of the river, he lit the fuse. The mule heard the sizzling noise and turned his head to see what was making it. Not seeing anything, he turned a little farther, then completely around, pointing the cannon at the officers. The brass hit the dirt just as the cannon roared, and the mule and cannon went flying out over the water from the recoil. Neither were ever seen again, and needless to say, the inventor didn't make the sale."

Sam chuckled, then said, "That's the goddamnest tale I've ever heard. Hell, I know some of that army brass ain't got much between the ears, but you'd think even they would have enough sense to know better than to fire a cannon from a mule. Are you sure you didn't make that up?"

"No, I swear to God it's the truth."

O'Bannon's eyes were glittering with satisfaction as he said, "Well, that's one blasted mule we got rid of."

That night, bathed in the light coming from a sliver of a moon, the vegetation on the twisted mass of rock all around them turned gray, making the mountains look ghostly and very forbidding.

O'Bannon looked around him warily and said, "'Tis the spookiest place I've ever seen. I hope the hell those mules don't get jittery and stampede. We need 'em to pull that damn gun."

"Oh, so you do appreciate the mules, after all," Sam commented with a hint of amusement in his voice.

"Hell, no, I don't appreciate 'em!" O'Bannon tossed back hotly. "But if those damn mules run off, then we'd have to hitch our horses to that wagon and gun—and I'd have to walk! I didn't join the cavalry to walk. Me feet ain't up to it."

O'Bannon rose and walked off. Sam watched him while the sergeant rolled out his bedroll, then commented to the trooper sitting next to him, "O'Bannon sure does hate mules."

"Aye, he does," the man answered. "Got the daylights kicked out of him by one. Broke his hip and half of his ribs and put him in the hospital for months. That hip still bothers him now and then. That's what hurts him when he walks too much, and not his feet, except O'Bannon would never admit a mule got the best of him."

When the fire burned down to glowing red coals, Sam took his bedroll and spread it out beside O'Bannon's. Laying in it, he spied Brant standing in the distance and gazing out at the ghostly mountains. "You asleep, O'Bannon?" he asked softly.

"No."

"How do you suppose the army is going to feel about what the Cap'n is doing? I've heard they're real particular about their equipment. They might not take kindly to him destroying a valuable gun, providing our trick works. Some of that top brass might feel he should have let the Indians have the hostages, or tried a suicidal attempt to rescue them instead. Why, I know a few that wouldn't make the trade out of nothing but pure bullheadedness. They'd let those captives die before they'd bow to an Injun's extortion. I'd sure hate to see the Cap'n get court-martialed because of this. He's too good an officer."

O'Bannon scowled. It had never occurred to him that the Cap'n might get in trouble with the brass because of his decision. In the rugged Irishman's opinion, it was the right thing to do. He had come to admire Brant, both as an officer and a man, and that was saying a lot, for the battle-seasoned cavalryman had seen a lot of officers in action over the years and was generally cynical of their performance. There was a long pause of thoughtful silence before O'Bannon answered, "There might be an inquiry, but here lately the army seems to be finally wising up. If an aggressive officer makes a mistake, but if it's on the bold and daring side, he's usually forgiven. Hell, that's what makes a good officer. Besides, Colonel Shafter will back him to the hilt. Why, he'd probably recommend the Cap'n for a medal, if we had any of the damn things, like those European armies do. The least he'd get is a promotion, if Shafter had anything to say about it. The Old Man don't take no shit from no one. He's tougher than any of that top brass, and they know better than to tangle with him."

The next day, they entered the mountains, and Brant found out that, compared to the Chisos, the Davis Mountains were tame. It was a land of twisted, towering rock and deep canyons where hundred-foot-high cattails grew, and everywhere around him were the marks of the perpetual struggle of wind, rain, and sun against the land. They passed through ancient Mescalero campgrounds with their circles of crumbling rock that marked their mescal pits and through a canyon that nature had painted

387

in a riot of colors. They climbed higher and higher, sometimes hugging the side of a mountain and looking down on deep, terrifying chasms, the far off Rio Grande River looking like a silver ribbon winding its way through the brown, parched land and the undulating foothills looking like breakers throwing themselves against sheer rock cliffs.

Then suddenly, as if out of nowhere, they entered a wide, grassy meadow surrounded by pinon pines and junipers, many of the trees covered with snapdragon vines that were blooming profusely in a riot of deep blue, while below them scarlet bouvardia added their brilliant color to the peaceful scene. Spying several low, iglooshaped wickiups in the distance, Brant knew they had reached their destination.

"Where is everyone?" Brant whispered to Sam. "The place looks deserted. Where are all the women and children, and those damn yapping dogs every Indian camp has?"

"This ain't their main *rancheria*. You don't think they're stupid enough to take us there, so we can lead the army back to it at a later date. Hell, this is just one of their outlying camps that they have scattered all over these mountains. And if you're wondering where all the braves are, just look around you."

Brant glanced quickly around him, seeing at least a hundred fierce-looking Apache warriors walking from where they had been concealed in the woods all around them, their rifles held menacingly in front of them.

It was a trap, Brant thought. He'd walked right into a goddamned trap! Fury rose in him, and he turned in his saddle, saying angrily to Colorado, who was sitting on his mount beside him, "I thought Chief Alsate was an honorable man? A man of his word. You lied to us! You never had any intention of trading for the captives."

"I did not lie to you," a deep voice said in Spanish from behind Brant.

Brant whirled in his saddle, seeing a leathery-faced Apache standing there. Even if he hadn't been taller than the other Apaches, his skin several shades lighter, his features less chiseled and his cheekbones lower, Brant would have known this was Chief Alsate. His proud, commanding bearing spoke of greatness, and he reeked power and dignity. No, this was no ordinary Apache, or chief for that matter. He was a cut above any chief Brant had ever seen.

"Chief Alsate, I presume," Brant said.

"Yes, I am Alsate."

Brant's blue eyes flashed dangerously. "If this isn't a trap, then why are your warriors holding guns on us?"

"Your men are armed. If you relinquish your guns, mine will lay their's down."

"Like hell we'll relinquish our guns!"

"Ah, I see you still don't trust me."

"No, I certainly don't," Brant answered in a steely voice.

A flicker of a smile crossed the chief's lips. "That is good. A man who is too trusting is a fool. But I am Alsate, chief of the Chisos, the bravest, fiercest Apaches on earth," he said proudly. "My word is my bond. I do not sink to deception like the others do. No man will call me a sneaky coyote. We will make the trade as you and my spokesman agreed."

"All right, but first I want to see the captives," Brant answered, still wary despite the chief's proud words.

Alsate gave a snort of disgust, then called out something in Apache. A moment later, the children were led from one of the wickiups and marched across the broad meadow. From what Brant could see, none appeared to be harmed, but they were obviously terrified. Then, seeing them, Major Bentley's son's face lit up, and the tow-headed boy broke away from his captor and ran towards them, calling out, "Sergeant O'Bannon! You came for us!"

O'Bannon swung down from his saddle, crouched, and caught the immensely relieved boy in his arms as he ran up him, saying, "Aye, Timmy, we came. Ye're safe now."

Even after the Mexican children had been led before Brant and his men, they hung back, as leery of these Anglos as they were of the Apaches. Brant's heart went out to them. He dismounted and hunkered down before the three, saying in Spanish to the older girl who held a smaller girl and boy protectively to her side, "There's nothing to be afraid of. We've come to take you home to your families. It's all over. You're safe now."

At Brant's softly spoken words, the three broke into tears of relief. Brant rose and motioned for his troopers to come and take the children.

As the troopers swept the Mexican children up in their arms and carried them to the rear, O'Bannon asked Timmy, "Did Mr. Lo harm any of you?"

"No, sir. Danny wouldn't let 'em. She kept us right by her side when we weren't riding. Then, yesterday, when we was in their big camp and they put that old woman to guarding us, Danny flat tore into her when she pushed little Maria, 'cause Maria wasn't walking fast enough to suit her. Danny told that Apache off right proper, she did. I ain't never heard such cussing in my life. She told that old woman if she laid one more hand on any of us, she'd tear her apart with her bare hands."

Brant frowned, saying, "I didn't know Danny spoke Spanish."

"She didn't speak Spanish," Timmy informed him. "She didn't have to. That old woman knew she was furious from the way Danny's eyes were flashing. And then, this morning, when they moved us to this camp and separated us from her, she fought like a regular wildcat. I'm telling you, that Danny ain't afraid of nothing or no one. She's the bravest person I've ever seen, even if she is nothing but an old girl," Timmy added, with typical nine-year-old male scorn for the opposite sex.

"What are you talking about?" Brant asked in alarm. "Why did they separate you? What did they do to Danny?" But before the boy could even open his mouth, Brant whirled on Chief Alsate and demanded, "Where's the woman? What have you done to her?"

The furious expression on Brant's face was enough to make a tingle of fear run up even Alsate's spine. "No harm has come to her," he answered in a soothing voice. "The wickiup was not big enough for all of them. We put her in another." Chief Alsate paused, then admitted, "But we had to tie her up. She was as wild as a female panther coming to the defense of her cubs. Personally, I will be glad to be rid of her. She has caused us nothing but trouble. She is not at all meek, as a woman should be. I pity the man who tries to tame her."

Any man who tried to tame Danny would be a fool, Brant thought. That was a big part of her beauty, her unbreakable spirit. "Which wickiup did you put her in?" Brant demanded.

Chief Alsate didn't have to answer. At that moment, Brant heard a loud, indignant voice crying out, "Let me go, you dad-blasted Injuns! Consarn it, iffen you've done anything to those young-uns, I'm gonna blast you from hell to breakfast as soon as I get my hands on a gun!"

Brant whirled and saw two Apaches struggling to drag Danny across the meadow. Danny spied Brant at the same minute. She came to a dead halt, her spirits soaring at the sight of him. Then she remembered her shame at being pitied by him. Dad-blasted, she thought, if she was gonna have to be rescued like some dumb-fool female, why did it have to be by him, of all people?

Brant walked swiftly across the meadow. Seeing him coming, the two Apaches let go of Danny's arms and retreated with wary looks in their eyes, not at all liking the angry glitter in the yellowlegs' searing-blue eyes.

Brant stopped before Danny, struggling with conflicting emotions. A part of him wanted to take her in his arms and crush her to him, another wanted to throttle her for endangering her life by fighting the Apaches. Danny sensed he was angry with her, although she had no idea why. But his anger was something she could handle. She just couldn't bear for him to pity her.

She tried the same tactic she had tried before to disarm him of his anger, saying brightly, "Howdy! Mighty glad to see you."

Brant knew any other woman would have thrown herself in his arms and dissolved into tears of relief. But not Danny. She stood there, acting as if nothing had ever happened, as if she had never been held captive for almost a week by fierce Indians, a captivity that would have terrified a lesser woman. His anger disappeared like a puff of smoke, but he had to know if she had been harmed. Knowing Danny, she wouldn't voluntarily tell him.

"Are you all right?" he asked in a deeply concerned voice. He paused, then asked, "Did they harm you in any way?" still fearing she might have been raped when the Apaches separated her from the children.

"No, they didn't hurt me. Scraped up my knees a mite, a-dragging me away that day at the fort, but otherwise I'm jest fine. Shore can't say much fer the Injuns' grub though. The meat was always half-raw, and those dad-blasted mesquite beans they eat tasted plumb awful. 'Course, it did keep my belly from a-rubbing against my backbone."

Well, Brant thought wryly, if all she could complain about was the food, she must not have been harmed. An immense wave of relief washed over him. He glanced down and saw she was wearing her canvas bag. "You have Charlie with you?" he asked in surprise.

"Yep, shore do."

"I'm surprised the Apaches let you keep him."

Danny glanced quickly around her, then whispered, "They don't know nothing about him. I kept him a secret fer fear they'd kill him."

"He's been in that sack for a week?"

"No, when we were on the trail, I let him out every night after the Injuns had gone to sleep, so he could fetch him some grub. He was a real good boy, always back before daylight. Then, when we reached the main camp and they put us in that willow wickiup, I had to rustle him up some grub and sneak it to him, so those Meskin young'uns wouldn't know. I was afraid they'd get scared and start a-hollering, and the Injuns would find out I had him. I did tell Timmy though. He was a real big help. Injuns didn't seem to think it strange when he started a-catching bugs. He could do it right out in the open, while

393

I had to settle fer what I could find in that little wickiup. I reckon all boys must do that, even those dad-blasted 'Paches."

Danny peeked around Brant and saw the troopers in the distance. "Where's the rest of yer troopers?" she whispered. "You got 'em hidden out in those woods?"

"No, only four and my scout came. The rest have gone back to Fort Stockton."

Danny was shocked speechless for a moment. Then recovering, she asked in a horrified voice, "Have you gone plumb loco? A-riding in this Injun camp with only five other men? Why, that's suicide!"

"We didn't come here to rescue you by force, Danny. Even if I had wanted to, I couldn't have, not with just forty men. Besides, even if I'd had a larger force, that would have been foolish. The Apaches would have killed you and those children at the first gunshot. No, we came to make a trade. The Apaches want the gun that we were taking to our post at Pena Colorado. That's why they captured you and those children. They'll give up their hostages, in return for that gun. They were the ones who dictated that I could only bring five men with me."

"Are you a-saying the Injuns went to all that trouble for a stupid gun?"

"This isn't any ordinary gun, Danny. It's a machine gun, a gun that can fire up to eight hundred shots a minute."

It seemed unbelievable to Danny. "You ain't a-telling me a sandy, are you?" she asked suspiciously.

"No, Danny, I'm serious."

As the full import of the deadly gun dawned on Danny, she said, "You have gone plumb loco! You can't

394

let those dad-blasted Injuns get their hands on a gun like that!"

"Sssh, keep your voice down," Brant cautioned. "And don't worry. They're not going to use that gun on anyone, at least not for long."

"But—"

"I haven't got time to explain right now. Just take my word for it and trust me."

Brant took Danny's arm and led her back across the meadow. Stopping before Chief Alsate, Brant said, "All right, Chief, we have the captives. Now you can have the gun."

As Brant walked towards his troopers and the waiting horses, Chief Alsate said, "No, Captain. You will not be allowed to leave until we have tested the gun to make sure it works."

Brant whirled and asked in pretended surprise, "You don't trust me?"

"No more so than you did me," the Apache answered. "Now have your men unhitch that gun and roll it into the middle of the camp. We will pretend that those trees over there are the enemy," Alsate said, pointing to a line of pinon pines to the left of the camp.

At Brant's order, the Gatling was unhitched and rolled to the center of the camp, then turned so that the muzzle was pointed towards the trees. Then O'Bannon and another trooper carried the heavy hopper from the wagon to the gun and loaded it, the Apaches carefully watching every move they made.

Pushing aside a curious Apache who was in his way, Sergeant O'Bannon manned the big gun. As he cranked the handle at the back, the Gatling rattled loudly as it spat a flood of bullets, the rapid staccato sound echoing off the mountains around them and multiplying to a deafening noise as branches and pieces of bark flew everywhere.

The cavalry mounts stood perfectly still while the Apache watched in stupefied awe, but not the mules. Totally undisciplined under fire, they went berserk at the loud, unnerving sound of the gun, the two that had been unhitched from the cannon tearing off for the woods, while the four that were still hitched to the wagon broke out at a dead run, braying shrilly as they raced into the crowd of Indians watching the demonstration.

Apaches scattered everywhere, running for their lives in every direction as the mules ran straight through the camp, the wagon bouncing and swaying precariously behind them. When the mules suddenly veered to go around a stand of pines at the opposite end of the camp, the wagon flipped on its side and hit the stand with a loud smash, sending broken wood and its contents flying through the air, but in no way impeding the mules flight. Still harnessed together, they raced away, dragging what little was left of the wagon behind them.

When the mules had stampeded behind him, O'Bannon hadn't noticed for a moment, because of all the racket the gun was making. When he did finally notice, he stopped firing the gun and watched the wild chaos that the mules were causing with secret glee, thinking he'd never thought he'd see the day when he'd applaud anything an ornery mule did. But seeing the fearless, fierce Apaches running for their lives before the beserk animals had more than made up for all his complaints against the stubborn, annoying animals. He even forgave the mule that had kicked the daylights out of him.

When the camp settled down, the brave Apache warriors who had run looked a little sheepish. Brant asked Alsate, "Do you want us to continue the demonstration?"

Brant held his breath. He had no idea how many bullets had been fired and how close they might be to the sabotaged layer. But Alsate had been unnerved by the unexpected pandemonium and was just a little embarrassed that his men had run. "No, that is enough." He turned and looked at the debris scattered all over the woods, then asked, "Was there more ammunition in that wagon?"

"More ammunition?" Brant asked, again pretending surprise. "You mean for the Gatling? Hell, what do you need extra bullets for? That damn hopper must hold close to ten thousand," Brant lied adroitly, knowing that the Apache had no earthly idea how many cartridges the hopper held.

Alsate walked to the gun, picked up the lid of the hopper, and peered into it, noting that it was full almost to the brim. Picking up one of the bullets, he examined it and discovered that it was the same cartridge that he used in his rifle. No, he didn't need extra ammunition. He had boxes and boxes of those bullets back at his main *rancheria*.

He placed the lid back on the hopper and turned to Brant, saying, "You may take the captives and go. Our business has been concluded."

Brant didn't dare let the Apache chief see the relief that he felt. He turned, calling out, "Mount up!"

Quickly, O'Bannon and the troopers swung the children into their saddles, then mounted behind them, while Brant led Danny to the horse that had been brought for her. Danny gave the small cavalry saddle a look of pure disgust, then mounted.

As soon as Sam and Brant were in their saddles, the group rode away, the tough old scout setting the pace at a leisurely speed. But once they were out of the Apaches' sight, Sam said to Brant, "Come on! Let's do some real riding. The sooner we get out of these damn Apache mountains, the better I'll feel."

The tough scout put his spurs to his horse, and the gelding sped off, with Brant and the rest of the group racing behind him.

Chapter 22

The ride out of the mountains was the wildest and most harrowing that Brant had ever taken. At breakneck speed, Sam led them through twisted canyons, then down narrow, perilous mountain paths that spiraled down the sides of the towering, jagged peaks, then through more canyons. As the scenery flashed by him, Brant vaguely recognized it as that he had seen on their ascent, and he didn't have time to worry about the Apaches laying in ambush someplace. His entire concentration was on his riding. What had taken them four hours to cover that morning, dragging the wagon and gun with them, was covered in less than an hour. It wasn't until they reached the last canyon that Sam slowed his horse to a walk, then circled back, saying to Brant with a big grin, "Well, Cap'n we pulled it off."

Brant wiped the sweat from his brow with the back of his hand before answering, "Yes, and I'm sure glad you memorized the way out of that mass of rocks when we traveled through it earlier. I might have found my way out eventually, but certainly not at that speed."

"That's my job," the Texan answered with his lazy drawl, "guiding you boys. Yours is to make the decisions."

Both men tensed in their saddles, hearing the faint but unmistaken rattle of the Gatling gun. It continued for a moment, then suddenly stopped, and an ominous silence fell over the canyon before Sam said in a disgusted voice, "Goddammit, those Apaches just couldn't resist playing with their new toy. Of all the rotten luck! I'd hoped we'd be halfway back to the fort before they used it."

"What's he a-talking about?" Danny asked Brant. "And what did you mean when you said those Injuns wouldn't be able to use that gun fer long?"

"We sabotaged all but the lower layer of bullets in that hopper so the gun would jam and be useless," Brant explained.

A big grin spread across Danny's face. "Well, I'll be a dad-blasted polecat. That was downright smart. And sneaky too. Who thought of it?"

Brant shot her a chagrined look, then answered, "I did."

Well, I'll be, Danny thought in amazement. She could have sworn he would answer the tough old scout. And she had noticed on that wild ride out of the mountains, how well Brant had ridden. As hard as she tried, she hadn't been able to even catch up with him, and if truth be known, she'd been just a little scared going down that steep, dizzying path that hugged the mountains. Goldurn, there must have been a thousand-foot drop on one side of her. Seems he could do more than just ride pretty. And now he'd gone and pulled a real clever trick on the Injuns. Why, he wasn't acting at all like a tenderfoot. Her admiration for Brant rose a few more notches.

"I'll bet those Injuns are as mad as a nest of stirred-up hornets," Sam said, breaking into Danny's thoughts. "Come on! Let's get the hell out of here!"

Sam tore off down the canyon with the rest of the party fast on his heels. Long before they reached the end of the deep chasm, they heard the hoofbeats of the Apache's horses behind them and the Indians' furious howls. Brant figured the only way they could have caught up with them so quickly was by taking a short cut that only they knew. He realized that his group couldn't continue to hold their lead. His men were riding double with those children, and he could tell by the sounds that the Apaches were slowly gaining on them. When they reached the end of the canyon, he raised his arm and called out to them, "Hold up!"

The party reined in their horses, the sweaty animals blowing from their hard run and their harnesses jingling. Brant glanced at the children held before the troopers, seeing their faces were ashen with fright. No matter what happened he couldn't let them fall into the Apaches' hands again, he thought with compassion. They'd already been through enough terror to last them a lifetime.

Brant turned to O'Bannon and said, "Hand me your rifle and that saddlebag filled with bullets. Sam and I will try to hold them off here while the rest of you make your get away. Don't stop riding until your horses can't go any further, and head straight for Fort Stockton. You should run into a force coming from that direction sometime tomorrow."

"But, sir, you can't hold off that horde of Apaches until we can get back here to rescue you," O'Bannon objected.

"I don't intend to hold them off that long. Just long enough for you to make your escape. Don't even bother coming back. The Apaches will be expecting that and waiting for you."

The Irishman's face paled at Brant's words. The two men would be giving their lives to buy the others time. "Then let me stay, sir, instead of you."

"No, O'Bannon. You get those captives the hell out of here." Seeing O'Bannon about to object again, Brant snapped, "That's an order, Sergeant!"

A crestfallen look came over the sergeant's face before he snapped, "Aye, sir!"

O'Bannon slipped his rifle from his shoulder and handed it to Brant, then the saddlebag of bullets. As he put his spurs to his horse he called out to his troopers, "All right, you dumb Micks! Get the lead out of your asses. I want to see some real riding!"

As the group tore off, Brant and Sam quickly wheeled their horses and galloped them up a pile of boulders, both knowing that it was an excellent spot to hold off the Indians. Not only would the rocks provide them cover, but they sat at the entrance of the canyon. The Apaches couldn't get past them to continue their pursuit, at least not from the direction they were coming.

Both men were in such a hurry and so engrossed with getting themselves under cover before the Apaches arrived on the scene that neither noticed Danny following them. They had assumed, just as Sergeant O'Bannon had when he raced away, that she had ridden off with the troopers. But Danny had no intention of leaving Brant. If he was to die this day, she wanted to die with him. Life wouldn't be worth living without knowing he walked the earth.

Brant and Sam were out of the saddle before their horses even came to a stop, grabbing their rifles as they swung from their horses and swatting the animals on the rump to send them behind the cover of some of the larger boulders. Brant turned just as Danny rode up, a shocked expression coming over his face before he recovered and thundered, "What in the hell are you doing here?"

"I'm a-staying with you," Danny announced, jumping from her horse and giving it a hard slap on the rump.

"Like hell you are! Get out of here!"

"No, I ain't a-leaving," Danny said stubbornly. "I'm a-staying with you. Three can hold those Injuns off better than two."

"Dammit, Danny this is one time you're going to do what I say. Get the hell out of here!"

"No, I'm a-staying, and you can't make me go," Danny threw back, her black eyes glittering with fierce determination. "I told you a long time ago I ain't one of yer troopers to be a-ordering around."

As Brant opened his mouth to toss back a retort, Sam stepped between the two and said, "Hold up there, Cap'n. Is she any good with a gun?"

"I shore am," Danny assured him, before Brant could answer. "I can outshoot anyone in this here state. Why, I bet I'm an even better shot than you."

Sam's lips twitched with amusement. She certainly didn't lack self-confidence. But he found himself believing her. "Let her stay, Cap'n."

"Are you crazy?" Brant roared. "She's a woman. She has no business being here. She should have ridden off with the others. Dammit, she could get killed!"

"In Texas, women fight Injuns right beside their menfolks, and yes, sometimes they die beside 'em too," Sam

403

answered, totally unperturbed by Brant's furious glare. "Besides, it's too late for her to leave now. Those Apaches are gonna be swarming down on us any second, and she'd be a sitting duck out there, riding off in the wide open."

Brant turned and saw the troopers riding like the wind across the rolling foothills. He knew they were out of the Apaches' gun range, but Danny wouldn't be. Then seeing O'Bannon wheeling his horse around and riding back, Brant knew the sergeant must have finally realized Danny wasn't with them and was coming back for her, the child he held before him presenting an excellent target for the Apaches that would be coming around the bend of the canyon at any second. "Go back!" Brant yelled, waving his hand. "It's too late! Get those damn kids out of here!"

The sergeant seemed to hesitate for a split second, then whirled his horse around and raced away.

The three barely had time to settle down behind the rocks before the Apaches came into view, tearing around the bend and thundering down the narrow canyon on their fleet mustangs. It was an awesome sight, seeing those furious, howling Indians coming down on them. It looked as if a dam had burst and was pouring out Apaches. Brant and Sam positioned their guns, peered through the sights, and let go with a volley of shots that sounded as if a hundred rifles had been fired as the loud cracks bounced back and forth between the walls of the canyon. Several Apaches flew from their saddles and hit the dirt, leaving the remainder momentarily stunned. They hadn't expected the yellowlegs to ambush them, but to keep riding. Recovering their senses, the Mescaleros scattered, jumping from their mounts and disappearing behind every rock, crag, and bush. For a moment, the deserted mustangs milled in confusion in the middle of the canyon, then trotted off the way they had come.

"Here's where the fun begins," Sam said, quickly reloading his rifle. "They'll pop out of their hiding places like so many jack-in-the-boxes and take a shot at us, then disappear so fast we won't know where it came from."

"I know there's a couple behind that big boulder to the right," Brant said. "I saw them when they slipped behind it."

"That's just a couple," Sam said, turning his head to spit out a stream of tobacco juice. "Where in the hell are the other ninety or so?"

"Which one of you fellas is gonna loan me a gun?" Danny asked in an irritated voice, breaking into the exchange between the two men. "Dad-blast it! I didn't even get a shot in."

"Can you fire a six-shooter?" Sam asked.

"Shore can. I'd prefer a rifle, since they got a longer range, but I'll settle fer that," Danny said magnanimously.

Sam chuckled and pulled his six-shooter from his holster, handing it over Brant's back to Danny.

"Thanks, mister."

"The name's Sam. Sam Eaton."

"Well, howdy, Sam," Danny said, tossing the gun to her left hand and holding her right out to Sam. "I'm Danny. Danny Morgan."

"Pleased to meet you," Sam said, his eyes shimmering with amusement as Danny pumped his hand.

A shot rang out, and the three ducked their heads behind their rocky barricade out of sheer reflex. The bullet whizzed over them and hit one of the larger boulders behind them, making a pinging sound as it ricocheted.

"Did you see where it came from, Cap'n?" Sam asked.

"No," Brant admitted in disgust. "Hell, they've got us pinned down."

"Yeah, we can't go no place, but then they can't either. Not without exposing themselves to our fire. And thank God, those canyon walls are too smooth and steep for 'em to climb."

Brant saw a darting figure from the corner of his eye. He raised his rifle and fired. The Mescalero barely had time to make a dive behind a small tree as Brant's bullet kicked up dirt where he had been just a split second before.

"Well, I reckon he'll think twice before he tries that again," Sam remarked.

"I missed him," Brant answered in self-disgust.

"A miss that close don't matter. They know they're up against sharpshooters now and they'll be doubly careful. Hell, it might get downright boring around here."

All afternoon, the gunfire was sporadic, an Apache popping out from his place of concealment and firing a quick shot now and then, and the three at the canyon's entrance shooting back at him. Only once was there a casualty, when Brant caught sight of a branch on a bush moving and blasted it. Even then they never saw the Apache. They only knew he had been hit by his cry of pain.

For over an hour, there wasn't a move or a sound from the canyon. Danny's eyes hurt from staring so hard as she peered out over the rim of the rock she was laying behind. She blinked her eyes, then heard the roar of a gun beside her. When she opened them, an Apache that had crept to a big rock not less than thirty feet from them went flying back in the air.

She turned her head to see Brant's rifle smoking. She couldn't believe it. Why, he'd seen that Apache jumping up and killed him before the Injun could even aim his gun, all in the blink of an eye. He sure was full of surprises today, she thought. Why, she'd never dreamed he was that good with a gun. And dad-blasted, she hadn't got a shot at those Injuns yet.

Another long hour passed with agonizing slowness. The hot sun beat down on the three unmercifully, making sweat trickle down their foreheads and sting their eyes. "Damn, I wish I'd thought to grab my canteen," Sam said. "My throat is parched. Thank God, that sun will be going down pretty soon, and we'll get some relief. Jesus, it's hot as hell out here."

"Are you crazy?" Brant asked. "If I could, I'd keep that sun up there till doomsday. Once it sets and darkness falls, those Apaches will attack in earnest. We don't know where they are, but they know exactly where we are."

"Wrong, Cap'n. Apaches don't attack at night. It's got something to do with their superstitions about spirits. As soon as that sun sets, the fighting is over for the day."

"Are you sure about that?" Brant asked.

"Positive. We can lay down and sleep like a baby, and they won't come anywhere near us."

"Then maybe we can slip out of here as soon as it gets dark," Danny said in an excited voice.

"Nope, I don't think we ought to try that," Sam replied lazily. "We've been out here about four or five hours, long enough for some of those Apaches to slip back up that canyon and come around that mountain on foot. By nightfall, or shortly thereafter, they'll have sneaked into those foothills behind us. Now, they won't

407

come in here at night looking for a fight—none of them wants to risk having their spirits roam the earth until eternity—but they sure as hell aren't going to let us escape."

"Then tomorrow, when we wake up, we'll find ourselves surrounded?" Brant asked.

"Probably."

As soon as the sun set, the three crept into the taller boulders to get a drink of water. Brant removed his canteen from his mount, uncapped it, and handed it to Danny, saying, "Don't drink it too fast, no matter how thirsty you are. It will make you sick."

"Hellfire, I know that," Danny replied irritably and raised the canteen. But despite Brant's caution, she was tempted to drink more than she should. The liquid was a blessed relief to her parched throat, even if it was warm.

As soon as they had assuaged their thirst, they unsaddled their horses, and the two men poured water from their canteens into their hats to water them. Brant glanced across at Danny and noticed that her face was a decided pink beneath her tan. "You've got a bit of a burn there. What happened to your hat?"

"I lost it that day the Injuns jumped me."

Brant remembered that Colorado had told him the Apaches had taken their captives by the cottonwood grove outside of the fort. That was the same place he had told Danny he loved her the night of the dance. Had she gone back there for sentimental reasons, to think of him and reflect on their lovemaking that night? "The Apaches told me that they captured you and the children down by the cottonwoods. What were you doing out there?"

Danny wasn't about to admit to Brant that she had gone there to commune with Emily, that she had been mooning over him when she got captured. "It's cooler out there under the trees, and a sight prettier than that dad-blasted dusty fort."

Brant was disappointed by her answer. He wondered if she said what she had because Sam was within hearing, and she would be too embarrassed to admit she was thinking about him in front of a virtual stranger, then remembered that Danny bluntly spoke her mind, regardless of who might be listening. For all practical purposes, she seemed to have reverted to the old Danny—and Brant was glad for that—but he sensed that things weren't the same between them. She seemed to have erected an invisible barrier between them, holding herself aloof and keeping her distance.

They ate tinned beans and hardtack that night, soaking the latter in tepid water until it was soft enough to chew. Even with the sun down, the place was sweltering, for the rocks held the daytime heat like an oven.

As soon as they had finished eating, Danny slipped her canvas bag from her shoulder and said, "Well, I reckon I'll let Charlie out, so he can rustle him up some grub. There ought to be enough spiders and insects in these rocks to fill his belly."

"Who in the hell is Charlie?" Sam asked.

"My pet grass snake," Danny answered, releasing the flap on the bag and laying it on the ground. "I keep him in this bag. It's his home."

"Did the Apaches know you had him with you?"

"Nope. I only let him out at night when they was asleep. Funny thing. They never did get curious about what I had in that bag. I reckon they thought it was jest my handbag and full of those silly things all white females carry."

As Charlie slithered off, Danny cautioned the snake, "Now, you be back way before sunup, you hear? With all these Apaches 'round here, I'm gonna have enough to worry about tomorrow morning without wondering where you wandered off to."

"You mean he'll actually come back on his own?" Sam asked in disbelief.

"Shore will. I'm the only family he's got."

And he's the only one I got, too, Danny thought, her spirits sinking again. Brant coming after her didn't mean a thing. He'd only done it out of compassion and because it was his job, just like he'd come after those young'uns. But after tomorrow, it wouldn't matter, not if they woke up to find those Apaches had surrounded them. No one was gonna have him, not her, or Elizabeth.

Long after Danny and Sam had fallen asleep, Brant lay awake, brooding over the day's events. He'd managed to save the children, but not the person he loved more than life itself. He looked across at Danny laying beside him, then gently pulled her into his arms.

"Oh, Danny," he muttered in anguish into her hair. "Why do you always have to be so hard-headed? Why didn't you flee with the others, like you were supposed to? Then I could have died in peace, knowing you were safe."

Chapter 23

The three were up before daybreak the next morning. Leaving Danny to keep an eye out on the canyon, the two men crept to the back of their rocky barricade and waited for the sun to rise. As soon as the sky in the east turned a rosy color and the sun tinted the wispy clouds hovering in the horizon in lavenders and oranges, Sam put his hat on the end of his rifle and poked the gun over the rim of the rocks that he and Brant were hidden behind. The crack of a rifle split the air, and Sam's hat went flying.

Sam sat back, saying glumly, "Yep, they're out there all right, just like I figured they would be. We're surrounded."

Brant hadn't expected to come out of this alive, but none the less, he had kept hoping. A black despair filled him. "Sam, I want you to do something for me. If I get killed before you and Danny, and it looks like the end is imminent, will you kill Danny? I don't want them taking her alive."

"Kill her?" Sam asked in a shocked voice. "Are you crazy? Why would you want me to do a fool thing like that?"

"I don't want her to be tortured."

"Apaches don't torture women, regardless of what wild tales you might have heard. And you've already heard my theories about raping 'em. They'd make her their slave. Now, there are some people that might say death is better than slavery, but I ain't one of 'em. Hell, as long as there's life, there's hope, and that little gal of yours is tough and smart. She might be able to figure out a way to escape. Hell, no, I ain't gonna kill her!"

Sam's assurances that Danny wouldn't be tortured made Brant feel somewhat better. And maybe she could eventually escape. Besides, he wasn't sure he had the courage to kill her, himself, to snuff out the light in those sparkling black eyes, to destroy something as beautiful and vitally alive as Danny. It hadn't been fair to ask another man to do what he couldn't.

"Sorry, Sam. I shouldn't have even asked you."

"Hell, it ain't that. If I thought it was necessary, I'd do it."

"No, if what you say is true, it isn't necessary. Besides, none of us may be taken alive." Brant glanced over his shoulder, then said, "I'm going back to the other side with Danny."

For hours, they lay beneath the hot sun, waiting for the Apaches to attack in earnest. They never did. It was a repeat of the day before, only sporadic gunfire, with no one on either side hitting the other. When the blazing sun had passed its zenith about two hours, Sam crawled to the side where Danny and Brant were and said in disgust, "Hell, it's a standoff. Neither one of us is getting anywhere."

"I guess they're in no hurry," Brant commented grimly. "They know we haven't got much water, if any.

All they have to do is wait us out and let the sun and time do it for them."

Sam scowled, saying, "I ain't so sure about that. I put myself in Alsate's shoes and decided he might be getting a little edgy. He's bound to know Colorado let the other troopers ride back to Fort Stockton and that a big force is probably on its way right now, and—"

"There isn't a force coming to rescue us," Brant interjected. "Didn't you hear what I told O'Bannon? Not to even try?"

"Yep, I heard. But Alsate don't know that. And if a force were to arrive, those Apaches out in those foothills would get caught in a crossfire. He's probably wondering right now if he should pull 'em back, or wait until one of his scouts spies the cavalry coming."

Brant was thoughtful for a moment, then asked, "Do you think he's edgy enough to make a deal?"

"What kind of a deal?"

"Suppose I offer to fight for our lives, man to man. You said he doesn't want to lose any of his warriors unnecessarily."

Sam gazed off for a long moment, saying, "Well, I reckon it's worth a try."

"Don't make too swift a decision, Sam. There's always the possibility that I'll lose. If I'm lucky, I'll get killed. But you won't be so lucky. They'd torture you."

"Yep, I know. But if we don't try that, the only other alternative is to sit out here and die of thirst. By nightfall, Alsate will know there ain't no one coming to our aid. Like you said, all he'll have to do is wait it out, and those goddamned Apaches don't think nothing about sitting for days in the hot sun as long as they got water. I've seen men who have died of thirst. Their lips and skin crack and bleed, and their tongue swells until they slowly suffocate. I don't think anything the Apaches could do to me could be any worse than that. At least, this way, we'd have a chance. I say let's give it a try."

Brant didn't ask for Danny's opinion. Both men knew it would be risking their lives, but what Brant was proposing was the only way to save Danny's. He lifted his head slightly and peered out at the canyon, then yelled, "Alsate? Are you out there?"

There was a brief silence before the answer came, the Apache's voice vibrating with angry undertones. "I am here."

"This is Captain Brant. I have a deal to offer you."

"A deal!" Alsate spat. "We made a deal, but you broke your word. You tricked us!"

"Goddammit, don't play noble with me!" Brant threw back, his own anger coming to the rise. "What do you call demanding that gun as ransom for those hostages, if it wasn't a trick? You tricked me and I tricked you. As far as I'm concerned, we're even on that score. That puts us right back where we were before all this started. The white man against the Indian."

Brant gave Alsate a few moments to mull over what he had said, then continued, saying, "I know you don't want any of your warriors killed unnecessarily. By the same token, I don't want any of my people to die needlessly. I propose that we settle this amongst ourselves, that just you and I fight it out. If I win, me and my people go free. If I lose, they'll already be in your hands to do with what you will."

"An Apache chief does not lower himself to fight hand-to-hand with a lowly white man."

Proud bastard, Brant thought, then said, "All right,

then. Pick your champion. Any man you like. And we'll pick ours."

There was a long pause before Alsate asked suspiciously, "Why are you doing this?"

"Because we don't have any water, and we're being fried alive out here in this sun. Waiting for something to happen is beginning to wear on our nerves. We've decided that we'd rather get what's going to happen over with." Brant paused, so that his words would have more impact. "Besides, I happen to think I'll win."

It was a bold challenge that Alsate found hard to turn down. Arrogant white bastard, he thought scornfully. There wasn't a white man alive that could beat an Apache in hand-to-hand combat. But as proud as he was, Alsate was a man who had survived the white onslaught by being cautious, and not rash. He carefully considered his position. If the yellowlegs were sending reinforcements, he would be forced to retreat to his main camp deep in the mountains and fight them another day, at a time and a place of his own choosing. If reinforcements did not arrive, it might take days for the white men in those rocks to die of thirst, and in the meanwhile, they might kill more of his warriors. It would be better to risk one man, than several, particularly when there was no real risk involved. There was no doubt in Alsate's mind that the weak white man would lose.

A smug smile played over the Apache's lips as he called out, "It is agreed then. You will choose your man to fight mine for your lives. But we will not fight here. We will go back to our camp where we made our previous exchange. Leave your weapons behind, mount your horses, and come out."

"Jesus, I hope he ain't tricking us," Sam said in a

worried voice, having second doubts.

"We'll soon find out," Brant replied grimly, coming to his full height and half-expecting to feel a flood of bullets ripping through his body. When none came, he said, "Well, so far so good. Come on, let's do what he said, before he changes his mind."

The three tossed their guns down, saddled their horses, and rode out of their rocky barricade. As Brant spied Alsate stepping from behind a crag to one side, he saw the frown on the Apache's face and knew the chief had thought there were more of them than three hidden in the rocks. That's why Brant had vaguely referred to Danny and Sam as his people, hoping to lure the Apache into agreeing to his proposal with the prospect of more victims.

As Brant, Danny, and Sam rode into the canyon, the Apaches slipped from their hiding places and surrounded them, their black eyes glittering with anger. Within minutes, the Mescalero's horses were brought from the back of the canyon, and everyone was mounted. At the end of the canyon, the Apaches veered onto another trail, and Brant knew it was the shortcut that they had taken the day before. He also knew, by their allowing them to see it, that the Chisos didn't expect them to leave their camp alive. Dead men revealed no secrets. He could only hope that it was the Apaches' arrogance that made the Indians so sure of his and Sam's fate, and not that they planned to kill them as soon as they reached the camp.

When they rode into the broad meadow an hour later, Brant noticed that the crank on the machine was broken off. Apparently the Apaches had tried to unlock the jammed mechanisms on the gun by brute force, only doing further damage. Without the crank, the gun was nothing but a piece of junk.

The Apaches reined in and dismounted. A group of about twenty quickly circled Alsate as he swung from his horse, all talking excitedly and gesturing wildly. Soon a heated argument broke out, and it was only by Alsate's firm command to cease, that the Apaches calmed down. "I bet I know what they're doing," Sam remarked dryly. "Arguing over who's gonna get the honor of being the chief's champion. They sure are counting heavily on one of us losing."

"One of us?" Brant asked in surprise. "I thought we agreed I'd do the fighting?"

"I don't recall us agreeing to any such thing," Sam said, swinging down from his horse. "You just assumed it, because you suggested it. I think we ought to do what Alsate is doing, pick the best man for the job."

"And I suppose you think that's you," Brant said with a strong hint of sarcasm, as he and Danny dismounted.

Sam might have thought just that, being as he was meaner, tougher, and more experienced, but having seen Brant in action over the past few days the scout had come to admire the Yankee. He was a cut above most of the officers Sam had known in the past, a man of action and decision, daring and fearless. Personally, Sam thought he'd make good Ranger material. "Not necessarily. It depends upon which weapons they choose. I might feel more comfortable with a war club, but you might feel you'd do better with a lance."

Sam had a point, Brant admitted silently. He'd felt he should do the fighting, since he was in charge, but that would be foolhardy if he knew nothing about the weapon.

He glanced over Sam's shoulder at the group of Apaches, seeing Alsate making his way through the circle of warriors and walking towards them. "I don't think we're going to have to wonder long what the choice of weapons might be. Here comes Alsate, and he looks awfully pleased with himself."

As Sam turned, Alsate stepped up to the two men, saying, "I have chosen my warrior. The contest will be tonight, after the sun has gone down, by his request. Until then, you will wait in the wickiups. You," the chief said to Sam, "will wait in the one to the far right, and you," Alsate said to Brant, "will wait in the one to the left with the woman."

"How come you're separating us?" Sam asked.

"I don't want you two plotting another trick," Alsate answered in a hard voice, his eyes flashing in remembered anger. "You will be brought food and water. I will not have you claim you lost because you were too weak to fight. We will come for you when we are ready for you. Do not try to leave the wickiups until then. We will consider it an attempt to escape and kill you on the spot."

"And the weapons? What will they be?" Brant asked.

A glimmer came into the Apache's dark eyes, and a smug smile crossed his lips. "Knives."

As Alsate walked away, Sam groaned and said, "I should have known those bastards would pick knives. I was hoping they'd say wrestling, since it's their favorite sport. I'm pretty good at that. But hell, I ain't worth a damn with a knife. I can't even whittle a stick without cutting the hell out of myself. The Rangers I used to ride with were always teasing me about how clumsy I was with one of the damn things. I just never got the hang of it."

418

"Well, it looks like I'm the man for the job," Brant commented.

"Cap'n, you may be used to wielding one of those damn sabers, but knife fighting ain't the same. And I feel I'd better warn you, Apaches are experts with those damn knives of theirs. Why, I reckon they're the best knife fighters among all the Injun tribes, and they're sneaky as hell."

"I think I can handle it," Brant answered.

The words had been spoken calmly, but there was something in the tone of Brant's voice that made Sam wonder if Brant knew more than he was openly admitting. Or was he just hoping the captain knew more.

Sam never got a chance to question Brant further. An Apache stepped up to them, saying angrily, *"Silencio!,"* then shoved Sam towards the wickiup he had been told to go to. Seeing another Apache bearing down on him and Danny, Brant didn't wait to be pushed. He took her arm and quickly walked to the wickiup they had been assigned.

Danny hadn't said a word since Brant had made his suggestion to fight man to man, an amazing quietness for her. At first, it had been because she was irritated that the two men hadn't even asked her opinion, treating her as if she didn't have enough sense to have one, just because she was woman. Her irritation had reached downright angry proportions when neither man even considered her as a possible candidate, again because she was a woman. But when it was decided that Brant would do the fighting and Sam had warned him that Apaches were experts, Danny's anger had disappeared, to be quickly replaced with an overpowering fear for him. He might have surprised her over the past two days with his cunning in tricking the Apaches, his riding, his shooting, but he was still a gentleman. Gentlemen didn't fight with knives. Only low-down, scum of the earth men did, like those river rats in the border towns her brother had told her about.

As soon as they stepped behind the brush windbreak in front of the low wickiup, she turned to him and said, "Let me fight that Apache. I'm real fast with a knife."

Seeing the absolutely furious expression coming over Brant's face, Danny quickly said, "Now don't get all het up. I don't mean to insult you, but you know about as much about knife fighting as a hog does Sundays, and I don't want you a-getting yerself killed. Now I—"

"Goddammit, when are you going to learn?" Brant thundered, making Danny almost jump out of her skin at the loud noise. "What does it take to get through that thick skull of yours that I don't want you to protect me? For Christ's sake, it's supposed to be the other way around. The man protects the woman! It's been that way since the beginning of time. Do you have any idea of how low you make me feel when you insist upon protecting me, instead of letting me protect you? What kind of a man would I be if I can't protect the woman I love? Why, I'd be no man at all!"

Danny was stunned by Brant's fury. Then her brain zeroed in on one phrase, "the woman I love." Her breath caught in her throat and her heart raced. "Do you mean it? Do you really love me?"

The anxious look on Danny's face tempered Brant's anger. He shook his head in exasperation, saying, "Danny, I told you I loved you the night of the dance. Don't you remember?"

"Yep, I remember, but I thought you was only

a-pitying me, 'cause I'd made such a dad-blasted fool of myself."

"Danny, I felt for you, but what I felt wasn't pity. Seeing you hurting, hurt me."

"But . . . but what about Elizabeth? I thought you loved her. You're gonna marry her."

"Danny, I never loved Elizabeth. Hell, I couldn't stand her. I was drunk the night she claimed I proposed to her. I couldn't remember a damn thing about it, but I felt obligated to keep my word. The more I've thought about it lately, though, the more convinced I am that she lied about the whole thing, that she deliberately tried to trap me. But I never had any intention of marrying her. That's one of the reasons I rejoined the army, to get away from her. I didn't ask you to marry me the night of the dance, because I was still engaged to her. I couldn't until I was free from her. I broke our engagement after I left you that night. The next morning, when Colonel Shafter ordered me to go to Fort Stockton to pick up that gun, I dropped by the Duncan's home to ask you if you would marry me before I left, but Julia said you weren't there. I couldn't wait for your return. I'd been ordered to ride escort to the stage, since there were Apaches reported in the vicinity, and it was time for it to leave."

"Then you meant everything you said that night, that you liked me just the way I am?" Danny asked in disbelief.

"Yes, I meant it. I don't want you to ever change. If you did, you wouldn't be the woman I love."

"And you really want to marry me?"

"I'd consider it an honor to have you as my wife."

Danny was filled with an overwhelming happiness that she couldn't contain. Any other woman would have thrown herself in her lover's arms, but not Danny. With a jubilant whoop, she leaped on Brant, wrapping her legs around his waist and her arms around his shoulders, almost bowling him over and knocking his hat from his head. Brant folded his arms around her and tried to capture her lips with his, but Danny evaded him as she smothered his face with excited kisses, her mouth darting here and there as she kissed his forehead, his cheeks, his nose, his chin, his ears, the top of his golden head, his throat, until Brant had to laugh at her extravagant show of joy.

"Does that mean your answer is yes?" Brant asked between his laughter.

Danny stopped her wild, exuberant kissing and gazed down at him, her black eyes dancing. "It shore does."

Brant squirmed, saying, "Then, if you'd kindly get the heels of your boots out of my back, I'd like to seal that with a proper kiss."

Danny dropped her legs, and Brant kissed her long and lovingly. When he raised his head, his blue eyes shimmering with emotion, she asked, "You really like me the way I am?"

"I love you the way you are. You're wonderfully fresh and natural, and very special. You're Danny, one of a kind. There's not another woman in the world like you. I don't want you to ever change."

"Does that mean I can wear men's clothes and a gun strapped to my hip?"

"Yes."

"And I can ride a horse astride?"

"Yes."

"And I can cuss?"

Brant's eyes twinkled with amusement. Danny's idea

of cussing was saying dad-blast it, consarn it, gol-durn, with an occasional hellfire thrown in. It was part of her colorful speech that he so loved. "Yes."

Danny was reveling in the power Brant's love gave her over him. She decided to test him a little further, to see just how far she could go. "Can I chew tobacco?"

The warm, benevolent expression on Brant's face was replaced with a firm, determined one. "No! Absolutely not!" Then seeing the mischievous twinkle in Danny's eyes, his voice softened as he said, "I'm afraid that's one thing I can't tolerate, Danny, that and your not letting me protect you like I want to, like I need to."

Brant's words reminded Danny of where they were and why, and her brief, but wonderful spurt of happiness was ended. She remembered Julia telling her that men needed to feel protective, or they didn't feel manly. At the time, she thought it was the silliest thing she had ever heard, but now, she had an inkling of understanding what Julia had meant. It wasn't simply a matter of pride for pride's sake. It was a matter of self-esteem, something a man needed to do, not just to prove his love, but to prove his manliness, his worth. No, it didn't matter what anyone else thought. What mattered was what the man thought of himself. She realized that if a woman really loved her man she wouldn't trample on his self-esteem, not a wise woman. There were times when a woman would have to stand back, even when she knew she could do something just as well, or better. And this was one of those times.

"I reckon I was just being silly, a-thinking I could fight that Injun. Hellfire, I don't know nothing about a-fighting with a knife. You probably know a durn sight more than I do. I was jest scared fer you and a-spouting off."

423

Brant knew only to well what it was to fear for the one you loved. Danny had scared the hell out of him more times than he cared to remember. But he strongly suspected that Danny was bowing out because of what he'd said, and not because of any great confidence in his ability. He hoped that night he could prove to her once and for all that he wasn't a weak, stupid tenderfoot. More than anything, he wanted her honest admiration, her respect. "Let's don't talk about what's going to happen tonight, or even think about it. Let's go inside and sit down. I want to see what you think about my plans for our future."

Brant had to bend almost double to enter the low, circular wickiup. Once inside, they sat on a bed of pine needles covered with a blanket. Having settled down comfortably, Brant said, "My enlistment is up in the fall, and I'm not rejoining the cavalry. But I don't want to wait until then for us to be married. I'd like to do it as soon as we get back to Fort Davis."

"That's jest fine with me, but how come you ain't reenlisting?"

"I don't want to devote my life to an army career. I want more. All of my life, I've been searching for something, a challenge that I could meet on a more personal basis. I've found it here in Texas. This is where I want to settle. I want to try my hand at ranching."

Danny was speechless with surprise for a moment. Then she asked, "You ain't a-telling me a sandy, are you?"

"No, I'm serious. When my enlistment is up, we'll go back to your ranch, but we're going to expand it, Danny. It's not going to be just another ranch. I have ambitious plans for us. We're going to have the biggest and best cattle ranch in Texas."

As Brant launched into more details on what he had planned, Danny listened quietly, wondering why he was telling her this now. Ordinarily she would be beside herself with happiness at the prospect of living her life with Brant on the land she loved so much, but she couldn't get excited over it, not with the terrible threat that was looming over them. They might not have any future together. Was he trying to distract her from worrying about what would happen that night? For his sake, she pasted a smile on her face, but she couldn't help but worry. She had stepped back, so he could keep his self-esteem, even though she still thought she was more skilled with a knife. But she didn't know if she could stand by and watch him be sliced into little pieces. Yet, she knew that's what everyone expected of her, the Apaches, even Brant. What was ahead of her was going to be the greatest test of courage she had yet to face. Dad-blast it, being a woman sure wasn't easy.

Chapter 24

By the time the Apaches came for them that night, Danny's fear for Brant was a living, clawing thing inside her. But she was determined to stick to her resolve not to trample on his self-esteem any more, even though she secretly longed to get down on her knees and beg him to let her do the fighting.

As they stepped from the wickiup, Danny couldn't understand how Brant could be so calm and cool. She hadn't seen a glimmer of fear in him, or for that matter, even concern. He acted as if this was an everyday occurrence for him, going to fight in hand-to-hand combat with a fierce Apache. He was either the bravest man she had ever seen, or the most stupid.

Sam stepped up beside them, saying in an ominous tone of voice. "Well, this is it." He gave Brant a penetrating look as the three walked towards the big bonfire that had been built in the middle of the meadow, then asked, "How are you feeling, Cap'n?"

"I'm as ready as I'll ever be, but what I can't understand is why they waited until tonight. I thought you said Apaches didn't fight at night."

"They don't ordinarily. Don't you remember Alsate saying the warrior who's gonna fight you made that decision? It's his way of saying he's so confident in the outcome that he's willing to take the risk of having his spirit roam the earth for all eternity."

When they reached the bonfire, Brant saw that a circle of ground had been cleared of every blade of grass and knew that it must be the arena in which the fight would take place. Alsate and another Apache materialized out of the darkness, coming from the other side of the camp. As they walked towards them, Brant studied his opponent thoughtfully. Stripped to nothing but his breechcloth, the Mescalero was taller than most Apaches, but Brant still had several inches of height on him. Ordinarily that would have given him an advantage, but Brant knew the wiry Apache would be light on his feet and fast. He was all thin muscle and bone, with not an ounce of spare flesh on him.

"You'd better strip down, too, Cap'n," Sam said. "Those clothes you're wearing are just gonna be a hindrance, particularly those heavy boots."

Brant could see the wisdom of the scout's words. He removed everything but his cavalry trousers, tossing the clothing well to the side of the arena so there would be no danger of him tripping on them. As he bent to roll up his pants to just below his knees, he gave the Apaches standing behind him an excellent view of the muscles on his shoulders, forearms, and broad back. Had the contest been wrestling, the sight of those powerful muscles might have given the Indians pause, but they knew this was not a contest of strength, but speed and skill. Those muscles were heavy and would only slow the yellowlegs down.

Brant was waiting in the circle of dirt when Alsate and the Apache stepped into it. The chief handed both men a wicket-looking knife, the long blade glittering in the firelight, then said to Brant, "I will explain the rules. If either of you places any part of your body outside of this circle, you forfeit the fight. Otherwise, you will fight to the death."

Brant glanced around him. The circle was no bigger than ten feet across. They certainly weren't going to give him much room to maneuver in. "I understand."

Alsate stepped from the circle, raised his hand, then brought it down as a signal for the fight to begin. The Apache in the arena crouched, holding his knife out before him, his dark eyes glittering with anticipation of the kill. Brant assumed the same stance, watching the Apache's eyes as the Mescalero slowly circled him, knowing that he would see the Apache's intent there before he even lashed out with the knife. At the slightest narrowing of his opponent's eyes, Brant jumped back, the knife in the Indian's hand ripping harmlessly through the air where Brant's midsection had been a split second before and bringing a groan of disappointment from the warriors on the sidelines.

A look of disbelief crossed the Apache's leathery face. How had the yellowlegs known when he was going to strike? This wasn't going to be the quick kill he had anticipated. The yellowlegs chief was a worthy opponent. He would have to be much more careful, much more cunning.

The warrior crouched and feinted, but Brant wasn't

fooled by his quick jab of the knife that was meant to bring a defensive lunge on his part, a lunge that would leave him wide open to the man's lethal blade. He stood motionless, not batting an eye, then when the Apache drew back as if in confusion, Brant's knife lashed out with lightning swiftness that almost caught the warrior completely off guard. The Apache barely had time to leap away, bringing a gasp of fear from the Indians who were watching from the sidelines.

Furious, the warrior lunged at Brant, their knives meeting with a clash of steel that made sparks fly before both men jumped back. Slowly they circled one another, the long blades glittering in the firelight, both knowing that the fight had taken on a deadly earnestness. The Apache's knife leaped out, catching Brant across the chest, and the Indians went wild as Danny gasped in sheer terror and turned away, burying her head in Sam's shoulder.

"He's okay, Danny," the scout assured her. "It's just a scratch."

Reluctantly, Danny turned to look and saw Brant still on his feet, the superficial laceration on his broad chest beaded with drops of blood. Then she gasped again as Brant and the Indian lunged at one another, the blades scraping down the length of one another before they met hilt to hilt. For a moment, the two opponents stood eyeball-to-eyeball, their hands with the knives trembling as each tried to force the other's down. Then, one of the Indian's legs flew out, wrapped behind one of Brant's and tripped him, and Brant went down, the Apache throwing his body over his so hard that it knocked the breath from him.

Brant didn't realize until it was almost too late what

429

the Apache's intention was. Suddenly he became acutely aware that his hand was outside of the circle of dirt, of the Apache bearing down with all his might on the hilt of his knife to force his hand back. The damn red bastard was trying to win by forcing him to forfeit the fight. Brant gave a mighty swing of his arm, forcing the Apache's back with such momentum that it rolled the Indian to his back. There they grappled in the dirt, rolling over and over from side to side as each fought to regain the upper hand, the blades of their knives glittering and their sweaty bodies glistening in the firelight.

The Apache balled the fist of his free hand and swung at Brant, but Brant caught the flying hand in his, then grunted as the Apache's knee slammed into his stomach. What had began as a knife fight had turned into a free-for-all. Well, if the Apache wanted to fight dirty, that was fine with him, Brant thought angrily. He jabbed him back with his knee, then released the Apache's hand and grabbed the wrist of the hand holding the knife. With a swiftness that brought a gasp of surprise from the onlookers, he rolled the Apache to his back, sitting on his midsection to hold him down with his weight.

Realizing the precarious position he was in, the Apache reached for Brant's hand that was holding his wrist where their knives were still locked hilt to hilt. But the yellowleg's fingers were like a vise, and no amount of tugging and clawing could break his hold. Then as Brant's fingers tightened and pressed on the nerve that ran down to his fingers, the Apache realized with horror that the white-eyes knew exactly what he was doing, that catching hold of his wrist had been deliberate. The hand holding his knife was turning numb. Frantic, he let go of Brant's hand, beating his arm, shoulders, and chest with his fist and jabbing his back with his knees, but to no avail. The fingers on his hand turned lifeless, and the knife slipped from them to fall to the ground. The second it did, Brant released the Apache's wrist, caught his flying arm with one hand and pinned it down beside his head, bringing the knife in the other to rest across the Apache's bronzed throat.

A stunned silence fell over the crowd as Brant held the knife to the Mescalero's throat. The moment that passed ticked by like an eternity of time as everyone waited for Brant to slit the man's throat and end the fight. Brant looked down and saw the fear in the Indian's dark eyes. The Apache knew he faced death and that his spirit was doomed to forever roam the earth, that his soul would never find rest.

Then, to everyone's surprise, Brant stood, stepped over the Apache's prone body, and threw the knife to the ground, burying the blade deeply in the dirt between the Indian's feet and the handle quivering from the force of the impact.

Without a backward glance, Brant walked from the circle to where Sam and Danny were waiting. "Why in hell didn't you kill him?" Sam asked as he approached them.

"I couldn't kill an unarmed man in cold blood."

"You damned fool!" Sam threw back. "Do you think they're gonna be impressed with your nobility? Hell, no! The only thing these Apaches admire is strength. They thrive on violence and cruelty. The fight was supposed to be to the death. They'll only interpret your compassion as a sign of weakness. By not slitting that bastard's throat, you forfeited the fight."

Brant turned and looked at the crowd of Apaches, and

knew from the scornful expressions of their faces that Sam spoke the truth. They'd still kill them, even though Brant had proven himself the better fighter. But Brant couldn't regret his decision to spare the Apache's life. A man had to live by his own beliefs, to follow his own conscience, or he was just a shadow of a man. He wondered if Danny scorned him, too, if she thought him weak? Had he gone through all that and still lost his bid for her respect?

He turned to face her. But a movement at her side caught his eye. It was Charlie, slithering out of his canvas bag. Christ, Brant thought, of all the times for that damn snake to decide it was time for his dinner, why did he have to pick now, with all these Apaches about? They were bound to notice him, and if they tried to kill him, Danny would fight to the death for her pet. Hell, not only were he and Sam going to die, but Danny too. They'd have been better off if they had stayed in the rocks.

The Apaches did notice the snake, just as they were approaching the two white men, their eyes glittering with anticipation of the slow torture they would use on them. Feeling something brush against her hand, Danny glanced down, saw the snake winding its way up her arm, and caught it by the neck, saying, "Dad-blast you, Charlie! Get back in your bag 'fore those Injuns see you. I swear you ain't got a lick of sense."

Brant was so busy watching Charlie and Danny that he didn't notice the Indians' reaction to the snake. The Apaches came to a dead halt, the looks of hatred on their bronzed faces changing to one of absolute horror.

An owl, sitting in a nearby pine, spied the snake at the same time the Apaches did. Thinking Charlie would make

432

a tasty meal, it swooped down on Danny's shoulder and made a grab with its beak for the snake. Danny jerked Charlie away protectively, looked up at the owl, and shrieked, "Get away from him, you consarn owl, 'fore I knock you to kingdom come! Iffen you think I'm gonna let you eat Charlie, you plumb got rocks in yer head!"

What happened next was sheer bedlam. The Apaches whirled around, tore away for their horses, flew on the animals' backs, and raced away in the darkness as if all of the demons in hell were after them. Brant watched their frantic exit in stunned disbelief, then turned to Sam and asked, "What in the hell got into them? Why are they leaving?"

Sam couldn't answer. He was doubled over with laughter.

Brant glanced at Danny and saw that she was occupied with defending Charlie from the owl, swatting at the bird with one hand and cussing up a blue streak while she held Charlie with the other hand at safe distance, the owl wildly flapping its wings and hanging on to her shoulder with a stubborn tenacity.

Brant looked at her, then at the scout who was laughing so hard that tears were streaming down his cheeks, then glanced across his shoulder in the direction the Apaches had disappeared. "Has everyone in this world suddenly gone insane but me?" he roared, adding the loud sound of his yell to Danny's angry shrieks, Sam's hysterical laughter, the owl's squawks, and the thundering hooves of the Indians' horses in the distance.

Brant reached for the owl on Danny's shoulder, caught it around its neck, jerked it free, and flung it into the woods. He whirled on Sam and glared at him, saying,

433

"Dammit, I asked you a question! Why did they leave like that? And what in hell do you think is so damn funny?"

"Give . . . give me . . . a minute . . . to catch my breath . . . and I'll . . . answer you," Sam gasped. Brant towered over the scout and glared at him, until Sam recovered and said, "You see, Apaches are terrified of snakes. All snakes. They think the spirits of the dead live in 'em. And it don't necessarily have to be a live one either. If they find a dead snake lying in their path, they'll go miles out of their way to keep from stepping over it. The only thing they're more terrified of is an owl. They think they've got evil dead spirits in them. So when that owl spied Charlie and came swooping down on Danny's shoulder, it was a double whammy. They figured she was a witch, if she attracted both snakes and owls, and beat the hell out of here before she could put an evil curse on them."

"A witch?" Danny asked, feeling highly insulted. "How dare those dad-blasted Apaches accuse me of being an ugly, mean old witch! I ain't got no warts on my nose."

Sam chuckled at Danny's indignation, then said, "You don't have to be old and ugly to be a witch in the Apaches' eyes, only able to practice sorcery. You don't even have to be a woman. They believe in men witches too. But they don't think you're just any witch, Danny. They think you're a powerful one, with medicine much stronger and more deadly than anything their shamans—their medicine men—could match."

"I can't believe it." Brant commented. "Are you telling me that Indians as fierce and savage and cunning as the Apaches actually believe in ghosts and witches?"

"They sure do. They're just about the most superstitious bunch of Injuns there are."

"But you wouldn't think they would be afraid of anything."

"Hell, every society has its weakness. For the Apaches, it's their fears of the supernatural."

Brant thought of the Irish troopers. They were the hardest fighting, bravest, most daring, devil-may-care men he had ever come across, yet they, too, were a superstitious lot. They believed in the evil eye, that a man could put an evil curse on another just by giving him a silent fixed stare, that a child born on the twenty-first of the month was destined to become a robber, that the seventh son of a seventh son possessed second sight and could foretell the future, that boots placed on a table or chair meant the owner would die by hanging, that if they found the tooth of a horse and always carried it with them, it assured them of never being without money. The list went on and on, and Brant guessed if the tough, fearless Irishmen could be so superstitious, so could the Apaches. As Sam had said, every society has its Achilles' heel.

"All right," Brant conceded, "so we scared the Apaches off for the time being, but will they come back in the morning?"

"Hell, no! They ain't never gonna come anywhere near us as long as we're with Danny. The dark don't have nothing to do with it. She's got powerful medicine. They ain't gonna get within miles of her." Sam glanced over at Danny and said, "I sure am glad Charlie decided he wanted a breath of fresh air and came out when he did. That snake saved our lives."

"Why, he shore did," Danny agreed, completely forgetting about how insulted she felt about the Indians calling her a witch. She raised Charlie up by his neck in front of her and said, "Did you hear that Charlie? You saved our lives. Why, you're a hero!"

Danny smiled broadly at the snake. Brant smiled at the snake. And, just as if he understood perfectly what Danny had said, Charlie smiled back. Watching the three, Sam wondered if he was losing his mind. Whoever heard of a goddamned snake smiling?

As Danny slipped Charlie back into his bag, Sam asked Brant, "Where did you learn to fight with a knife like that? And don't tell me you learned it in the army. I know better."

"Well, actually I did, at least on army time. My first sergeant during the war taught me. I saw him in action one night when some cutthroat attacked us in an alley of a little town we were bivouacked near. I thought it might come in handy some day, and there wasn't much going on with the war at the time, so it helped relieve our boredom. He'd been born and raised in the Irish Channel in New Orleans. Apparently, it was one of the roughest, toughest places on the Mississippi, and he'd learned to wield a knife at an early age out of sheer survival. He knew every knife trick there was."

"Well, it sure did come in handy," Sam agreed, "but I wished you'd told me that sooner. It would have saved me a heap of worrying."

"I didn't want to be overconfident. I thought I could handle it, but that remained to be seen. I'd never actually fought a man with a knife before, just practiced a few of the moves he taught me."

"Why, you looked like a dad-blasted expert out there," Danny said, her eyes gleaming with pride and totally forgetting how terrified she had been. "I ain't never seen nothing like it. You moved as quick as greased lightning, yer knife jest a-flashing here and there and a-making that

Apache jump around like he was a-standing on a bed of hot coals. And the way you forced him to drop his knife, even though he was a-beating on you. I wish you could've seen the look on those Apaches' faces. They looked like they'd been struck by a bolt out of the clear blue."

"That was another trick the sergeant taught me. He told me if I ever got in a pinch, to squeeze the man's wrist at a certain spot that was guaranteed to paralyze his hand. To be honest with you, I was beginning to fear he'd been wrong. It seemed an eternity before that Apache let go."

Brant's admission that he had been afraid didn't change Danny's opinion of him in the least. She thought he was the greatest man that ever walked the earth. Why, he could ride like Meskin, shoot just as good as her, knife fight better than any Apache, and was smart as a whip. And he was kind, too, letting that Apache live. He was as brave as all get-out, but he didn't have a mean, spiteful bone in his body, and she purely couldn't stand mean, spiteful people.

"Well, if he hadn't of made him drop that knife, you would have beaten him anyhow," Danny said with utmost confidence. "There ain't nothing you can't do!"

Brant had wanted Danny's admiration and respect more than anything in the world. He relished his victory, but typical of Danny, she carried her feelings on her sleeve, and Brant soon became embarrassed by her blatant admiration. He hoped she wasn't going to go to the opposite extreme and go around with that silly, adoring look on her face all of the time. It made him feel as foolish as her scorn had.

"Thank you for your vote of confidence, Danny, but I'm afraid I'm far from perfect." He turned his attention back to Sam and said, "If you're positive the Apaches aren't going to come back, we might as well spend the night here. Then we can get an early start back to the fort in the morning."

"Sounds good to me. That pallet back in the wickiup was beginning to look mighty tempting before the Apaches came for us."

"Well, if we're gonna stay here, I'm gonna have a bath 'fore I go to bed," Danny announced. "Ain't had one in a week. I stink so bad I can't stand myself."

Brant seriously doubted that Danny smelled that bad. If she did, he certainly hadn't noticed it. But then he didn't smell like any bouquet of roses himself. "Where are you going to bathe?" he asked. "I haven't seen any stream."

"There's one over there in the woods," Danny answered, pointing to the back of the camp. "I saw it that day they brought me here. Was the first thing I spied when they took that dad-blasted blindfold off."

So the captives had been blindfolded when they had been brought here from the Apaches' main camp, Brant thought. Alsate wasn't going to take any chances of them leading the army back to their *rancheria*. It was disappointing news. After having seen these wild mountains, he feared the army would never be able to flush them out. Hell, they couldn't even blast them out.

Danny broke into his thoughts, saying, "Well, I'm a-heading fer that stream. I'll see you fellas later."

As Danny walked off, Sam saw the longing look in Brant's eyes and knew the captain wanted to join her but was too much of a gentleman to do so in his presence. He faked a yawn and said, "Well, if you two will excuse me, I think I'll go on to bed. I'm getting too old for all this chasing around and excitement."

After Sam had walked away, Brant glanced around him. He saw their horses standing in the distance in the flickering firelight, still tied to a part of the roped-off corral that the Indians hadn't slashed in their terrified exit, but saw no sign of their belongings. He turned and looked towards the wickiups, spying their saddles piled up in front of the center one.

With swift, long strides, he walked to the wickiup and searched until he found his bedroll and saddlebags. Then, with a smile on his face, he followed Danny, his heart racing in anticipation of their night together.

Chapter 25

Brant didn't have any trouble finding the stream and Danny after he left the Apache camp, even though there was no moon. It was one of those beautiful nights that he had seen only in the mountains in west Texas, a night in which the sky was filled with billions of glittering stars that looked close enough to reach up and touch.

Brant stopped beneath a pine tree when the stream came into view, drinking in the sight of Danny standing thigh-deep in the water. With her bare skin glowing in the soft light, and the water reflecting the glittering heavenly bodies from above, she looked like an angel bathing in sparkling stars. It was a breathtaking, ethereal sight that made Brant wonder if he was dreaming it, or if it was real.

Danny quickly proved she was real and no angel who had fallen from heaven, saying, "Howdy. I've been a-waiting fer you."

The spell was broken, but Brant couldn't regret it. He much preferred a flesh and blood woman he could hold in his arms. Besides, Danny had a magic all her own.

As he stepped from the shadows of the tree, Danny said, "I've been a-having to scour myself off with sand, since I don't have no soap. But still, it feels mighty good, a-getting all this dirt off me."

"I think I have a sliver of soap left in my saddlebags," Brant answered.

"You do?" Danny asked in an excited voice.

"Yes, give me a minute, and I'll join you."

Brant set his bedroll and saddlebags down on the grass and slipped out the thin bar of soap. He stripped off his pants and, carrying the soap in his hand, waded into the cool water.

As he approached her in all his naked, masculine glory, Danny took in the sight hungrily, then said in an awed voice, "Gol-durn, you shore are beautiful."

A flush rose on Brant's face. Danny had told him she thought him "purty" before but "beautiful" was a gross exaggeration. Then his lips twitched with amusement as he said, "Men aren't beautiful, Danny. They're . . . handsome."

"Well, maybe other men are, but you're downright beautiful," Danny answered in a tone of voice that told Brant she wouldn't brook any argument. "Of course, that don't mean you ain't manly," Danny added, her eyes sweeping over Brant's magnificent physique. "Why, you just ooze it from every pore, like a horse does sweat when he's been run hard fer a spell."

Brant chuckled, thinking no one but Danny could compliment a man and compare him to a horse in the same breath.

"I'd thank you kindly if you'd hand me that piece of soap," Danny said, a shiver running over her. "This here water is a-getting a little chilly. Must be spring fed."

"I'll bathe you."

Danny knew by the husky timbre of his voice and the warm look in his eyes that the bath would be much more than a washing of her body. It would be a preliminary to their lovemaking. Another shiver ran over her, one that had nothing to do with the chilly water.

As Brant bathed Danny, each touch was a caress that was filled with promise, and he didn't miss an inch of her skin, lingering at her breasts and then again between her legs. By the time he'd finished, the water no longer felt cold. A warmth suffused her body, and she tingled all over.

As he wordlessly handed the bar of soap to her, Danny didn't hesitate for a second. She could hardly wait to touch him, to love him back. She, in turn, lingered over his broad back, his tight buttocks, his chest with its sprinkling of crisp, golden hair, glorying in the feel of those powerful muscles between her fingertips. Her hands slipped lower, washing the proud, rigid proof of his desire for her, her fingers moving with tantalizing purpose, then dropping to soap down his corded thighs.

Suddenly, she was swooped up in Brant's arms. As he carried her to deep water to rinse off the soapsuds on their bodies, she objected, "But I wasn't finished yet."

Standing in water almost up to his shoulders, Brant chuckled, saying, "I couldn't stand anymore. This cold water serves more than one purpose than rinsing us off. Maybe it will cool me off a little."

"Hellfire! What you want to cool off fer?" Danny asked in frustration. She was primed and ready, and the feel of Brant's erection brushing across her buttocks was driving her wild with yearning.

Brant looked deeply into her eyes and answered, "I

442

don't want this to be a hasty loving. I want to delay it, savor it to its fullest. This is a special night for us, Danny. One that we'll cherish for the rest of our lives. It's our wedding night."

"Our wedding night?" Danny asked in disbelief, his surprising announcement accomplishing what the cold water hadn't been able to do to her heated senses. "But there ain't nobody here to marry us."

"Marriage is a lifetime commitment between a man and a woman in the eyes of God," Brant answered solemnly. "We're all here. Do you think a man saying the words over us is more important than God's blessing our union? No, that just makes it official in the eyes of man. We'll do that when we get back to Fort Davis. But I don't want to wait until then to make you my wife."

And Danny didn't want to wait until then to make Brant her husband. She buried her head in the crook of his neck so he couldn't see the tears of happiness in her eyes, muttering, "Yes, oh, yes. Let's do it tonight."

Brant carried her from the water, set her gently down on the grass, then spread his blanket out and pulled her down beside him. Kneeling before her, he took her hands in his, looked her directly in the eye, and said softly, "Before God, I take you for my wife, to love, cherish, and protect to my dying breath, and then, God willing, to spend eternity with you."

Danny was so choked up with emotion that she could hardly say her vows. "Before God, I take you as my husband to love, cherish, and . . ." Danny hesitated, wondering if she dared to say protect. But if that was the man's role, as Brant professed, what was the woman's? Danny wondered. Surely he didn't expect her to say obey, like some meek female. A sudden inspiration came

443

to her. ". . . and carry yer young'uns beneath my heart, to nourish them and bear them in joy, to raise them to be fine men and women, jest like their father, as living proof of our everlasting love."

A smile came to Brant's lips and a mistiness to his eyes. He had never even thought of children. Yes, long after he and Danny had gone to their eternity, their descendants would walk the earth, proof of their love and their oneness, to carry on the work that they had left behind. There was such a thing as undying love.

With hands that trembled with deep emotion, Brant took something from his saddlebags and slipped it on Danny's finger. Danny looked down in disbelief, then asked, "Where did you get the wedding ring?"

"I bought it at the post store at Fort Stockton. I hope you're not disappointed with it. It's just a simple gold band, but I couldn't see you wearing diamonds or precious jewels."

"You're dad-blasted right I don't want any of those silly stones on my ring. Why, they'd probably get caught in my lariat when I'm a-roping and yank my gol-durn finger off." An apprehensive look came to Danny's eyes. "You are gonna let me rope and brand cattle, ain't you? I hope you ain't expecting me to jest stay in the house, and cook and clean and take care of young'uns. I purely love a-being outdoors."

Brant had known that he wasn't going to get an ordinary wife when he proposed to Danny. No, she'd be like the other settler's wives, working right beside their husbands. And that was fine with him. He didn't want a shadow, a pretty ornament, a built-in housekeeper and cook. He wanted a woman that would share everything with him, the labors as well as the rewards, the disappointments as well as the joys. That was real oneness.

Aware of Danny anxiously awaiting his reply, Brant answered, "No, I don't plan on keeping you cooped up in the house all the time. If it's going to be our ranch, then we're both going to have to work it. Of course, I don't imagine I'm going to be a very good waddy at first. It will take some learning."

Danny was vastly relieved. "I'll teach you. Why, as smart as you are, you'll be a-roping and a-branding and a-herding cattle as good as me in no time."

Brant hoped so. He certainly didn't want to go back to looking foolish in Danny's eyes. He picked up her hand and kissed the ring, saying in a husky voice, "Do you realize we're married now?"

"Well, gol-durn, I reckon we are," Danny said in an awed voice.

Brant lifted his head and said, "And now, I'd like to love my wife."

Danny was suddenly breathless; her heart racing in anticipation at the warmth shimmering in Brant's eyes, a look that promised heaven and more. He kissed her as he lay her back on the blanket, a long, excruciatingly sweet kiss that brought tears to her eyes, as his hands smoothed over and caressed her, speaking eloquently of his love.

It was a prolonged loving, each striving to keep their passion at bay. It was an expression of their deep mutual love, a celebration of their lifetime commitment to one another, and they wanted to savor it to the fullest. It was too beautiful, too meaningful to be rushed.

Each tried to give the other the most possible pleasure, and in giving, received much more in return. Brant kissed each inch of Danny's satiny skin, and she adored him in return. He brought her to a shuddering peak of rapture with his mouth, over and over, and then to his utter surprise—mixed with just a little gentlemanly shock—she eagerly reciprocated.

"You don't have to do that, Danny," Brant gasped, trying to pull her head up.

"Yes, I do. I jest gotta show you how much I love you, jest like you did me."

Brant surrendered to the exquisite torture that Danny's mouth and tongue lavished on him, until his skin felt as if it could no longer contain him, that he would burst if she continued. He lifted her head and rolled her on her back, then looking her deeply in the eyes, entered her, slowly—ever so slowly—savoring the feel of her velvety heat surrounding his pulsating, rigid flesh, welcoming him into her sweet, tight warmth. Then when he was buried deep inside her, he sighed, feeling as if he had come home, a deep contentment filling him.

Danny felt it, too, that wondrous contentment, that utter bliss. They were truly one in body and spirit, no longer Danny and Brant, but one being, with one heartbeat, one soul, one mind.

For a long time they lay, savoring their joining, their closeness, their unity, both feeling awed by this miracle of love that could make them one. Then Brant bent and kissed her tenderly as he began his thrusts—slow, exquisitely sensuous strokes that gave and gave again. Each powerful, deep thrust was pure rapture, each kiss ecstasy. Breaths quickened, hearts raced against the other, lips met with feverish abandon, bodies strained with urgency, blood turned to liquid fire as they steadily climbed to that sweet, glorious pinnacle. Time seemed suspended as they held at that quivering zenith, breathless and trembling in an intense anticipation, until they climaxed in a sweet, overpowering burst of rapture amongst a golden shower of stardust.

Their breaths were still ragged and Danny was still spinning when Brant lifted his head, gazed down at her, and said softly, "I love you. Oh, God, how I love you."

"I love you, too," Danny responded with a catch in her throat. "So much it hurts."

As Brant started to lift himself from her, Danny pulled his head down to her breast, saying, "No, don't leave me."

Brant shifted his lower body to relieve her of the burden of his weight and slipped his arms around her back, relishing the sound of her heartbeat against his ear, feeling utterly sated and blissfully contented.

Danny wrapped her arms around his shoulders, her fingers stroking the soft golden hair that curled at the back of his ears. She had never known such sublime happiness.

She recalled everything Brant had told her the day before about his plans for their future. She was glad that they would renew their vows to one another at Fort Davis, solemnizing their commitment in the eyes of man where Julia and John could be present. The two were more than friends. She had come to think of them as her parents. Why, she might even wear that pretty white dress Julia had made her for the occasion. She supposed she could tolerate the silly female garment just that once, since Julia had put so much love into it. And their children would have a wonderful set of grandparents in the loving couple who had welcomed her into their hearts. Oh, yes, she and Brant were going to have a wonderful future together.

Danny glanced up at the sky, and the full impact of

Brant's proposal and their union as man and wife hit her. She'd done it, she thought in silent, joyous exaltation. Actually done it! As unbelievable as it seemed, she'd kept her feet firmly on the ground, reached up, and caught herself the biggest, most beautiful, most glittering golden star in the heavens—and she wasn't ever going to let him go.